Debby Giusti is an award-winning Christian author who met and married her military husband at Fort Knox, Kentucky. Together they traveled the world, raised three wonderful children and have now settled in Atlanta, Georgia, where Debby spins tales of mystery and suspense that touch the heart and soul. Visit Debby online at debbygiusti.com, blog with her at seekerville.blogspot.com and craftieladiesofromance.blogspot.com, and email her at Debby@DebbyGiusti.com.

Mary Davis is an award-winning author of more than a dozen novels. She is a member of American Christian Fiction Writers and is active in two critique groups. Mary lives in the Colorado Rocky Mountains with her husband of thirty years and three cats. She has three adult children and one grandchild. Her hobbies are quilting, porcelain doll making, sewing, crafts, crocheting and knitting. Please visit her website, marydavisbooks.com.

DEBBY GIUSTI

Amish Rescue

&

MARY DAVIS

Courting Her Amish Heart

⟨H⟩ HARLEQUIN® LOVE INSPIRED®

LOVE INSPIRED BOOKS

Recycling programs
for this product may
not exist in your area.

ISBN-13: 978-1-335-47009-6

Amish Rescue and Courting Her Amish Heart

Copyright © 2019 by Harlequin Books S.A.

The publisher acknowledges the copyright holders
of the individual works as follows:

Amish Rescue
Copyright © 2018 by Deborah W. Giusti

Courting Her Amish Heart
Copyright © 2018 by Mary Davis

www.Harlequin.com

Printed in U.S.A.

CONTENTS

AMISH RESCUE

Debby Giusti

This story is dedicated to children at risk.
Please join me in praying for their protection
and well-being so the forces of darkness
will not prevail against them.

Then spake Jesus again unto them,
saying, I am the light of the world:
he that followeth me shall not walk in darkness,
but shall have the light of life.
—*John* 8:12

Chapter One

Sarah Miller's heart pounded in sync with the footsteps that echoed up the stairway leading to the third story of the old antebellum home. Rats scurried in the attic as she crouched in the closet, pulled her knees to her chest and fought back tears that burned her eyes. The rats didn't frighten her, but Victor Thomin did.

The shuffle of his feet on the landing signaled his approach. Keys rattled as he unlocked the door, sending another wave of panic to ricochet along her spine. The locks—all three of them—were to protect her from those who hoped to do her harm…or so Victor claimed.

"Sarah?"

Her lungs constricted at the sound of his voice. She gasped, struggled for air and wished she could be anywhere except in his mother's house, where he said she was safe.

The door creaked open.

In her mind's eye, she could see his pallid skin, deep-set eyes and shock of red hair as he glanced around the room.

"Where are you, Sarah?" Anger rose in his voice. "Are you hiding from me?"

He knew too much about her, about being left alone as a child, about the fire and the fear that continued to eat at her even though she should know better. Why had she told him so much in her drugged stupor? At least he no longer forced her to take the pills.

"You can't hide from me, Sarah." His voice made her tremble all the more.

The closet door flew open. She startled, gasped for air and wanted to run but was too frightened to move.

He grabbed her arm.

"Don't hurt me." She struggled to pull free. "It was the dream that made me hide."

"Did you dream of being dragged from the car along with Miriam?" he asked, seemingly concerned. His hold eased. "Tell me about it, Sarah."

His voice was syrupy sweet now. How could he be such a Jekyll and Hyde? Hateful one minute, feigning compassion the next.

If only she could remember all the details of the car-jacking instead of hazy flashes that clouded her mind.

He leaned closer. "I told you about the bad men, Sarah, the men in your dreams. They captured your sister, but I'm working to get Miriam back before she's transported so far away that you'll never find her again."

Sarah's stomach roiled, sickened by the horrific thought of her sister gone forever. All her life, Sarah had relied on Miriam in times of need. But it wasn't just Miriam she could count on. Even her eldest sister, Hannah, had offered support, though the two of them had not been as close.

"If Miriam can't help me, then Hannah will."

He clicked his tongue. "She left you years ago. Remember, you told me how you cried after Hannah was gone."

Frustrated that he had manipulated even that information from her, she raised her chin in defiance. "I don't believe what you said about Miriam. You're wrong, Victor. She hasn't been taken away. She'll save me."

Sarah eyed the open door to the hallway. Without thinking, she shoved past him and ran toward the stairs.

He chased after her, grabbed her arm and threw her down.

Her shoulder crashed against the floor. She groaned, then scrambled to her feet. He caught her hair and yanked so hard she thought her scalp would rip from her skull.

His other hand wrapped around her neck; all the while he pulled her hair until her face pointed to the ceiling, exposing her throat, where his fingers tightened, constricting her airway.

She clawed at his arm and kicked, her lungs on fire. She couldn't swallow, couldn't scream.

"Don't ever doubt me, Sarah."

Hot tears seared her eyes. She tried to nod, but the movement caused more pain along her scalp.

Her ears rang, something gurgled in her throat, blackness swirled around her. Her knees gave way. In the split second before she would have slipped into unconsciousness, he released his hold. She fell to the floor, gasped for air and clawed her way back to reality.

"Are you going to obey me?" he demanded, standing over her, hands on his hips and eyes glaring.

She opened her mouth, hoping he hadn't seriously

damaged her vocal cords. A raspy "Yes" filtered out along with a whimper.

"That's my good Sarah."

She wasn't good and she wasn't his. She never would be. After her mother's transgressions, she would never belong to any man, and especially not a crazed lunatic who had suddenly become abusive. His verbal threats had unnerved her and made her tremble, but until today, he had never touched her inappropriately or raised his hand in anger. Seemingly in the blink of an eye, all that had changed. She couldn't fathom why. The only thing she did know was she needed to escape from Victor's control.

Not that she'd had an opportunity to elude him in the past. He kept close watch on her during the day and made sure she was locked away each night.

With a huff, he yanked her to her feet. "Mother has been asking for you."

"She wants Naomi." From what Sarah could tell, Naomi was a local Amish woman who had taken care of Ms. Hazel before Victor had brought Sarah here. Ms. Hazel repeatedly asked for her.

"You're taking Naomi's place."

Something in his tone chilled Sarah to the core. "Wh-what happened to Naomi?"

His gaze turned somber. "She disappeared, leaving Mother brokenhearted."

More likely, Victor had arranged for Naomi's disappearance.

He touched Sarah's cheek. She turned her head away.

"Listen to me." He grabbed her jaw and forced her to look at him. "A man is bringing your sister here in a day or two. I'll pay George off. Then you and Miriam can take care of Mother together. If you want to see your sister, do as I say."

His thin lips twisted into a hateful smirk. "But if you disobey me, if you try to escape, I'll—"

He let the threat hang.

She uttered the first question that came to mind. "Then will I disappear like Naomi did?"

He bristled.

Evidently, she had struck a chord that rang a little too true.

"I'm not afraid of you, Victor." Could he hear the tremble in her voice?

He leaned closer. "What if I turn off the power and use candles to light the house? Remember what you told me about the fire when you were a little girl?"

Her chest constricted. She struggled to pull air into her lungs.

"Do everything I say, Sarah, so you and Miriam can be together again, and so you can be safe. Do you understand?"

She cocked her head and furrowed her brow as if listening to a rustling sound coming from the unfinished portion of the attic.

He bristled. "What's wrong?"

"Do you hear them?" she asked, feigning an unfounded confidence in her voice.

His face blanched.

"Rats, Victor. They're in the attic."

"I don't believe you."

The fear that flashed from his eyes proved what Sarah had assumed was true.

"Feed Mother her breakfast," he ordered as he hurried out of the room.

From the open doorway, Sarah watched him race down the stairs to save himself from the rats. If she could only escape as easily.

Her momentary euphoria at having unsettled him was short-lived. Exhausted from lack of sleep and weeks of confinement, Sarah dropped her head in her hands. Hot tears burned her eyes. Would she ever be free again?

"Send someone to help me, Lord," she pleaded, her heart breaking at the hopelessness of her plight. "I don't want to die trapped in this old house."

Joachim Burkholder guided the buggy along the mountain road. He had come home like the prodigal son. Except he had not squandered money or lived a life of debauchery. He was, instead, coming home to reconcile with his father. At least that was his plan.

Metanoia, some called it, a conversion or transformation, which was what Joachim had started to experience. Now, he needed to piece his broken life back together. He had tried to live *Englisch*. His heart remained Amish.

Jostling the reins, he encouraged the mare forward. Together he and Belle had traveled from farm to farm to farm. Joachim had worked odd jobs and saved his earnings until his yearning to come home had caused him to slowly retrace his steps.

Belle increased her speed as Joachim took in the rolling hills and lush valleys. How deeply he had missed the beauty of this land and the serenity of the Amish way of life.

Gott, he silently prayed, *forgive my obstinate pride that forced me away from family and faith when I sought to place my will above Thy own.*

The tranquil setting soothed Joachim's troubled soul.

He breathed in the loamy scent of Georgia clay mixed with fresh pine from the trees that dotted the side of the roadway. The cool morning air tugged at his black jacket and lulled him into a sense of peaceful calm that dissipated as soon at the buggy rounded the bend. At the bottom of the incline, a level plain stretched out in front of him. His gut tightened as he recognized this particular section of the road home he had inadvertently taken.

Was he trying to add more burden to his already guilt-laden shoulders? Why had he guided Belle to the very spot he had never wanted to pass through again? Some memories were too hard to bear.

He glanced back, debating whether to turn around, retrace his journey and take the longer route that would circumvent this place of pain.

Joachim squared his shoulders, refusing to cower. He needed to face the past to heal. He felt sure that was the advice the bishop would provide when and if he sought to return fully to his Amish faith.

As he turned his gaze to the intersection ahead, Joachim's chest constricted. The morning sunlight filtered through the gray sky overhead, yet for a moment, he stepped back in time as the memory of that night assailed him. He heard the rhythmic clip-clop of horses' hooves against the pavement and the creak of the two buggies as they strained along the ill-fated path.

In his mind's eyes, he saw Eli turn and laugh at Joachim, who followed close behind in the second buggy. The ongoing competition between the two brothers had taken a tragic turn that night.

At eighteen, Joachim should have known better than to go along with the seemingly innocent challenge. He did not blame his brother. Nor had his *datt* blamed Eli. Instead, his father had blamed Joachim.

Once again, he remembered how Eli had egged him on, ignoring the roar of the oncoming vehicle and the headlights speeding too fast.

Joachim had raised his voice in warning. "A car approaches on the road." But Eli had not heard and had not reacted.

The crash of metal and splintering wood echoed in Joachim's memory, along with the horrific cry that had come from his own throat as he screamed his brother's name.

Five years had passed, yet Joachim's grief was still so raw. "*Gott*, forgive me," he whispered as he hurried Belle through the intersection.

Perhaps coming home to the mountains had been a mistake. What had happened could not be undone. No matter how Joachim tried to reconcile the past.

He needed longer to decide if he was ready to contact his father. Work would help. Using his hands and carpentry skills to transform disrepair into integrity would allow him to see more clearly. If he could hole up somewhere, he might be able to stem the figurative bleeding of his wounded heart and come to terms with his future and the way he wanted to live his life.

Belle flicked her head.

"You want to go home, girl. I know. But I need more time."

The turnoff to the old Thomin homestead appeared in the distance. The house had needed work five years ago. If Hazel Thomin were still alive, the elderly lady might hire Joachim to do odd jobs around the property while he tried to decide how he was going to piece his life together.

He pulled back on the reins to slow Belle's pace, then nudged the mare onto the path that led to the grand home. The property had been in Mrs. Thomin's family for generations, but what he saw made his spirits plummet even more. The house that had been regal in its day—some called it a mansion—now appeared wasted from neglect.

Joachim grimaced, noting the peeling paint and the sagging facade. The stately beauty had come under hard times and was in need of a steady hand that could restore her original beauty as well as her once-sturdy understructure.

He guided the buggy toward the front of the house and glanced up to see a young woman near Joachim's age peering from a second-story window. Blond hair hung around her slender face. She stared at him, wide-eyed, for a long moment. His chest tightened in response to the need he recognized, even at this distance, in her pensive gaze. Before he could acknowledge her presence, she stepped away, leaving him confused by the tangle of emotion that wrapped around his heart.

Joachim pulled the horse to a stop and jumped to the ground as the front door opened. Victor Thomin stepped outside, coffee mug in hand. Tall and skinny with unkempt red hair, Hazel Thomin's only child had not improved in looks—or, it seemed, in temperament—over the last five years.

With a surly grunt, Victor raised the mug to his lips and drank deeply, his beady eyes intent on Joachim, even as he wiped the back of his hand over his thin lips. A cut festered that had spattered his knuckles with dried blood.

Recalling the baleful glance of the woman at the window, Joachim made a connection that caused his eyes to widen in horror—though he immediately reminded himself that it could be wild speculation and not credible in the least. He had no proof of abuse, yet Joachim could not and would not ignore his instincts. Victor had been a scoundrel in his youth, and from the downward pull on his drawn lips, there was no reason to think he had changed.

Extending his hand, Joachim introduced himself. Instinctively, he knew from Victor's menacing expression that the red-haired man had failed to recognize him.

Victor reluctantly accepted the handshake. "Is there something you want?"

"I'm looking for work." Joachim glanced again at the overhead window, feeling a sense of loss at finding it empty. "Carpentry, painting or any handyman jobs you might need done. I can provide references."

Victor pursed his lips. "You're from around here?"

Joachim would not lie, but he saw no reason to provide more than a minimum of information. "I worked in North Carolina for a number of years. Folks said there might be jobs in this area of North Georgia."

He studied the once-beautiful home, pausing to gaze at each window, hoping for another sign of the illusive woman. "Looks like they were right. Your house could use a bit of upkeep."

Victor shrugged. "I doubt this old place is worth the effort."

"A few repairs will make a big difference," Joachim assured him. He touched the dry rot around the front door and peered inside the house through the sidelight. His heart skittered in his chest.

The woman he had seen moments earlier now stood poised on the landing. She raised her index finger to her lips as if pleading for him to remain silent about her whereabouts. The furtive look on her oval face made him even more concerned about her wellbeing.

Joachim turned back to Victor. "I can do as little or as much as you want. But you should know that the value of your property would improve with the repairs, in case you decide to sell any time soon."

Victor arched a brow. Seemingly, the mention of financial gain brought interest. "You think I could find a buyer?"

Joachim nodded. "*Yah*, if you are willing to fix some of the problems."

"I've got rot around the back porch, too," Victor volunteered. "Plus, the kitchen door is warped and won't close easily."

"Let me have a look," Joachim suggested. He motioned Victor to take the lead and then glanced again into the house. The woman had disappeared.

Joachim sighed at his own foolishness. He knew better than to play hide-and-seek with an *Englisch* woman. He needed employment, not involvement in a domestic dispute. Although she and Victor seemed an unlikely match. Perhaps she was a caregiver for his mother. Still, something did not seem right. Whether she was there as an employee, a spouse or a guest…no woman should look so afraid.

After rounding the house, Joachim climbed to the back porch. Quickly he inspected the sagging roof and rotting soffits, trying to get his mind off the woman who continued to tug at his heart.

His gaze turned to the kitchen window. He stepped

closer in pretense of examining the sill, all the while peering through the glass, searching the kitchen and hallway beyond for some sign of the woman.

Victor stood to the side. "If I do hire you," he warned, scratching his chin, "I won't stand for laziness or slip-shod work."

Movement caught Joachim's eye. Something or some-one hurried across the entrance hallway to the front door.

"I understand your concern, but you will not find me to be lazy or my work slipshod," Joachim said, hoping to keep Victor's attention on the disrepair instead of what was happening inside the house.

Feeling the need to provide a distraction, Joachim tapped the sill and pushed on the wood before moving to the next window and repeating his assessment.

"Yah," he finally said. "There is much work to be done. I could start tomorrow. Pay me only if you are satisfied with the completed job."

"I'll think it over." Victor took another slug of his coffee. "Stop by tomorrow, and I'll let you know."

Joachim nodded. "Sounds *gut.*"

Leaving Victor on the porch, Joachim returned to the front of the house. He glanced at the outbuildings and barn in the distance. Had the woman left the house? Was she now hiding close at hand, or was he making more out of that which was innocent?

"Sarah?" Victor's voice sounded as he entered the house.

Joachim climbed into the buggy and flicked the reins. Thankfully, Belle responded with a brisk trot.

Although Joachim kept his eyes on the road, he knew he was not alone. He had seen the tarp—which had been neatly folded and stowed away earlier—strewed over the back of the buggy. Someone was hiding under the thick covering.

He hurried the mare along the driveway and felt a sense of relief as he guided Belle onto the main road.

A sports car raced by, going much too fast. The woman in the passenger's seat turned to stare at Joachim as if she had never seen an Amish man.

Too soon, the sound of another vehicle filled the air.

Joachim looked back, seeing a red pickup truck turn out of the Thomin driveway. Victor sat behind the wheel. The tires squealed as he gunned the engine.

Would he pass by as the other car had done or stop and demand to know who or what was hiding under the tarp in Joachim's buggy?

Coming home had been a mistake. More than reconciling with his father, Joachim needed to reconcile with himself as to why he was so eager to help an *Englisch* woman on the run.

Chapter Two

Sarah blinked back tears and tried to calm her heart before it ricocheted out of her chest. She had been a fool to think she could escape. The squeal of tires and the whine of a vehicle approaching the buggy made her realize the full extent of her mistake.

She curled into an even smaller ball and prayed the tarp would keep her hidden. After two months of captivity, she shuddered at the thought of what her punishment might be if Victor found her. Plus, she had put the Amish man in danger, and now he would be subject to Victor's wrath, as well. The man driving the buggy was innocent of any wrongdoing and had stepped, quite literally, into a perfect storm that was getting worse by the moment.

That she had grabbed the opportunity to run away from Victor still stunned her. An action she never would have taken if not for his abuse earlier this morning. She had planned to escape with Miriam after they were reunited. Her sister would have known what to do and where to go. Miriam had saved Sarah from the fire. She would have saved her from Victor, as well.

Instead, the Amish man with the broad shoulders and

understanding gaze had been the catalyst that had Sarah running for her life. Even when peering down at him from the window, she had felt an instant surge of hope when their eyes met, as if he knew she was in danger and had come to her rescue.

The hope evaporated with the deafening roar of the motor vehicle. She fisted her hands and bit down on her lip, willing herself to remain still while internally she wanted to kick her feet and wail like a small child who didn't want to be punished for some misdeed. Yet she had done nothing wrong.

Victor was the one at fault, a fact she needed to remember. How thoroughly he had filled her mind with lies so that she sometimes confused her innocence with guilt.

"You're the reason, Sarah, that we have to hide from the police," Victor had complained on more than one occasion. "If I didn't need to protect you, I would be free to come and go. Instead, we must hole up and hide out so the corrupt cops won't find you and sell you into slavery along with your sister."

He had brainwashed her with his constant badgering about her guilt. Fear, fatigue and her dulled senses, caused by the drugs he forced on her, had added to her confusion.

Thankfully, today, she was able to think rationally enough to seize the opportunity to escape. Pulling in a fortifying breath, she smelled the musty scent of the tarp mixed with the damp cool air of the encroaching storm. If dark clouds hung overhead, hopefully, they weren't a harbinger of what would happen to her in the next few moments.

Instead of the weather, she focused on the clip-clop

of the horse's hooves on the pavement and tried to ignore the blast of a horn and the revved acceleration of the vehicle that forced the buggy to the side of the road.

"Hold up there, Belle." The deep voice of the Amish man quieting his horse should have calmed her unease, but knowing Victor was the reason brought another volley of fear to wrap around her spine and underscored the seriousness of her situation as the buggy came to a stop.

God help me, she silently prayed. *Help the Amish man. Save both of us from Victor.*

"Hey, Amish." Victor's voice. "Did you see a woman leave my house?"

"Your *mudder*?"

"Not my mother." Victor's sharp retort reminded Sarah of the caustic tone he often used with her. "A twenty-one-year-old woman wearing jeans and a sweater."

"She is your *schweschder*?" The Amish voice was deep and calming.

"What?" Victor didn't understand.

"Your *schweschder*," the Amish man repeated. "Is your sister the woman for whom you are searching?"

"I don't have a sister," Victor spat. "I'm looking for the woman who works for us, helping my mother. Did you see anyone?"

"A car passed by, heading toward Petersville. A woman sat in the passenger seat. The man driving had a bald head."

"What color was the woman's hair?"

"Blond. This is perhaps the woman you are seeking?"

Victor grumbled. A car door slammed and tires squealed as he drove away. Sarah held her breath and listened to the sound of the engine disappearing into the distance.

"He's gone." The Amish man's voice was low and reassuring. "You can come out now."

He had known she was under the tarp?

She raised the edge of the covering and stared up at a square jaw, furrowed brow and deep-set eyes filled with question.

"Did he hurt you?" he asked.

She hadn't expected his concern or the tears that filled her eyes. "Not until today."

"He will return soon. Plus, a storm is approaching."

She looked at the darkening sky.

"I will take you someplace safe. Do you have family in the area?"

She glanced at a nearby road sign—Petersville 5 miles, Willkommen 30 miles—and shook her head. "My sister will be here tomorrow or the day after. She'll make sure I'm safe once she arrives."

"But today you need lodging," he said, calmly stating the obvious. "Stay under the tarp in case Victor returns."

Without further discussion, he turned his gaze to the road and clicked his tongue. The buggy jerked as the horse responded. Sarah found the sound of the horse's hooves on the pavement and the sway of the carriage mildly soothing.

She didn't know anything about the Amish man, yet he had helped her escape. She had to trust him, at least for the moment. From what she knew about the Amish, they kept to themselves and had little to do with law enforcement. If so, the man in the buggy might help her elude the crooked cops who had hijacked Miriam's car and were searching for both sisters even now. He might also help her reconnect with Miriam and take both of them to safety. But where would that be?

Sarah had moved from town to town her entire life with no place to call home except the short-term rentals where she and her mother and sisters had lived for a month or two at most, before moving on to the next temporary lodging. How foolish she was to think her life in the future would be different, no matter how much she longed for stability and a home of her own.

Relieved though Sarah was to be free of Victor, she worried about his mother now left home alone with her crazed son. Over the last few weeks, Ms. Hazel's condition had deteriorated much too quickly, making Sarah wonder if Victor was doing something to speed up her decline.

Concern for the older woman weighed heavily on Sarah's shoulders, but she couldn't do anything to help Ms. Hazel at the moment. Right now, she needed to close her eyes and rest. Sarah had escaped, although she felt anything but free while hiding under the tarp with Victor prowling the area in search of her.

Should Victor return to question her rescuer again, would the Amish man whose faith embraced peaceful nonresistance be able to save her? Or would Victor find her? She shuddered at the thought, knowing that if he got his hands on her once more, Victor would ensure Sarah never escaped again.

The dark sky mirrored Joachim's inner struggle. Passing through the intersection where Eli died had been Joachim's undoing earlier. Now he was hiding a woman he did not know. The added complication only made him more conflicted.

All too clearly, he had recognized the pain on the woman's face as she glanced down at him from the window and again as she stood on the stairway inside the Thomin house, her finger to her lips and her eyes pleading for mercy. Her expression had reminded Joachim of his own sense of hopelessness and despair that had overwhelmed him following his brother's death.

Was that what had drawn Joachim to the woman and made him long to protect her?

He glanced at the rear of the buggy, where she lay under the tarp. By the steady rise and fall of the heavy covering, he presumed she had fallen asleep, which was probably for the best. Fatigue had lined her face along with fear that made him grateful he had come to her rescue.

The wind picked up, and the temperature dropped as dark clouds billowed overhead. Joachim needed to find shelter before the storm brought more chaos to this already confusing day.

He flicked the reins, hurrying Belle. Instinctively, she knew the route he had chosen to take.

The woman needed a place to hole up for a day or two until she could connect with her sister. Petersville was the nearest town, but that was the direction Victor had gone. When he failed to find her there, he would more than likely retrace his route to search more thoroughly in the local area.

The Burkholder farm adjoined the Thomin property, but the road connecting the two homes took a circuitous route around the fields and pastures. Glancing at the sky, Joachim wondered if Belle would get them to shelter in time.

If his father was tilling the soil in the distant acreage,

Joachim might be able to signal his sister, Rebecca, especially if she was working in the garden. She had written him faithfully while he was away, telling him about the family. In spite of the breezy news she shared, Joachim had read between the lines, all too aware of the emotional anguish Eli's death had caused his family.

More than anything, Joachim longed to see *Mamm* again, yet his mother would abide by the rules his father established. Having to watch her turn her back on him would be almost too hard to bear.

And the woman hiding in the back of his buggy? If his father forbid Joachim entry into the house, he would hole up in the barn and give the woman as long as she needed to decide where she wanted to go. Until that time, Joachim would stand guard, ensuring Victor did not find her.

But would she want Joachim's help?

He shook his head. An *Englisch* woman was not in his future, yet whether he liked it or not, she was very much in his present. More than anything, Joachim wanted to keep her safe from Victor and from anyone else who might cause her harm.

Chapter Three

In her dream, Sarah watched Victor raise his hand to strike her. She screamed, then flailed her arms and tried to free herself from the shroud that covered her.

"You are safe." Hands reached for her, removed the heavy covering and pulled her into an embrace.

Not Victor, but the Amish man.

"Shh," he soothed, cradling her like a child.

It was the first comfort she had felt in far too long. She buried her head against his neck, wanting to remain forever enveloped in his warm and protective hold.

Tears filled her eyes and spilled down her cheeks, wetting his cotton shirt. Hearing the rain, she was more than grateful to be under cover and out of the storm, and even more grateful for the human contact.

The rapid thump of his heart proved the Amish man wasn't a figment of her imagination. She nestled closer, not wanting to open her eyes or leave the security of his embrace for which she had hungered too long.

Thunder crashed overhead.

"Joachim?" A woman's voice said the name, her tone filled with surprise.

Another clap of thunder.

Her Amish protector tensed and pulled back ever so slightly.

Sarah clung to him for a moment before her eyes fluttered open.

His head was turned. She followed his gaze to the woman dressed in a calf-length blue dress, white apron and bonnet, who stood just inside the open barn door.

Outside, rain pummeled the earth. The day had turned dark as night. Or was it night already? She wasn't sure how much time had passed. The woman's questioning frown seemed equally dark. Perhaps she was the man's wife. The thought cut through Sarah's heart. She had been such a fool.

Embarrassed by her neediness and the way she had reached out to the man, she untangled her arms from where they had wrapped around him.

He glanced down at her, a glint of confusion flashing from his dark eyes.

Was he upset that his wife had found him giving comfort to a woman who wanted nothing more than to return to his embrace?

"I—I'm sorry," she stammered, trying to make sense of what had happened. "I was asleep. I didn't realize…"

"Who are you?" the Amish woman demanded, glancing first at Sarah and then turning her frosty gaze to the man. "Joachim, is there something you did not tell me in your letters?"

"She needs help, Rebecca."

"*Yah*, and it looks like you need help as well from the way you clutched the *Englischer* to your heart."

"Father is in the house?" he asked, seemingly side-tracking the issue at hand.

Rebecca shook her head. "He and *Mamm* are visiting Aunt Mildred and Uncle Frank in Kentucky. They will be gone for a few more days. Had you written that you were coming home, they might not have left."

Sarah was trying to follow the conversation and understand the undercurrent of what was really being said. The man had mentioned his father. No, his tone implied that it was *their* father. Was the woman not his wife?

"Excuse me," Sarah said, pulling away from him and peering at both of them. "You're not married?"

The woman huffed. "Why do you think this?"

Evidently, Sarah had jumped to the wrong conclusion. She held up her hand. "I'm sorry. I don't want to offend either of you."

She turned to Joachim. "Thank you for bringing me here. If I could stay in the barn until the storm passes, I would appreciate it."

His brow furrowed. "You plan to leave?" He shook his head. "This cannot be."

He climbed from the buggy and motioned to the Amish woman. "We must take our guest into the house."

Glancing back, his gaze burrowed into hers. "Your name is Sarah?"

She nodded. "Sarah Miller."

"I'm Joachim Burkholder." He pointed to the other woman. "My sister, Rebecca."

The weight on Sarah's shoulders lifted ever so slightly. Sister. Not wife. Tears again stung her eyes.

"She needs food and lodging, Rebecca."

The Amish woman stepped closer. Her earlier scowl softened but she seemed hesitant to offer Sarah a hearty welcome.

"We must hurry," Joachim said. "Before Victor returns."

Rebecca grasped her brother's arm. "Victor Thomin?"

"*Yah*. He is staying at his mother's house."

"*Ach*," his sister groaned, with a shake of her head. "Naomi said he is not a good man."

"You know Naomi?" Sarah asked. "Victor's mother kept asking for her."

Rebecca nodded. "Naomi lived nearby. She cared for Ms. Hazel while Victor was away."

Joachim pointed to the open barn door. "The rain eases. We must go inside."

He reached for Sarah and helped her from the buggy. Taking her hand, he hurried her out of the barn.

Dark clouds rolled overhead. Another storm was approaching, but Sarah breathed in the cleansing air, feeling a sense of relief. She had escaped Victor. She had a place to stay. At least for now, she was free.

A bolt of lightning pierced the sky and struck nearby. The almost-immediate crash made Sarah realize everything could change in an instant.

She would never be free of Victor, not until the hateful man was stopped.

The rain intensified just before Joachim and Sarah reached the porch. Another sound was discernable over the rain. He glanced at the drive and tensed. A horse and buggy scurried along the main road. For a long moment, Joachim stared after the buggy and then let out a deep breath.

"You thought it was Victor, didn't you?" she pressed.

He squeezed Sarah's hand, hoping to provide reassurance and bring comfort to her seemingly still-anxious heart. "Victor will not find you here."

At least that was Joachim's hope.

Together they climbed the steps to the porch. He opened the door and motioned her inside. She wiped her feet on the latched rug and hurried into the kitchen.

A sense of calm and right order enveloped Joachim as he stepped over the threshold and stopped to take in the peacefulness that pervaded the space. Glancing at the familiar furnishings—the table and chairs, dry sink and cabinets—his *datt* had made, Joachim soaked in the aura of home and family he had missed for the last five years.

"Rebecca can brew coffee," he said, hoping his voice did not reveal the mix of emotions that had welled up within him upon entering the house. He turned to the newcomer. "Perhaps you would prefer tea?"

Sarah glanced at Rebecca, who hurried in behind them.

"I have cold cuts and cheese and fresh baked bread if you are hungry."

"Thank you both," Sarah said. "But first, I need to wash my hands and face, if you don't mind."

"Of course." Rebecca pointed to the stairs. "I will take you to the room where you will stay the night. Joachim must tend his mare. We will eat after he returns from the barn."

His sister turned as if to shoo him outside. But despite her prompting, he was slow to head to the door. He did not want to leave the home to which he had only now returned. He also did not want to leave Sarah.

He gently touched her shoulder. "So much has happened, but you are not to worry. Victor is in town, searching for you there."

"And if he comes here?" she asked.

"I will not let him into the house."

Belle needed to be groomed and fed. Rebecca would take care of Sarah until he returned. Still, leaving the house this time was almost as hard as leaving the mountains had been five years ago.

How could he have grown so attached to a woman—an *Englisch* woman—in such a short period of time? He knew nothing about her except that she needed a safe place to stay for a day or two. He and Rebecca would open their home to her, but Joachim needed to be careful. As taken as he was by her in such a short time, he feared what might happen in the days ahead. He must guard not only Sarah, but also his heart.

Chapter Four

Joachim had said that he would keep her safe. As much as Sarah wanted to believe him, she was worried. Victor was unpredictable, and his mood swings had grown progressively more extreme. He had warned her never to leave him, but she'd done just that. Given how angry he'd been before over smaller infractions, what would his response be to this?

Rebecca filled a pitcher with water and motioned for Sarah to follow her. "A diesel pump runs our well, so we always have water in the house," the Amish woman explained as they climbed the stairs. "Propane heats our water for washing and bathing. Later I will fill a tub for you."

On the second floor, she ushered Sarah into a small but spotlessly clean bedroom. A beige patchwork quilt pieced with blue triangles covered the single bed. A chest of drawers, table and straight-back chair filled the room.

Rebecca placed the pitcher on the chest next to a large porcelain bowl. She opened the bottom drawer and pulled out a thick terry-cloth towel, a bar of soap and a glass bottle.

"I made the soap and shampoo and added natural oils to both products. I hope you will find them to your liking."

"Thank you, Rebecca. You and your brother have been so thoughtful."

Rebecca seemed to appreciate the compliment that hopefully would wash away her earlier concern about Sarah. The Amish woman offered a weak smile. Her cheeks glowed pink with a mix of embarrassment and appreciation. "Come downstairs when you are ready to eat."

Sarah glanced at the inviting bed, wishing she could hide under the covers and curl into a ball. Maybe then she wouldn't worry about Victor finding her again. Was she safe here? Sarah needed to learn more about Joachim Burkholder and his Amish family. Thanks to them, she had a place to stay, at least for now.

She scrubbed her face and hands and dabbed water through her hair, appreciating the clean, fresh scent of the bar soap and eyeing the liquid shampoo. Using the bath products Rebecca had made would be a welcome treat, although so much could happen in the hours ahead. Sarah needed to focus on figuring out what she needed to do to remain free from Victor instead of on creature comforts like having a long soak in a hot tub.

After patting her face and hands dry, she returned to the kitchen.

"The coffee is hot," Rebecca said in greeting. "Or as Joachim mentioned, I could make tea."

"He's still in the barn?" Sarah asked, knowing nothing about farm life and feeling somewhat awkward around his sister.

"*Yah*. Joachim feeds his horse before he feeds himself."

"You seemed surprised to see him."

The Amish woman nodded. "He has been gone from our home for a number of years. It is *gut* to have him back again."

"Do you have other siblings?"

"A brother, Eli, died a few years ago."

"I'm sorry."

"It was *Gott*'s will."

Sarah didn't want to think about a loving God taking anyone's life. At the moment, she longed for something to keep her mind on anything other than death. "May I help you prepare the lunch?"

"You can slice the bread. It is cooling on the counter." Rebecca pointed to the raised loaf. A knife lay next to a cutting board.

"It's homemade?" Sarah asked, admiring the plumpness of the loaf and the golden brown crust.

"*Yah*." Rebecca arranged the meat and cheese on a platter. "I always make extra bread and sell it to tourists who stop at our driveway."

Sarah looked out the window, suspicion growing within her. "Do people often come to your house?"

"It is not something that should worry you," Rebecca assured her.

In spite of Rebecca's comment, Sarah couldn't shake off her concern about strangers visiting the Burkholder farm while she stayed there. She continued to peer from the window, hoping for some sign of Joachim—and for no sign of anyone else. The door to the barn hung open, and the interior looked dark and foreboding.

Rebecca claimed Joachim was caring for his horse, but what if she was wrong? Victor could have returned and overpowered Joachim when he wasn't looking. Perhaps Victor was ready to barge into the house and capture Sarah again.

Minutes ticked by, only increasing her worry. "Why is Joachim taking so long?" she finally asked, unable to calm her unease.

"You could go to the barn and ask him yourself," Rebecca suggested. "Or you could join me in the main room where I have my mending. Joachim will come inside shortly."

Joachim had assured Sarah earlier that she was safe, but it felt to her as if too much time had elapsed since he had left the house. Rebecca moved into the main room and started humming. The tune, a childhood favorite, should have calmed Sarah's unease. Instead, it only added to her concern. What was she doing in a strange house with people she didn't know?

She glanced at the oil lamps on the wall, the candles on the sideboard and the matches on the table. Her chest constricted and her pulse raced. A ringing sounded in her ears that failed to overpower the voice screaming through her mind.

Fire!

She wrung her hands. The memory of that night so long ago returned, constricting her lungs and leaving her gasping for air, overcome by the same panic that filled her every time she even thought about flames.

She had to leave. Now.

Ever so quietly, she opened the kitchen door and

gulped in the damp air, all the while the voice continued to warn her.

While in the buggy, she had seen a sign for Willkommen. Victor had mentioned Miriam was being held somewhere in that area. Their aunt lived in Willkommen, as well. At least that's what their mother had told them. If Sarah could get to Willkommen, she might find her aunt, and together they could search for Miriam.

She pulled in a fortifying breath and then raced down the steps and scurried past the barn, heading toward the pasture and a line of trees on the far side of the field. She would hide there until the roadway looked clear. Then she would cross to the opposite side where a thick patch of trees flanked the road. Hidden by dense underbrush, she would make her way to the narrow two-lane that veered off from the main road, where she had spotted the sign for Willkommen.

As much as Sarah had appreciated Joachim's help, she couldn't rely on him to keep her safe. He was Victor's neighbor.

She checked the road for cars, saw that it was clear and crossed the pavement. The approach of a vehicle sounded in the distance. Her pulse raced. She turned to glance over her shoulder.

Her heart stopped as a red pickup crested the nearby hill. Victor!

She ran toward the trees, needing to disappear in the brush. She wouldn't let him capture her again.

The truck accelerated.

She ran faster.

The screech of brakes made her heart lurch.

Victor had seen her.

Footfalls pounded the pavement. He was coming after her.

She'd been so foolish. Victor was more of a threat to her safety than the matches and candles and oil lamps. She never should have traded the security of Joachim's house for the outdoors, where she was so vulnerable.

"Sarah!" Victor screamed her name.

She hesitated for a fraction of a second, then chastised herself for being so easily swayed.

Fighting against the pull of his voice, she forced herself forward, remembering how he had choked her this morning until she couldn't breathe.

She pushed through the bushes, needing to escape his voice, his control. To escape him.

"You won't get away, Sarah," he called, as if reading her mind. "I'll follow you. You can't escape from me."

The branches scraped her arms and pulled at her sweater, but she kept going, ignoring the cuts to her flesh. She couldn't listen to her body. She had to listen to her mind, warning her to run fast, run hard, run away.

She made a sharp turn to the right and ran all the faster. The only sound she heard was her own raspy breath and pounding heart. For an instant, she thought she had eluded him until the sound of his footfalls returned along with the rustle of leaves.

If only she had stayed at Joachim's house. He would have protected her.

"Sarah!" He was close. Too close.

She tripped.

He grabbed her.

She fought to free herself from his hold.

No! She tried to scream, but his hand clamped around her mouth.

"Sarah?" Victor called again. This time, he was farther away and moving in an opposite direction.

If Victor wasn't holding her, then who was?

Soft. Her skin was so very soft.

Joachim dropped his hand, releasing Sarah from his hold.

She stood ever so still, as if afraid to move.

"He's heading back to his truck," Joachim whispered. "You lost him when you made that sharp turn to the right. I saw you cross the street when I left the barn, but it took me a while to catch up to you."

"Oh, Joachim," she said, pulling in a deep breath. "Victor was following close behind me."

"But you outsmarted him, Sarah."

She turned to gaze up at Joachim with blue eyes that were crystal clear and filled with sorrow. His heart tripped in his chest, making him want to move even closer.

"I never should have left your house," she said, seemingly oblivious to the way her nearness affected him. "It wasn't because of any distrust for you or your sister. It was me. I didn't want to cause you any problems. If Victor found me at your house, I'm not sure what he would have done. Plus, I need to get to Willkommen. My sister Miriam—"

She shook her head. "I haven't mentioned my aunt. My sister, my mother and I came here to find her, but dirty cops hijacked our car. Miriam and I were taken and our mother was killed. Victor said he bought me so I could take care of his mother. I'm still so confused." She pulled in a ragged breath. "It was crazy of me to think I could have found my way to Willkommen, yet it seemed like the best choice I had in that moment. I don't have any place else to go."

"You have my house. Victor will not find you there. I will protect you."

At least Joachim hoped he could keep her safe. "Willkommen is a two-hour buggy ride from Petersville," he tried to explain. "Even if you were strong, the trip would be difficult for you to manage on foot. You have been held captive. You must gain your strength first. I will take you when you are ready."

"I wasn't thinking." Sarah tugged at a strand of her golden hair. "Or maybe I was thinking too much about getting away from Victor."

Joachim held out his hand. She placed hers in his, her touch light, but she was trembling and her pale face gave him even more cause for concern. She needed time to rest and gain her strength. Good food and lots of sleep would help build up Sarah's reserve. Then they could think about traveling to Willkommen.

"Rebecca will wonder where we are," he said. "We will go now and take a path that leads through the woods. The spot where we will cross the road is thick with trees on both sides of the pavement. We will move slowly and keep watch lest Victor be close at hand."

"I'm all right, Joachim. You don't have to worry about me."

But he *was* worried. He was worried about the fatigue written so plainly across her sweet face. She was too thin and too pale, and no matter how strong she tried to appear, she needed rest and nourishment.

He had to get Sarah to his house to keep her safe. Hopefully, she wouldn't run away again because next time he might not be able to save her.

* * *

Once they arrived back at the Burkholder house, Joachim held the kitchen door open for Sarah and motioned her inside.

"Rebecca has lunch ready," he said, as they stepped over the threshold and into the warmth of the Amish home. "A good meal is what we both need."

His eyes were filled with understanding as he looked at her and smiled. "Is that not right?"

"I am hungry," Sarah admitted, grateful for Joachim's focus on food instead of mentioning her foolish mistake of thinking she could outwit Victor.

Just as Joachim had mentioned, she needed to gain strength before she journeyed to Willkommen. Besides, Victor said Miriam might be arriving at his house in a day or two. This wasn't the time for Sarah to run scared.

"Joachim, you are ready for a cup of coffee?" Rebecca asked as she entered the kitchen, her needlework still in her hands. From her casual gait and nonchalance, she evidently had not realized what had transpired after Sarah left the house.

"Yah," Joachim said with a nod. "I will wash my hands, and then I will also be ready for the meats and cheeses you have placed on the table."

He and Sarah both washed at the sink. Rebecca filled mugs with coffee and motioned Sarah to sit next to her at the table.

Joachim sat across from both women and bowed his head.

Sarah and Rebecca followed suit, with each person praying silently.

Thank You, Lord, Sarah mentally intoned, *for Joachim rescuing me in the woods, and thank You for providing this place of shelter from the storm. Send Miriam and let me help her escape whoever is holding her captive so she and I can be together again.*

She glanced up to find Joachim staring at her. Her chest tightened, and a warmth tingled her neck. Glancing away, she reached for the meats and cheeses and placed a slice of each on a piece of bread.

Hungry though she was, Sarah kept thinking of Victor's mother, knowing Ms. Hazel was at the mercy of her son. What would become of the frail woman if Victor left the area for good?

"You are thinking of Victor?" Joachim asked.

"His mother. She's bedridden. A sweet lady who is too infirm to help herself."

"Victor is not to be trusted." Rebecca said with a decisive nod.

Sarah reached for her coffee, not willing to let her expression reveal her own struggle, knowing she had wanted to believe Victor when he'd first taken her from the cabin where she and Miriam had been held. He had told her he would keep her safe from the men who planned to traffic both sisters across state lines. Had it been the drugs that made Sarah believe—at least for a day or two—that he would protect her?

Joachim placed his mug on the table and cocked his head. "A vehicle approaches."

Sarah recognized the sound. Her stomach tightened, and she clutched her hands. "What if it's Victor?"

"Stay inside." Joachim left the table. "Do not let anyone see you."

He opened the door and stepped onto the porch. Rebecca ran to open the window over the sink.

"It is a pickup truck," she relayed to Sarah. "A man is driving. Red hair."

She glanced back at Sarah. "*Yah*, it is Victor."

Sarah wanted to find a closet and hide.

"The pantry." Rebecca pointed to the walk-in alcove. "He will not see you there."

Sarah's heart nearly pounded out of her chest. She hurried into the pantry. Peering around the curtain that divided the cupboard area from the kitchen, she watched the truck pull to a stop.

"Hey, Amish." Victor's raised voice floated through the partially open window. "I spotted the woman I told you about. She disappeared in the woods. If you see her, let me know."

"Why do you need to find this woman?" Joachim asked, his voice calm and rational in contrast to Victor's nervous high pitch.

"Sarah worked for my mother. Now she's gone. In fact, if you know of an Amish girl who wants a job, I need to hire someone."

"Dependable help is hard to find," Joachim said.

"As sickly as my mother has become, I doubt she'll live long. I plan to get the house ready to sell. Come over tomorrow. I have work for you, and remember to let me know if you see that woman."

Victor turned his truck around and drove off.

Sarah's heart hammered in her chest. If she had been outside on the porch, or even standing next to a window, Victor would have spotted her.

Joachim entered the kitchen and hurried to where she stood, her eyes wide and back to the wall.

"He is gone," Joachim assured her.

Sarah was too frightened to move. Victor had found her once. He could find her again no matter what Joachim did to try to stop him.

Fear. Joachim had seen it in Sarah's pretty blue eyes when he had come back inside the house after Victor had driven away.

"He is gone," Joachim assured her again. From the look on her face, he knew his words did little to quell her upset.

A knock sounded at the front door. Sarah took a step back and gasped.

Joachim glanced at Rebecca. "You are expecting someone?"

"Levi Plank has been helping me while *Mamm* and *Datt* are away." She peered from the kitchen window. "*Yah*, it is Levi."

Her voice took on a lilt Joachim had not heard, and the blush to her cheeks made him pause.

"Levi is a friend," Rebecca assured Sarah. "You do not need to be afraid."

But her words did little to change the concern written so plainly on Sarah's face. She backed even farther into the pantry and covered her mouth with her hand; all the while her eyes sought out Joachim. He nodded his encouragement before he stepped toward the door.

Years before, the young Amish man had been his brother Eli's friend. Both the same age, Levi had been the quiet, pensive one whose personality contrasted sharply with Eli's charisma.

Rebecca opened the door, her eyes twinkling with interest, a warm and welcoming smile on her face as she invited Levi inside. "I have a surprise that I did not expect. Joachim has come home."

In the five years that Joachim had been away, the quiet youth had grown into a muscular man whose grip was strong and firm when the two men shook hands.

"This is a *gut* surprise," Levi said. Then as if overcome with enthusiasm, he pulled Joachim close and slapped his back. "You have been missed."

The sincerity of his welcome touched Joachim. "It is good to see you, my friend."

"Our parting was difficult. I trust you have been well. It was time for you to come home, *yah*?"

Joachim nodded. "It was time."

Levi's gaze turned to the alcove where Sarah peered with wide eyes at the gathering.

"You have brought someone home with you?" Levi asked, a hint of confusion evident in his tone.

Sarah took a step forward as Joachim introduced her to Levi. "Sarah needed a place to stay," Rebecca quickly volunteered. "She will remain with us for a day or two."

"You have found a good house," Levi said with a nod. "Plus, Rebecca is known for her pies and cakes."

He rubbed his stomach. "Often she asks me to taste her baked items after the chores." He smiled at the young Amish woman. "Perhaps today we will all be able to enjoy a slice or two of pie."

Rebecca laughed. "*Yah*, that is possible after the animals are watered and fed. You know I cannot resist you, Levi, with all the help you have provided."

"Then I will hurry to the chores as my mouth waters for the special treat that awaits."

Joachim nodded. "I, too, am grateful for your help, Levi. We will go together."

"I will bake something while you both work," Rebecca assured them. She glanced at Sarah. "We will both remain in the house and watch for Victor."

"Victor Thomin?" Levi asked.

"Yah." Rebecca nodded. "He is a dangerous man. I do not know how Naomi could work so long in his house."

"My sister helped Ms. Hazel, but she had nothing to do with Victor. Ms. Hazel lived alone back then."

Sarah stepped from the alcove. "Your sister was the Amish woman Ms. Hazel mentioned? She misses Naomi."

"We all miss her," Levi admitted.

"I don't understand," Sarah said.

Levi pursed his lips and thought for a moment before responding. "Victor came home. She did not like being around him, but we fear something else could have happened because she left not only the job but also the area. We have not heard from Naomi since then."

Sarah's brow furrowed. "Did you go to the police?"

"The Amish in this community do not trust the Petersville police. It is commonly known that they can be bribed and bought. My *datt* would not have gone to them, except for his concern for Naomi's welfare." Levi's voice took on an angry edge as he continued. "They were no help and said Naomi must have left for a better life among the *Englisch*."

Rebecca patted his shoulder, offering support.

He nodded his thanks and then continued. "It was not what my father wanted to hear. We will not go to the police again. They do not understand our ways. Some say they are only interested in their own gain."

"Victor told me the police were corrupt," Sarah shared. "Although he is corrupt as well, so I don't know if I can believe what he said. Still, my sister's car was hijacked by men claiming to be police." She quickly explained being sold to Victor and how Joachim had helped her escape today.

Levi was right, Joachim thought. The Amish did not trust the police, but Victor needed to be stopped by law enforcement. Perhaps Sarah would change her mind about notifying the authorities if she knew them to be honorable. Right now, she was exhausted and still traumatized by what had happened. Joachim would broach the subject again later. In the meantime he would do everything possible to keep her safe.

Chapter Five

Sarah appreciated the bath Rebecca drew while the men worked outdoors. The fragrance of the sweet-smelling soap she provided filled the air like a spring bouquet. Sarah stepped from the tub feeling rejuvenated and grateful as she slipped into the Amish dress Rebecca had provided.

"With a clean body, you must also have fresh clothes," Rebecca stated as she instructed Sarah on how to pin the fabric and then adjust the apron around her waist.

"What about the bonnet?" Sarah asked.

"It is a prayer *kapp*. Amish women cover their heads when they pray."

"But you wear it all the time?"

"This is true. We are always ready to pray when our head is covered."

"I pray but perhaps not often enough," Sarah admitted.

"The *kapp* will remind you to do so."

Sarah thought of being in the closet as a child. The smoke had seeped under the door, making her even more afraid. God hadn't saved her even though Sarah had prayed. Thankfully, Miriam had come to her rescue.

"Did you ever pray for something that didn't come about so that you felt God refused your prayer?" Sarah asked.

"*Gott* does not refuse prayer, but sometimes that which we desire is not according to His will." Rebecca sighed. "I told you that Joachim and I had a younger brother named Eli, who died in a buggy accident. My *mamm* prayed for him to live."

"I'm so sorry about your brother."

"As I mentioned earlier, it was *Gott*'s will." Rebecca smiled ruefully. "This is what my *mamm* believes."

"And your father?"

Rebecca's face clouded. "My father does not blame *Gott*." She hesitated as if weighing whether to say something else, then shrugging, she added, "He blames Joachim."

Before Sarah could question her further, Rebecca picked up the white bonnet from where she had placed it on the dresser and handed it to Sarah. Earlier, she had pulled her towel-dried hair into a bun, and she now placed the bonnet on her head.

Rebecca stood back and nodded her approval. "You look like an Amish woman. Victor will not recognize you if he returns to talk to Joachim."

Sarah's stomach roiled thinking again of the hateful man who had held her against her will for too long. How could his mother, who seemed sweet and unassuming, birth a baby who would grow to be so vicious?

What had caused Victor to turn out so bad? She shook her head at the issues within families. Sarah's oldest sister, Hannah, had left three years ago. Sarah had pleaded for her to stay, but Hannah said she had to leave. Sarah hadn't understood her reasoning or why Hannah had never contacted them again.

When she begged her mother to reach out to Hannah and ask her to return home, her mother had shoved the request aside, just as she ignored anything that didn't suit her. Sarah never understood how she could turn her back on her own child. Although too many times her mother had turned her back on Miriam and Sarah. At least Sarah had always had Miriam, but where was she now and would the two women ever be reunited?

The rain returned. Fat drops pounded the barnyard, and thunder rumbled overhead. Joachim and Levi hurried to finish the chores.

Glancing at the upstairs window, Joachim thought of when he had first seen Sarah. Had it been only a few hours since their eyes had connected at the Thomin home?

He followed Levi into the barn. The two men spoke little as they worked, but the silence was comfortable, and the physical labor relaxed the tension in Joachim's shoulders. Some of his earlier concern about Sarah evaporated, and instead of confusion, he felt a sense of purpose and right order.

"Your father is a *gut* farmer, but he is getting old," Levi confided as he paused for a moment to wipe his brow.

"*Datt* planned for Eli and me to work the land with him," Joachim admitted. "Now he needs to find help. You are good to aid him, Levi."

"I help only when he is not in town. He is too proud to take on another person the rest of the time."

Joachim nodded. "*Yah*, he is proud."

"He will be glad to see you."

"You are good to give me comfort by your hopeful words, but I do not think my *datt* will welcome me home."

Levi narrowed his gaze. "You come asking forgiveness, *yah*?"

"I do, but my father and I must both bridge the divide between us. I will walk halfway. I hope he will walk halfway, as well."

"Sometimes the son must walk farther, especially if the father believes he is right."

Joachim pondered Levi's words while he added feed to the troughs and watched the horses eat the newly offered grain.

Levi might think his father would be open to Joachim coming home, but what if his homecoming brought back too many memories of what had happened? Maybe when he faced his father again, Joachim would discover that he had been foolish to think reconciliation was possible.

Once the horses were fed, the two men rolled up their sleeves and washed their hands and arms at the water pump, and then ran to the house as lightning split the sky.

Joachim opened the door and hurried into the kitchen ahead of Levi.

Rebecca stood at the stove, holding a pie that she had just pulled from the oven.

"The storm comes again," he said as he crossed the kitchen to the towel hanging on a hook.

He dried his hands, then glanced up as Rebecca turned to face him. His heart lurched in his chest, sending a new wave of confusion over him. He stared open-mouthed at the Amish woman.

Not Rebecca. The face he saw beneath the white *kapp* made his breath catch in his throat.

Sarah.

"Rebecca provided the clothes." Sarah's hand wrapped through the fabric of the skirt. "Your sister said Victor would not recognize me like this."

"My sister is right." Joachim struggled to find his voice. "I did not recognize you at first glance."

"You think I look like Rebecca?"

Her blue eyes reached into his heart. She was beautiful. Not because she was in the Amish dress or because her hair was pulled into a bun but because some of the pain she had worn earlier had eased. The lines that tugged at her face had lifted, and the open honesty of her gaze hit him anew.

"Joachim, you haven't answered me," she said, her eyes filled with concern. "Is something wrong?"

"Nothing is wrong and you do not look like Rebecca, but I am surprised to see you as an Amish woman."

"Am I offending you?"

He shook his head. "You could never offend me."

Levi hurried inside and stopped by the door to wipe his feet. Bewilderment washed over his face as he glanced first at Sarah and then at Rebecca, who stepped back into the kitchen.

"You are both staring as if you have never seen a woman in an Amish dress," Rebecca said with a laugh.

Levi pointed to the stove. "I was wondering if you could spare a cup of coffee and a slice of pie for a hungry man."

"*Yah*, of course." Rebecca's cheeks glowed with a

hint of embarrassment. "But I have ham and cheese on the table, along with fresh baked bread. You need to eat something substantial before you have your pie."

Levi smiled as he accepted the cup of coffee she offered. "You know what I need even before I do."

The twinkle in her eyes warmed Joachim's heart. Rebecca's interest in the young man was more than evident, and Levi seemed taken with her, as well. Joachim was happy for his *schweschder* and hoped Levi would start the courting process soon. Perhaps Joachim could chaperone and take them for rides in the country. He would occupy his mind with thoughts of pretty Sarah in her blue dress and white apron while Rebecca and Levi chatted with each other.

If only Sarah was wearing the Amish dress as a woman of their faith instead of as an *Englischer* who needed to hide her identity and had nothing else to wear.

Joachim and Sarah sipped coffee as Levi ate the lunch Rebecca had provided. Although Sarah said little, her eyes took in the conversation he and Levi had about the farm and what could be done if his *datt* were open to accepting help to make the fields more productive.

"The Amish Market in Willkommen is a fine place to sell produce and baked goods," Levi shared. "My uncle goes twice a week as do many of the other Amish farmers. The *Englisch* come from as far away as Atlanta. They buy handcrafted items, too—including woodwork. You could do well in this area, Joachim, if you opened a shop in town."

He shook his head and laughed. "I am a carpenter, Levi, not a store clerk."

"Yet you charge for your labor when you go house to

house. How different would that be from selling chairs and tables and lawn furniture to walk-in customers?"

Although Levi had a point, Joachim saw only the folly in his comment. Once his father returned home and Joachim had a chance to talk to his parents, he doubted they would want him to remain at home. In fact, Rebecca would probably be chastised for allowing Joachim to stay in the house while their parents were out of town. There would be no point in Joachim staying in the area and opening a shop if he was shunned by his family.

Suddenly, his mood dampened, and the coffee tasted bitter in his mouth.

"You will have pie?" Sarah asked as she and Rebecca cleared the table once Levi had eaten.

Joachim nodded. "Only a small slice. There is much yet to be done. The fences need repair. The barn, as well. Tomorrow I will go to Victor's house. Today, I will work here."

"I'm sure your father will appreciate your help."

If only that would be so, yet Joachim suspected his *datt* would be hard-pressed to appreciate anything his son did.

Sarah accepted a small piece of pie from Rebecca and carried it to table.

"Denki," Joachim said as he took the plate from her.

She glanced at Levi. "I'm sure you would like pie."

"Yah, but a much larger slice than Joachim," the younger man said with a grin. He glanced at Joachim. "I must work for my father this afternoon, and tomorrow is the barn raising. Did Rebecca tell you?"

Joachim shook his head.

"The Byler barn burned," Levi continued. "Samuel

had wood delivered, and he has asked us to arrive in the morning. We could use your help, Joachim."

"Of course. Samuel is a *gut* man. If he needs help, I will be there."

As Joachim and Levi ate the pie, Rebecca wrapped cheesecloth around a second pie and tied the edges together. "I baked extra for your *mamm*. Tell her thank-you for the onions she sent yesterday. They were sweet and will keep in the root cellar."

Levi smiled. "She will like to hear that her gift was well received."

"*Yah*, of course, it was."

"She always asks about you, Rebecca. You should come to visit."

"Perhaps when *Mamm* and *Datt* return."

"They will not be gone much longer?" Joachim posed.

"Only a few more days," Rebecca responded. "But, Levi, I will see your *mamm* tomorrow at the barn raising. She will be there, *yah*?"

"Probably not. Her arthritis is bad, especially when it rains."

Levi bid Joachim and Sarah farewell and accepted the pie from Rebecca. She walked outside with him, and the couple stood talking on the porch.

Joachim glanced at Sarah. She rinsed dishes in a bucket of water at the sink. "You will be all right here in the house with Rebecca if I am working in the barn?" he asked.

"Of course, I'll be fine. Don't worry."

"I was not worried."

"Then you were concerned."

"Perhaps," he said with a shrug. "I know you were frightened when Victor drove onto the property earlier."

"You should tell him to stay off your land."

"*Yah*, this I could do. But that is not how a good neighbor acts."

She narrowed her gaze. "Is it necessary to be a good neighbor to a man who is so hateful?"

"If I want him to think I have nothing against him." Before he could explain what he meant, the back door opened and Rebecca returned to the kitchen.

"I am interrupting something?" she asked.

"No," Sarah insisted. "But I am tired and would like to rest."

Joachim peered through the window at the darkening sky. "Black clouds roll overhead. The storm may turn the day to night. Perhaps you will need a candle in your room."

Sarah's face tightened. She shook her head. "There's still plenty of daylight. Besides, I don't like candles."

Joachim didn't understand her comment, nor did he understand the fear that returned to her face and the way she clasped her hands together. Something about candles had set her off, but what? And why?

"Perhaps the oil lamp would be better," Rebecca offered.

"I'll be fine," Sarah insisted. "The room has a window. I will awake before nightfall, if I can even sleep."

Sarah grabbed her skirts and hurried upstairs. Her footfalls echoed in the house and made Joachim's heart ache.

He had to let her go, but he wondered what the *Englischer* was hiding. Sarah feared Victor, but there was something else she feared.

Chapter Six

Sarah hadn't realized how exhausted she was until she removed the bonnet and apron and lay on the bed. She draped the quilt over her legs and turned her head away from the diffused light coming from the windows. In less than a minute, she was sound asleep.

Sometime later, a noise startled her awake. She turned to glance out the window, seeing the failing light. The steady rhythmic pitter-patter of raindrops on the roof made her want to close her eyes again.

She began to drift back into a light slumber when someone pounded on the downstairs door. She sat up, slipped her feet into her shoes and hurried to the window. She peered around the curtain, but all she could see was the barn, not the drive where a car or buggy, undoubtedly, sat parked.

Not a red pickup truck.

But what if it was Victor?

Her breath caught in her throat as the banging started again.

Where were Joachim and Rebecca?

And what if the person at the door *was* Victor?

Sarah's hand rose to her throat. She glanced around the room, searching for a closet in which to hide, but the Amish bedroom had no closets and only one door that led to the hallway. She backed into the corner beyond the bed, as far as she could get from the window, her pulse racing.

She spied the prayer *kapp* on the dresser where she had placed it. Rebecca's mention of an Amish woman always being prepared to pray circled through her mind.

"Lord, he-help me," she stuttered. The words stuck in her throat.

A voice sounded outside. Joachim's voice.

Slowly, she approached the window, making sure she was not visible from below.

Joachim stood at the doorway of the barn talking to someone. Her stomach churned. She rubbed her hand across the waistband of her dress, hoping to calm her internal unrest, all the while she silently beseeched Joachim not to reveal her whereabouts if he was talking to Victor.

A sinking feeling settled over her. If she'd trusted the wrong man and Joachim and Victor were actually friends, she could end up back in the attic, being held under lock and key, which was the last thing she wanted.

"Help me, Lord," she mumbled as she tied the apron around her waist, settled the bonnet onto her head and hurried downstairs in hopes of seeing for herself who had come knocking at the door.

Joachim did not expect to be just as broadsided when he saw Sarah for the second time dressed in Amish clothing. Maybe it was her flushed cheeks or the question he read in her gaze that made him stop as he entered the kitchen and stared at her until she seemed ready to flee up the stairs again.

"Who was at the door?" she asked, her eyes hooded. "I heard knocking. It was Victor, wasn't it?"

"It was a man from town who came to buy fresh eggs. He has come often in the past and did not realize Rebecca had taken down the sign about having eggs and baked goods for sale. I told him none were for sale today."

"But—" She shook her head.

"But you thought it was Victor," Joachim said.

"I don't know what I thought. The pounding woke me. I couldn't see the drive—"

"I told you I would keep you safe." But she had not believed him. Joachim let out a frustrated breath, knowing too well that Sarah's trust would be hard earned.

"You're going to his house tomorrow," she said as if to justify the assumption she had incorrectly made.

"I need the work, Sarah. Plus, what better way to keep my eye on Victor? He held you against your will. What if he does the same thing to the next woman he brings home to care for his mother? The police need to be notified so he can be stopped from hurting anyone else."

"No." Her voice was firm. "The police are already too involved."

"Involved in capturing you?"

She turned her back on him and hung her head.

Joachim mentally chastised himself. He had caused her upset, which was the last thing he wanted. "I do not understand," he finally admitted. "Perhaps you can explain everything."

She stepped toward the kitchen table and slipped into a chair. Her face was tight with emotion.

"It is difficult to talk about, *yah*?" he said, following her to the table and sitting across from her.

She offered him a weak smile as if to acknowledge

what he said was true. "Until recently, my sister Miriam and I lived outside Knoxville with our mother. She had shown signs of dementia over the last year or so. A few months ago, she started talking about a long-lost sister with whom she wanted to reconnect. Her name is Annie Miller." Sarah stared at him expectantly. "I believe my aunt lives in Willkommen."

Joachim nodded. "The next town."

"A road sign said it is thirty miles from here."

"*Yah*, that is right."

"On the way to find my aunt, we got lost. It was night. A police car pulled us over. At first I was relieved, thinking they would help us, but then—"

She clasped her hands and held them tight against her heart.

"Something happened," he prompted, knowing the retelling must be difficult.

"There were two police officers, although I wonder if they truly were law enforcement. One of them grabbed Miriam and pulled her from the car. My mother became agitated and opened the passenger door. She wanted to protect my sister, but a second man—he was in the police car."

She hung her head and blinked back tears that filled her eyes. Joachim reached for her hand.

"I can't remember everything, but a second man— the one in the police car—shot my mother."

Joachim hadn't expected her comment. "*Gott* help you, Sarah, for what you had to endure."

"They took Miriam and me to a cabin and held us in separate rooms. Everything after that was a blur. Victor hauled me away at some point. I know he forced me to take drugs that he said would help me. I stashed them in the corner of my mouth and spit them out whenever

I could. But I couldn't get rid of all of them. I was in a drugged stupor for too long. Eventually he took me to his mother's home. All told, he held me against my will for two months. When I saw your buggy, I knew I needed to get away. I hadn't taken the pills he offered for a few days so I was clearheaded and able to think for myself." She glanced up at Joachim. "You came at the right time."

Joachim had been drawn home for some reason. He had thought it was to reconcile with his father. Maybe it was because of Sarah's need.

"Now," she continued, "I'm not sure what I should do. Perhaps I should leave."

"Leave?" Had he or his sister done something to upset her? "Surely Rebecca said nothing that caused you concern."

"No, Joachim, your sister has been very helpful and welcoming."

"Then you think I do not want you here? That is not true."

"Victor is your neighbor. Perhaps he's a friend, although I cannot see how you would want anything to do with such a hateful man." She glanced down at the dress she wore. "You were kind to invite me to stay, and I'm grateful for the clean clothing Rebecca has provided. I'll remain here tonight and leave in the morning."

Joachim could not believe what she was saying. The fact that she thought he would have anything to do with Victor was unsettling.

"Victor is not the type of man I would ever call friend. It troubles me, Sarah, to have you think that I would not see with clear vision who he really is. But you have been through so much, and often our minds jump to incorrect conclusions."

His own father had done exactly that. "I told Victor I

would start work tomorrow, not because I like the man but because I want to ensure Victor does not cause more harm. When I work at his house, I can see what he is doing and hopefully keep him from harming any other woman. Plus, you were concerned about his mother. I am, as well. I will find a way to check on her."

Sarah stared at him for a long moment. "I want to trust you, Joachim."

He took her hand. "And you can. If I was a friend to Victor, I would have told him where to find you. He never would have left my father's farm alone if he thought you were here."

She sighed as if weighing his words. "I want to believe you."

"Then *do* believe me, Sarah. It is that easy. You are safe here. Victor will not enter this house, I will make certain of that. You must decide what you want to do and where you want to go. If you want to go to Willkommen, I will take you, but that would be in a few days. First you must get stronger."

Sarah had been held captive for too long. Rebecca's cooking and the peace that even Joachim could feel in the Amish house would replenish Sarah's strength and her health.

That night when they sat at the table, Sarah had little to eat, and the sadness in her eyes worried him even more than her hesitancy to enter into a conversation.

After they finished eating, she started to clear the dishes, but Joachim took her hand. "I will help Rebecca. You need to rest."

"Joachim is right," Rebecca encouraged. "You do not need to help me tonight. You need to sleep."

"But—"

Joachim took her plate and placed it near the sink. "It is dark. You'll need a candle to go upstairs."

Her eyes widened, and she shook her head. "I don't want a candle."

"Perhaps the gas lamp then. You can adjust the wick so only a small flame will light the room all night if you do not want to remain in the dark."

"The dark doesn't frighten me," she insisted.

But something frightened her.

"I have a flashlight in my buggy. Wait here and I will get it."

"You are Amish, yet you can use a flashlight?"

Rebecca nodded. "We do not run electric wiring into our homes, but flashlights, which are battery powered, are allowed."

Joachim hurried outside and returned soon thereafter with a flashlight in hand. He turned it on. "You will be safe tonight."

She took the flashlight and nodded. "Thank you, Joachim."

Glancing at Rebecca, she added, "Thank you for dinner. Don't let me sleep too late in the morning."

Joachim watched as Sarah slowly climbed the stairs, her footsteps heavy as if she had little or no energy. Would she be able to get over the pain she had experienced?

He thought of her future and wondered where she would go once she gained her strength. To Willkommen to find her aunt and perhaps track down her sister? Or farther away where Joachim would never be able to see her again?

She was *Englisch*. He was Amish.

Whether he liked it or not, the two could never mix.

Chapter Seven

Sarah woke the next morning to the smell of bacon and eggs. Her mouth watered, making her realize how hungry she was. Last night with Joachim sitting across the table from her, she had eaten little. Thankfully, she had slept well and now hurried to dress and go downstairs.

Rebecca was clearing the table and turned as Sarah entered the kitchen. "What is wrong this morning? You look worried."

Sarah glanced around the room, seeing the empty skillet on the wood-burning stove. Dirty dishes were piled in the sink, and the butter and jelly sat on the counter.

"I missed breakfast?" *And Joachim*, she wanted to add.

Rebecca motioned her toward the table. "I have kept a plate of bacon warm in the oven. Your place is still set at the table, and eggs will not take long to fry. I can toast the bread or you can eat it as is."

"Thank you, Rebecca, but I hate for you to go to all that trouble."

"It is no trouble. Joachim has already eaten."

Sarah stepped to the window and peered toward the barn. "Is he hitching the horse to the buggy?"

"He is in the east pasture, repairing a fence. One of our cows got out. Thankfully, he got her back, but now he must fix the breach."

Sarah felt a sinking in her stomach. The nervousness she had felt last night returned, and her appetite left her. "Maybe I don't need breakfast."

"You must start the day with food," Rebecca insisted. "I will fetch more eggs from the chicken house."

"Let me. It's the least I can do."

"If you insist." Rebecca handed her a basket. "The nests are just inside the coop. You will see them. There should be plenty of eggs."

Sarah hurried outside, relieved to be of help, and inhaled the fresh country air, enjoying the sense of freedom with the open spaces all around her. For too long, she had been locked in the old Thomin house, which smelled of dust and mildew.

She looked for Joachim, but couldn't see him. She did, however, see a barking dog, which ran from one of the fields, wagging his tail and warming her heart. She bent to pat his head and scratch under his neck. "Aren't you a cute Yorkshire terrier. I'll have to ask Rebecca your name. I'm glad you want to be friends."

The dog licked her hand. "You're what Victor needs. Did you know your ancestors were bred to hunt rats?"

The playful terrier wiggled all the more. His antics made her laugh, which she hadn't done in so long. Even before Victor she couldn't remember the feeling of acceptance that flowed over her with the playful dog so eager for her attention.

She laughed again as the dog danced at her feet. "I

need to get the eggs before Rebecca comes looking for me." Sarah scratched the dog's head and then hurried to the hen house with the pup scampering along beside her.

"Don't scare the hens," she warned playfully.

The clucking coming from the hen house assured her she would find eggs, which she quickly did. After filling the small basket Rebecca had given her, Sarah started back to the house.

The sound of a vehicle caused her to turn toward the main road. Her heart stopped.

A car sped by going much too fast. A tan sedan.

She let out the breath she had been holding and hurried to the porch, the pup at her feet.

Rebecca met her at the door, holding a large bag of dog food in one hand. "I see you have met Angelo. He is lovable, *yah*? Maybe too much so at times."

"Angelo?" Sarah smiled down at the dog. "That doesn't sound like an Amish name."

Rebecca chuckled. "He belonged to a local man named DeCaro. When he moved away, he could not take Angelo so we agreed to keep him. The dog is a wanderer. He visits lots of farms and comes back when he's hungry."

She handed Sarah the bag. "We will make a trade. I will begin cooking your eggs if you fill Angelo's bowls. You will find his dishes at the side of the porch."

Sarah enjoyed being useful, and Angelo seemed to appreciate the attention she showered on him as she filled his food dish and a second bowl with fresh water.

Hurrying back inside, she ate the eggs Rebecca had prepared along with the crisp bacon and a thick slice of bread slathered with butter.

"I'm so full," Sarah admitted. "Breakfast was delicious." She stood and carried her empty plate to the sink.

A buggy turned onto the drive. Rebecca hurried to the window and peered outside. "It is Levi. He will take us to the barn raising."

"What about Joachim?" Sarah asked, feeling a knot form in her stomach.

"He will join us later at the Byler home."

"I'll wait for him here."

"Joachim did not want you alone in the house, Sarah. You are to go with us."

"But what if we pass Victor on the road?"

Rebecca smiled. "You will sit in the back of the buggy. Victor will not see you there. Besides, being dressed as an Amish woman protects you from Victor even if he still searches the area. He would not think to look for you among us, and he would not be able to spot you just from passing the barn. The women work in the kitchen getting the lunch ready. He might drive by on the road, but he will not come into the Amish home."

Sarah bit her lip, trying to weigh the pros and cons of leaving the protection of Joachim's home. She had made an almost disastrous mistake by leaving yesterday and didn't want to repeat her error.

"What about the other women?" she asked. "They'll realize I'm not Amish and Victor might find out."

"*Ach*, this is not something that should cause you worry. After what happened with Naomi, the Amish give Victor a wide birth. His true self is known and not admired, to say the least. The Amish ladies you will meet today will not talk to Victor, of this you can be certain."

"But won't they ask questions about where I came from and why I'm with you?"

"We will tell them the truth. You are visiting from Tennessee. We will not mention anything more. You are used to *Englischer* gatherings where perhaps people are inquisitive. The Amish do not pry." She tilted her head. Her eyes twinkled. "At least most of us try not to pry, but there are busybodies even among the Amish. I will make certain you stay away from anyone like this today."

Sarah had to smile at Rebecca's insights. Human nature was human nature no matter the culture. Some people thrived on knowing everything about everyone else.

"You're sure Joachim will join us later?" she asked again.

"*Yah*, I am certain." Rebecca picked up a basket from the table and handed it to Sarah. "Carry this potato salad to the buggy. Levi will tuck it in the rear where it will not turn over. I will bring the pies."

Sarah pulled in a fortifying breath and grabbed the wicker basket. "Did you make the basket?"

"*Yah*, I did. In the winter I weave, and sell my baskets in the warm weather along with the produce from the garden, fresh eggs and my baked items to the people from town."

She handed Sarah a black bonnet with a wide bill, and a lightweight black cape. Once both women were properly attired, they grabbed the baskets and hurried outside to where Levi waited with the buggy.

He arranged the food in the rear and then helped Sarah onto the back seat. Rebecca sat in front next to him.

Sarah peered from the buggy, hoping she was hidden from roving eyes, especially if Victor happened by. She rubbed her right hand over her stomach to still the unrest within her. If only Joachim were at her side.

Levi flicked the reins, and his mare headed to the road. Thankfully, both directions were clear. Sarah settled back in the seat, soothed by the side-to-side sway of the buggy and the clip-clop of the horse's hooves on the pavement as Levi turned the mare onto the main road.

The crisp morning air mixed with the musky scent of the still-damp earth. She turned her gaze to the distant pastures, hoping to catch sight of Joachim. All she saw were a few horses on the hillside and newly tilled fields waiting for planting.

The repetitive cycle of tilling, planting, harvesting year after year had to bring satisfaction to the farmers who worked the soil and depended on God's providence to provide an abundant harvest.

Thinking back on her own life, she saw little fruit, no matter how hard she worked to be productive. She had tried to be a dutiful daughter and sought ways to help her mother, although her efforts always fell short of her mother's expectations. Yet she had continued to try to prove herself.

It had started with the fire that was never talked about, never forgiven. Outrage from her mother would have been better than the silence. At least then the issue could have been discussed and resolved. Instead, it remained a gaping hole in their relationship. A hole that never closed and always festered.

"You are all right?" Rebecca turned to ask, probably hearing another of Sarah's sighs.

"I'm fine. The air is refreshing and the scenery is so picturesque. I'm glad you invited me to join you today."

"We will be there soon. The barn is to be built on the Byler land. As you probably heard Levi mention yesterday, Samuel and Ester lost their barn in a recent fire."

Sarah tugged the cape tight around her neck, trying to push aside the memories from the past.

"Did…did a candle overturn?" she finally asked.

"Lightning caused the fire," Rebecca shared.

"I'm sorry."

"*Yah*, but it is a reason to gather today. The men will work to build the barn, and the women will work in the kitchen so the men have food when their stomachs grumble."

"My stomach is grumbling now for a slice of your pie," Levi joined in with a laugh.

Rebecca poked his arm playfully and turned back to face the road. Levi leaned a bit closer to her, and Rebecca's laughter carried an even stronger lilt.

Sarah's heart warmed to the attraction between them that was so obvious. For half a second she longed for someone in her own life who could make her laugh and take away the pall that hung across her shoulders.

She was being foolish. Such a relationship was not in her future. Her mother had made mistakes in the men she chose. Sarah had learned wisely to guard her feelings lest she, too, succumb to a man who would break her heart or her spirit. Love was not for everyone. Her mother was proof of that.

The ride to the farm took a little more than twenty minutes. Levi helped Sarah climb down from the buggy and then handed her the same basket she had carried earlier.

A two-story Amish house stood nearby with small outbuildings directly behind the main structure. A stream of women climbed the porch steps and entered the house carrying baskets and bowls and boxes. Sarah imagined the delightful offerings loaded within the containers—cakes and cookies and freshly baked bread.

In the distance, lumber was neatly piled in stacks on the ground. Giant frames lay waiting to be raised. Beyond the location for the new barn, she saw the charred remains of a former structure, now little more than burned rubble. The acrid smell of smoke wafted past her and made her turn from the destruction and focus on the men milling close to the woodpiles. They chatted amicably among themselves, and laughter punctuated their conversation.

Sarah had read somewhere that the barn and house raisings combined neighborly help with social time and were important mainstays of the Amish life. Even as an outsider, she could sense the excitement and an energy that was almost palpable.

Although buoyed by what she saw, thoughts of Victor returned and brought Sarah back to her own predicament. Longing for the protection of the house, she hurried in that direction, unwilling to be out in the open for long, especially with Joachim nowhere in sight.

Levi joined the other men while Rebecca fell in step next to Sarah.

"The women will know I am not Amish." Sarah repeated her earlier concern. Surrounded by the Amish, she realized how much she stood out, in spite of the clothing she wore. Surely the women would recognize her attempt to be something she wasn't.

"Do not worry," Rebecca said. "I told you before, all you must say is that you are a friend visiting from Tennessee. This is true. You do not need to enter into long conversations with the other women. Just smile and nod."

Which sounded so easy when Rebecca said it, but as Sarah stepped into the house overflowing with women, she felt totally out of place. Following Rebecca's lead, she removed her cape and black bonnet and hung them on a peg by the door.

Lowering her gaze, she walked behind Rebecca into the kitchen and was relieved when someone handed her a whisk and a half-filled mixing bowl.

"The cream needs to be whipped," the woman instructed before she moved to the stove to stir a pot of what looked like homemade noodles.

Complying with the woman's wishes, Sarah stood in the corner, beating the cream with a steady motion. Thankfully, the women were so busy preparing the meal that they paid little attention to the newcomer.

Once the cream was whipped, Sarah helped grate cabbage for the slaw and clean carrots and kale fresh from the Bylers' garden.

The smells of succulent meats and vegetable casseroles, mixed with the warm scent of baked goods, made her look forward to the luncheon in spite of the hearty breakfast she had eaten this morning.

Glancing through the window, she smiled at the young children playing close to the house, watched over by older girls who hauled food to the long tables set up in the shade of the mighty oaks.

"You will help me?" Rebecca asked as she lifted a large container of lemonade from the sink. "We will use a small wagon to take this to the men."

Sarah wiped her hands on a nearby towel and followed Rebecca outside. Together, they pulled the wagon to where the men worked. The frame had been raised while the women were busy in the kitchen. Now the barn had a sturdy outer structure upon which men climbed.

The steady tap of their hammers filled the air, along with the grinding of hand drills and the grating rasp of saws, cutting through the four-by-fours. The smell of fresh wood overpowered the earlier scent of the fire, and Sarah breathed in the clean aroma as she scanned the structure.

Her heart leaped in her chest when she spied Joachim, big and strong, perched high atop the massive support frame. He hammered a crossbeam into place, seemingly oblivious to the danger of being so precariously poised.

"Joachim doesn't fear heights, it seems," she said, her eyes focused on his long legs and strong arms.

Rebecca followed her gaze. "My brother has been a climber since he was a boy. *Yah*, he fears little."

Once the beam was nailed in place, he glanced down, finding Sarah in the swarm of people as if he had eyes only for her.

Her spine tingled and a smile parted her lips. Joachim waved in response, filling her with a sense of well-being.

Rebecca poured lemonade into glasses, and Sarah distributed them to the men who eagerly accepted the refreshing drink.

Grabbing Sarah's arm, Rebecca pointed to the road.

Sarah's breath caught. Victor's pickup pulled into the drive and braked to a stop near the house.

He stepped out and stood for a long moment, staring at the gathering of workers.

Sarah clutched Rebecca's hand in fear. Victor was near the porch, blocking her path to the kitchen. Her pulse raced. Exposed and in danger of being discovered, she searched for a hiding spot.

Her only recourse were the outbuildings. Trying not to be obvious, she wove her way between the men.

A barking dog drew her attention to the open field. Angelo appeared in the distance racing toward her, his tail wagging.

She glanced back. Victor turned in her direction at the same moment. His eyes widened, and he pushed through the children playing on the lawn.

Sarah ran. Skirting the first shed, she edged around a second building to where another structure stood.

If only the door was unlocked. She climbed the stairs, grabbed the knob and pushed on the door, relieved that it opened. Slipping inside, she saw the pile of sawdust in the corner and the various woodworking machines. She pulled in a deep breath and closed the door behind her.

From the window, she caught sight of Victor. He glanced again at the house and then walked with determined steps toward the workshop.

A dog barked. She peered through the window. Angelo stood at the door, demanding entry. Victor rounded the second outbuilding and was heading straight for her.

She climbed behind a pile of plywood.

Her heart pounded. A roar filled her ears. Her pulse raced so that she was sure the entire workshop must be shaking in sync with her trembling body.

Angelo continued to bark. He wanted to be let in, right now.

Footsteps sounded outside. The door creaked open. She held her breath. Sawdust tickled her nose so that she wanted to sneeze but she managed to stay silent.

"What's going on, you stupid mutt?" Victor demanded, his voice gravelly and laced with anger. "Did someone come in here?"

She envisioned Angelo clawing at the plywood, drawing Victor's attention to where she hid.

If the dog didn't reveal her presence, the unbridled pounding of her heart would alert him for sure.

Angelo barked again.

Please, Lord.

"What'd you find, boy?" Victor drew closer. "What's behind that pile of plywood?"

"Is there something you need?" Joachim's voice as he entered the workshop.

Victor growled. "I saw that woman who cared for my mother. She came in here."

Joachim laughed. "You are seeing things unless she is Amish. No *Englischer* is here."

Victor stepped closer to the plywood. Angelo sniffed at the opening to where she huddled.

"The dog's found something, Amish. The woman's hiding."

Something scurried across the floor. Angelo chased after it.

Victor gasped.

"It was only a mouse," Joachim assured him.

Sarah held her breath. Victor hated rats. Hopefully, his dislike of rodents included mice.

"I saw the commotion from the road and wondered if I would find you here. Why aren't you at my house?" Victor groused.

"This morning I must help with the barn. Perhaps you will stay and eat with the Amish? The women have been cooking for days. Later, I will come to your house."

Victor huffed. "I need to go to town this afternoon so don't keep me waiting."

"And the lunch?" Joachim asked.

"I don't want your food." Victor stomped out of the workshop. The door slammed behind him.

"Sarah?" Joachim was moving the wood.

A flurry of fine wood particles filled the air. Then his arms were around her, pulling her from her hiding spot.

"Are you all right?"

"Oh, Joachim." She let out the breath she had been holding. "Victor almost found me. If you hadn't—"

Joachim pulled her closer. "Angelo is the one who saved you by scaring that mouse out of its hiding spot."

"Angleo may have saved me, but he also caused the initial hoopla that drew Victor's attention. By the way, I don't like mice," she admitted, "but anything to keep Victor away."

Rebecca opened the door and peered inside. "He is gone."

Joachim stepped away from Sarah, leaving her feeling vulnerable. She wanted to be back in his arms, but she resisted the urge to move closer.

Why was she letting down her guard around Joachim? Sarah was an *Englisch* woman who had no place in his Amish world.

Chapter Eight

Joachim hated the disrepair he found in the Thomin home. Sagging gutters, peeling paint, broken shutters, but the worst problem was the dry rot. When Victor's father, Mr. Thomin, was alive, he had kept the house in tip-top shape. A woodworker by hobby, he had taken pride in ensuring the house was well maintained. The father had died when Victor was a teen. Ms. Hazel had maintained the home until her health started to fail. In her declining years, she struggled to care for the inside of the house and did little for the exterior. Joachim could work on the house for weeks and still not shore up all of the more deep-seated structural problems that would require even more extensive work.

He glanced at the drive and wondered how long Victor would be gone. A niggling voice kept playing Sarah's words in his head, especially her concern for Victor's mother. Joachim needed to check on the elderly woman. He would never forgive himself if something happened to her.

He placed his tools on the porch, wiped his hands on a rag and stamped his feet, not wanting to track dirt into the home. After peering again at the driveway, he reached for the kitchen doorknob.

"Joachim?"

He turned, surprised to see Sarah running toward him from the path through the woods. Concern clutched his heart.

"What are you doing here? Is something wrong at the farm?" Instantly he regretted the harshness of his tone when he saw the grimace on her face as if she had been offended by his question.

"Did Rebecca send you?" he asked.

She shook her head. "But she told me about the shortcut through the woods. I thought it would be safe to come because Victor said he would be gone this afternoon. I'm worried about my sister. He promised me Miriam would join me either today or tomorrow. I should have mentioned it this morning, but after what happened at the barn raising, I wasn't thinking straight. Did you see anyone? Miriam's tall with brown hair."

"You need to go home, Sarah. Victor left for town, but who knows when he will be back. I was going inside the house to see about Victor's mother when I heard you call my name. I will check on her and see if any other woman is being held inside, but first, you must return to my house."

"No, Joachim. Victor will be gone for a while. I need to see how Ms. Hazel is with my own eyes. Maybe she'll know something about Miriam."

"It is too dangerous," he insisted.

Sarah pushed past him and opened the door.

As frightened as she was of Victor, Sarah seemed determined to see his mother for herself.

"You are making a mistake," he warned.

"Guard the door and let me know if you see Victor."

Joachim shook his head. "You are not going anywhere without me. Besides, we will have a better view of the road from the upstairs window. I will keep watch from there."

Sarah hurried up the stairs, and Joachim followed. At the top of the landing, she tuned left and opened the door to a large bedroom. Mahogany furniture filled the room. Ms. Hazel lay on a king-size bed, looking tiny and frail against the large pillows and down comforter.

Sarah hurried to the bed and touched the woman's arm.

Joachim stepped to the window, relieved that he could see the roadway in the distance and the route Victor would take home.

"She's asleep, and I can't wake her," Sarah said, her voice filled with concern. "Ms. Hazel, can you hear me?"

Finally, the woman groaned. Her eyes fluttered open for a minute, long enough for a sweet smile to cover her lips before she drifted to sleep again.

A tray sat on a small table near the bed with the remains of a piece of toast and a soft-boiled egg. "It looks like she had something to eat not too long ago," Joachim said. "Maybe Victor is taking better care of her than you thought he would."

"If only that were true. He left her alone in this big house."

"I was working outside."

"And would you have heard her cry out if she needed help? Plus, you weren't here this morning when he stopped by the Bylers' farm."

Sarah moved to the dresser, pulled open the top drawer and took out a pill bottle. "The label is made out to Hazel Thomin, but the bottle is empty. It's for Cardoxin, which sounds like it might be a heart medicine. All the while I've been here, Victor has never refilled her prescription."

She pulled out another bottle. "This one has remained empty, too. It's Lasix. Mother took that. It's a diuretic to eliminate fluid buildup within the body."

"Perhaps Victor keeps the filled bottles of pills in his own room."

Sarah flashed him a look of frustration and opened a second drawer. Her eyes widened as she held up a third bottle. "Over-the-counter sleeping medication. Half the pills are gone."

She looked at Joachim. "Do you know what this means?"

"That Victor needs to refill her medication?"

Sarah frowned. "The sleeping pills are one way to ensure an infirmed woman doesn't try to get out of bed or wander around the house. If Victor is sedating his mother, he's despicable. Even more so than I had initially thought."

Joachim flicked his glance back to the road and his stomach soured. "His truck, Sarah. He is turning into the driveway. Hurry. You must leave the house now."

She returned the pills to the drawers and then raced from the room and down the stairs.

Joachim followed her. On the first floor, she peered through a window. Victor parked his truck and then stepped out of the vehicle onto the driveway with a scowl on his face.

"You have to hide," Joachim warned.

But where?

She opened the door to the basement and scurried down the steps. He closed the door behind her.

"What are you doing?" Victor's voice.

He burst into the kitchen, his eyes filled with fury as if ready to lambast anyone who stood in his way.

Victor stopped short, seeing Joachim at the sink, holding a glass of water to his lips. He drank it down in one large gulp, then smiled at Victor. "I trust you had a good trip?"

"What are you doing inside the house?"

"I did not think you would mind me getting a drink of water. If this is a problem, I will bring a jug of water with me tomorrow."

Victor flicked his gaze around the kitchen as if to make certain nothing was disturbed. "Did you go anywhere else?"

"I told you I needed a drink of water. Is this a problem?"

"No, of course not. Did anyone stop by the house?"

"You are expecting someone, perhaps?"

"No one. I just thought—"

He let the sentence hang.

Joachim pushed past him. "I must return to my work, but first you should see what I found on the opposite side of the house. You have time for me to show you now?"

"More problems that will cost more money?"

"I believe you have spare wood in one of the sheds outside. I saw this, *yah*?"

"My father's shop. You can use anything from there."

"That was my hope." He motioned Victor forward. "Come, let us walk to the front of the house. I will show you the problem."

Joachim had been digging out dry rot all afternoon,

never thinking he would be able to use the disrepair as a decoy for Sarah.

He squared his shoulders, knowing he needed to distract Victor long enough for Sarah to escape.

If he only could.

The basement was dank and smelled of mildew. Light from a small window allowed Sarah to make her way down the stairs and then to the far corner of the basement where she stood, listening for any sign of Victor opening the kitchen door and descending to where she hid. She had been foolish to enter the house, even if she'd wanted to ensure Ms. Hazel was all right.

Muffled voices came from the kitchen, followed by footfalls as the two men walked through the house and left through the front door. She hurried to that side of the basement and peered through a mud-splattered window. Joachim was talking to Victor and pointing to the house.

If Joachim could distract Victor long enough, Sarah could leave through the kitchen and pick up the path just beyond the barn.

She started for the stairs and then stopped. A scratching sound came from the other side of the basement. She had little time to waste but paused as the scratching repeated.

Moving even farther into the rear of the basement, Sarah noticed a small alcove and a padlocked door. The scratching came again.

Sarah tapped on the door. The scratching continued.

Her heart stopped. Was someone signaling from behind the door?

She searched for keys to open the locks but found none. Knowing she had to be careful, she put her mouth to the door and whispered, "My name's Sarah. I'll come back to help you. Can you hear me?"

Silence.

She glanced back at the window. Joachim couldn't keep Victor occupied much longer. Sarah would be of no help to anyone if she fell into Victor's control again.

She hurried up the stairs and slowly opened the kitchen door. The muffled sounds of the men's voices filtered through the house.

"Thanks for showing me the problem, Joachim." The front door opened. "Right now, I need to check on my mother."

Sarah stepped back into the basement and pulled the door closed behind her.

Hovering on the top step, her heart nearly pounded out of her chest.

Footsteps sounded in the hallway. Was Victor heading up the stairs or coming into the kitchen?

Sarah clutched her stomach to still its rumblings.

He entered the kitchen. Glasses clinked. Water ran in the sink. She heard movement below and glanced down, seeing a small, brown creature with a long tail run across the floor. Sarah pretended rats didn't bother her when she was with Victor, but she didn't like rodents of any kind, especially ones with beady eyes and long tails. Her gaze landed on something else that troubled her—an old tin of rat poison sat open on a workbench. Victor must have used the poison to control the rats in the house.

She thought of Ms. Hazel's lethargy and rapid decline. The woman's shallow complexion was troubling, as well.

Was Victor poisoning the rats…and his mother?

Sarah gripped the basement handrail as a wave of vertigo swept over her. The rapid pounding of her heart and her accelerated pulse were probably making her feel woozy. The walls started to cave in around her in a sweep of claustrophobia.

She closed her eyes, hoping that might calm her anxiety, but it only made the symptoms worse. She gripped the handrail more tightly and opened her eyes to get her bearings.

Victor's footsteps came again. This time, he neared the basement door. She glanced down, seeing the doorknob turn.

No! she silently screamed.

The phone rang. A landline. Victor hurried into the front parlor to answer the phone.

Sarah had only a minute or two. Opening the door, she crossed the kitchen and slipped outside. She didn't look back to see if she could find Joachim. She had to get away, back to the path before Victor returned to the kitchen.

The memory of being held captive flashed through her mind. The attic room, the dark nights she lay hearing the rodents running through the attic. The candle Victor would bring to light the room, knowing she was terrified of the open flame.

She couldn't and wouldn't go back again. No matter what happened, she needed to remain free.

What about the scratching in the basement? Brushing it off as rats would make everything so much easier. But she had been held against her will. What if Victor were holding another person? A chill scurried down her spine. What if the sounds were a call for help from someone beyond the padlocked door? Sarah couldn't ignore her gut feelings nor the sounds. She had to find a way to learn where that door led. Maybe then she'd know if another woman was being held captive.

Chapter Nine

The day could not pass fast enough for Joachim. He had watched Sarah run out of Victor's house and scurry back to the path. Just as she disappeared into the woods, Victor had stepped onto the porch, demanding to know why Joachim was not working.

He had welcomed the chastisement. It showed that Victor had no idea who had been in the house. Sarah had made it safely to the path and, hopefully, had made it home, as well.

A storm blew in later in the afternoon, which provided a good reason for Joachim to pack up his tools earlier than he would have normally. Victor had grumbled, but the dark billowing clouds and flashes of lightning that ripped across the sky overrode his discontent.

Belle was skittish on the way home as thunder clashed overhead. A car raced by much too fast, throwing water against the buggy. If only the *Englisch* realized how their cars could unsettle a horse, they might be a bit more cautious. Too many accidents happened on back roads even in good weather; add water to the mix and the situation got even more risky.

Joachim thought again of the fateful night his brother had died so tragically. Had the driver of the other vehicle been tried for recklessness? Probably not. The Amish with their slower moving buggies usually bore the blame, and the cases rarely went to court.

His spirits were bolstered when he turned onto his father's property. He leaped from the buggy and hurried to the back door, needing to assure himself that Sarah was there before he tended to his mare.

He pushed open the door.

She stood at the dry sink, kneading dough. His unexpected entrance startled her. A gasp escaped her lips, but when she turned and recognized him, her fear disappeared and was replaced with an awareness that connected them just as had happened that first time she had glanced at him from inside the Thomin home. Joachim's chest constricted, and the world stood still for one electrifying moment.

Sarah was on an emotional roller coaster. Hearing movement behind her, she feared Victor had entered the Burkholder kitchen. When she turned, her eyes locked on Joachim, standing there baring his soul in the intensity of his gaze. Her heart stopped beating for one brief second as if both of them were suspended in time and had gone someplace far away from the fear and confusion that had existed in her life for too long.

"Joachim, I thought you were someone else." She raised her hand and patted her chest as if to start her heart beating again. "You scared me."

He seemed to search for words, and then shook his head and headed back outside to his buggy. Had she said something wrong?

Hurrying to the window, she watched him lead his mare into the barn. Knowing Joachim, he would remain there caring for his horse while she wondered what had transpired. The moment of connection had taken her to a special place only to have his rejection topple her back to the reality of the moment. She was foolish to give her feelings such free rein. After her mother's less than wise choices in male companions, Sarah had shielded her heart. Now here in this Amish home, she had let down her guard and was making another huge mistake.

She turned from the window and picked up the dough only to slam it down on the dry sink and pound her fists into the plump flour mix. Over and over again, she pushed and folded and stretched the dough until her arms ached from the strain. Kneading the dough eased her frustration until the door opened again. This time she could sense Joachim's presence even without seeing him, as if there had been a trigger within her body signaling his nearness. How could she hide her true feelings if even her body gave her away?

She dropped the dough into a greased mixing bowl, covered it with a dish towel and placed it on the back of the stove, where the warmth could help the yeast to rise.

She turned and tried to smile in spite of the tangle of confusion that swirled within her.

"Let me wash my hands, and then we'll have coffee." She struggled to hide her inner turmoil. "Rebecca is gathering potatoes from the root cellar. Although she also planned to clean the shelves and rearrange the canned goods. She said the task would take quite some time. While she is gone, we need to talk. But first I must tell you what I heard while I was in Victor's basement."

* * *

Talk? Joachim wondered what Sarah wanted to discuss and what she had heard. He took a seat at the table and watched as she filled two mugs and placed one in front of him.

"You take yours black?" she asked.

He nodded and waited as she added cream from the pitcher to her own cup and a teaspoon of sugar. After stirring the hot brew, she reached for a plate of cookies on the counter and placed both the plate and her cup on the table as she slid effortlessly into the chair across from him.

"I apologize for startling you earlier," he said. "I hurried inside to ensure you were home and all right. The last I saw, you were running toward the path. I stood by the door ready to distract Victor in case he came outside."

"He remained on the phone?"

"For only a minute or two, talking to someone named George."

Sarah's eye widened. "George is the man who is supposed to bring Miriam here. Did you hear him mention my sister's name?"

"I only heard a bit of the conversation and nothing about Miriam. Victor disconnected and stepped outside just as you disappeared into the woods. I feared he had seen you, but his only concern was my need to get back to work. Thankfully, the storm came up this afternoon so I could come home early."

She touched his sleeve. "You are wet from the rain."

"*Yah*, and from the cars that sped around the buggy, never realizing the water their tires stir up."

"Perhaps you should change into something dry."

He shook his head. "You said we should talk. What do you want to discuss?"

She leaned in closer. "What I heard in the basement."

"You heard Victor talking to me, no doubt."

"Only your muffled voices. I ran to the far end of the basement, needing to hide in case Victor came downstairs. I thought he might have heard the basement door close. Thankfully, the water ran in the sink. The sound must have drowned out the closing door."

"I was sure he would not believe that my only reason for being inside was to draw water into a glass. As hateful as Victor seems, he can be a bit of a *dummkopf*, as we say."

Sarah wrinkled her brow. "I need a translation."

"Stupid. A dummy who lacks common sense. His father was a learned man, well-thought-of in the local community. His mother was known for her big heart and sweet disposition. Somehow Victor missed out on the fine qualities seen in both parents."

"Children do not always take after their parents, which is a relief to me," Sarah said. "I never wanted to be like my mother."

"She was an authoritarian and demanding of you?" he asked.

"Not really. I longed for structure and stability, but she could never settle down. We were nomads traveling from one rental property to another across the United States. Two or three months in one place was the norm. Then my mother would become dissatisfied and decide it was time to move. Often the bills she couldn't pay would mount up, and she'd wake us in the middle of the night so we could sneak out of town undetected."

"I left this area five years ago," he shared. "Before that, this house was the only home I had known."

Sarah smiled. "We're both so different."

"Yet sometimes opposites are attracted to one another."

She glanced down as if unsure of how to reply, perhaps even unsure what he was alluding to with the comment. Joachim understood her confusion. An Amish man and an *Englisch* woman were as extreme opposites as two people could be. They had found each other because of her need to escape and his willingness to come to her aid. Otherwise, it was unlikely their paths would ever have crossed.

"We have gotten off the topic," she quickly added. "I wanted to tell you what I heard in the basement other than your mumbling voices."

He raised his cup to his lips and took a long pull while she gathered her thoughts.

"I have been in the basement before," Sarah began, "but Victor has always gone with me. Ms. Hazel kept extra canned goods there, so I would help Victor carry the items upstairs. One day we saw a rodent. He was especially unsettled by the small creature."

"This is what happened today. The mouse frightened him."

Sarah nodded. "His house is infested with rodents, so he has reason to be anxious. Ms. Hazel kept old rusted tins of rat poison in the basement. The kind that contains arsenic, although I'm not sure how effective it might be as old as the cans look. Today the poison sat open on a basement workbench."

"Which means he is trying to solve his rat problem."

"Probably. I went to the very back of the basement

where I hadn't been before. That's when I heard the noise."

"A rat?"

"Maybe, but I don't think so. It was a scratching sound. I found a corner alcove and a doorway."

"You opened the door?"

"I couldn't. A metal bar ran from one side of the wall to the other and was padlocked. I looked but couldn't find a key."

"A secret room perhaps?"

"I'm not sure. Could it be a door that leads outside?"

Joachim shook his head. "I have been all around the house, checking for damage, and have not found a door from the basement level. The only entrances appear to be the one that leads to the kitchen and the other into the main foyer. Besides, the basement sits almost entirely belowground. Stairs would be needed, or a ramp to climb from the basement to ground level. I have seen nothing like that which you have mentioned."

"It's an old house, Joachim. Perhaps the stairway has been filled in."

"This could be, but then the door would lead nowhere. Are you sure the scratching sounds came from behind the door? The basement is large. A sound on one side could echo in another area. Besides, a scratching sound does not mean a human being is involved, especially when rats and other rodents seem to have taken up residence in the house."

She sighed. "It sounds crazy, doesn't it? You probably think I'm a *dummkopf*, like Victor."

Joachim laughed. "You could never be like Victor, nor do I think you are being foolish. Maybe you heard exactly what you think. Victor is an evil man, and it would not be surprising if there are other victims of his cruelty. But it is also possible that your fear is causing you to jump to conclusions. You were held captive for a period of time. Perhaps you heard a sound, but your imagination took it to the extreme. You have a big heart, Sarah, and would not want another human to be held against his or her will. I will check the outside of the house tomorrow and will look for anything that could have been filled in or a door that could have been walled off. If I see something, I will let you know."

He hesitated. "The Amish are not prone to calling in law enforcement, but so much has happened. I understand you want to avoid the police, but…"

"I can't and I won't trust the local law enforcement. Victor said the police were involved. They might tell Victor where to find me."

"Suppose Victor captures someone else?"

"Perhaps he already has, if the sound I heard in the basement was caused by another person."

"Then all the more reason to involve the police."

"Maybe when I'm ready to leave and return to Tennessee."

"You are not leaving any time soon?"

"I can't stay here much longer, Joachim. I need to find my sister Miriam, if she's even alive. I also have an older sister, Hannah, who left the family three years ago. She was going to Atlanta. I might find her there."

"Atlanta is a big city. A person could get lost in such a place."

"Are you saying I shouldn't try to find Hannah?"

"I would think involving law enforcement might be the best way to find both your sisters."

"Corrupt law enforcement won't help me, Joachim. I would have to trust the person I tell."

"You have told me, which must mean you trust me."

She smiled. "You saved me, Joachim. You could have revealed my whereabouts to Victor a number of times, and instead you've chosen to keep me safe. I have to trust you. At least for now."

She scooped up the empty mugs and took them to the sink just as Rebecca entered the house, carrying a basket filled with potatoes. Her face was flushed. Levi followed her inside. He was laughing as if he did not have a care in the world. Would Sarah ever be able to laugh with such abandonment, or would she carry the weight of all that had happened on her shoulders forever?

Chapter Ten

"Is something wrong, Joachim?"

Rebecca stood staring at him. Her smile was gone, and she looked concerned as she glanced from him to Sarah. "Did something else happen? Did Victor come to the house again?"

He shook his head. "I left Victor at his mother's house."

"Yet you look as if something is very wrong."

He glanced at Sarah, giving her the opportunity to share what was troubling her.

"The coffee is hot," she said, as if to deflect the tension that filled the room.

Levi grabbed a cup from the cabinet and headed to the stove. Sarah filled his cup, refilled hers and Joachim's, and then poured coffee for Rebecca.

His sister seemed surprised to be the one served for a change. "You should sit at the table, Sarah, and let me pour the coffee," Rebecca said. "I am not used to being waited on."

Sarah smiled and appeared to appreciate Rebecca's

comment. "You and Joachim have done so much for me. It is the least I can do."

When everyone was at the table, sipping coffee, Sarah joined them and waited for a lull in the conversation before asking, "Do you remember seeing a basement door at the Thomin house?"

She looked at Levi. "Did your sister ever mention the basement?"

He shook his head. "I cannot remember Naomi saying anything about the basement. Why do you ask?"

"Joachim and I wanted to ensure Victor's mother was all right. Victor was away, so we went to check on her. We found her empty prescription bottles that Victor has not refilled. We also found sleeping pills. As lethargic as his mother has been, I fear he might be sedating her."

Rebecca sighed and shook her head. "Victor is not to be trusted, that is for certain. It troubles me deeply that he might not be providing adequate care for his mother."

"It troubles me, as well. But there is something else." Sarah recounted hiding in the basement and the scratching sounds she heard.

"Surely it was the rats that you say have nested in the house," Levi suggested. "Perhaps Victor needs a few cats to scare the rodents away."

"It sounds as if more than one cat would be needed," Rebecca added.

Sarah nodded and then continued, "The barricaded door could lead to a storage closet, but it could, at one time, have been an outside exit from the cellar. Do either of you recall hearing of a basement door on the exterior of the house in years past?"

Levi shook his head. "I have not seen a basement exit, although I do not recall ever walking around the house.

A few times, I took the buggy and picked up Naomi after she finished working. She always came out of the kitchen door."

Rebecca nodded in agreement. "I have been to the kitchen entrance, but have not walked around the house either. Nor would I have had any need to look for an old door. But I do know someone who might provide information."

Joachim leaned closer. "Someone in the area?"

"*Yah*, that is so. Do you remember Mamie Carver, the *Englisch* woman who used to buy eggs from me?"

"The Carver family lived in a small house that sat back from the road. As I recall, they rented a tract of land from the Koenigs and grew vegetables that Mamie's mother canned."

Rebecca nodded. "That is right. Her mother died a few years ago, and Mamie's eyesight is failing, but she is still able to tend her garden. You must visit her, Joachim."

"How would she be able to help us?" Sarah asked.

"Her mother worked for Ms. Hazel's parents, who owned the home before Ms. Hazel married. Miss Carver's grandmother worked there, as well."

Sarah's face brightened. "So she might recall information about the basement."

"Perhaps she visited the house. It was customary for the owners of the big houses to provide for their staffs at Christmastime. Often there would be a day of celebration with food and activities. The children of those employed on the property would take part. Miss Carver may have been involved, or she might recall her mother or grandmother talking about the event."

Sarah glanced at Joachim. "We must find Mamie and talk to her."

"Tomorrow. If the rain continues, Victor will not expect me to work."

"And if the sun shines?" Sarah asked.

"I will work in the morning and tell him I must tend to my father's farm in the afternoon."

He glanced at Levi. "You will be here?"

"*Yah*, I told your *datt* that I would help Rebecca with the chores until he returns with your *mamm*. He knows that day after tomorrow I must go to Willkommen to help my uncle at the Amish Market."

Joachim's heart sunk. "Day after tomorrow? Our *datt* is returning home that soon?"

"This I do not know for sure," Levi admitted. "I only told him when I would be gone."

"You know our parents," Rebecca added. "They only schedule when they will go on their visits. They rarely plan their return."

Joachim nodded. What his sister had said was true. His parents could stay away longer...but perhaps not. Which meant it might be no more than forty-eight hours until Joachim would have to talk to his father. If their meeting did not go well, Joachim might be forced to leave home again. He glanced at Sarah, knowing he was not ready to leave her.

He would hold on to each precious hour. There was so little time. Would it be enough time to tell Sarah how he felt? Or would he leave never sharing how special she was to him?

Chapter Eleven

The deep rumble of thunder woke Sarah before the first light of dawn. Rain fell in torrents, but she was grateful for the downpour. The storm would provide a reason Joachim would not be able to work for Victor today.

She and Joachim needed to visit Miss Carver and learn more about the padlocked doorway. Sarah thought again about yesterday when she heard the scratching noise. Could the sound have been made by a mouse or a rat or some other creature?

Throwing back the quilt and sheet, she dropped her feet to the floor and reached for the flashlight, grateful again for Joachim's thoughtfulness. She hadn't wanted to tell him about her childhood and the fear that still troubled her.

The fact that her mother had never again mentioned the incident had made it even more difficult to bear. She longed to be forgiven, but forgiveness had never been provided.

Once she had mustered the courage to mention the fire to Miriam. Even her sister had shoved aside her comment. "That was the past," Miriam had told Sarah. "We need to focus on the present."

But the guilt she carried had followed Sarah into the present and remained a weight around her neck. No matter how hard she tried, Sarah would never be rid of the memory.

Footsteps sounded in the hallway. From the lightness of the step, Rebecca was hurrying downstairs to add wood to the stove and begin her day of cooking. Sarah dressed quickly and followed her to the kitchen.

The tin coffeepot sat on the burner. Water dripped through the grounds and filled the house with the rich scent of the morning brew.

"You are up early," Rebecca said in greeting. Her eyes were bright and her smile welcoming. Levi had stayed after dinner last night, and the two of them had sat on the front porch until well after sundown. Sarah envied the relationship they had, an easy and familiar connection even when they weren't conversing. A bond connected them as surely as if their hearts were actually tied together with a ribbon.

As much as Sarah longed to have someone in her life to lean on, she couldn't trust her instincts. She had seen the destruction caused by love wrongly given. That was one of the reasons she had encouraged her mother and Miriam to drive to Willkommen. Sarah had wanted to find her long-lost aunt, her mother's sister, but she had also wanted to breathe new life into her own daily routine. Secretly, she had dreamed of remaining with her aunt when her mother and Miriam returned home. Foolish though it seemed, she had hoped the rural mountain community would provide an opportunity for her to start fresh without the constant shadow of her mother's disapproval.

She poured coffee into a mug and sighed as she reached for the pitcher and added a dollop of the rich cream and a teaspoon of sugar.

Now she wondered if she would have stayed in Willkommen if Miriam and her mother returned home to Tennessee. Sarah had relied on Miriam to guide her through the first twenty-one years of her life. It was doubtful to think Sarah would have become more independent in Willkommen.

"You seem pensive this morning." Rebecca's statement pulled her from her thoughts.

"I'm still tired," Sarah admitted.

"You should have slept longer."

"I wanted to help you with breakfast, yet here I am pining over my coffee. What can I do?"

"We have bread from yesterday. Joachim likes it with butter and jelly. Could you fetch the butter from outside? It sits in a jar in the cool tub of water near the pump. You'll find a bottle of milk there, too. Bring both inside, if you do not mind."

Sarah glanced out the window. The pitter-patter of rain on the tin roof of the kitchen had eased, although the sky remained gray and overcast. She opened the door and stepped into the damp morning air, relishing the clear freshness of a new day washed clean by the earlier storm.

She hurried down the steps and followed the well-worn path to the pump. To the side was a tin tub half filled with cold water, as Rebecca had mentioned. The butter sat in a half-submerged glass jar next to the milk jug. She lifted both from the tub, shook off the excess moisture and turned back to the house.

The sound of a car's engine made her heart lurch. She hurried for the protection of the porch and ducked behind the railing, her eyes straining to see the vehicle on the road this early. Surely it wasn't a red pickup.

Peering through the gaps between the fence posts, she realized her folly. If Victor was on the road and turned his truck into the Burkholder farm, she would be seen instantly.

She held her breath and stared at the road as the sound of the engine grew louder.

"Please," she whispered.

A black sedan zipped along the roadway and passed the farm.

She let out the air she was holding and clutched the two jars close to her heart.

"Sarah?"

She jumped, nearly dropping the milk and butter. Hands reached to grab them and locked around her arms. When she looked up, she stared into Joachim's questioning eyes.

"I have startled you again," he said, contrition evident in his tone.

She tried to cover her surprise. "I thought you were still asleep."

"The Amish rise early. Animals must be fed and watered. Stalls mucked."

"You haven't forgotten about visiting Mamie Carver, have you?"

He smiled. "I have not forgotten. It appears more storms are brewing in the distant sky, which provide the excuse I need for Victor. He will not expect me this morning. After breakfast I will take the buggy to Miss Carver's home."

"I'll go with you," Sarah insisted.

"Storms may continue throughout the entire morning. You should remain here and stay dry."

"I'm not made of sugar, Joachim."

He laughed and his eyes glanced down at her shoes, wet from the rain. "You have not melted yet, that is true. You can go with me, but we must be careful in case Victor is on the road."

"He sleeps late and doesn't like to get his truck dirty when the roads are wet. I don't think we'll run into him."

"You know him well."

Sarah hesitated. Joachim was right. After weeks of being held captive, she knew Victor's idiosyncrasies, of which he had many. Somehow all that knowledge hadn't helped her escape until Joachim came into her life. She owed him her gratitude.

"I don't know if I ever thanked you for saving me. If you hadn't come along—"

"As I recall, Sarah, you were the one who snuck from the house and hid in the buggy. You saved yourself. The only thing I did was drive my buggy off Victor's property."

"Did you know I was hiding there?"

A smile twitched his lips. "I saw that the tarp had been moved. You had raised your finger to your lips when I glanced through the window. It was easy to realize you did not belong with Victor."

"He had grown increasingly antagonistic," she shared. "That particular morning, we were in the attic. I mentioned the rats, which probably added to his agitation. He choked me until I could not catch my breath. I knew then that I had to escape."

"Then I arrived at the perfect time."

She nodded, feeling the pull between them that made

her want to step closer. Instead, the clip-clop of horses' hooves on the road caused her to draw back. She was too visible, especially with the sun rising in the east. She would be safer inside. And her heart would be safer if she put some distance between herself and Joachim. But was safety what she really wanted when it came to him? He had saved her. Was she letting down her guard because of what he had done? She would forever be grateful, but she could not confuse gratitude with affection.

"Rebecca is fixing breakfast," she said. "You must eat, then we will find Miss Carver and learn what we can about the Thomin basement."

"You still believe a person made the scratching sound?"

"I don't know, but I won't have peace until I ensure that no one else is being held captive."

She hurried up the stairs to the porch, relieved to have Joachim follow close behind her. For a moment, she thought of Rebecca and Levi entering the kitchen last night with that special bond between them so evident.

Would Rebecca be aware of a connection between Joachim and Sarah? She sighed at her foolishness. She was putting too much emphasis on a moment in the early morning before she had a chance to think clearly. Joachim was Amish. His faith intrigued her, and if truth be known, he intrigued her as well, but the handsome carpenter needed to look for someone within his own community to capture his heart.

Sarah stamped her feet on the rug as she entered the sweet-smelling kitchen. She was acting like a *dummkopf*. Better to guard her heart and her head until she could get safely away—from Victor and perhaps from the handsome handyman, as well.

* * *

In a moment of weakness, Joachim had agreed to Sarah accompanying him to visit Miss Carver. Hopefully, he had not allowed his heart to override his head. Even if Victor usually slept late and kept his truck off the road during wet weather, the man's actions had become more erratic according to Sarah.

Joachim would never forgive himself if his moment of weakness, giving in to her pleading to come with him, put Sarah at risk. He blamed it on her crystal-blue eyes, which shimmered like a placid lake, reflecting the sun's bright rays. One glance at her and he was lost in another world, a world without the restrictions that came from an Amish man having interest in an *Englisch* woman. As much as Joachim needed to be Amish, he longed to be with Sarah.

Their time together was passing much too quickly. His father would be home soon. Joachim had moments of despondence when he was convinced he had been a fool to think reconciliation could be achieved. At other times he had hope that his father would accept him back. Pride was the wall that stood between them. At the present moment, Joachim believed his *datt* would not change his mind or his heart.

He sighed, pondering whether he had been foolish in coming home. Yet if he had not, he never would have met Sarah. The thought that she would still have been under Victor's control made Joachim grateful that he had journeyed back to his Amish roots. He only wished Sarah could embrace that which gave meaning to his own life. But a *fancy* woman could never embrace the *plain* life. Of this, he was sure.

Chapter Twelve

"I do not think this is a good idea," Rebecca told Sarah. Both women stood at the sink filled with breakfast dishes and peered through the kitchen window as Joachim disappeared into the barn to hitch Belle to the buggy.

"The sky is dark," Rebecca cautioned. "More rain will fall, and there will be lightning and thunder. Belle spooks in storms. You are tired and still healing from what you have endured. The seat of the buggy is not what you are used to. Stay here and let Joachim go alone to talk to Miss Carver."

Sarah appreciated Rebecca's concern, but she would not be content to stand at the window and watch for Joachim's return.

"Didn't you tell me that Miss Carver lives close?" Sarah asked. "Surely a short trip won't be a problem. Joachim was worried about me getting wet. You are concerned that I will not be comfortable in the buggy."

Her frustration mounted the more she thought about Rebecca's and Joachim's desires to coddle her.

"I was not comfortable locked in an attic room or

being tied up in the passenger seat of Victor's truck," she said. "The drugs didn't help my comfort either, especially when I didn't have any food and reacted to the heavy medication on an empty stomach."

She hadn't intended to be so adamant, but she wasn't a prima donna. She had endured a lot over the last few weeks and none of it good.

Rebecca turned, her gaze filled with compassion. "I was thinking only of your well-being, Sarah, but you are right. You have endured so much. I am not sure I would have survived. You are a strong woman and independent. I was wrong to want to hold you back."

Independent?

No one had called her that before. "But I'm not strong," she countered. "I've always relied on my sister Miriam."

"Your sister was not with you at the Thomin house, *yah*? You escaped by yourself."

"I escaped because of Joachim."

Rebecca tilted her head. "You worked together to escape Victor. I want you to remain safe so that you and Joachim can share more moments in the future."

Sarah took a step back. "I can't think of the future, Rebecca. I can only think of today. Plus, I have to focus on the sound I heard. Suppose a person is being held captive? That's what's most important, not whether I am comfortable or dry."

"*Yah*, you are right. I will pray Victor is holding no other women against their will, and I will pray he does not find you again."

Rebecca grabbed the cape hanging on one of the pegs by the door and draped it over Sarah's shoulders. Reaching for the black bonnet, she smiled. "The wide bill will offer protection from buffeting winds. It will also keep you hidden from view should Victor be on the road." After tying the bonnet securely under Sarah's chin, Rebecca nodded her approval.

"It limits my vision." Sarah adjusted the bonnet, still mildly upset by Rebecca's somewhat overly protective nature. Then she felt embarrassed by her curt tone. Rebecca was merely concerned for her safety.

"I'm sorry, Rebecca. You're kind to let me wear your cape and bonnet. I'll get used to the wide bill, even if it limits my vision."

Rebecca chuckled. "A woman can sometimes hide her feelings within the hat."

"I doubt you want to hide your feelings from Levi." Sarah couldn't help but counter.

Rebecca's cheeks turned pink. "Levi is a good friend and a good man, but he has many women who are interested in him."

Sarah raised her brow. "Yet he comes here every day."

"Coming here is a job. My *datt* hired him."

"Your father did not tell him to have a twinkle in his eye or laughter on his lips. I've seen the way he looks at you."

"Do you mean he is laughing at me?" Rebecca's own eyes sparked with mischief.

"You know exactly what I mean."

"I see something in Joachim's gaze as well, when he looks at you. He has been away for five years, yet I know my *bruder*."

Sarah held up her hand. "Your *bruder*, as you say, came home to talk to your father. Anything you see in his gaze is his concern about how that meeting will turn out."

Rebecca lowered her eyes. "I worry about that meeting, as well. My *datt* is a strong man who has been deeply hurt by the death of his younger son." She glanced up. "He has also been hurt by the absence of his oldest son."

"Have you told Joachim?"

"Some things he must find out on his own. Besides, I see through my own eyes. Perhaps I do not see as Joachim would."

The sound of the buggy caused both women to glance outside. "It is time to go." Sarah pulled the cape tight across her neck.

"I almost forgot." Rebecca ran to the pantry and returned with a basket draped with a dark blue cloth. "This is for Miss Carver. There is bread and cheese, eggs, butter, and a pie. She does not have anyone to help her with her baking."

"She'll enjoy the food, I'm sure. I'll tell Mamie you were thinking of her."

"Perhaps she can come for supper after my parents return. They would like to see her."

"Be careful while we are gone, Rebecca. I worry about your safety with Victor so close."

"I will lock the door. Do not worry about me. Take care yourself." She readjusted the bonnet around Sarah's face.

Her thoughtfulness touched Sarah. Without forethought, she hugged Rebecca. "Be on guard lest Victor comes searching for me. You must remain safe."

"*Gott* will provide," Rebecca said as the two women parted.

Sarah opened the kitchen door and stepped onto the porch, thinking of Rebecca's words. God hadn't provided protection for her mother or Miriam or herself when they had been carjacked. Would He protect Rebecca today? What about Joachim?

All of them were in danger, and it was because of Sarah. She had brought danger to this peaceful Amish farm. She had been thinking only about herself and her own well-being. She hadn't truly considered Rebecca's or Joachim's safety.

The last thing she wanted was to have anything harmful happen to either of them. Rebecca was a lovely woman who had a full life ahead of her with Levi, even if she wasn't ready to admit that. And Joachim?

He had so much to offer a woman. The right woman. An Amish woman to whom he could give his heart.

If only Sarah could be part of his future, but that was a silly thought that needed to be erased from her mind.

Joachim helped Sarah into the buggy and climbed in next to her. He spread a protective throw over her legs.

"The rain won't hurt me, Joachim," she politely informed him.

"*Yah*, but you have not ridden in the front of an Amish buggy when so much moisture covers the road. The cars do not understand how their wheels throw the water. I do not want you drowning before we talk to Miss Carver."

She laughed. Not what he had expected.

"You think my words are funny?" he asked.

She shook her head and touched his arm. He liked the feel of her fingers and the way she leaned into him. Perhaps riding together was a good idea after all.

"I wasn't making fun, Joachim. I was laughing about the seriousness of your expression. You are always so concerned about my safety."

He relaxed a bit and allowed his mouth to turn up

in a responsive smile. "I have never found anyone else in the back of my buggy, Sarah Miller. There is a certain amount of responsibility I must take to ensure you remain safe and protected. Do you consider this a bad thing or an inconvenience?"

Her fingers rubbed his arm, making a ripple of current flow along his spine. She had too much of an effect on him, especially sitting so close.

"I've never had anyone concerned about me before, Joachim." Suddenly, her face was serious, and her words struck an even deeper chord within him. He stared into her eyes and lost all sense of time and space and where they were to go and why they were going there. Instead, all he could focus on was her beauty and the pureness of her gaze and the way his heart lurched whenever she smiled.

Rebecca opened the kitchen door and pulled him back to reality. "Sarah, you forgot the basket."

She seemed equally as confused as she pulled her eyes away from Joachim and glanced at Rebecca. "Oh yes, I'm sorry. I wasn't thinking."

Joachim hoped she *had* been thinking, thinking about him.

He took the basket from his sister's outstretched hand and placed it on the floor of the buggy behind them. After waving farewell to Rebecca, he reached for the reins and with a flick of his wrist, Belle trotted along the drive. He pulled her up a bit at the edge of the road to check traffic in both directions before the buggy turned onto the main road.

"We will hope the rain will keep the *Englischers* with their big cars at home," Joachim said, steering the conversation to practical matters of the head instead of the heart.

"Rebecca said Miss Carver's house is not far."

"Not far in miles, but the drive will take time. You are used to vehicles with engines. We have only Belle."

"She'll get us there," Sarah said with confidence.

Joachim liked her optimism. He smiled again and flicked the reins. Belle increased her speed to a steady trot and ambled along the roadway, heading away from Petersville and the Thomin home toward the cluster of Amish farms. Would Sarah appreciate the beauty of the land and the bounty of *Gott*'s providence for providing such a fertile area to farm?

Joachim hoped she would. He wanted her to like everything about the Amish and their way of life. The truth was he wanted her to like him, as well.

Chapter Thirteen

The Amish farms rolled by one after another, each picturesque in its simplicity. Young children stood on their front porches and watched, wide-eyed as the buggy passed.

Sarah inhaled the country air and the musky smell of the red Georgia clay. Joachim seemed lost in thought, so she kept her gaze on the homes they passed. She wondered about the women working in the kitchens or helping the farmers in the field. Had they been raised Amish or had some of them lived the life she knew? If so, how had they decided to embrace the *plain* life? Surely the transition would be a challenge, yet she had found nothing difficult about being in the Burkholder home. She would have liked a mirror to check that her bonnet was on straight, but she could see enough of her reflection in the windowpane. She had never worn makeup or done much with her hair, so that wasn't a problem.

Sometimes she caught Joachim looking at her, and his gaze made her realize she must have done something right concerning her grooming, even without a mirror.

"The farms are lovely, Joachim. You will have one someday like your father?"

"*Yah*, although I like working with wood so I would have fewer fields and a larger workshop for my carpentry."

"You did carpentry work while you were away?"

"I did. There was more than enough work."

"Do you plan to stay here in the Petersville area or return to the Carolinas?"

"It depends upon my father. If he will have me in his house again, then I will stay."

"And if not?" she asked.

"Then I will find my own way and a new place to live."

"But you will remain Amish?"

"*Yah*, Amish is who I am."

For some reason, his response took the joy she had been feeling out of her heart.

Joachim turned the buggy onto a dirt side road and encouraged Belle onward. The path was pockmarked, and the ride became bumpy. Sarah bounced from side to side and began to understand Rebecca's concern about the buggy ride.

When the back wheel dropped into an especially large hole, she gasped and reached for the handle on the seat to steady herself.

"Do people ever fall off?" she asked in all seriousness.

Joachim put his arm around her and drew her closer. "I will not let you fall."

His words and the strength of his touch relieved her concern. She settled against him. In spite of the bumpy road, she liked sitting close to Joachim.

The ride soon came to an end at a small house. A tin roof hug over the raised porch and cast the door and two windows in shadow. A wooden rocking chair sat idle as Joachim helped Sarah climb from the buggy.

"The house could use some repair." Joachim kept his voice low. "I will come back with my tools once I have finished at the Thomin home."

He rapped on the door. "Miss Carver, it is Joachim Burkholder and a friend. We have brought food from my sister, Rebecca."

Silence greeted them. Joachim knocked again. He glanced at Sarah and then over his shoulder, eyeing the road they had just traveled. "I will check the barn. You stay here."

"I'll go with you."

He nodded, but before they left the porch, the sound of footsteps caused them to glance at the corner of the house. A wizened woman appeared, stooped with age; her white hair contrasted sharply with her brown skin. She carried firewood and seemed out of breath with the effort. Seeing that she had company, her eyes widened and a smile pulled across her full face.

"Don't know if my eyes are making a fool of me, but I see Joachim Burkholder standing on my front porch big as life."

Sarah smiled at the humor in the woman's tone.

"Your eyes have not fooled you," Joachim responded as he flashed an equally warm smile back at the sweet woman. "I have come home."

Mamie nodded. Her gaze fell to Sarah. "And you have brought a pretty girlfriend to brighten my day."

Joachim hurried to where Mamie stood and took the

wood from her hands. "You have a heavy load. Allow me the pleasure of helping you."

Mamie laughed. "You can help me any time, Joachim. Any time at all."

She climbed the stairs and held out her hand to Sarah. "Mamie Carver, ma'am."

"My name is Sarah," she replied, feeling strength in the woman's handshake and seeing the twinkle in her eyes. Miss Carver might be advanced in years, but she still had a spring in her step and a charisma that made Sarah feel instantly at home.

"Come inside. The coffee is hot. Joachim, you can set that firewood by the stove. Don't mind Butch. He's old, but friendly."

Sarah bent to pet the beagle who ambled toward them after Mamie opened the door.

"You would like Angelo," Sarah told the pup. "He's small, but friendly."

"Butch used to be a good hunter," Mamie bragged. "Now his nose doesn't smell much. Same as mine. Although I'd be interested to know what's in that basket you're carrying."

Sarah laughed. "Rebecca's pie and fresh baked bread, cheese and butter. Also some eggs."

"Which I appreciate. You folks come in and sit a spell."

She motioned them into the small but tidy house. The kitchen was to the left. A table and four chairs sat in the middle of the room with a stone fireplace to the right. Close to the hearth was a second rocking chair with a straight-back chair positioned nearby.

Peering through an open door, Sarah noticed a small

bedroom. The single bed was covered with a quilt, and a latched rug covered the floor.

Sarah slipped out of her cape and took off her bonnet.

"Sit at the table, please." Mamie pointed her toward a chair. "I'll pour coffee."

"May I help?" Sarah asked.

"I'd like that. Milk's in the refrigerator. There's sugar on the counter. Why don't you slice that bread Rebecca made? I haven't had breakfast, and I'm hungry. Surely you and Joachim would like something to eat, as well."

"I'm still full from breakfast," Sarah and Joachim said in unison and then laughed.

Sarah opened a cabinet and found a plate and a serrated knife in the drawer next to the sink. She cut a thick slice of bread and slathered it with butter and strawberry preserves Rebecca had thoughtfully included.

As Mamie poured three cups of coffee, Sarah peered into the pantry and noticed the near-empty shelves, making a mental note to share the information with Rebecca.

Once Mamie finished eating her bread, she took a long drink from her coffee and wiped her hand over her mouth.

"Joachim, your sister makes pies like my mama and grandmamma used to make. Mama always said it was the lard that made her crust so flakey. Now the doctors tell us lard is bad for our health."

"Do you have any brothers or sisters?" Sarah inquired.

"I've got a younger brother. He and his wife live near Willkommen. I don't see much of them these days. His wife has rheumatism and stays close to home."

Sarah perked up at the mention of Willkommen. "Do you know of anyone named Annie Miller in that town?"

"Not that I recall, although I don't know many folks

on that side of the mountains. Next time I see my brother, I could ask him. Is she a friend of yours?"

"My mother's sister."

"Yet you don't know her, child?"

"My mother left home at a young age. She never returned to this area. In fact, she never told us that she even had a sister until not long ago."

"Sometimes we stay away for a number of reasons." Mamie glanced knowingly at Joachim.

"And sometimes we return home seeking to mend any broken fences," Joachim added.

"Which is a very good thing," Mamie stated with a nod. "The good Lord says not to focus on the speck in another's eye, but rather to recognize the plank in our own. My brother and I had a tiff some years back. Can't remember what it was about. One day, I drove to his house. Even before he could say hello, I told him I was sorry. I wanted the divide between us to end."

"What happened?" Sarah leaned closer. She noticed Joachim was focused on the old woman's story, as well.

"My brother just stood there looking at me. In fact, he paused so long I was ready to turn around and get back in my car. Before I did, he stepped toward me, looked deep into my eyes and said he was sorry for the time we had wasted with the anger. He said it was time for healing. Then he pulled me into a bear hug, and we both laughed until tears ran from our eyes."

She stared at Joachim for a long moment, then turned her gaze to Sarah. "Your mama would do well to reconnect with her family."

Sadness flitted over Sarah. "She was killed not long ago."

"Oh, child, I'm so sorry. I saw pain in your eyes. I didn't know the reason. You need to find your aunt and be that conduit of peace and unity in the family. You can bridge the gap even after all those years."

"But suppose I can't find her?"

"Have you asked the Lord's help? He listens and responds when the request is for our good. I'll ask Him to help you."

Warmth swept over Sarah. A feeling of being loved, which was something she always had hoped to feel from her own mother. Miriam and Hannah had loved her but not in the same way as a parent, and she'd always felt the lack. Mamie, a sweet woman who had only just come into Sarah's life, had shown her how to fill the hole in her heart. Sarah needed to put her trust in the Lord.

Mamie covered Sarah's hand with her own and squeezed ever so gently. "You turn to God with your needs, child. He'll make everything right. I know what I'm talking about."

She glanced at Joachim. "Your father made a mistake. You reacted because you were young and hurt by Eli's death and your own confusion. I'm glad you've come home."

"*Yah*, but my *datt* is visiting relatives. He and my *mamm* return home in a day or two. I am not sure how he will react to seeing me again."

"In his heart, he loves you. Remember that, Joachim. You are his son."

"But you know my father is a proud man."

"What does scripture tell us? *Pride goeth before a fall.*" She nodded as if appreciating her own wisdom. "You ask the Lord to make you the better man, Joachim. You can do that. But first, you must erase any pride in your own heart."

As Mamie took another drink from her cup, Sarah

scooted closer. "There is something else we need to ask you, Miss Carver. Rebecca and Joachim told me that your grandmother and mother worked for Ms. Hazel Thomin's parents. Perhaps you went to the house as a girl?"

She nodded. "Sometimes I helped to move furniture or polish shoes or the silver. A house that big takes constant care. After Mr. Thomin passed, Ms. Hazel needed even more help. My brother and I were there often." She rubbed her cheek. "If you see Ms. Hazel, you tell her I said hello. She's a good woman."

"Her health has declined and she's bedridden," Sarah said.

"I'm so sorry about her failing health. I heard Naomi Plank was caring for her."

"Naomi left the area almost a year ago."

"Then who's taking care of Ms. Hazel?" Mamie narrowed her gaze. "Don't tell me that son of hers is back."

"That's the problem," Sarah said. "He *is* back, and I worry that he's not giving her good enough care."

"I'd like to give him a piece of my mind."

Sarah smiled, knowing Mamie would not mince words with Victor about his lack of concern for his mother. "We need your help on something else, Mamie, that involves Ms. Hazel's home."

Joachim leaned closer. "I am making repairs to the Thomin house. There is a boarded-up doorway in the basement, but I cannot see an opening on the outside of the structure. Do you recall a door leading from the basement?"

Mamie shook her head. "The only doors to the outside that I knew about were the one leading into the main hallway and the kitchen door. I've been in the basement enough to know I had to leave the house by the back door."

"Was there a closet or cubbyhole, perhaps?" Sarah asked.

"I wish I could help you, but nothing comes to mind."

Discouraged, Sarah glanced at Joachim. He nodded as if it was time for them to head back to the farm.

"Is there anything we can do for you before we leave?" Sarah asked, grabbing her mug and Joachim's off the table.

"You can pour me another cup of coffee and bring me my Bible." Mamie pointed to a small table near the rocker by the fireplace. "And my glasses. I always take time to read the Lord's word each day. My eyes may be bad, but not so bad that I can't read my scripture. The Lord always has something to tell me."

"I wish He would tell us about the basement," Sarah admitted as she quickly washed the mugs at the sink and placed them in the strainer. After drying her hands, she poured Miss Carver a fresh cup of coffee and placed it on the table, along with the Bible and glasses.

"Don't forget to take that basket back to Rebecca," Mamie added. "Hopefully, she will take pity on an old woman and bring me another pie in a week or so." Her eyes twinkled.

"I'll be sure to let Rebecca know how much you enjoyed what she provided. I'll also tell her that her pie rivaled your mother's. I'm sure Ms. Hazel loved your mother's pies, too."

Mamie chuckled. "You've got that right. Ms. Hazel would come to the kitchen house in the summer just to check on when the pies would be pulled from the oven. Course I'd be waiting on them, too."

"The kitchen house?" Sarah asked.

Mamie nodded. "It sat about thirty yards from the big house. Stoves gave off too much heat in summer before air-conditioning to be attached to the main house. The old homes all had a free-standing kitchen used in the summer. The root cellar was there. My mama used to send me down to get the apples for the pies. Mighty nice to have an excuse to visit a cool spot in the heat of the summer."

"Where exactly was the kitchen house located?" Joachim pressed.

Mamie thought for a moment. "To the rear of the house, but more to the east side so the hot afternoon sun wouldn't shine on it. The cool of the shade trees would help, too."

Joachim glanced at Sarah. She shook her head. "I'm not good at understanding distances, but it seems that was a long way to carry food back to the house. What happened if it rained?"

"Why, they used the tunnel when it rained," Mamie was quick to reply.

Sarah looked at Joachim. "A tunnel? From the root cellar?"

Mamie nodded. "Sure enough. It led to the big house so when the rain came, the food could be carried to the dining room without getting wet."

"But the tunnel didn't lead to the dining room," Sarah said.

"No." Mamie shook her head. "The tunnel led to the basement."

Chapter Fourteen

After saying goodbye to Mamie Carver, Joachim helped Sarah into the buggy and guided Belle along the dirt path to the main road. More rain had fallen while they were inside, and a thin layer of water lay across the asphalt once they turned onto the main road.

"The barricaded door has to lead to the tunnel," Sarah said as she adjusted the bonnet on her head and pulled the cape tight around her neck. "But I never noticed a kitchen house."

"Mamie talked about it sitting in the shade under trees. Perhaps the woods have grown around the old structure. Or maybe it was torn down when air-conditioning was installed and they did not need it anymore. The only buildings I know of are the barn and the few outbuildings located on that side of the house. Mr. Thomin was an expert carpenter. There is a wood shed nearby and also another small building that houses garden tools."

"Look around the grounds the next time you're there."

He nodded. "*Yah*, that I will do for certain."

The rain started again and the wind gusted, sending a sheet of water against the buggy. Sarah lowered her head against the pummeling rain.

Thunder rumbled overhead. Joachim hurried Belle. He needed to get Sarah home and out of the storm.

In the distance, the sound of an approaching car made his pulse quicken. *Please,* Gott.

Sarah lifted her gaze. Her face was lined with worry. "Surely it can't be Victor."

"It is probably someone else on the road, but no matter who it is, lower your head as the car passes," Joachim cautioned.

He flicked the reins to encourage Belle. The buggy creaked as the horse trotted up the small hill.

The approaching car crested the rise, taking up more than half of its lane. Joachim steered Belle to the edge of the road as the car zoomed past. It was a big, boxy SUV painted white, with tinted windows that made it impossible to see the driver or passengers.

The car was going much too fast for the narrow road. The wheels splashed a wave of water against the buggy, soaking both of them.

The SUV screeched to a stop. Joachim glanced back. Had the driver realized his mistake and stopped to offer an apology?

The SUV backed up and pulled next to the buggy. The driver's window rolled down partially, and a man peered through the opening. He had a full face and small eyes, which glared at Joachim from under bushy brows. A scar ran along his cheek and disappeared under his jaw.

From the frustration written so plainly across his face, rather than the remorse Joachim had hoped to see, the guy was probably not going to ask forgiveness for his negligent driving. Someone huddled in the back seat. Joachim could not see the person's features through the tinted glass, although the person did appear to have long hair.

"You folks know of a man name Victor Thomin?" the bushy browed guy asked. "I thought he lived along this road, but I can't find the turnoff to his house."

Sarah bristled at the mention of Victor's name.

"You must turn your vehicle around and head back toward Petersville, the way you came," Joachim replied. "You will see a brick mailbox on the left about two miles ahead. Turn onto that driveway. His house sits back from the main road."

The guy nodded but failed to offer thanks. Instead, he pulled his car into a nearby drive, backed onto the road and then gunned his engine and squealed past Joachim and Sarah, sending more water to splash over them. The close proximity of the massive car as it barreled past made Belle skittish. She pranced and shook her head, causing the buggy to edge off the road. The back wheel angled up a small rise.

The whole carriage tilted. Sarah screamed.

Joachim reached for her. Before he could grab her arm, she slipped through his hands and flew out of the buggy.

"Sarah." His heart lurched. He leaped to the pavement and knelt next to where she lay. Her eyes were closed, her mouth open ever so slightly.

"Sarah, are you all right?"

She moaned. Her eyelids fluttered open.

Relief swept over him. He touched her hand. "Tell me you can raise your hand."

She wrinkled her brow. "My hand...why?"

"Just do as I ask."

She raised one hand and then the other.

"What about your neck? Does anything hurt?"

"Everything hurts, but I didn't break anything—at least I don't think I did." She rolled to her side and started to raise herself.

"Go slowly. You had a bad fall." Joachim grabbed her arm and helped her stand.

She wobbled for a second and then brushed the dirt from her dress. "Rebecca's pretty outfit is ruined."

"It will wash. Are you sure you are all right?"

"Yes, but I'm getting cold. Who was that man?"

"One of Victor's friends perhaps. You have seen him before?"

She shook her head. "Never. Did you notice someone in the back seat with long hair? I couldn't see clearly through the windows. Do you think it was Miriam?"

"I do not know, but we must get you home now."

Joachim lifted her into the buggy, overwhelmed with gratitude that Sarah had not been badly injured. Much as he did not want to think of another buggy accident, he could not help but remember what had happened five years earlier. Eli had lain on the road in almost the same way Sarah had fallen. Only Eli had remained where he was, unable to move and struggling for air as the life ebbed from him.

"Are you sure you are not badly hurt?" Joachim asked again as he spread the blanket over her legs and crawled into the buggy next to her.

"I'm still shaking inside, but I'll be fine once we get back to your house."

"The rain has eased. That is good." He moved the reins, signaling Belle to start walking. The buggy creaked as the wheel came free from the mud, and the buggy moved back onto the roadway. Joachim made a sound with his mouth to encourage Belle. The mare increased her gait.

Holding the reins with one hand, Joachim wrapped his other around Sarah, pulling her close. The thought of what could have happened made his stomach sour.

She had mentioned her shaking insides. His felt no better. The shock of watching helplessly as she fell to the ground made him want to take out his frustration on Victor's friend, who had caused the mishap. If Joachim ever saw him again, he would explain the importance of giving a horse and buggy a wide berth. But would an explanation even have a small effect on the man? He seemed to be absorbed by his own needs and uncaring about the consequences of his actions to anyone else, including beautiful Sarah.

Joachim thought again of the person slumped in the rear of the car. All his instincts told him something was not right, but he did not want to alarm Sarah.

No other cars passed them on the way home, for which Joachim was grateful. He pulled Belle to a stop by the back porch and then hurried around the buggy to help Sarah down. Rebecca came out to greet them.

"I have been worried with the storm." Her frown grew more pronounced as she looked at Sarah. "Something has happened."

"Sarah fell from the buggy," he said.

"*Ach!* No!"

"A car passed us going too fast. Belle got skittish and moved off the road. There was an upward incline that caused the buggy to tilt."

"I was anything but graceful." Sarah smile ruefully.

"Did you hit your head? Perhaps you should take her to the doctor, Joachim."

Sarah held up her hand. "No to the doctor. I'm not seriously injured, just cold and a little bruised. I want to get dry and pretend that I didn't slide off a buggy seat." She glanced at Rebecca. "You were right to warn me. Riding in a buggy is not easy, especially in the rain."

"Or when cars drive too close and too fast," Rebecca added.

"The driver of the car knows Victor." Sarah touched Joachim's arm. "I keep thinking about that person sitting in the back seat. I couldn't see her through the glass. What if it *was* Miriam?"

"I am going to Victor's now. Hopefully, I will learn more about this man and his passenger."

Sarah grabbed his hand. "Be careful, Joachim. The man had an evil look in his eyes. I don't want anything to happen to you."

He wrapped his fingers through hers and stepped closer. Sarah had an effect on him that made his head swim and sent everything else into oblivion so that all he saw was her.

"I will be fine," he assured her. "Victor will wonder where I am since the rain has stopped. Besides, if he has houseguests, he will be less interested in the handyman doing repairs."

"Victor sees more than you would think. He has ways of appearing when you don't suspect him of being anywhere in the area. Be cautious, Joachim. And remember that Victor is not to be trusted."

"I will remember."

He did not want to leave Sarah, but he needed to get to the Thomin home before the next volley of rain started. If the storms continued, he would come home after working for a bit under the overhang of the porch to escape the rain.

Stepping away from her was difficult.

"Get dry and stay warm," he told her. "I will return soon."

Rebecca stood on the porch, her face drawn and looking as forlorn as Sarah. He was aware of the danger of going back to the Thomin home, but he needed to see what was happening there for himself. As Sarah had mentioned, Victor was not to be trusted. The arrival of the second man and the passenger in his car made Joachim even more concerned.

Sarah was worried about what Victor could do to Joachim. She was also worried about the man in the SUV, as well as his passenger. Could the woman be Miriam? Would her arrival at the Thomin home be a good thing or would it place her sister in even more danger? The last time Sarah had seen Miriam had been in the cabin where they had been held captive after the carjacking. Victor had claimed that a man named George had her now. If only Sarah had more information.

Rebecca and Joachim had cautioned Sarah to keep her head down, which was what she had done when the man pulled his SUV to a stop beside the buggy, yet that hadn't kept her from catching a glimpse of the guy at the wheel. He looked menacing and evil. Just like Victor. Which made her all the more concerned about her sister and worried about Joachim's safety.

Could the newcomer be George, the man who was supposed to deliver Miriam? Sarah shivered at the thought of her sister being considered a delivery, like property or chattel. This was the twenty-first century. Women weren't supposed to be owned or controlled by anyone. But life in this part of Georgia was a free-for-all with corruption run amuck. That was why she couldn't go to the police. They were corrupt, as well.

At least she had found Joachim, a man of virtue and integrity. She appreciated all he had done for her, but she worried about his safety. *Protect him, Lord*, she prayed, hoping her prayer would be heard. *And protect Miriam.*

Chapter Fifteen

The ride to the Thomin property seemed especially long today, no doubt because Joachim was thinking of the way Sarah had gripped his arm and the plea he had heard in her voice.

Eventually he turned onto the Thomin driveway and guided Belle toward the barn, where she would stay while he dug through the decaying wood and replaced the rotten areas on the back porch. Once the rain stopped and the wood dried, he would paint the new patches to make them identical to the old.

The white SUV that had caused problems earlier sat parked at the front porch. Joachim stared into the rear seat, seeing nothing of interest. On the porch, he noticed a large duffel bag leaning against the side of the door frame. The arms of a man's brown dress shirt poked from the drawstring closure. Would the filled bag, if propped up in the back seat, have given the appearance of a person with long hair? He shook his head and sighed, suddenly not sure of what he had seen through the tinted windows. He flicked the reins and guided Belle around the vehicle and into the barn. After unpacking his tools from the buggy, he hurried to the back porch.

The kitchen door opened. Victor sneered. "Where have you been? I thought you *plain* people got up early in the morning?"

As much as Joachim did not like Victor's tone, he steeled himself and gave a brief nod as he set his tools on the porch. "The storm was severe. It is dangerous to be on the road when lightning strikes so close."

"That's a lame excuse," Victor said with a wave of his hand.

"I do not offer it as an excuse" Joachim was quick to point out. "I have provided the reason I was delayed arriving. Would you prefer that I leave you now?"

Victor shook his head. "No need to get huffy."

Joachim was not huffy, but he was concerned about what might be happening inside the house. The television was tuned to a sporting channel and cheers from the crowd filtered through the back door.

"Victor, bring me a beer," a male voice demanded.

"You have guests today?" Joachim asked, glancing around Victor in hopes of seeing into the house.

"Get to work," Victor growled before he disappeared back into the kitchen.

Joachim glanced through the windows on the side of the house, searching for some sign of a woman. Seeing nothing except empty rooms, he glanced into the wooded area where Mamie mentioned the kitchen house had been located. Over the years, a thick forest had encroached within twenty feet of the Thomin home. If the kitchen house had been left standing, the woods would have surrounded the small outbuilding by now.

The sounds of the game on the television and the cheers

of the onlookers bolstered Joachim's determination to continue searching. Convinced the men would remain focused on the TV, he hurried to the rear of the house.

Victor found him there. "I'm a little miffed at you, Burkholder," he said, his voice raised. "What didn't you understand about doing a day's work?"

Joachim placed his hand on his forehead as if to shade his eyes from the sun, which had only just peered through the dark clouds.

"I wanted to see the rotting areas on the second and third stories of the house. To do so, I must stand here at the back of the structure." He eyed the upper floors and nodded. "*Yah*, there is more work to be done on the second and third floors. I can see the rot. I must go inside and open the windows to check the sills."

"Not today," Victor insisted. "We'll do it another time. Now get back to work."

Joachim complied with Victor's wishes, but he continued to peer through the windows, hoping to catch sight of the newcomer and whomever might have ridden in the rear seat. Joachim also studied the forested area in hopes of spotting some sign of the kitchen house. Victor kept appearing at the kitchen door—no doubt, checking on him. Tomorrow would be a better day. At least that was Joachim's hope.

Sarah fretted all day about Joachim and whether Miriam was at the Thomin home. Rebecca was worried as well, and both women spoke little. Instead, they busied themselves with sewing. Rebecca was piecing a quilt and taught Sarah how to cut the squares and sew them together on a treadle sewing machine. The rhythmic cadence of the machine filled the house. Sarah enjoyed the repetitive work, but the hours still dragged by too slowly, and her concerns failed to ease.

Late in the afternoon, they put away the sewing and turned to cooking the evening meal. Sarah chopped onions for a stew and almost cried, not from the acrid sting of the onions but from her own worry.

"When will Joachim get home?" she finally asked, no longer able to hold in her emotion.

"Victor will want Joachim to work until five o'clock at least," Rebecca said as she peeled carrots. "He might demand Joachim make up the hours he missed this morning due to the rain."

"Which means Joachim won't be home until after dark," Sarah said with a sigh.

A dog barked near the barn. Sarah peered from the window. "It's Angelo. He's back from his day's escapades."

"And probably hungry," Rebecca added. "Would you mind feeding him?"

"Does he ever come inside?"

Rebecca shook her head. "Dogs are creatures *Gott* created for the outdoors." She lowered her voice and looked stern as she recited the statement. Then she smiled at Sarah and returned to her usual tone of voice as she explained, "That's what my *datt* says."

"He is a gruff man?" Sarah asked.

"On the outside, *yah*, but—" Rebecca patted her heart. "On the inside, where it really matters, he is softer, although you must not tell him I said that. I think he enjoys having people think he is stern."

"And your mother?"

"*Mamm* does not let his caustic tone bother her. She is strong, but in a loving way. You will like her, Sarah."

"And what will she think of having an *Englisch* woman in the house?"

"It is not what *Mamm* thinks that concerns me. My *datt* is the one who will have questions."

"Perhaps it would be best if I leave before he and your mother return home."

"And where would you go? You said your mother has died. Your sister Miriam has disappeared, and you have lost touch with your eldest sister, Hannah. You have nowhere to call home."

"I have an aunt who supposedly lives in Willkommen. At least that's what my mother claimed, but her mind had become addled and I'm not sure if she knew what she was saying."

"I hope you can find your aunt someday."

Which seemed highly unlikely at the present time. Whether she wanted to admit it or not, Rebecca was right. Sarah had no place to call home.

She thought of the sound she had heard in the basement and wondered again if Victor was holding someone else captive. Perhaps someone who had a home and loved ones who were worried about her.

"Have you heard of anyone who has gone missing in the area?" Sarah asked.

Rebecca looked up from the carrots. "Naomi is gone if that is what you mean."

"What about other Amish women? Do you know anyone who disappeared without explanation?"

"Once, about a year ago, a man came to this house. He said he was a policeman, but he was in an unmarked vehicle and asked if we had seen a young woman named Rosie. I do not remember her last name. She was Amish and lived near Willkommen. He claimed the authorities were looking for her."

"Had Rosie done something wrong?"

"I asked, but the man said he could not say anything more." Rebecca shook her head. "He mentioned that she was Amish and had gotten mixed up with the wrong people."

Victor would fit the wrong people category. "Did you ever see her?"

"I saw a woman once at the Thomin house after Naomi was gone. That day, I had baked a cake and took it to Ms. Hazel, thinking she would be lonely without Naomi."

"That's when you saw the Amish woman?"

"*Yah*, at an upstairs window. She turned away when she saw me. I knocked on the door, but she either did not hear me or chose not to answer my knock."

"You think she could have been the missing Amish girl?"

"I wondered if she could be. Not long after that, a policeman stopped by our roadside stand and bought some of our homegrown tomatoes. I told him about the girl I had seen, but he did not seem concerned. I am not even sure if he inquired at the Thomin home. He bought three pounds of tomatoes and then did not have enough money to pay for them. He said he would come back and bring the rest of the money. I was foolish to believe him."

"You never saw him again?"

"Never."

"Joachim says I need to talk to the police."

"I do not know if that is wise," Rebecca said with a shake of her head. "The Amish do not involve law enforcement when there is a problem. We handle things ourselves. But even if we accepted the idea of contacting law enforcement, I do not believe I would trust these policemen. The Petersville police have not helped the Amish in the past."

"Victor told me the police are not to be trusted, but then that's coming from Victor."

"Yet Victor must be stopped from repeating what he did to you," Rebecca said.

"If I go back to Knoxville, I'll tell the authorities there."

Rebecca's brow raised. "Will they care what happened in the mountains of Georgia?"

"I don't know. My mother always ran from the police. When they came looking for us, it meant we had too many bills that hadn't been paid. Even before I met Victor and he told me I couldn't trust the police around here, I had a fear of anyone in law enforcement."

Rebecca patted her hand. "You have had a hard life, *yah*?"

Sarah shrugged. "I never thought of it as hard. It was my life and the only way to live that I knew. Although seeing the peace in this house shows me another way, a way I would like to follow."

"You would like to be Amish?"

"What I want is to sink roots down somewhere and have a home to call my own."

Rebecca nodded her approval. "And a good man to share that home with you as your husband?"

"You're getting ahead of me, Rebecca."

"You do not want a husband?"

"I don't want to be my mother. She made bad choices with men."

"But you are not your mother," Rebecca assured her. "You are your own person."

"A person who can't seem to stand on her own. I need to be more independent, to take care of myself and to be able to make my way in life."

Rebecca nodded. "Perhaps you yearn for a life in the world you left, instead of being holed up in an Amish house."

"The world is not what I want. I want this." She looked around her. "I want the peace and love I feel in this house. I want to work hard and have a sense of accomplishment at the end of the day."

"You have worked hard before, I can tell by the way you always help me and the way you learned to use the sewing machine so quickly today."

"But it wasn't the same in Knoxville. There was always an undercurrent of unease. I never knew if my mother would get upset and become volatile. Maybe it was the yearning for her affection, for words of acceptance that made me a hard worker—even if it never paid off. Growing up, I wanted to please her, but I always seemed to miss the mark, as the saying goes. If I tried to coax her into affirming me, she would ridicule my attempt or walk away as if she had never heard me."

"Mothers are not all the same. Some have big hearts. Others have small hearts. Hopefully, their hearts, no matter the size, are filled with love for their children."

"Yet shouldn't a mother with even a small heart, let her child know the loves she feels for that child?"

"*Yah*, it is so, but *Gott* loves you, Sarah. You are a *gut* person. You should open your heart more to Him and see if you find that acceptance for which you are searching."

Sarah wished it would be as easy as Rebecca implied.

At that moment, she heard the welcome sound of a buggy turning onto the drive and ran to the window.

She smiled when she saw Joachim. She threw open the kitchen door and stepped onto the porch.

He looked tired and worried as if he carried too much on his shoulders. Sarah's heart skipped a beat as she was confronted once more with the truth. She had brought pain and struggle into Joachim's life. Anything good that she sensed in this house was there in spite of her. Yet anything that brought concern and even danger was *because* of her.

Joachim and his family had lived their years in this home and on this farm situated next to Victor's parents. All families had problems, but as far as she knew during that time, nothing had happened to upset the harmony between the Thomins and the Burkholders. Her seeing Joachim through the window at Victor's home had changed everything.

He looked at her from the buggy. Her knees became weak, and she felt light-headed. Silly reactions that didn't do anything to help Joachim. She had to control her emotions and her inner feelings. She had to guard her mind and her heart. She needed to leave the area as soon as possible because staying here, staying close to Joachim, would ruin his life.

Her spirits plummeted as she accepted the truth— leaving the peace and security she felt in this home would be the worst thing to happen to her. She had found something here. Something she wanted to hold on to, but something that didn't belong to her. Something she would only ruin if she stayed.

Her mistake. She had to leave, but leaving would break her heart.

Chapter Sixteen

Joachim had not wanted to stay so late at Victor's home. He had wanted to come back to Sarah. Thoughts of her had carried him through the afternoon. Now that he was home, his heart nearly burst with joy seeing her on the porch waiting for him. If only Sarah were an Amish woman instead of a woman of the world.

Some things were not meant to be. His mother had told him that years ago when he had a crush on a non-Amish girl he had met at the lake where the teens sometimes gathered. The girl was visiting her Amish uncle and aunt, but all too soon she had returned to Atlanta, back to the life she knew. She had promised to write. He had waited for the mailman every day that summer, his heart becoming more and more saddened with each passing day he did not hear from her.

His mother's words back then brought no comfort, but they had provided the wisdom he held on to when he was on his own in North Carolina.

He had come home to find where he was meant to be, but now that he was here, all he could think about was a woman who would soon leave him. Sarah, like that young teen so long ago, would not write, and once her life returned to normal, she would probably not even remember the Amish man who had helped her escape.

"You stayed so long," Sarah said in greeting. "I was worried."

"Victor was insistent that I finish the back porch. He and the man with the scar were drinking beer as they watched sports on television all day."

"Did you see a woman with long hair?"

"I saw no one else. Now I wonder if the form in the back seat was a figment of my imagination."

Sarah furrowed her brow. "Meaning what?"

He explained about the puffy duffel bag he could have mistaken for a person.

"Oh, Joachim, I thought it could have been Miriam."

He shook his head. "I do not think there was anyone else in the house, Sarah. I am sorry."

"Did you search the woods for the kitchen house?"

"I tried, but Victor spotted me through the window and came running outside to call me back."

"Maybe he didn't want you discovering something in the woods."

"I thought he was more concerned about the work not getting done."

"What about the man with the scar?" she asked. "Did you see him?"

"*Yah*, each time he pulled another beer from the refrigerator. I wrote his license plate number on a scrap of paper. We will give it to the police."

"Not the Petersville Police—they can't be trusted. But there should be law enforcement in Willkommen. We could go there. I need to find my aunt. She may have news of Miriam."

"Yet all you know is your aunt's name."

"Isn't that enough?" Sarah asked.

"People move. They get old. She could be infirmed and receiving medical care someplace."

"Then I'll check the nursing homes. Surely there's one in the area."

"We will wait until my parents return. With Victor and the strange man next door, I do not want to leave Rebecca alone. Then I will take you."

"What about Ms. Hazel?" she asked.

"Through the kitchen window, I watched Victor fix a tray and carry it upstairs. It was probably for his mother."

"Did you see a can of rat poison in the kitchen?"

"What are you saying, Sarah?"

"I'm worried about his mother."

"You think he would poison his own mother?"

"The old rat poisons contained arsenic, which can cause lethargy, confusion. Those are all symptoms that Ms. Hazel had."

"Yet you said yourself, she is old and infirmed. She would not have to be poisoned to appear confused or dazed."

"Except she was caring for herself while Naomi was there if what Levi said is true. I got the impression Naomi was more of a housekeeper than a caregiver."

"I do not doubt Levi."

"Nor do I, but it seems suspicious to me that Ms. Hazel's health would fail so quickly."

"Naomi has been gone for almost a year. Many things can change in a year. Ms. Hazel could have had a stroke. She could have gotten pneumonia, which would cause serious complications and setbacks."

"And she could be ingesting small doses of arsenic," Sarah said again.

"What about the sleeping pills we found in her dresser drawer?"

"I'm not counting those out either. Victor might give her sleeping pills so she will stay in bed while he drives round the countryside looking for women."

"And if he had someone holed up in the basement, why would he not use that person to help with his mother?"

From the look on her face, Joachim's statement had stopped Sarah like a brick wall. Surely she realized he was right.

"Why would Victor lock someone in an underground cellar if he needed care for his infirmed mother?" Joachim asked again.

Sarah raked her hand through her hair, nearly knocking off her bonnet. She caught it before it dropped to the ground. Strands of her hair pulled loose and fell over her cheek. He reached out his hand to weave them back in place.

"I don't seem to be getting the hang of this Amish thing, Joachim."

She was being truthful, and he knew it. Sarah was not suited for the Amish life. She needed her world and not his.

"Sometimes we want what cannot be."

She stared into his eyes for a long moment. "The problem is, Joachim, I'm not sure what I want."

With a heavy sigh, she walked to the door, pushed it open and slipped back inside.

Joachim felt as confused as Sarah seemed to be.

Surely she realized they were not meant for each other. No matter how much he wanted what could never be.

Sarah entered the kitchen and washed her hands, then seeing the pot of boiled potatoes in the sink, she grabbed the potato masher and took out her frustration on the spuds. By the time Joachim stepped inside, the pot was filled with creamy mashed potatoes that would be a perfect side dish to the roast Rebecca was cooking in the oven. The rich aromas filled the kitchen and made Sarah's mouth water.

She refused to look at Joachim and then hated herself for being so petty. He was thinking of her safety and was trying to be cautious. If the Amish didn't trust the Petersville police, there had to be a good reason, but Joachim was right. They needed law enforcement somewhere to run the license plate and then investigate whether the man with the scar had anything to do with Miriam.

Ever since Victor had turned against her in the attic the day she had escaped, Sarah had wondered if she would ever see her sister again. For all she knew, Miriam might be dead. Something Sarah was not able to admit aloud.

Tears sprang to her eyes, but she blinked them aside. She had to be strong and hold on to the hope that Miriam was alive. If so, Sarah had to find her.

Again she thought of the scratching sound in the basement. Suppose Miriam was being held captive in some other place and had tried to alert others to her whereabouts. What if her signal for help had been ignored? Miriam wasn't in Victor's basement, but if some other woman was being held captive, Sarah had to act.

Joachim entered the kitchen and stood for a long moment just inside the door, staring at her.

Sarah's heart ached. "I have to find the kitchen house. If my sister was being held in a place like that, I'd want someone to try to save her. I can't stay here in safety when someone might be locked away in an underground cellar."

"I will go tonight," Joachim said. "When it is dark and when Victor's friend is gone or has passed out from his drinking. You will stay here with Rebecca."

"No, Joachim. I'm going with you. I have to go. I can't save my sister, but maybe I can save someone else. Sometimes we have to sacrifice for another. Isn't that what your faith teaches you? It's what I believe. Christ gave up his life so we might be saved. Surely you believe that, too. So you have to understand why I need to go with you."

"What if I don't go?" he asked.

"Then I will go alone. Either way, I have to make sure no one else is trapped in Victor's snare."

"And if something happens to you, Sarah. What will happen to me?"

"The same thing that will happen when I leave here. You will go on with your life." She glanced around the kitchen. "Your future is here with your family. I have to make a new life for myself, but I would not be able to go on if I didn't find that root cellar and determine if someone is being held there."

She looked at him. "Can you understand?"

He nodded. "*Yah*, I understand. But it puts you in more danger, which is not what I want. I want something more for you, Sarah."

"Then go with me, Joachim. We'll find the kitchen

house and search for someone held against her will. Then when I leave Petersville, I'll know I did the right thing."

"What about Ms. Hazel?"

"I'll alert the authorities in Willkommem or the next town or Atlanta if need be. I'll keep talking to law enforcement until someone listens to me. That's what Miriam would do." She grabbed the pitcher of milk and poured some into the potatoes, then mixed in a large scoop of butter.

As good as the mashed potatoes appeared and as wonderful as the smells were in the kitchen, Sarah suddenly wasn't hungry. Everything was about to change. Joachim's parents would return soon, and they wouldn't want an *Englisch* woman underfoot, which made Sarah sad.

For all her bluster, she didn't want to leave this Amish home. Even more important, she didn't want to leave Joachim.

Chapter Seventeen

Joachim tapped on Sarah's bedroom door. "It is time," he whispered, hearing her stir. He turned on the flashlight as she opened the door.

"I fell asleep," she admitted, rubbing her face.

"Are you sure you want to do this?"

"We discussed it earlier. I have to, Joachim. I appreciate you going with me."

"I told you that I would go alone. I had hoped to search the woods today, but Victor kept too close of a watch. He seemed nervous, like a skittish colt."

"Maybe his friend frightens him. The guy looked like he was used to pushing his weight around."

"He is a big man, *yah*. I do not even want to think what happened that caused his scar."

"Perhaps too many beers in a bar someplace."

Joachim held his laughter in check so as not to wake Rebecca. "Let's hope both he and Victor are sleeping off their beers and will not arise from their slumber."

"I'd like to feed both men those sleeping pills we found in Ms. Hazel's room. Then they wouldn't hear us as we search the property."

"We will find the kitchen house tonight," Joachim assured her. "Tomorrow we can determine how to help Ms. Hazel."

She glanced at the small arch of light. "You brought a flashlight instead of a candle. Thank you, Joachim."

"The flashlight will help us find the root cellar."

He stretched out his hand and was grateful when she placed hers in his. Her skin was soft and smooth, and her nearness made his heart skip a beat. He needed to control his emotions tonight lest he do something foolish that might alert someone in the Thomin house.

Sarah's safety was the most important thing to him. Actually, if truth be known, it was all that mattered.

"We will take the path through the woods on foot," Joachim whispered when they left the house and headed along the drive. "The buggy would make too much noise. Stay behind me on the trail. I must turn off the flashlight so Victor does not see us. The trees will block the light from the stars, forcing us to move slowly."

They made their way along the narrow path. Joachim had traveled it many times in daylight. Tonight, the sounds of the forest seemed especially ominous. Leaves rustled, perhaps from a squirrel or some night creature crawling through the underbrush. Snakes were common, but he would not mention that complication to Sarah.

"Wait, Joachim," she whispered. "My skirt caught on a bush."

She tugged it free and then headed on. "It's so dark."

He squeezed her hand. "We are almost there."

Except the trail seemed to stretch forever.

Eventually, they came to the edge of the tree line, where Joachim stopped. He put his finger to his lips as a reminder for them to remain quiet.

For a long moment he studied the house and surrounding area, then motioned Sarah to follow him. Slowly they wove behind the outbuildings and the barn.

"We will cut through the trees until we get to the area where the kitchen house should be located."

Sarah glanced at the Thomin home. "All the windows are dark. Victor used to leave a small light on in Ms. Hazel's room. When I took breakfast to her in the morning, it would still be on."

Joachim squeezed her hand again, hoping to provide reassurance. "We must stay focused. Tonight we will find the kitchen house and determine what caused the sound you heard. As I mentioned, we will decide how to help Ms. Hazel tomorrow."

She nodded. Even with the darkness, he could see her eyes, wide with worry.

"Do you see the SUV that belongs to the man with the scar?" she asked.

"No, but it was parked in front of the house earlier. We would not be able to see it from here. As much as he drank today, I hope he did not try to drive home."

"He's probably staying in one of the guest bedrooms on the second floor. Victor's bedroom faces the front of the house, but the windows in the guest room overlook the back lawn. We need to be careful in case he happens to wake."

"He won't see us, Sarah."

Joachim took the lead. Without a path to follow, he had to pick his way through the underbrush.

"Be careful," he cautioned as he navigated an especially thick area of bramble.

If only he had been able to search the woods in the light of day. Tonight, everything lay in shadows so that even the most common tree or shrub took on a strange appearance.

At long last they arrived in the area where the kitchen house most likely would have been located. Joachim stared into the darkness, seeing nothing.

"What do we do now?" Sarah asked, leaning closer.

"We start searching and walk in a grid fashion so we cover all the ground to make sure we don't miss any trace of it. Remember, it might have been torn down, or fallen apart due to disrepair. But hopefully, we will find some sign of an older structure."

"And if we don't?" Sarah asked.

"Then we will return home without any answer to your question about the noise in the basement."

"I don't want to give up, Joachim."

"I do not want that either. Let us walk next to each other so we can cover two times the amount of area," he suggested.

She glanced over her shoulder at the large Thomin house. "The windows in one of the guest bedrooms are open. That may be where Victor's friend is staying."

Joachim put his finger to his lips. "Then we will be quiet so he has nothing to hear."

He grabbed her hand. "Come, we must walk."

Traversing the area in the dark was a challenge. The smallest bush or tree root caused Sarah to stumble. Joachim caught her each time and helped her regain her balance.

"I'm beginning to think this is impossible," she admitted.

"We will keep looking. Do not get discouraged."

"It's not that."

"You are tired."

She nodded. "You must be, too. I keep thinking about the scratching sound and whether Miriam is being held someplace far from here."

"We can go home and return tomorrow," Joachim offered.

"No. I want to keep searching."

They walked in silence for the next fifteen minutes.

Sarah stopped to lean against a tree. "I'm sorry, Joachim. You would do better without me."

"We will leave now."

Her shoulders slumped. "I feel like a failure."

"You are no such thing. You are tired and still not strong enough. Do not be discouraged."

"Maybe just another ten minutes," she suggested.

He nodded, and they set out again. A break in the trees surprised them. The clear area was easier to navigate with the stars visible overhead, which shed light on the ground.

Joachim pointed to a raised area just a few steps away. They hurried forward and then stopped to stare at what appeared to be stacked bricks.

"It looks like part of an old chimney," he said. "We have found the kitchen house—or at least what remains of it."

He glanced around, searching for some sign of a root cellar or opening for a tunnel. If only they had more light. Glancing over his shoulder, he saw the big house through the trees. They were close to finding what they came searching for, but would the remains of the old structure reveal anything about the scratching sounds Sarah had heard, namely whether a person was being held captive?

Sarah's heart pounded with excitement and anticipation. They'd found at least a portion of the old kitchen house. And even though the building was mostly gone, surely the tunnel had remained. Now they needed to find what was buried belowground.

"No telling how much dirt and debris has settled over this area," she said, glancing around.

"We will walk a few steps away from the chimney," Joachim suggested. "Perhaps ten or twelve feet, and then walk around the periphery of what would have been the outbuilding."

"That sounds like a good plan." They paced off the steps, and then each turned in opposite directions. Sarah walked to the left and took tiny steps, her gaze on the ground. Knowing they had discovered the location of the actual kitchen house gave her confidence. Her foot stumbled over a raised area. She bent and touched the rock that had caught her foot.

"I've found the foundation for a wall," she whispered to Joachim.

He hurried to join her. "*Gut*. We will keep walking, hopefully around the outer wall of the old structure."

Together, they slowly moved forward. Sometimes the stone wall disappeared, but they continued on until they found another section of the old wall.

When they were almost three-quarters of the way around, Sarah stopped. "What's that?" she asked, pointing to a metal slab on the ground.

Joachim bent and worked his hands over the flat surface then down the edge of the covering. "I have found a padlock."

Sarah's heart raced. "It's the door to the cellar."

Joachim nodded. "You are right."

He glanced at the house that sat less than fifty feet away. "If only the windows in the house were not opened. If we are going to explore the tunnel, then I will need to break the lock, which will make noise."

"We don't have a choice, Joachim. We can't turn back now."

"*Yah*, it is true. We must continue our search." He pulled a hammer from his waistband and knelt on the ground next to the metal slab.

Hammer in hand, he glanced up at her. "If you hear anyone coming, run through the woods and angle around, keeping the barn as a point of reference. It will be dark so you will need to be careful, but you should find the path back to my farm on the far side of the barn."

"You're worrying me."

"That is because I am worried, Sarah."

"If Victor and his buddy are sleeping off all the beer they drank, the sound of the hammer might not wake them."

"This we can only hope to be true. Let me know if you see anything change at the house."

She stared at the windows, dark and devoid of life.

Joachim raised the hammer.

She held her breath.

Her heart jerked as his hammer hit the padlock. The clank of metal striking metal echoed through the forest, shattering the night and the stillness.

Sarah continued to stare at the windows. Would she be able to see anyone as dark as it was?

She glanced down. The padlock was still attached. Joachim raised his hammer and struck again.

A light went on in the house.

"Joachim?" She pointed to the window.

He fiddled with the padlock and then held it up triumphantly. Quickly, he stepped aside, grabbed the edge of the metal door and lifted it open.

They both stared into a dark hole.

"Watch the house," Joachim whispered. "Run if someone comes outside, but warn me first. I am going down into the cellar."

She grabbed his arm. "Be careful."

He nodded. Pulling out his flashlight, he stepped onto the wooden stairway that led into the darkness.

Sarah's heart lurched. She wrung her hands, wishing she and Joachim could be anyplace else except at this root cellar in the middle of the night.

She focused her eyes on the light in the window. The minutes passed too slowly. Leaves rustled behind her. She glanced back, half expecting to see Victor. Relieved when he didn't appear, she bent and stared into the darkness.

"Joachim?" she whispered.

Her heart pounded. The sound of her pulse roared in her ears. Where was Joachim and what had he found?

From out of the darkness down the tunnel, a face appeared. Not Joachim's, but a young woman.

Slender, pale, wide-eyed.

Sarah stretched out her hand and helped the woman up the stairs. Tears glistened on her dirt-smudged cheeks. She pulled in a ragged breath. Sarah's heart broke thinking of what she had endured.

"I'm Sarah." She opened her arms and pulled the woman into her embrace.

"My…my name is Rosie Glick."

Sarah smiled. "You're safe now. Victor won't hurt you again."

Rosie gripped her tightly for a long moment and then turned as Joachim climbed from the cellar.

He held a pile of blankets in his arms. Rosie hurried forward and took the blankets from him, a look of relief on her slender face.

Sarah stepped closer. Her heart bursting with wonder and surprise as she stared down, seeing the tiny newborn infant in Rosie's arms.

Chapter Eighteen

"We must hurry," Joachim warned both women. He lowered the metal covering into place and motioned them to head deeper into the woods, away from the house.

A door slammed.

"Victor?"

A man stood in the backyard, the big guy they had seen in the car. He called out for Victor a second time and then started jogging toward them.

"Hurry," Joachim whispered.

Rosie clutched the baby and tried to keep up. Joachim grabbed Rosie's arm. Together, he and Sarah helped the young woman move faster.

Joachim glanced over his shoulder.

The darkness prevented him from seeing the man, but he heard his heavy footfalls.

Again the visitor called out for Victor.

Joachim would not let Rosie be captured again, especially with the baby.

The barn appeared on the right. If only they could clear the outbuildings and find the path.

A kitchen light flicked on in the house, and a person stepped onto the back porch. Shoulder-length brown hair, medium height, slender build.

Sarah stopped and stared at the figure. Her eyes narrowed. "Miriam?"

Joachim turned just as Sarah started to run, not away from the big house, but toward it.

He pointed out the barn to Rosie. "Wait there with the baby."

Joachim hurried to cut Sarah off before Victor's friend saw her. Thankfully, he caught up to her and grabbed her arm.

She turned on him, anger flashing from her eyes. "It's my sister. I have to save her."

"Look again, Sarah. What you see is a man with shoulder-length hair. Your eyes are playing tricks on you."

She shook her head and glanced again at the slender, but very masculine, figure on the porch. "Oh no," she groaned, realizing her mistake.

Joachim took her hand. "Come. We must hurry."

They started to run, but not toward the barn. Joachim did not want to lead the men to Rosie. Instead, he turned back the way they had come.

Victor's friend chased after them. The long-haired man, as well. Sarah gasped for air. Her foot caught and she stumbled. Joachim helped her up. She was winded and frightened. The big man with the scar was gaining on them, his friend lagging some steps behind.

Joachim's heart pounded, fearing Sarah would be captured again. He would rather die himself than let that happen, but she could run no farther, which meant they had to hide. But where?

Think! Think!

"Go on without me, Joachim."

He wrapped his arm around her shoulders and guided her deeper into the underbrush. Both men followed too close behind them.

"It's no use," Sarah gasped.

She was right. Running would not work.

The clearing appeared ahead. "Hurry, Sarah. Just a little farther."

Gott, help us, he prayed.

Dark clouds filled the night sky, blocking the starlight and making the clearing even more difficult to traverse. They were close. He knew it, but the men were close, too, gaining on them.

Joachim stumbled. He stopped short and dropped to the ground.

"What's wrong?" Sarah cried.

His fingers found what he had been looking for. He lifted the metal slab, exposing the black void.

"Hurry, Sarah, crawl into the cellar."

"No, I can't."

"You have to. Now." He took her hand and ushered her forward. "I will not leave you. We will hide together until the men return to the house."

"But—"

"Now, Sarah." The men's footfalls echoed in the night. They were close. So. Very. Close.

With a faint whimper, Sarah climbed down the wooden stairs and disappeared into the darkness. Joachim followed her. He lowered the slab over them. The musty scent of the damp earth filled his nostrils. Sarah grabbed his arm. He pulled her close, feeling her body tremble as the men ran across the clearing, searching for them.

* * *

"I will not leave you." Sarah kept playing Joachim's words over in her head as they waited silently for Victor's friends to give up their search and return to the house. Her head rested against Joachim's chest. She heard his heartbeat, which calmed her racing pulse and helped her endure the time they remained underground.

Finally, Joachim stirred. "I'm going to raise the covering ever so slightly. Do not make a sound."

He moved away from her. A lump filled her throat, and she blinked back tears that burned her eyes. She had to be brave and remain still. At least she was with Joachim. Her heart went out to Rosie, who was alone with her baby. Just so the men wouldn't find her.

A gust of fresh air floated over Sarah as Joachim pushed up on the metal slab. She could see the outline of his profile as he stared motionless through the opening.

Finally, he nodded and reached for her hand. "The house is dark. I trust they have gone back to bed."

Together they climbed from the cellar. Sarah sucked in a deep breath of fresh cool air, grateful to be free. Joachim replaced the covering over the root cellar and pointed toward the barn.

Slowly, they moved away from the house. If they only would find Rosie and her baby waiting for them.

Sarah glanced back at the house that stood black against the night. She recalled the men who had chased them—the large, scarred man they had met on the road, and the other man who she had mistaken for her sister. The slender man with shoulder-length brown hair had been the passenger in the SUV and not Miriam. Just as Joachim had said, her eyes had played tricks on her. Another mistake. She had made so many.

Joachim squeezed her hand as if he could read her mind. He pointed to a path through the woods that allowed them to move more quickly.

Her heart pounded as they approached the barn and entered through a side door.

"Rosie?" Joachim called, his voice little more than a whisper.

Silence.

He walked by the stalls and peered into the nooks and crevices. Had Victor or one of the other men found her and taken her back to the house?

Sarah wanted to scream with frustration and anger at herself. If she hadn't made the mistake about Miriam, Rosie and her baby would have escaped.

Oh, God, help her!

A soft mewing made Sarah turn. She glanced through the open doorway to a second outbuilding. There on the ground, with her back against the wall, sat Rosie, holding the baby in her arms.

Rosie was exhausted, and the trip back to Joachim's house sapped what little strength she had.

"Only a little farther," Sarah whispered, taking the baby and cuddling the infant close. Joachim picked Rosie up in his arms and carried her back to his house.

Sarah knocked on the kitchen door and Rebecca let them in. "Where have you been? I heard you leave the house, and I have been so worried not knowing what happened."

Joachim carried Rosie inside. Rebecca guided him to the rocker by the fire. "It is warm here. I will make tea."

She hurried to the kitchen and passed Sarah, only now noticing the bundle in her arms. Rebecca stopped short.

"Oh my, Sarah. Do you have what I think you have?"

She nodded. "Rosie's baby."

Rebecca turned to look at her brother. "Victor was holding her captive?"

Joachim nodded. "In the morning, I will go to Petersville. The police need to be told. If one officer is corrupt and not interested in getting involved, then I will find another one who will listen. And if not Petersville, then I will drive to Willkommen. Victor must be stopped. He must be stopped now."

Sarah's heart soared with emotion as she rocked the baby who slept in her arms. She had never held a baby so small or so beautiful.

Rebecca prepared food for Rosie, who ate and then asked for more. She kept looking at Sarah and making sure her baby was still sleeping.

No one asked her questions. There would be time for that later. Right now, she appeared too tired and had been through so much.

"There's a spare room upstairs and a bed," Sarah said. "We'll care for the baby down here while you get some sleep."

"Are you sure?" Rosie asked.

Sarah nodded. "Tell me his name."

"Joseph. My baby's name is Joseph."

"Don't worry about your little one," Sarah assured her. "Get the rest you need. Tomorrow we can talk."

Rosie gave a weak smile. "Thank you for saving Joseph and me."

"I heard scratching on the wall when I was in the basement of the big house. That was you, wasn't it?"

Rosie nodded, her face still so pale. "Victor locked me in the root cellar, but he did not remember the tunnel."

"How did you find it?"

"I searched for some way to get out and found the doorway. Dirt had piled up around it. Before the baby came, I cleared the dirt and pried open the door."

"You went into the tunnel?"

Rosie nodded. "Victor left a candle for me. I used that to see my way. I thought it would lead to an exit. When I got to the end and found it blocked, I cried." She glanced at the baby. "That night, my pains started."

"You went into labor and delivered the baby by yourself?"

Rosie nodded, then closed her eyes.

The memory was either too difficult or the young woman too fatigued to go on.

"You need to rest," Sarah insisted. "Tomorrow we will decide what to do next. You are from around here?"

"My parents live near Willkommen."

Sarah glanced at Joachim. If he took Rosie and her baby home to her parents, perhaps Sarah could go with them and make inquiries about her aunt.

Before she could mention her plan to Joachim, he headed to the door.

"Stay here with Rebecca and Rosie," he told Sarah. "I will go back along the path and make certain we were not followed."

Her heart lurched. "Oh, Joachim, be careful. Victor is a terrible man, and his friends seem equally as bad. I'm afraid of what could happen to you if they see you. Please, don't go," she pleaded.

"It is important to stay on guard, Sarah. This is what I must do."

"But suppose you find them. You don't have a

weapon. Your faith does not allow you to respond to their violence."

"Sometimes a man must do what he knows he must do."

"Which means you could get hurt."

"When I was working in North Carolina, I was forced to confront two men who thought being Amish meant being weak. They had no love for *Gott* in their hearts, Sarah, and they left me no alternative but to protect that which was mine."

"What do you mean?"

"I had to show them the fallacy of their ways. Did not Christ drive the money changers from the temple?"

She nodded. "Would your minister approve of your actions?"

"We do not have a minister, Sarah. A bishop leads us and he, more than likely, did not approve of me leaving my home. For a period of time, I had my feet in both worlds, trying to be both Amish and *Englisch*. For that, I must ask forgiveness."

Sarah didn't understand how one man could hold so much power over Joachim. "And what if the bishop says you cannot stay in the area?"

"If I ask forgiveness of *Gott* and of my Amish community, he will not deny my request. He wants what *Gott* wants, and that is for me to live by the *Ordnung*, the rules established for our community."

"What does the *Ordnung* say about matters of the heart?"

His brow furrowed. "A man takes a wife and the two become one. This is the way we have lived through the years. Perhaps I do not understand your question?"

"What if the woman is not a member of the Amish faith?"

Joachim lowered his gaze and sighed. "Then the relationship could not continue. An Amish man marries an Amish woman. Marriage to someone outside the faith is not allowed."

"Isn't that narrow-minded, Joachim?"

He shook his head. "It is the way we keep our faith and our way of life. As much as I tried, I could not walk on both sides of the fence. The choice must be made, either to fully embrace the Amish faith or to leave it altogether. A person must decide which way he or she is to live life." He smiled weakly. "Sometimes that is a hard choice."

Then he turned and walked to the door. After grabbing his hat off the wall peg, he reached for the knob.

Cool nighttime air blew into the kitchen as the door opened, making Sarah shiver. Joachim had clearly explained the choices available to a person drawn to the Amish way of life. Where did Sarah stand?

She was attracted to Joachim and, as she suddenly realized, to his faith, as well. Although she wasn't ready to fully embrace the *plain* life. She needed longer to consider her options, but she was running out of time. Remain *Englisch* and say goodbye to Joachim, or embrace his Amish faith and remain in the area. If only she knew what the future would hold.

She glanced though the window, seeing Joachim hurry toward the pathway. She was running out of time.

Amish or *Englisch*? The decision was one she wasn't able to make. At least not tonight.

Chapter Nineteen

Less than three hours later, the first rays of dawn pulled Sarah from a light slumber. The baby was still asleep in her arms. She glanced around the room, hoping to find Joachim in one of the chairs. Instead, she realized, with a heaviness in her heart, that she was alone.

Too much time had passed since he had left the house. Thoughts of what could have happened stabbed her like a knife. A tiny cry escaped her lips, making the infant stir.

She rocked the little one and tried to force the vision of Joachim being locked in the attic room from her mind. Even worse were visions of him thrown into the dark, dank root cellar.

If Victor was holding him captive, then she couldn't let him remain there. She had to do something to set him free. But what and how?

The baby stretched, then wrinkled his precious face and started to root for a feeding. She patted and rocked, hoping to soothe him back to sleep, yet little Joseph continued to search for nourishment. A shrill cry escaped his thin lips.

As much as she didn't want to wake Rosie, the baby

was hungry and needed to be fed. His cries quickly became inconsolable. Sarah carried him upstairs. The door to the extra bedroom jerked open, and Rosie stretched out her arms to take the child. The baby nestled against his mother. She nodded her thanks to Sarah and then retreated into the bedroom and closed the door behind her.

Sarah stood in the hallway and longed to hold the baby in her arms again. The unconditional love she had felt for the small infant surprised her. A love without reservation. The little one had accepted her love unconditionally as well, and had slept in her arms with absolute trust.

Sarah had always wanted that type of love from her own mother. Instead, she had received criticism and scolding and had grown up sensing she was unwanted. If Sarah ever had children, she would ensure they knew how much she loved each of them and how special they were to her.

She sighed and shook her head, surprised by thoughts of children when she had never allowed herself to consider marriage and family. Surely it was this house with the love and acceptance she had found here that was changing her mind.

But Joachim had told her without hesitation that he could not be interested in an *Englisch* woman. She did not need to be told twice. He had made his feelings on the matter perfectly clear. With all that had happened and as confused as her life had been, she wasn't ready to commit to the Amish faith. At least, not yet.

A swell of melancholy filled her as she headed back downstairs. She walked slowly through the house, seeing the simple beauty of the rockers by the wood stove, the calendar hanging on the wall in the kitchen, and the gas lights sitting on stands in front of aluminum disks that magnified the light and helped to brighten the rooms. She still had an aversion to matches, but the long-necked fireplace lighters and the gas lights with tall hurricane chimneys that encircled the flames were no longer threatening.

She ran her hand over the silky smooth wood of the dry sink and marveled at the workmanship. Had Joachim made the piece for his mother perhaps? Or had his father, who Joachim claimed was a farmer at heart, crafted the kitchen work area long ago for his new bride?

She stepped to the window, seeing the warm glow of the first light on the horizon. The barnyard came into view. As she watched, a small animal bounded along the drive and raced toward the house. Sarah hurried onto the porch and bent to welcome Angelo home.

"Oh, it's good to see you, boy." She scratched his neck. The pup nosed at Sarah's hands and jumped to lick her face. She laughed at his excitement and attention, and again, she was filled with a sense of acceptance and love.

Footsteps sounded. Her heart skidded to a halt. She stood, ready to flee into the house, but before she did so, her eyes caught sight of the man walking toward her.

Her heart went from a standstill to an erratic thumping that warmed her neck and made her want to run to welcome this man home.

"Oh, Joachim," she said as he drew closer. "I was so worried about you."

He opened his arms and reached for her. She stepped into his embrace, the thoughts of their differences fleeing so that all that mattered was being with him.

"The night is over, Sarah, and we are both safe."

She lifted her face to his, longing to remain forever in his arms. He lowered his lips to hers, but before they kissed, a car turned into the drive and captured both of them in the arc of its headlights.

Sarah raised her hand to her forehead, shielding her eyes from the glare as the vehicle pulled to a stop.

A man stepped to the ground. "Joachim Burkholder?"

Sarah felt Joachim tense. *"Yah?"*

The man moved to the front of the car, his dark blue uniform now visible in the headlights.

Sarah blinked and saw the logo for the Petersville Police Department on the side of the car.

"I'm here to take you into headquarters for questioning," the officer said. "You're wanted in connection with the death of Eli Burkholder."

"What?" Sarah looked from the policeman to Joachim.

Shock registered on his face. "Eli died five years ago."

"Did you not flee the area immediately after his death without leaving the statement that law enforcement specifically requested?"

"I do not remember being told to do that."

"Maybe you'll remember more clearly if you come down to headquarters."

"This is not something I want to do."

"Are you resisting arrest, sir?"

Resisting arrest? Everything was going from bad to worse. At first the policeman had mentioned questioning Joachim. Now he talked about making an arrest.

"You've made a mistake," Sarah insisted. "Joachim has done nothing wrong. You need to question Victor Thomin. He's at his mother's house. It's the next property on the road to Petersville. The turn is about a mile and a half from here."

"Ma'am, the Thomins are one of the oldest and most respected families in this area."

"I'm not disparaging the family, I'm talking about their son, Victor. He—"

Joachim grabbed her hand. "Sarah, be quiet. This is not the time."

Rebecca stepped onto the porch. "Joachim, what is happening?"

"Go inside," Joachim insisted. He glanced at Sarah. "Both of you."

"Why do you want to question him?" Sarah demanded of the officer.

"Lady, we received a tip that Mr. Burkholder was in town. We've been wanting to talk to him for years about that old investigation. And now that he's back, he has also been incriminated in illegal operations happening in this local area that involves human trafficking."

"If you're investigating human trafficking, then you definitely have the wrong man. I told you to question Victor Thomin," Sarah insisted, but the officer ignored her and moved to handcuff Joachim.

"I will go peacefully," he told the cop.

The officer ushered him to the squad car, where he frisked him and then clicked the handcuffs into place.

Seeing Joachim handled like a common criminal made Sarah shake inwardly. What was happening? Her world was falling apart. Victor was the kind of man who should be taken in for questioning, not Joachim.

Rebecca hurried from the porch to stand next to Sarah. Both women watched the officer open the rear door of the squad car and shove Joachim into the back seat. The door slammed shut, sending a shiver down Sarah's spine.

The officer climbed behind the wheel, started his car and backed onto the main road. The police sedan turned toward Petersville and drove off.

The stillness was overpowering. Sarah stared at the road as the taillights disappeared from sight.

Angelo nuzzled Sarah's leg and then started to howl.

Joachim glanced back through the window of the police squad car and caught a last glimpse of Sarah standing in the drive, her eyes wide and fear wrapped around her slender face.

After what she had just heard, he was certain she thought he was a killer, just like the heinous man who had killed her mother.

Any chance of convincing her that the Amish way of life—and particularly life with him—would be something she should consider had disappeared the moment the police officer had clasped the cuffs around his wrists.

The night of the buggy accident, Joachim's world had fallen apart. In the years since, he had tried to rebuild it, but all his efforts had fallen apart in the last few moments. He felt vile and unwanted, like a snake that needed to be squashed underfoot lest its deadly venom strike someone down. He had looked into Sarah's eyes and seen her gaze go from one of affection to disgust.

Moments earlier, he had come so close to kissing her that he could almost feel her sweet lips on his. His heart had soared as high as the eagle flies, and he had thought of nothing else except holding her close and keeping her safely protected and with him for the rest of his life.

Then everything had plummeted and his future, the

one he had envisioned with Sarah at his side, disappeared with the click of the cuffs.

Thoughts of going to prison and all the humiliation that accompanied incarceration ate at his gut. Surely he would be exonerated of guilt, yet even the accusation of wrongdoing would mark him. He shook his head, seeing another option, one that was also troubling. He envisioned the loneliness of a vagabond carpenter traveling from job to job, never with a place to call home and never with a *gut* woman like Sarah—no, not a *gut* woman, an amazing woman—to walk with him through life.

The officer was talking on the radio, unaware of the pain Joachim was experiencing. Would he realize his mistake, or would Joachim be held behind bars and forced to face a trial where he would be accused of being responsible for his brother's death?

Perhaps his father had been right. Joachim did not deserve to remain part of the family. He had been shunned and rightfully so.

Gott, *forgive my transgressions. I came home to reconcile with my datt. That reconciliation will never be.*

He turned again to glance back at the farm where he had grown up and where he and Sarah had shared such a short period of time. He now knew what he wanted in life. He wanted his Amish faith, and he wanted Sarah walking through life next to him.

This morning, riding in the back of the police car, Joachim realized he had wanted too much.

Chapter Twenty

Sarah's heart was heavy as she returned to the house and climbed the stairs without saying anything to Rebecca. Joachim, with his concern for others and his willingness to help those in need, was not a man who would take a person's life. Nor did he have anything to do with trafficking. Sarah couldn't believe such nonsense, yet she herself had watched as he had been handcuffed and locked in the back of a patrol car.

Joachim, who had come to her rescue, who had saved her from Victor, who looked at her and made her knees weak and her stomach turn to jelly, was the most wonderful man she had ever known, yet she couldn't stay around and hope there was a chance for them. Joachim had said as much himself when he had discussed the differences between them.

Sarah was an *Englischer*.

Joachim was Amish.

And never the two shall meet or mix or fall in love or declare their love or get married and have a family.

His arrest had nothing to do with her upset. Even if the police officer had not appeared, Sarah would still be struggling to make levelheaded decisions about what to do next. How foolish she had been to have given her heart to Joachim. He wasn't meant for her. After all the legal problems were ironed out, Joachim would find a wonderful Amish woman who would cook his food and sew his clothes and help him in the fields and with milking the cows and slaughtering the pigs. All the things about which Sarah knew nothing. Although she was willing to learn.

She lightened her footsteps when she passed Rosie's room and headed to her own chamber. Pushing open the door, she stepped inside and then quietly closed the door behind her.

The tension that had welled up within her since she had been in Joachim's arms burst loose. Tears fell from her eyes. She stumbled to the bed and collapsed onto the thick quilt as she struggled to control her outburst. She didn't want to concern Rosie or Rebecca with her tears. Hopefully, they wouldn't hear her when she left the house. She could no longer stay here, where everything reminded her of Joachim.

But where would she go and what would she do? A trip to Willkommen to inquire about her aunt? Yes, that made sense as a first step. If the woman couldn't be found, Sarah would board a bus and return to Knoxville.

She wiped the tears from her eyes, and in spite of the heaviness of her heart, she eventually fell asleep. Awakening a few hours later, Sarah headed downstairs and hurried into the kitchen. Rosie sat at the table sipping from a mug of coffee.

"Did you sleep?" Sarah asked.

"Not with the baby in bed with me. I had slept earlier, but after he nursed, I kept wondering how I would face my parents."

"They love you, Rosie. They want you home with them." At least that's what Sarah hoped.

She poured a cup of coffee, weighing how she would leave this wonderful Amish home and how she would get to Willkommen to find her aunt.

"Joachim had said he would take me home," Rosie said. "Now I'm not sure how I will get there."

Sarah nodded. "Perhaps I will go with you, Rosie. I need to find an aunt who may live in Willkommen."

"You are not staying here with Rebecca and Joachim?"

Joachim isn't here, Sarah wanted to remind her. Instead, she asked, "How long did you help Ms. Hazel?"

"More than seven months."

"You didn't try to escape?"

"Where would I go? I was an unwed mother. I could not go home. I could not go anywhere."

"What about Joseph's father?"

"His name was William." Rosie lowered her eyes. "William is dead."

"I'm so sorry." Sarah's heart went out to the young woman. "For those reasons you never tried to escape?"

"That is true, although if I had known that Victor would lock me in the root cellar close to my delivery time, I would have tried to escape. He was not abusive except with his words, but I was foolish to think he was a better man than he proved himself to be."

"What led to him forcing you into the cellar?"

"I told him the baby was due, and that I needed help. He did not want to bring in a midwife. It was easier to

lock me away than to have a doctor or midwife find out
he was holding me in his mother's house."

"How did Ms. Hazel seem when you first arrived?"

"She was sick, and her condition grew worse. I told
Victor she needed to see a doctor. He refused to take
her. Instead, he gave her sleeping pills."

"You saw him give her pills?"

"*Yah*, many times."

"You need to tell the police."

Rosie shook her head. "I do not want to talk to the
police. They cannot be trusted. You must know this for
yourself. After all, they have Joachim. From the window, I watched as the officer put him in the police car."

Sarah's heart ached, thinking of Joachim in custody.
She had run away from law enforcement as a child each
time her mother woke her in the middle of the night, saying they must leave town before the police came knocking at their door.

She had vowed to never live like that again. She didn't
trust law enforcement, but she wouldn't do anything to
be under suspicion again, and tying herself to Joachim
would do just that. He had helped her escape Victor and
had provided a safe place for her to stay until she gained
her strength and was ready to move on with her life, but
he wasn't the man with whom she wanted to spend the
rest of her life, especially if he had problems with the law.

Tears burned her eyes. Tears for Joachim and his
plight, but also for herself. She had made another mistake. She needed Miriam. What would her sister advise?
After considering the matter, Sarah decided that Miriam
would say to leave the area and to forget about Joachim,
that he wasn't the man for her.

Sarah had to find a way to take Rosie and the baby

home, alert the authorities and then find her aunt. If her aunt couldn't be found, Sarah would have to find a way to earn enough money for a bus ticket. She had to go somewhere. Home to Knoxville or south to Atlanta or maybe to Birmingham or Montgomery. She had to leave the area to get free of Victor and find a place where she could start over.

In that new spot, she would try to forget Joachim, although she doubted he would ever be erased from her memory or her heart.

Joachim peered through the bars of the jail cell. His life had gotten more complicated. Officer Nelson had hauled him into police headquarters, fingerprinted him and then ushered him quickly into a holding cell.

No telling how long Joachim would remain behind bars. His mind returned to Sarah with her crystal-blue eyes, silky skin and lips that begged to be touched. If only he could go home.

"What're you in for?" a guy asked from an adjoining cell.

"The officer mentioned manslaughter. Actually, it was a buggy accident that killed my brother five years ago."

The guy nodded. "Ask to talk to Sergeant Evans. He's the only sane cop in the bunch."

Joachim appreciated the tip. He would try to talk to Sergeant Evans, but as the minutes ticked by too slowly, all Joachim could think about was Sarah and whether she would still be at his house when and if he was released from jail.

Rebecca hurried into the kitchen and pulled biscuits from the oven. "Where is Rosie? I heard her talking to you?"

"She's upstairs with the baby."

"I'm worried about her."

"I am, too. That's why we need to hitch Belle to the buggy and drive Rosie and Joseph home."

"What are you saying?"

"This is our chance to get help for Ms. Hazel. We will take Rosie and her baby home and then find Levi in Willkommen. He said he would be working with his uncle at the Amish Market. Levi will know how to locate the police, a law-abiding officer we can trust. The good cops will save Ms. Hazel and arrest Victor and insist that Joachim be released."

"I'm not sure that is the best idea," Rebecca reasoned. "Rosie is weak and her face is flushed. I fear she has a fever. If so, she must stay here and rest."

"Then I'll go to Willkommen alone."

"You are a smart woman, Sarah, but you do not know about horses or how to guide the buggy." Rebecca wiped her hands on a towel. "Let me give Rosie something to eat, then I will get the buggy ready. We will go together."

Relief swept over Sarah. "We'll locate Levi. He'll help us."

"*Yah*, he goes often with his uncle to the market there. He will know about the police and who we can trust. I am frightfully worried about Joachim with the Petersville police, especially if Victor was the informant who called them. Think of how many lies he will tell them about Joachim."

Sarah took a tray with biscuits and ham upstairs to Rosie and quickly explained that she and Rebecca were leaving to get help and that Rosie needed to remain inside with the doors locked.

"Are you sure my baby will be safe here? I am not worried about myself, but I am worried for my child."

"You'll both be safe."

But would they be? *Please, God, let nothing happen to this young woman and her precious infant.*

Sarah hurried to the kitchen. She grabbed the cape off the peg and put the bonnet on her head and tied it under her chin. Looking around the kitchen one more time, Sarah saw the chair where Joachim had sat and the towel where he wiped his hands. Mentally revisiting the past few days, she saw his warm smile and the acceptance and understanding in his brown eyes. She had to say goodbye to his memory and to this home where she had found something she had never experienced in her life. She had found love and acceptance and the true meaning of Christian charity and a heartfelt concern for others. She would carry that memory with her forever.

Rebecca led Belle, now hitched to the buggy, out of the barn. With no time to spare, Sarah opened the door and hurried outside. Dark clouds covered the sky and blocked the warming rays of the sun, as if all of nature was mourning Joachim's arrest and the hateful crimes that had happened in the house next door.

Sarah needed to get help for Ms. Hazel and Rosie and the baby, and yes, Joachim, too. Then, unless she could find her aunt, she would leave the area never to return again.

She climbed into the back of the buggy, missing Joachim's strong arms to lift her onto the seat. She could no longer rely on him. She had to rely on her own wherewithal.

Rebecca had called her strong, although she felt weak and unsure of the future. What would it bring? All she saw was loneliness and sorrow in the days ahead as she began to realize she wanted to remain in this Amish community.

Did Joachim have something to do with that?

She nodded imperceptibly. He had everything to do with the way she felt and the sorrow that pulled at her heart.

Chapter Twenty-One

Rebecca was right. Sarah wouldn't have been able to navigate the roads. Belle was a well-trained mare, but she still needed a competent person handling the reins.

"Once we get on the main road to Willkommen, we will not have to worry," Rebecca said with assurance. "Belle will continue straight along that road, but first we must make a turn at the next intersection and watch for approaching vehicles. The *Englisch* demand the right-of-way, so we must be careful."

"I'll be on the lookout for cars while you handle Belle."

Rebecca reached back and grabbed her hand. "We must pray for our trip."

"Pray for Joachim, as well. I am worried about his safety."

"*Gott* will provide," Rebecca said with confidence. "And do not worry about Victor. He will not see you in the back seat nor will he recognize you even if he passes us on the road."

Sarah hoped Rebecca's statement held true.

Both of them bowed their heads and offered a quick prayer. Rebecca squeezed Sarah's hand and then flicked the reins. Belle trotted to the gate and slowed of her own volition while both Rebecca and Sarah checked for oncoming cars. Once they confirmed both directions were clear, Rebecca encouraged the mare onto the roadway. With another flick of Rebecca's wrist, Belle increased her gait to a rapid trot.

Sarah glanced back at the Burkholder farm. Rosie was inside with the doors locked. Hopefully, she and the baby would be safe.

Lord, if You're listening, protect Rosie and that precious baby. Keep Victor far from them and let no other vile men come near the farm.

"We must pass the driveway to the Thomin property," Rebecca said, as if reading Sarah's mind. "Just after that, we will turn right at the intersection. The road heads over the mountain toward Willkommen. Once we enter the town, we must follow the signs for the market. We will find Levi there. You can tell him what happened, and he will take you to the sheriff."

Sarah couldn't control her nervousness when the fence around the Thomin property appeared on their left. As if realizing her upset, Rebecca hurried Belle along. The mare's brisk trot made the buggy creak and groan as it swayed. Sarah's stomach roiled in sync with the back and forth motion. The Thomin driveway came into view.

Her heart stopped and a gasp escaped her lips.

She couldn't look away from the sight of Victor's red pickup idling at the end of the drive. He sat at the wheel, his gaze on the buggy as it approached.

Sarah lowered her head. The black bonnet had a wide bill, but would it hide her from Victor's view?

Please, do not let him see me.

Rebecca acted unfazed and unaffected by the red pickup. If only Victor wouldn't recognize either of them.

Sarah focused her attention on the clip-clop of Belle's

hooves and attempted to drive out the fear of seeing Victor, knowing he could swerve onto the roadway, at any second, and brake to a stop in front of the buggy.

Thankfully, the pickup remained stationary. When the buggy was more than fifty yards along, Victor pulled his truck onto the road. Sarah recognized the hum of the souped-up engine. The intersection lay ahead.

"Get going, Belle." Rebecca flicked the reins. The mare increased her pace.

Sarah peered at the oncoming intersection, relieved that no cars approached from either direction. Instinctively, Belle slowed then stepped into the turn, following the slight pressure Rebecca had put on the reins.

The wind tugged at Sarah's bonnet. She raised her right hand to hold it in place. The sound of the truck's engine roared behind them.

Tires squealed and a blur of red passed on the left, then braked to a stop. Her heart hammered in her chest. Rebecca pulled up on the reins. The buggy eased to a stop.

The door of the pickup flew open. Victor jumped to the pavement.

Sarah's heart lodged in her throat. She looked to her left and right, hoping for some way to escape, but she couldn't escape Victor. He had found her once again.

Twilight descended over the farmland and painted the hillside in shadows as the police car drove along the country road. Joachim sat in the rear, fearing what had happened to Sarah and Rosie and the baby and his sister in his absence. How foolish of him to have considered, at one time, going to the police for help. They had turned a deaf ear to his recounting of all that had happened.

Thankfully, Sergeant Evans had come on duty at the end of the day shift. He had listened to Joachim and was sympathetic to what he had to say.

"I read your statement about your brother's death," Evans said, "and don't see any reason to hold you. The guy who brought you in tries to be a tough dude at times. He hauled you in for questioning, but there isn't any evidence to charge you. If we need to talk to you again, we know where to find you. I'll drive you home. Tomorrow I'll explain what happened to the captain who's been out of town. I have a strong feeling the officer who called you in will be disciplined."

Joachim was grateful for the officer's honesty. At least there was one trustworthy cop in Petersville.

When the police car turned onto the Burkholder property, Joachim should have felt relief and a sense of anticipation to be reunited with Sarah again. He would explain everything to her about his bother and what had happened that night as well as his father's anger, which had forced Joachim to leave.

Would she understand? He would not know until he told her how he really felt.

Hopefully, he would not be too late.

But when the police car pulled to a stop in front of the house, Joachim's stomach soured, seeing his father's face staring down at him from the upstairs window.

He had not expected such a homecoming.

Joachim stepped from the car. The officer turned the patrol cruiser around in the drive and headed back to Petersville.

Mamm opened the kitchen door. Tears streamed down her cheeks at the sight of him. Joachim longed to open his arms and run to embrace her. Then his *datt* eased around her and stepped onto the porch.

His father's eyes were hooded, but the scowl on his face cut into Joachim's heart.

There was no welcome to find in his father's expression.

"Is this the way you come home," his father asked, "in the back of a police car, like a criminal?"

His mother's faint gasp broke Joachim's heart.

"Once again, you are reacting without learning what really happened." The words of reconciliation Joachim had planned to utter refused to issue forth. Instead, he felt the need to vindicate himself.

Joachim fisted his hands, then opened them, consciously trying to overcome the frustration that welled up within him. "You were reacting to your grief when you closed me out of the family and forced me to leave home, but you were wrong, *Datt.* I had done nothing wrong. Rebecca will tell you. Have you talked to her?"

"Rebecca is not here," his father said.

"The only ones here are a young Amish woman who appears scared to death and her infant," his mother added.

Joachim tensed. "What about Sarah?"

Confusion washed over his father's face.

"Who are you talking about, Joachim?" his mother asked. "What happened while we were gone?"

Which was the question Joachim wanted answered, as well.

A sickness filled his gut and he turned in the direction of the Thomin home, fearing Victor had struck again.

Without waiting to explain to his parents, Joachim started running along the drive to the path that cut through the woods. His heart pounded in his ears. The rhythm of his feet hitting the ground kept time with the internal voice that kept screaming Sarah's name.

Victor had captured her. Joachim was to blame because he had left her alone. His gut clenched and pain cut through his heart.

Joachim had saved her once, but would he be able to save her again?

Chapter Twenty-Two

"Where are you taking me?" Sarah demanded.

Victor yanked her out of the attic closet where he had kept her locked up throughout the past day. She struggled to free herself from his hold, but he slapped her face and shoved her down the stairs.

All around her candles flickered, their light casting eerie shadows over the yellowed wallpaper. The smell of smoke rose from below and burned Sarah's eyes.

Memories of her childhood circled through her mind.

She tried to pull out of Victor's grasp. "What did you do with Rebecca?"

Maniacal laughter was his only response.

"You're insane, Victor."

"That's what my friend George said. He thought he could overpower me, but I proved him wrong."

"George? Was he the man who had Miriam? You killed him, didn't you?"

"Like I killed Naomi. She planned to leave me. I told her to stay, that we would have a good life together. It's fortunate I didn't kill you, Sarah."

She fought against his hold. "I'm not going with you."

"Don't disobey me," Victor screamed, his hand tight on her arm.

"You can't control me," she insisted, struggling to maintain her courage. "I'm not the same person you held captive in your attic. I'm stronger now and I see things more clearly."

"You said you started a fire when you were young. You told me all about it when you were drugged. Your mother left you alone in the house with her boyfriend, and you hid in the closet with the candle. You tried to light it and the fire started. You would have died except Miriam saved you, but she can't save you this time, Sarah. You'll either die in the fire or go with me."

She squared her shoulders and raised her jaw. "I won't go anywhere with you."

He grabbed her by the throat and dragged her down the next flight of stairs. She tripped over her feet and fell. She tried to crawl away from him. He kicked her, then pulled her upright.

The air was thick with smoke. "What about your mother, Victor? She won't survive the fire."

He laughed. "Does that worry you? She doesn't die as easy as you might think. I've tried everything with her, but she's too strong. I stopped her heart medicine, then I gave her sleeping pills. I even tried rat poison, but I must have not given her enough."

"You can't leave her in a burning house."

"Maybe I'll come back for her later. After I take you someplace safe. A guy in Savannah wanted you, Sarah, but I bought you first. You're mine, and you'll do what I say."

"I don't belong to you." She kicked and pummeled him with her free hand. He caught her wrist and bent her arm up behind her. The pain made her breath catch. She gasped for air.

Her knees went weak and she fell. He kicked her down the steps and ran after her. She landed at the bottom of the stairs. Her gaze turned to the kitchen, where the man with the scar lay bleeding on the floor, his chest rising and lowering ever so slightly. That must be George. From the amount of blood he had lost, she was certain George couldn't live long.

"Where's the other man?" she asked, thinking of the slender guy with shoulder-length hair, the guy she had mistaken for her sister.

"Karl? He's in the basement, dead."

"Why, Victor?"

"Because I had to strike back at someone or something. The electric company said I didn't pay my bills, so they turned off the power." Victor fumed. "Don't they know I'm a Thomin? My family is the wealthiest in this county."

She had to get away from him—but he was stronger and could easily overpower her. Sarah's only chance was to distract him and catch him off guard.

She glanced up the stairs. "Look, Victor. They're coming out of the attic because of the fire. Do you see them?"

He glanced up. "What are you talking about?"

"The rats that live in the attic. They're coming down the stairs."

"No!" He slapped her across the face.

"They're coming after you."

"That's why my mother has to stay here. She never tried to save me."

"Save you from what?"

"From my father. He wanted a son who loved what he loved, woodworking and finance and this house. When I didn't fall in line, he'd lock me in the woodshed. You know what I'd hear?"

"You'd hear the rats."

He nodded, his crazed eyes wide. "At night, they'd crawl over me to get to the food he placed on the floor to attract them. I'd scream, but my mother ignored me. Now, everyone will ignore her."

Victor grabbed Sarah's arm and dragged her to the pickup parked near the front of the house.

She fought against his hold.

He struck her again.

Her knees gave way once more. He shoved her into the truck and climbed in the driver's side. He pulled a weapon from his waist and jammed it into her ribs.

"Do as I say or you'll die."

He gunned the engine and screeched away from the house. She saw movement near the barn.

Her heart lurched.

Sarah jammed her face against the glass and screamed, but he was oblivious to what had happened.

If only Joachim had seen her.

Chapter Twenty-Three

Joachim saw the red pickup pull out of the driveway, going faster than seemed possible. While he didn't like the idea of the man driving recklessly on the road where others could get hurt, Joachim was still glad he was gone. With Victor out of the way, he could search the house and find Sarah.

"Joachim?" A voice sounded behind him.

He turned to see Levi. "Your father said Rebecca is gone and that you took the path leading to the Thomin home."

Levi pointed to the once-stately home. Joachim turned to see flames licking the roof. They started running.

The front door hung open. They dashed inside and climbed the stairs to the second floor.

"Ms. Hazel." Joachim pointed to her bedroom door. Both men ran to the master suite.

The frail lady lay in bed.

Joachim pulled her free of the coverings and placed her in Levi's arms. "Get her outside. She needs fresh air. I'm going to the attic where Victor kept Sarah."

He climbed the flight of stairs, taking them two at a time.

At the top of the landing, he saw the door and tried the knob. Locked. He pounded on the door. "Sarah?"

Why wouldn't she answer?

Joachim hurled his weight against the door, once, twice, three time before it splintered. He kicked it open and ran to where Sarah crouched, huddled in the corner.

When she looked up, he didn't see Sarah.

Instead, he saw Rebecca.

"Where are you taking me?" Sarah demanded.

Victor was driving like a crazed man. Surely they would wreck before they arrived at their destination.

"We'll go to Savannah and get onboard a ship and head to one of the islands. You belong to me, and you'll do as I say."

"I always obeyed you, Victor," she said, hoping to calm his outrage.

"Until you ran off. Joachim helped you, didn't he?"

Wanting to distract him from thinking about Joachim, she asked, "Why did you keep Rosie and not give her medical care when the baby was born?"

"She never told me she was pregnant. The people I bought her from didn't tell me either. I brought her home to care for my mother. Then after a few months, I realized the truth."

"Are you sure it wasn't your baby, Victor?"

"No!" He shook his head. "I never touched her, but I let her stay until she got too big. I was sickened that she would bring a child into the world."

"She gave the child life," Sarah tried to reason.

"The child didn't deserve to live. Neither of them did. Besides, I provided food and shelter."

"You call the root cellar shelter? You buried her alive."

"At least she didn't have the rats."

"How do you know? Did your father put you in the root cellar, too?"

Victor nodded. "My mother never questioned my father. Didn't she wonder why I wasn't sleeping in my bed? She had to have known."

"I won't let anyone hurt you again, Victor." Sarah made her voice sickeningly sweet. If she could make him believe she was on his side, maybe he'd let down his guard—giving her an opportunity to get away. "You can trust me."

He shook his head. "I can't trust anyone. The police captured some of the men I've worked with in the past. They're coming after me."

"What about Miriam?" Her heart swelled with hope.

"She's gone. I don't know where they took her. No one knows."

Sarah grabbed his arm. "Someone has to know how to find her."

Victor shoved her away.

Being sympathetic hadn't worked. Sarah needed to try another tactic. She had to get away from him somehow.

"Stop the car," she demanded. "I need to get out. You'll be okay on your own, but let me live."

"I can't, Sarah. You have to come with me."

"The police will find you. You'll go to jail. Let me go now, and you'll be able to get away."

"We need to stay together. I'll dress Amish. We'll

live in the country in a small house. They won't find me if I'm with you."

Victor, with his hateful heart, would never fit in with the Amish. "You would stand a better chance on your own. You can save yourself," she encouraged.

"It's too late."

Sarah reached for the door handle. He struck her. Her vision blurred. She grabbed the handle again.

He wove his fingers through her hair and slammed her head against the dashboard.

Pain zigzagged down her spine. Her body went limp and darkness surrounded her.

Chapter Twenty-Four

Joachim hurried Rebecca through the smoke and down the stairs. "Victor took Sarah," his sister explained. "I saw them drive away in his pickup. He acted like he was crazy, screaming about his father and rats."

"Where did he take her?" Joachim demanded.

"When he was locking me in the attic, he talked about driving to the interstate."

"To get there, Victor will travel along the main road. I will head him off by taking the shortcut. If I can get to the intersection first, I might be able to stop them."

Rebecca grabbed his arm. "No, Joachim. Eli died there. I cannot lose you, as well."

"Then pray I will arrive there before them, Rebecca. Pray Victor will stop his car and will have done no harm to Sarah."

Levi met them at the front door and helped Rebecca flee the house and the fire.

"Oh, Levi," she cried. "I never thought I would see you again."

"I notified the sheriff in Willkommen about what

has happened here, but I do not know if he will arrive in time."

Joachim ran for his buggy, the buggy Sarah and Rebecca had taken earlier.

"Hurry, Belle. We have to save Sarah."

The mare seemed to understand the emergency or maybe it was the flames licking the dried wood of the Thomin home that caused Belle to charge out of the drive and onto the roadway. Joachim led her to the bypass, the shortcut locals used that intersected with the main road.

Eli had planned to come home that night so long ago, but he had gotten too carried away with his need to prove himself. If only Joachim had stopped him.

The smell of smoke followed Joachim for some distance; the acrid stench hung on his clothes and filled his nostrils. Ms. Hazel and Rebecca were safe. Now he needed to get to Sarah in time.

He flicked the reins to spur Belle on and glanced into the night sky where stars hung like lanterns, their light helping to guide him.

"*Gott*, I made mistakes and cut you out of my life for too long while I traveled far from home. Forgive me. Forgive my iniquity and my prideful heart. I give You my life to do with as You will, *Gott*, but let no harm come to Sarah."

The wind whipped at his shirt. He tugged his hat down more tightly on his head and strained to see the road ahead.

The ride never seemed so long.

The intersection loomed in the distance. Joachim's gut tightened, the memory of that night five years ago played over in his mind's eye. Eli's buggy barreling headlong into the intersection. His brother's gleeful laughter as he looked back and taunted Joachim for straggling behind. He had not heard Joachim's cry of warning, nor had Eli seen the headlights approaching the intersection.

Eli had lived life on the edge, always wanting more than the *plain* life offered. He pushed at every chance to break the *Ordnung* and experience life as he chose to live it. Why had their father not seen the truth about his younger son? Joachim had tried to save him that night, but Eli was too reckless and headstrong to listen.

Instead, his buggy had run headlong into the path of the oncoming vehicle.

Seeing it play out again in his thoughts, Joachim cringed, his stomach churned and he wanted to wrench the horrific memory from his mind.

Headlights appeared in the distance. This time, Eli was not in harm's way. Sarah was.

Joachim needed to stop Victor at any cost. He was willing to give up his own life so that Sarah would live.

He guided Belle into the intersection, then pulled her to a stop. He jumped from the buggy, hoping it would provide a barricade, and unhitched the mare, then slapped her on her rump.

"Yah, yah," he screamed, waving his hat and sending the confused horse running into a nearby clearing so she would be out of harm's way.

Joachim turned, seeing the pickup approach. He waved his arms to signal Victor to stop, knowing the crazed man would never do so.

If only Sarah would be safe.

Chapter Twenty-Five

Sarah groaned and blinked her eyes open. In the glare of the headlights, she saw Joachim. The strong man she had grown to love in such a short time. He flailed his arms, warning Victor of danger. Only Victor was the danger. He continued to push down on the accelerator and steered his truck straight for Joachim.

"No!" she gasped, anticipating the crash and knowing she had to act.

"Rats," she screamed. "At your feet."

Terror flashed from Victor's eyes. He glanced down as if believing a rat was in the car. In that instant with his guard down, she grabbed the steering wheel. The truck veered off the road, jumped a ditch and crashed into a stand of trees. Airbags exploded. Sarah was knocked back, unable to see. All she knew was that Joachim had been saved.

A warm trickle of moisture seeped down her forehead. She touched the wound and pulled her hand back, seeing the dark stain that covered her fingers. Even in her stupor she knew it was blood, her own blood streaming from a gash to her head that she only now began to feel. Gritting her teeth, she ignored the pain. She couldn't waste this opportunity to escape.

She tried to reach for the door handle. The airbag, twisted around her, prevented her escape.

The memory of being in the closet so long ago returned. She smelled smoke from the fire that had started in the main room of the tiny duplex. But thinking back on it now, Sarah realized she hadn't started the fire by her own negligence. He had. The man her mother was seeing. The man who was supposed to watch Sarah when her mother worked. The man who had gotten angry and forced Sarah into the closet. His anger had sent him into a rage so that he knocked over the candles he had lit and later blamed the fire on her, a child only six years old.

All this time, she had thought Miriam had saved her. Now Sarah saw it play out. Sarah had saved herself. Miriam and Hannah were in the adjoining duplex visiting with a friend. Sarah had alerted them to the fire. All the girls, as well as the neighbors, had been saved that night from Sarah's fast action.

Along with the clarity came a sense of relief. She no longer needed to depend on others because she didn't trust herself. She had made good decisions even as a child.

Smoke filled her lungs, along with the pungent smell of gasoline. She untangled her hands from the airbag and grabbed the door handle, but it wouldn't budge. She looked at the rear of the truck, seeing the flames, knowing she was trapped. This time she wouldn't be able to save herself.

"Sarah?"

Joachim was running toward the pickup. Flames curled from under the hood of the truck. He couldn't save her, and if he tried he would be burned and maybe even killed.

"No!" she screamed. Unwilling to have him sacrifice his life for hers.

* * *

Joachim knew he had only a few seconds before the fire would accelerate, sending a fireball of flames into the air.

Please, Gott!

Sarah stared at him through the passenger window, her eyes drooping as she became overcome by smoke.

Victor's head lay against the steering wheel, blood seeping from his mouth.

Joachim grabbed the door handle and pulled, but the door refused to budge.

His heart jammed in his throat, a roar filled his ears along with the sound of the fames licking at the truck bed. He needed to act. Now.

He grabbed the handle and tugged with all his might. The door sprang open, sending him flying backward. Regaining his balance, he raced forward and pulled Sarah from the truck. Lifting her into his arms, he ran as fast as he could away from the fire to a clearing, where he placed her on the ground, relieved to see her breathing in spite of her closed eyes and the blood that matted her hair.

He ran back to the truck, this time going to the driver's side. The door opened on the second try. He dragged Victor out of the truck and away from the fire, just as it accelerated, sending flames into the air. Burning embers fell on Joachim, searing his arms.

Leaving Victor well away from the truck, Joachim ran again to Sarah. Sirens sounded. An ambulance and a sheriff's car from Willkommen were heading toward them. Levi had alerted them. Thankfully, they had jurisdiction in this area near the interstate and had responded to his plea for help.

But would they arrive in time to save Sarah?

He touched her neck, searching for her carotid artery and fearing she was already dead.

Chapter Twenty-Six

Joachim sat in the waiting room at the hospital, his head in his hands, unable to think about anything except Sarah and the surgeon who was working on her.

The doctor had been guarded in his assessment of her condition, using words like *dislocated shoulder, possible head trauma* and *broken femur*. Even more frightening was the threat of internal bleeding.

"We won't know the extent of her injuries until we open her up. What she needs now is prayer."

Except Joachim's mind was numb, and he could not put the words together into some type of a coherent order. The only word that he could utter was her name.

"Sarah" he kept saying over and over again.

Rebecca entered the waiting room along with Levi.

She touched Joachim's arm, offering support, then gasped, seeing the gauze bandages wrapped around portions of his arms. "You have been hurt in the fire?"

He shoved her hand aside. His own injuries were minor compared to what Sarah had experienced, and nothing, not even his sister's concern, could reach

Joachim at this moment. All he could think about was Sarah.

"Have you heard anything from the doctor?" Levi asked, sitting in a chair next to Rebecca.

Joachim shook his head, unsure whether he could muster the energy to actually speak.

"I have been praying," Rebecca assured him. Usually, her prayer support would have touched Joachim, but at this moment, her words had no more effect than if she was talking about the weather instead of having asked *Gott* to save his Sarah.

His Sarah. He should have told her how he felt. Why had he kept pushing her aside, never explaining the way she made him feel, like a man who could face any hardship as long as they were together?

"Victor came through his surgery," Levi offered, as if thinking Joachim would get some closure with the information. "I heard two of the sheriff's deputies talking. They will guard him during his recuperation until he can stand trial for his wrongdoings. Not only is he a killer, but they mentioned a trafficking operation that stretched to Savannah and involved shipping women out of the country."

"How could this have taken place here in the North Georgia mountains?" Rebecca asked, sorrow evident in her voice.

Joachim heard footsteps and the swish of a woman's skirt as people entered the waiting room. He ignored the newcomers, intent on his own pain and concern for Sarah.

A hand touched his shoulder. He looked up into his father's face, lined with worry.

He blinked. Surely he was dreaming. Why would

his *datt* be here at the hospital—and looking at him that way?

"I was wrong," his father said, his voice deep and sorrowful. He glanced at Levi and then Rebecca. "I have learned the truth about what happened that night."

Joachim did not understand. He rose from the chair, needing to stand eye to eye with his *datt*. Over the last five years, the father who had once seemed strong and self-assured had aged, his shoulders somewhat slumped as if from the heavy weight he carried. In his hand, he held his hat and with the other, he again patted Joachim's arm.

"Some things are too painful to discuss, son, yet I can no longer contain the sorrow I feel about what happened."

Joachim felt that same overpowering sorrow. "I ask your forgiveness for anything I did that night to encourage Eli. He wanted me to race him home, but this was not my desire. I was not racing. Instead, I was following to ensure he got home. But I should have done more—should have tried harder to stop him. He would not listen to my warnings, and I still do not understand why."

His father's eyes were filled with remorse as he spoke. "Only tonight, Levi told me that Eli had boasted about what he had purchased from some of the *Englisch* boys in Petersville. I do not know if he had taken the drugs, and I am grateful the police did not test his blood, but his actions were not what I would have wanted for him."

Joachim's heart went out to his father. Never before had he heard his *datt* say anything negative about his younger son. Eli had always been the favorite one who could do no wrong.

"You know he was driving Levi's buggy?" his father added.

"Yah," Joachim nodded.

Levi stepped closer. "Eli did not ask to use my buggy. He took it without asking because I had left the singing and was talking with someone behind the building."

"He was talking to me," Rebecca admitted. She lowered her gaze. "I should have told you all of this five years ago, but I was too ashamed. You see, I was at fault for drawing Levi away that night so we could talk about the future. When Eli could not find Levi, he took the buggy without permission. I felt so burdened with guilt that I refused to see Levi for the past few years and I refused to reveal what really happened. It was only with *Mamm* and *Datt* leaving that I needed someone to help me with the farm. Levi volunteered."

"I am the one to blame," his father said. "Eli had not done his chores that day. I had found him in the hayloft with an *Englisch* girl. I told him he would stay at home that night instead of going to the youth singing. But when he asked again that night, I was weak and allowed him to go. I should have kept him home. I was afraid he would leave us for good if I was too hard on him."

"Yet, we lost him forever all the same," Joachim's mother said, stepping around her husband. She opened her arms and wrapped Joachim in her embrace. "I feared I had lost you as well, my son."

He smelled the sweetness of her and knew the fullness of her heart, which had always made room for him. Eli had been his father's favored son, but his mother had loved all her children equally, without censure. Joachim knew that she had never stopped loving him.

"My heart has cried for both of my sons. *Gott* has blessed me by bringing you home again."

"I'm sorry, *Mamm*, for everything."

"*Yah*, we are all sorry about Eli. He lived fast and died fast. As much as it hurt to have him taken from us at such a young age, it was *Gott*'s will."

"Levi has told us of all that has happened while we were away. How is the woman?" his father asked.

Rebecca's eyes were heavy with concern. "The nurse at the front desk said they will know something in the morning. She has been through so much."

His father looked at Joachim. For the first time in perhaps his whole life, he saw pride for his elder son in his father's eyes.

"You saved the woman and both Hazel and Victor Thomin, as well. This is what we were told."

"Victor has come through surgery. I am not sure about Sarah or whether she will survive."

He thought of the truck heading straight for the buggy, then it had turned sharply, leaped over the ditch and plowed into the trees.

"Her shoulder is dislocated and her leg is broken. There are internal injuries, as well."

The nurse came into the room. The sorrowful cast of her eyes made Joachim's heart nearly break.

"You have news?" he asked, hesitant to hear what the nurse would say.

"Ms. Miller is out of surgery and has been moved to intensive care. They're getting her settled. A nurse will notify you if she's able to have visitors."

Moving to ICU could mean her condition had taken a turn for the worse. Joachim swallow hard, trying to remain optimistic.

His mother reached for him. "This woman is *Englisch*?"

He nodded.

"You have known her long?"

He thought back to the first time he had seen her peering down at him from the window of the Thomin house. Had it been only a few days ago?

"I have not known her long, yet I have been waiting for her my whole life."

His mother drew him close and patted his shoulder. "I will pray for *Gott*'s will."

He wanted to contradict her and insist she pray for what he, Joachim, wanted. He wanted Sarah to live. Most of all, he wanted her to stay with him, but if she could not embrace the Amish faith, then she would leave the area and move on with her life. As difficult as that would be for Joachim, at least he would know she was alive and doing what she wanted.

"When you were a little boy, you had little problems," his mother said, her eyes filled with warmth. "Now that you are a man, you have big problems that weigh upon the heart and soul. I have prayed for you every day of your life and especially over these last five years when you were away from me. I will continue to pray for you and for Sarah. Remember you must use your head as well as your heart, Joachim."

"*Yah*, that is true. But right now all I can think about is Sarah with both my head and my heart."

Chapter Twenty-Seven

Smoke burned Sarah's lungs. She struggled to breathe and tried to fight her way out of the truck. The door wouldn't open. She wanted to scream.

Then she saw Joachim. He was staring at her through the window. His mouth was open. Was he calling her name?

"Joachim," she wanted to shout, but she couldn't move her lips. Nor could she open her eyes or lift her hand. She was trapped in her body, in the truck, sur-rounded by fire.

"Sarah? Open your eyes." Joachim's voice. He must have opened the truck's door, or was she hallucinating because Victor had given her more drugs? She thought she saw the man from her childhood, her mother's old boyfriend, pointing at her and saying that all of this was her fault.

She thrashed her arm, needing to get away from Vic-tor and the fire and the man who said she had started the fire, when he was the one who had turned over the candles.

"Sarah, it is Joachim. You are in the hospital. You need to lie still. Stay calm and rest."

She wanted to see Joachim, but nothing worked right and her eyes remained closed.

Her head ached. Her left arm felt weighted down.

A hand touched hers. She wiggled her fingers.

"That's right. You can hear me, I know you can, Sarah. I'm here with you at the hospital. I won't leave you."

"My...my sister?"

"What? I saw your lips move, but I couldn't hear what you said. Say it again, Sarah."

But she couldn't. She was too tired, and her mind was starting to drift. Hopefully, she wouldn't go back to the fire. She didn't want to be there.

Please, Lord, I want to stay with Joachim. He always keeps me safe.

She felt his fingers grip hers, then she slipped into darkness and couldn't feel anything.

The waiting room was empty when the nurse ushered Joachim out of Sarah's ICU room. "When can I see her again?" he asked.

"I'll come and get you in an hour. Right now, she needs to rest."

"Can she not rest while I am with her? I will not talk to her. Just being with her is all I ask."

The nurse's eyes filled with compassion. "I understand how you feel, Mr. Burkholder, but nonfamily visits are limited to only fifteen minutes each hour."

"But she has no family. She only has me."

The nurse nodded. "I'm sorry, but I still have to follow the rules."

Rules Joachim did not like and did not understand, even if the nurse felt they were necessary. He walked across the waiting room to the far windows. Staring into the parking lot, he wondered what would happen in the next twelve to twenty-four hours that the nurse said were so important. Sarah had been through so much, yet she was a fighter. If only she would continue to fight for her life.

"Mr. Burkholder?"

Joachim turned as a big man, probably midthirties, entered the room. He was dressed in the uniform of the Willkommen sheriff's department.

"I'm Acting Sheriff Dan Quigley. The nurse said I would find you here. Levi Plank spoke to one of the deputies when he was at the Amish Market in Willkommen. The deputy notified me. I'm sorry we didn't get to the Thomin house before the fire. Everything burned to the ground."

"But no one was harmed?"

"Correct. That's thanks to you and Levi Plank. Mrs. Thomin is being medically evaluated. She's weak and malnourished, but the doctors are cautiously optimistic."

"Victor was giving her sleeping pills."

"He was doing worse than that. The test results haven't come back yet, but the doctors believe that arsenic may have been involved."

The rat poisoning about which Sarah had been concerned.

"Nothing surprises me about Victor," Joachim admitted. "Is he still being held?"

"He's under guard here in the hospital. We won't let him get away. He killed two people today. We think there may be more victims. He'll stand trial in a month or two."

"And Ms. Hazel? Will she testify against him?"

"I can't tell you. It would probably depend upon the judge and how he feels about parent-child privilege. Right now, she's still too weak to communicate very effectively. With Victor out of commission, she would be wise to rent a room in the senior care complex located just outside Willkommen. That is if—"

The sheriff paused a long moment. "Tell me what happened once you arrived at the house."

Joachim recounted trying to find Sarah and instead finding his sister.

"Did you smell gasoline or any type of accelerant?" Quigley asked.

"I smelled only smoke, but the house is so old and made of wood. An accelerant would not be needed."

The acting sheriff made note of what Joachim shared in a small tablet he pulled from his pocket. He pressed for more information and pursed his lips at times as if envisioning what had happened in his mind's eye.

"Rebecca Burkholder is your sister?" he asked.

Joachim nodded. *"Yah."*

"She talked about seeing rats."

"That does not surprise me. Sarah said she heard them in the attic and the basement. I would expect that they ran from the house to escape the fire."

"You had worked on the house. Did you see anything that could have caused the fire?"

"Before my sister left the hospital this evening, she told me Victor had become crazed. Candles were burning. He knocked them over in his rage."

"Then he caused the fire."

"You would have to ask my sister."

"The electric company said Ms. Thomin had failed to pay her bills, and the power had been turned off."

"Perhaps that is why he lit the candles. Ms. Hazel was bedridden, but I thought Victor would take over payment of the bills."

"If there was money."

Joachim looked up. "The Thomins seemed to want for nothing."

"Yet Victor's father died some years ago. A house that size could be expensive to heat and cool. Money can run out."

Joachim knew that too well. He had had to watch his finances over the last five years. "Victor planned to sell the home once his mother passed. He must have tried to hurry her along."

Joachim explained about the scratching sound Sarah had heard and the root cellar. "You know about Rosie Glick and her baby?"

"I plan to talk to her next."

"Talk also to Levi Plank about his sister, Naomi. She worked for Ms. Hazel until Victor came back to the area. She told her family she did not want to work there when Victor was home. Soon after that, she disappeared. The Petersville police thought she had left the Amish way and had run off, perhaps with an *Englisch* man, but the family feared foul play."

"You think Victor had something to do with her disappearance?"

Joachim shrugged. "It is a possibility. A very sad one, but this could be."

"I'll check it out."

"Will you also check out the Petersville police? Some of their actions have been questionable."

Joachim recounted his experience with the officer who had hauled him in for questioning. "The officer's name was Nelson. He mentioned Victor's name a few times as if they were friends. I do not believe this man is above reproach."

"The Petersville chief of police has had problems in the past. I'll talk to him and see what he says about Nelson."

"The Amish do not always trust the police."

"Is that any police or just those in Petersville?" Quigley asked.

"In Petersville. Once trust is broken, it is hard to heal."

Joachim thought of his own father and the trust that had broken between them. Eli had been loved, and in loving indulgence he had been trusted perhaps more than he merited, even after he had broken that trust. Regrettably, his father had given Eli another chance. If only Joachim could have prevented his brother from taking Levi's buggy when he and Rebecca were spending time together. Everyone had a little part to play in his brother's death, but Eli was to blame for his actions that night. He should not have died, but things happened and there was no going back to make them right once tragedy struck.

Joachim would carry the memory of that fateful night his whole life. At least now, he would be free of the guilt.

Once Acting Sheriff Quigley had asked all his questions, he shook hands with Joachim. "I'll be in touch."

"I have a question," Joachim said before the sheriff left. "What about Sarah's sisters?"

Tired eyes, a drawn face that hung low, a downturned mouth. Sarah blinked at the image.

A dream or...

He moved closer.

"Jo… Joachim?"

"Oh, Sarah, seeing your eyes open has made my heart leap in my chest with relief and joy. I have been so worried about you. Everyone has been worried."

She smiled weakly. "You…saved…me."

He shook his head. "You were the one who saved yourself. You grabbed the wheel and turned the car off the road."

"Victor…would have run…you over."

"I would have jumped to safety, but he needed to be stopped. If he had gotten through the intersection, I would not have been able to catch up to him. Or to you. The police were coming from Willkommen, but Victor would have gotten on the interstate first. He was involved in trafficking, Sarah. He could have known places to hole up. I would not have been able to find you."

He took her hand. "But you are safe now, and that is the only thing that matters. You must get strong and let your shoulder heal and your broken leg mend. You were bleeding internally, but that has stopped. The doctors were so worried, and so was I."

"What of Rosie and her baby?"

"They are both with Rosie's family. I am sure her parents were happy to have their daughter home."

Sarah nodded. "And…a new grandbaby."

"It will be hard for Rosie. She has been through so much. You saved her, Sarah. You heard her in the basement. If you had not insisted that we investigate…" He did not finish his statement.

Instead, he offered her water from the glass on the bedside table. She took a long sip and smiled with gratitude that he knew what she needed, even before she knew it herself.

"Victor's father locked him in the woodshed as a boy when he disobeyed," she said, her voice gathering strength. "He would hear rats. Sometimes they crawled over him. He thought his mother should have protected him, yet he loved her."

"Until she got old and he wanted her money."

Sarah nodded. "Ms. Hazel might not have known what her husband was doing."

"Or perhaps she was like Amish wives who follow their husband's commands within the family."

"You're thinking of your own mother," Sarah said, noting the sorrow in his eyes.

"*Yah*, but *Mamm* never stopped loving me."

"You father loves you, too, Joachim."

"I know that now. Mamie Carver was right. I had to ensure pride did not rule my heart in order to reconcile with my *datt*."

"Does that mean you're staying in Petersville?"

He nodded. "For now. I want to make certain you get stronger so you can decide what you want for your future."

Sarah already knew what she wanted, but she wouldn't tell Joachim. Not now. She needed to rest and, as he had mentioned, regain her strength before she made plans. If only Joachim could be part of those plans. They still had so many obstacles that stood in their way.

She couldn't think of that now; now she wanted to think of the wonderful man who was smiling down at her. He had rescued her from Victor and from the fire and from the guilt she had carried for too long.

Chapter Twenty-Eight

Eight days later, Joachim stepped into Sarah's hospital room, hat in hand. "The taxi will arrive within the hour," he told her. "You are feeling up to the trip?"

She nodded, her eyes bright in spite of the brace on her arm and the cast on her leg. "I'm still amazed that the Amish are allowed to hire taxis. Are you sure the bishop would approve?"

Joachim laughed. "He uses them himself for long journeys. Our trip to my parents' home is not long in miles, but the doctors were concerned about your comfort in the buggy."

"Did you mention that I fell out of the buggy?"

"Some things need to be forgotten," he said with a twinkle in his eyes. "I did not want the doctors to question my ability to lead my mare."

"As I recall, it was my fault for not holding on."

"In truth it was my fault for not holding on to you. That is exactly why we are using Ralph's Taxi Service. Plus, his car has air-conditioning. The day is warm, but we will remain cool as we travel."

"What about your parents, Joachim? Are you sure

they don't mind me staying at your house while I recuperate?"

"My mother has been cooking and baking for two
days. She always wanted more than one daughter and
is happy to have another woman in the house."

"And your father?"

"He gave his nod of approval. Currently, he is busy
in the fields. I have been helping him, but thankfully,
he has not asked me to join him there today. He knew I
needed to be with you at the hospital."

"I promise not to be demanding while my leg and shoulder heal. You need to help your father. I'll stay busy cutting
quilt pieces and learning to sew a dress for myself. Rebecca
said she would teach me." Sarah looked at the brace on her
arm. "At least I'll cut and sew after my shoulder heals."

"You will continue to dress Amish?" he asked.

"Of course."

Her response warmed Joachim's heart.

"Which reminds me," she added. "The nurse said
she would help me dress for the trip home. Can you tell
her I'm ready?"

Joachim found the nurse and waited in the visitor's alcove until Sarah was dressed. She was sitting in a wheelchair with her leg propped up when the nurse pushed
her into the hallway.

"Remember to follow the instructions the doctor gave
you," the nurse advised. "He wants to see you in two weeks.
Until then, have this handsome guy take care of you."

Sarah smiled. "He'll be getting dirty in the fields
working with his father, but his mother and sister will
provide plenty of help."

After waving goodbye to the nurse, Joachim pushed
Sarah to the elevator and hit the button for the next floor up.

"Aren't we going to the street level?" Sarah asked.

"There is someone I thought you might enjoy seeing before we leave the hospital."

"You're being very secretive for an Amish man," she chided.

"Have you read from scripture that patience is a virtue?"

"Evidently, it's a virtue I need to master."

They rode the elevator to the next floor. Joachim stopped the wheelchair outside one of the rooms. He knocked. A woman's voice bid them enter.

He pushed Sarah into the room and smiled as he saw a very perky and alert woman sitting up in bed.

"Ms. Hazel," Sarah gushed, as Joachim guided the wheelchair next to the older woman's bed.

"I was hoping you would have time to stop by before you left the hospital," Ms. Hazel said with a warm smile. "Joachim has visited me each day and told me about your progress. I am so glad you are doing well."

"The last time I saw you," Sarah said, "I feared you wouldn't survive the night."

Hazel nodded. "The night of the fire." She glanced at Joachim. "I owe my life to Joachim and Levi. They saved me." She patted Sarah's hand. "And you saved me from my son."

"I'm sorry about Victor."

"Victor was a troubled child. My husband thought I was too lenient and insisted our son needed more discipline. I didn't approve of my husband's tactics. He could be an obstinate man and difficult at times, although most people saw only his positive attributes. Today, some might call him bipolar or manic depressive, which only added to Victor's confusion growing up. He never knew how to take his father. And I fear he inherited some of his father's infirmities—most especially the mood swings and the difficulty controlling his temper."

She looked down and sighed. "I didn't know about the rats in the woodshed. Victor never told me, and I'm sure his father thought our son should be man enough to withstand the punishment. Undoubtedly, those nights terrified Victor, and I pray he will forgive me someday for not stepping in." She glanced up with sorrowful eyes. "Hindsight is always easier."

"We all make mistakes," Joachim assured her, thinking of his own mistake. He should have remained in Petersville and dealt with his brother's death and his father's anger instead of running away. But if so, he would not have found Sarah.

She had taught him a lot about facing fear. She had returned to the Thomin home to save Rosie. Her determination meant the Amish woman and her son survived.

"I'm sorry about your house, Ms. Hazel."

"There's nothing to be sorry about, Joachim. The memories of what happened there were difficult. I'm relived it's gone."

"But where will you live?" Sarah asked.

"A new assisted-living home is being built not far from here. I've reserved an apartment and arranged for a woman whose mother worked for my mother to live across the hall. Her eyesight isn't good, but we'll help each other."

"Would that be Mamie Carver?" Sarah asked.

"Why yes. How do you know Mamie?"

"Joachim introduced us."

"You'll have to visit once we move into our apartments. Meals are provided in the main dining room. Come for Sunday supper once you're feeling stronger."

"I'd like that, but if you don't mind me asking, can Ms. Mamie afford such accommodations?"

Ms. Hazel smiled. "Mamie and I have an agreement. She'll help me with my day-to-day needs and I'll cover the cost of her lodging. My husband left me financially secure, which is a blessing. Because of his concern for Victor's poor skills in managing money, he made sure our son never knew the extent of our estate. Plus, I never gave him power of attorney, which is why he couldn't pay the electric bill when I was so infirm. That might have been a mistake on my part, but my husband had everything worked out with a lawyer before he died. I also regret letting the house fall into disrepair. As I struggled with age and my failing health, I left too many things undone."

She turned to Joachim. "There's one more thing I need to mention. Now that the house is gone, I no longer need the land."

The sweet lady smiled at Joachim. "You have always been a good neighbor. I'd like you to have the acreage, Joachim. You're just starting out, and property values are going up. Finding your own farm would be costly. I'll sell you the property for one hundred dollars."

Joachim's eyes widened. "As much as I appreciate your offer, that is far too little," he insisted. "I could not even buy a tenth of an acre for that price."

She shrugged. "My husband always said I wasn't good at math, but that's the price I'm asking if you're interested in buying. You'll have to build a new house, but I don't think that would be a problem."

"Thank you," Joachim said, his voice husky with emotion. "I will buy your land for that amount, but as I mentioned, you are too generous."

"I'm grateful, Joachim. You'll allow me to live the rest

of my life knowing some good came out of the land. Perhaps you'll bring me fresh produce from time to time."

He laughed. "You will have your fill of tomatoes, beans and cucumbers. In the fall, we'll gather apples from the trees. Sarah will bake you pies."

Hazel's eyes twinkled. "I like the sound of that. There's one more thing. Mamie Carver has a beagle who needs a home."

Joachim nodded. "He'll enjoy romping with our own dog, Angelo."

The older woman smiled. "Then it seems that we have a deal. I'll have my lawyer stop by your home next week to work out the details."

"I don't know what to say."

"You don't have to say anything, Joachim. Your actions have always spoken louder than words."

The taxi driver was a kindly man who was waiting for them when they arrived at the first floor. Joachim was quiet on the way home, no doubt thinking about Ms. Hazel's generosity. Perhaps he was making plans for his new home.

Sarah mused over his comment about her baking pies for Ms. Thomin. Not that she would question Joachim. There would be time later to talk about his plans. Now she needed to meet his parents. Hopefully, they wouldn't regret their offer for her to recuperate at their home.

Once she was healed, she would need to decide where she would go. She reached out and took Joachim's hand. Perhaps by then they would know what the future would hold.

The taxi turned into the Burkholder driveway and braked to a stop next to the back porch. Two buggies stood near the barn, and horses Sarah had never seen before were in the paddock.

"Your parents have guests," she said, suddenly worried about intruding. "I hate to be a bother."

He squeezed her hand. "A bother you would never be." After paying the driver, he hurried around the car to open her door.

"I will carry you to the porch."

Sarah saw the ramp Joachim had built.

"The wheelchair should have been delivered," he continued. "It will help you get around in the house."

"You've thought of everything, Joachim."

The kitchen door opened and a full-figured woman with big brown eyes and a warm smile stepped onto the porch. No doubt, she was Joachim's mother.

"Welcome." Mrs. Burkholder hurried down the steps and wrapped Sarah in a gentle hug. "We are so glad to finally meet you and to have you in our home."

A man, Joachim's height but with a thinner frame, pushed a wheelchair onto the porch. "Here is your transportation for the next six to eight weeks."

He looked like Joachim but with less bulk.

"Thank you, Mr. Burkholder," Sarah said. "You all are so generous and thoughtful."

Rebecca hurried outside. "Look at you, Sarah. You have color in your cheeks, which I have not seen before. Joachim, bring her into the house."

"I'm sorry to interrupt your company," Sarah said as Joachim settled her into the chair.

"You must come inside to meet them," his mother insisted.

Joachim pushed Sarah through the kitchen to the main room. She didn't understand his hurry. Meeting the guests was not as important as visiting with Rebecca, who looked like she was ready to burst with anticipation.

Glancing over her shoulder, Sarah saw Levi enter the kitchen, hat in hand. No doubt that was the reason for Rebecca's excitement.

"Here we are." Joachim brought the chair to a stop.

Sarah turned to greet the two couples who had risen from the chairs and were staring at her, their faces filled with expectation.

She blinked.

Her heart stopped. Tears flooded her eyes. Standing before her were Miriam and Hannah, her sisters, whom she'd feared she would never see again.

In one fell swoop, they swarmed around her with hugs and kisses and laugher along with tears of joy.

"How can this be?" Sarah asked once they stepped back to catch their breath.

"Miriam, I thought you were dead or taken by some crazed man named George." Sarah looked at her eldest sister. "And Hannah, I thought you were in Atlanta."

"I was until I drove to Willkommen to find you and Miriam."

"Only we couldn't find you," Miriam explained as she wiped the tears from her cheeks.

For the first time, Sarah noticed the clothing they wore. "You've dressed Amish?"

"Yah," both sisters answered in unison.

"And we're married." Miriam tugged on the arm of a handsome man in black trousers, white shirt and suspenders. "Meet your brother-in-law Abram Zook."

"And…" Hannah drew an equally good-looking Amish man closer. "Your other brother-in-law, Lucas Grant."

"There's much you need to tell me," Sarah said as her heart nearly burst with joy.

Rebecca invited them into the kitchen for lunch, where they talked about all that had happened since they had last been together.

Sarah had never seen her sisters so happy. Joachim stayed at her side, eager to help when she needed something. She glanced around the table, realizing everyone she loved was in this kitchen. She had thought the past was over and that she would have to make a new life for herself, but God had reunited her with her sisters. At long last, the three girls were together again.

"We have room for you to stay with us," Miriam insisted as the afternoon waned.

"Lucas and I would love for you to stay with us, as well," Hannah added.

Sarah glanced at Mr. and Mrs. Burkholder and then at Rebecca and finally at Joachim. His face was tight with concern.

"This wonderful Burkholder family has been kind enough to open their home to me. I'll stay here."

"You've made a good decision," Joachim said as he squeezed her hand.

"I'm glad I can stand on my own two feet." Then she looked down. "Well, maybe not stand, but at least know what I want. I like being an independent woman."

"An independent *Englischer*?" he asked.

She shook her head. "I'm no longer *fancy*. I'm an independent Amish woman."

"*Yah*? Are you sure?"

"Cross my heart."

He smiled. "This is a good decision."

Joachim was right. Being Amish was a very good decision.

Chapter Twenty-Nine

Eight weeks later, Joachim lifted Sarah into his buggy. "You are lighter without your cast," he joked playfully.

"The doctor said I can do anything I want. My leg and shoulder have healed, and he doesn't need to see me again."

"This is good."

"Now tell me where you're taking me, Joachim Burkholder. You've been so secretive recently."

He laughed. "Just because I do not chatter on like Rebecca and Levi."

"They have much to talk about with their wedding this fall," Sarah said with a smile.

"*Yah*, they are both excited. This is as it should be."

"The wedding brings joy to the Plank family after the sorrow of the police finding Naomi's remains."

Joachim nodded. "Levi said Victor confessed to killing her because she would not stay with him, which is what he had told you."

"If you hadn't rescued me, Joachim—"

Before she could finish her statement, Angelo ran toward the buggy. Butch followed slowly behind the younger pup. The two adorable dogs brought a smile to Sarah's lips. "Angelo and Butch want to go with us."

"Maybe next time," he said with a twinkle in his eyes. "Today we will go alone."

He flicked the reins and Belle headed for the road.

The day was warm, and Sarah adjusted her bonnet, enjoying the sunshine and the blue of the sky. "Your mother asked me about my plans for the future."

"What did you tell her?"

"I said I needed to make up my mind about what to do and where to go."

"I thought you wanted to stay in Petersville."

"Hannah told me that help is needed at the Amish Inn where she and Lucas met. I am eager to see it for myself when we go there for lunch on Saturday."

"I thought we planned to simply visit with your family. I did not know you would be applying for a job."

"I'll see what the inn looks like and make my decisions then."

He steered Belle along the main road and withdrew into himself. Sarah didn't need conversation. She enjoyed the ride and being with Joachim.

"I want to get your opinion about something," he said, turning Belle into the old Thomin driveway.

"I must start thinking of this as the Burkholder place," Sarah said, taking his hand. "You've working hard planting the fields, but I don't want your woodwork to suffer."

"After harvest there will be time."

"The barn remains standing by the burned-out home site?" she asked.

"*Yah*, but I do not want to build the new house there. I have found a better spot."

He tugged the reins to the right and encouraged Belle up a small incline. At the crest of the hill, he and Sarah looked down onto a lake surrounded to the rear by hardwoods. In the distance, deer grazed and geese flew overhead.

Joachim pointed to a clearing. "I thought a house on the rise would be *gut*. The beauty of the hills and lake would be visible from the porch."

She nodded. "It's so peaceful, Joachim."

"You like the spot I have chosen?"

"Yes, it's perfect."

"And you are meeting with the bishop next week?"

"He is coming for dinner. Your mother said I will be able to talk to him after we eat."

"You are asking for baptism."

She nodded. "Living Amish is what I want. Is that all right with you?"

"It is what you chose, Sarah. You are an independent woman who knows her mind."

She smiled, appreciating his comment. "And the Amish will accept an independent woman into their community?"

"My *datt* has already told the bishop that you are a woman of faith. My *mamm* has assured him of your sincerity of heart." He winked. "Plus, she wants a good wife for her son."

Sarah titled her head, her heart nearly bursting with excitement. "What?"

"She knows her son's heart." He wrapped his arm around hers. "My mother sees the way I look at you and knows how I feel."

Her cheeks warmed and she couldn't stop smiling. "How do you feel?" she asked coyly.

"I feel that life has no meaning without you." He

pointed to the hillside and the lake. "All this means nothing to me if I cannot share it with you, Sarah. I love you."

She saw the truth in his gaze and felt overcome with gratitude. "I love you, Joachim."

He pulled her closer. "Will you marry me, Sarah? If you do, I will be a happy man."

"Of course, I'll marry you. I've been waiting for you to ask."

He smiled. "I thought perhaps an independent woman would ask first."

She nestled closer and lifted her lips to his. "First kiss me, then we can talk about how demanding I can be."

"There is something good about a woman raised *Englisch*."

"Oh?" Sarah raised her brow.

"*Yah*, she knows what she wants."

"Joachim, you're all I've ever wanted."

He lowered his lips to hers and they kissed. Sarah's heart nearly burst with happiness and anticipation of their future together.

A new home built on the rise with the water in the distance. Children to bring even more joy and laughter to their home, and a love that would grow stronger with the years.

The trip to the Amish Inn was pleasant. Sarah talked about wedding plans and what she needed to make for her new home with Joachim, curtains and quilts and the special dress she would sew to wear at their wedding.

Joachim smiled and nodded in agreement, letting her talk and thinking how his life had come full circle. He now had everything he had ever wanted with Sarah at his side.

They arrived at the inn to find both of Sarah's sisters

and their husbands stepping from their buggies. Miriam and Hannah greeted them with hugs and then stared expectantly at Sarah.

"What?" she asked.

"I have a feeling there's something you need to tell us," Miriam said with merriment in her eyes.

"You know me too well," Sarah admitted. She grabbed Joachim's hand and pulled him close. "We're getting married."

The women hugged and the men shook hands, and as they walked together into the inn, the conversation turned to wedding dates after the fall harvest and their new home and furnishings.

An older Amish woman greeted them in the dining room. Hannah introduced Sarah and Joachim to Fannie Stoltz, who owned the inn. "I am pleased to meet you," she told them with a warm smile. "The corner table is for your family."

Again the sisters continued to talk, planning the upcoming wedding and catching up on what had transpired since their last visit. The lunch was delicious, and after dessert as they sipped coffee, the talk turned to their mother.

"She is buried on property Hannah and Lucas own," Miriam told Sarah. "We will go there one day."

"I would like that. Mother wanted to find her sister, but none of us ever imagined that we would find a new life and a new faith for ourselves here in the mountains."

"I wish she could have connected with her sister," Hannah said. "I have a feeling some of her struggle and search for happiness was because of the family she had left behind. We've continued the search, but we haven't been able to find any clues."

"No one in the area has heard mention of Annie Miller?" Sarah asked.

Fannie placed the coffeepot on the table and turned to stare at the girls. "What was your mother's name?"

"Leah Miller," Sarah said.

"Miller or Meuller?" Fannie asked.

"Miller is all we ever knew."

"And what was her sister's name, the aunt you have been looking for?" Fannie pressed.

"Annie Miller."

Tears welled in Fannie eyes. "I cannot believe this, but it is true."

The girls waited expectantly.

"My maiden name was Meuller. Fannie Meuller. My baby sister could never pronounce Fannie, so she called me Annie. My sister's name was Leah."

"Mother must have changed her last name when she left Willkommen," Sarah said, putting the pieces together.

"Which means our mother was raised Amish," Miriam said with astonishment.

"And all of us," Hannah added, looking at each of her sisters, "have found our way back to our Amish roots."

Fannie nodded. "If what you said is true, then I am your mother's sister, your Aunt Fannie or Annie, whichever name you choose to use."

The girls circled the sweet woman and hugged her close. She joined them at the table and told them stories of their mother growing up, of her hopes for the future and her dreams of the family she would someday have. Their aunt also mentioned their mother's struggle with her authoritative father, who never showed his love.

"Mother searched for love and affirmation her whole

life but never realized her three daughters loved her more than any man ever could," Miriam said.

Sarah smiled sadly. "And as her dementia started to take hold, she sought to return home to the sister she loved."

Fannie patted Sarah's hand. "I am sure she loved each of you girls deeply. Showing that love was the problem."

Joachim appreciated the importance and healing of the stories and the insights Fannie shared. The three sisters might have questioned their mother's love, but there was no way they could fail to see the compassion and concern that exuded from their aunt.

The family was growing, and Joachim felt sure that in the not-too-distant future, God would bless the couples with children so that the table would grow even fuller in the years ahead.

Going home that evening, Sarah rested her head on his shoulder. "What are you thinking?" he asked.

"I was thinking how God made good come from all the pain of the carjacking. We came to Willkommen to find our aunt, and we also found three wonderful men to love. I'm free of the memory of the fire. Miriam and Hannah both said they never talked about it because of our mother. She knew the man she was seeing had been at fault. Blaming it on me meant that he wouldn't have to face criminal charges, so she forbid them to mention what had taken place."

"Now you do not have to be afraid of fire."

"I don't have to be afraid of anything, Joachim, with you by my side."

"Have I told you how much I love you?" He pulled the buggy to the edge of the road.

"You've told me, but I want to hear it again."

"I love you more than myself, Sarah Meuller. You are my life, my breath, my heart, my soul. You are my everything."

The sun started to set in the west as Joachim pulled her close and kissed her, which was what he had wanted to do every day since he had first seen her peering at him from the Thomin window.

"You rescued me, Joachim," she said. "I'll be forever grateful."

"And I'll be forever grateful for having you as my wife, Sarah. We have much to look forward to."

"Yah," she said, turning her lips to his. *"Gott* brought you into my life at the perfect moment."

He nodded. "And *Gott* brought me home to find you, the woman I will love forever."

They kissed and kissed again. Then Joachim flicked the reins, and Belle continued the journey that would take them to the Burkholder farm. In a few months, they would marry and move into their own home where Joachim would cherish Sarah all the days of her life.

As if reading his mind, she snuggled even closer and sighed. "The pain of the past is over for both of us, Joachim, and tomorrow awaits us." Sarah thought for a moment and then added, "We have a lifetime ahead of us filled with blessings."

"Blessings and love," he added, and then he kissed her again.

* * * * *

COURTING HER
AMISH HEART

Mary Davis

Dedicated to my awesome sister Kathleen Shogren.

Aller Anfang ist schwer. "All beginnings are hard."

For do I now persuade men, or God? or do I seek to please men? for if I yet pleased men I should not be the servant of Christ.
—*Galatians* 1:10

Chapter One

Kathleen Yoder stood in front of the motel room mirror, fussing with her hair. She had to look just right. She needed to be viewed as a proper Amish woman if her community was going to welcome her home. She pulled the pins from her hair and started over. What did the English say? Third time's a charm.

Even though all through her medical training she had continued to dress Amish and put her hair up, she hadn't had another Amish woman to measure her ability against. It wasn't *gut* to compare oneself to others, but she could gauge if she had been getting her clothes and hair put right. Iron sharpens iron. Had the fourteen years in the English world whittled away at her Amish standards? Probably. However, she would quickly fall back into Amish life.

She snugged her *kapp* on her head and smoothed her hands down her blue Plain dress. At this point, no more amount of labor would make her appearance any more appropriate. She would need to trust *Gott* to pave her way.

She zipped her suitcase closed, lowered it to the floor

and extended the roller handle, holding it tight. With her other hand, she slung one strap of her backpack of medical supplies over her shoulder and draped her coat over her arm.

Rolling her suitcase behind her, she opened the door and stepped out into the sunlight. The only things that stood between her and home now were the bus ride to Goshen and the walk to the farm. If she could convince the bus driver to let her off outside of town, she would have only eight miles to trek.

She traipsed to the bus station three blocks away, purchased her ticket and sat in the seat behind the driver. "Could you let me off outside of Goshen?" She gave him the country road names of the intersection.

"Sorry. I'm not authorized to make a stop there." He tipped his head up and glanced at her in his rearview mirror. "Is someone meeting you at the station?"

"No." She hadn't had the courage to contact anyone to come get her. It would be harder to turn her away if she were at the door.

"How you getting from town out to the country?"

"I'll walk."

"That's a long ways. Well over ten miles."

Thirteen point two from the city limits and another two or three from the bus station. "I'll be fine." She needed to get used to traversing these stretches. No time like the present.

"I'm sure one of your people would gladly come into town to get you. Or you could take a taxi."

If someone knew she was returning today. But she hadn't told anyone. "The walk will do me *gut*." It would help transition her back into the slower pace of life. As well as giving her something to occupy herself with instead of dealing with idle chatter. Giving her a chance to prepare herself for the meeting of *her people*. She hoped they still *were* her people.

She stared out the window at her home state's terrain sweeping by. As the Indiana countryside grew increasingly more familiar, snippets of her past surged through her. Places she'd been. People she'd seen. Homes she'd visited. Her life among the English fell away with each passing mile.

The bus slowed, and the driver pulled onto the shoulder of the highway and stopped under an overpass. The one she'd hoped he could have taken to shorten her walk. The driver stood and faced the passengers. "I need to check something on the bus outside. Won't be but a minute." The driver gazed directly at Kathleen. "Could you accompany me?"

Kathleen stood. "All right." She didn't know what help she could be.

With a broad smile, he motioned for her to precede him down the steps.

Once outside, he handed over her medical pack and coat. He must have taken them from her seat. He pointed to the lower storage compartments. "Which one's your luggage in?"

"Excuse me?"

He faced her. "You see, I'm not supposed to stop along the way, but if I think there could be a problem with the bus…well, that's a different story. And if, while I'm checking the bus, a passenger was to get off, and if I wasn't able to talk her into getting back on, there's nothing I could do about that. And if a particular piece of luggage were to 'fall' off, there wouldn't be anything

I could do about that either. Seeing as I wouldn't notice it until I got to the station."

She smiled. "I appreciate your kindness."

"I don't know what you're talking about. I'm just checking on the bus." He winked. "I believe the problem could be in the back compartment. I'll need to move a...dark blue roller case?"

She nodded. She shouldn't encourage this kind of deceptive behavior.

He opened the section and pushed a couple of bags aside before pulling hers free. "You going to be all right by yourself?"

"I'll be fine." She felt safer already being here than she'd ever felt being at the university or in any of the hospitals or clinics where she'd worked. "Thank you." She appreciated him cutting her walk in half.

Giving her a nod, he climbed back into the bus. "False alarm. Everything is as it should be." He winked at her again, then closed the doors.

She waved in return, and several passengers waved to her. As the bus pulled away, she pressed a hand to her queasy abdomen. Almost home. Regardless of the reception she would receive, she was back in her Elkhart County New Order Amish community. She draped her coat over the top of her suitcase, balanced her medical backpack on top of that, gripped the roller handle and struck out on the very last leg of her fourteen-year journey. Up the off-ramp, down the road, along the country lane, and toward home.

After trudging along for fifteen minutes or so on the edge of the blacktop, she realized this was not at all like walking the halls of a hospital. She was out of shape and shifted her suitcase handle to her other hand.

The familiar reverberation of horse's hooves clomping on the pavement came from behind her. The comforting sound both thrilled her and caused her unsteady insides to knot. In all her daydreams, she hadn't pictured seeing any Amish until her family opened the front door. How foolish. Who would this be? Someone she knew? Would anyone still recognize her?

As the horse and buggy drew closer, her midsection twisted tighter and tighter. She dared not turn around though she wanted to know whom it was. But at the same time, she didn't want to know. Let them pass her by.

First, the horse came alongside her, then the buggy. The driver slowed the horse to her pace. *"Hallo."*

She glanced up into the sun and raised her hand to shade her eyes. The bearded face held a kind smile and sparkling brown eyes that sent a small thrill dancing through her. Shame on her. His beard signified he was a married man. Though he seemed familiar, she couldn't place him. Maybe it was just because he was Amish. And all her emotions, negative and positive, were heightened.

"Hallo." She stopped, welcoming the respite. Or did she welcome the delay in arriving at her destination?

He reined in the horse and spoke in *Deutsch.* "Can I give you a ride?"

It had been so long since she'd heard her language. She replied in kind. "That's very considerate of you." She was tired, not used to this amount of walking in the late-spring heat. "But I'm fine. Walking is *gut.*" Nevertheless, she remained rooted in place, not wanting to part company from this man yet for some strange reason.

He set the brake and jumped down. He stood between her and a passing pickup truck as though protecting her from it. His gaze flickered to her suitcase then back to her face. "I'm Noah Lambright."

No doubt he thought she was running away with her suitcase in tow. "I'm Kathleen Yoder."

His eyes widened slightly as though her name were familiar. Why wasn't his? *Noah?* She had known many Noahs in her youth, both young and old. But now she'd spent nearly as much time away as she had at home. Certainly such a handsome Amish man she would have remembered. "I'm sure my strolling alongside the road with my suitcase must have you confused. I'm not running away, if that's what you're thinking." Quite the opposite. She was finally running home. Home to her family. Home to her community. Home to her Amish way of life. And for some reason, it was important that this man—this Noah—knew that.

"If you were running away, you'd be heading in that direction." He pointed down the road the way she'd come. He picked up her medical pack and coat in one hand and hoisted her suitcase in the other.

Kathleen reached for them. "What are you doing with my things?"

He put them in the back of his open buggy. "Even if you refuse a ride, I can at least take your belongings to your destination so you don't have to cart them along behind you." He held out his hand to her. "Are you sure you don't want a ride? This is the hottest part of the day."

"What would your wife say to you picking up a woman you don't know?"

Pain flickered across his features and left just as quickly. "I'm widowed."

"Oh. I'm so sorry."

"Don't worry about it. She passed three years ago."

"I thought with your beard…" She needed to just stop talking. But why did he still wear one? It wasn't her place to ask. So he *wasn't* married after all. That was *gut* to know. *Ne*, it wasn't. The poor man had lost his wife. And she had no room in her life to consider courting and marriage.

He must have noticed her staring because he rubbed his jaw. "I've been meaning to shave this off. Thought about doing so this morning."

Three years? And he still wore a beard? That was none of her business.

"So what do you say to that ride?" His mouth quirked up on one side.

That caused her insides to dance. Though she didn't want to hurry her journey along, she certainly wasn't enjoying the hike. She *had* wanted this time alone to gather her thoughts. But her hand reached out for his.

Strong, calloused and work worn. Comforting.

He helped her up into the front seat and with him came the distinct aroma of fresh-cut wood and something sweet.

She had rarely ever ridden in the front. This was an open buggy and still daylight, so there wouldn't be anything inappropriate about accepting his offer. For what she had spent the past fourteen years doing and what she planned to do in the near future, she needed to make sure everything else she did was beyond reproof. She didn't want to give the church leadership any more reasons than necessary to refuse her offer of help.

He climbed in next to her and set the buggy into motion. Strangely, he didn't dive into conversation and questions like the English, who felt the need to fill every silence. He just drove. Down one road and then another.

Turning here and there. How odd that the silence wasn't in the least awkward. Sitting next to this man—this stranger—was comfortable.

And honey. He smelled of wood and *honey.* Very comforting, indeed.

Solar panels winking off a roof caught her attention. An *Englisher* must have bought that farm. When she'd left, it had belonged to one of the Lehman families. Another house also had solar panels. And then the next one. They couldn't have all been sold out of the community. Amish liked to keep Amish property in the family, and if not, sell it to another Amish. "Did *Englishers* buy several of these farms?"

"Ne."

"But what about the solar panels? They aren't allowed."

"They are now."

She'd thought about how nice this form of electricity would be for the Amish and planned to bring it up to the leaders—after she got her clinic going. What other changes had taken place in her absence? Did her parents have solar panels?

When he turned onto the road that passed her parents' home, she faced him. "How did you know where I was going?"

"You're Kathleen Yoder. Your parents are David and Pamela Yoder."

"How did you know?"

"Everyone knows who you are. The girl who went away to become a doctor."

She couldn't tell if that was sarcasm in his voice or something…something less negative. Dare she hope admiration? What was she thinking? Of course not. Her devout Amish neighbors would never condone her actions without permission from the bishop. But that didn't matter. She would help them whether they liked it or not. She had a plan. In time, she hoped they would see the *gut* in what she'd done.

Lord, let them see I did it for them. For all of them.

Noah clucked to the horse and flicked the reins to keep Fred moving. He still couldn't reconcile the strange sight that he'd found on the roadside.

Kathleen Yoder. Strolling along like a distant memory or faded dream.

She wasn't at all what he'd pictured. He'd heard so many stories about her that he'd thought she'd be taller. More of a person to be reckoned with. He'd expected her to be more forceful. Not demure. How was she ever going to forge her way to be a doctor in their community? A doctor close at hand could prevent many senseless deaths. He admired her tenacity to do what no other Amish would. Woman or man.

And if she could come back after nearly a decade and a half, that gave him hope that another might too.

He certainly never anticipated her to be pretty, with her dark brown hair, steady blue eyes and heart-shaped face. Why would she have wanted to leave and pursue something like medicine against the leadership's wishes? She could have married any man she wanted. Every young man must have had his sights on courting her.

"Stop the buggy." Her words came out half-strangled.

"Why? We're almost there."

"That's why. Please stop. Please." She grabbed the reins and pulled back. Her hands brushed against his.

Fred eagerly obeyed.

Her touch sent a tingle shuddering up Noah's arm. Before he could put on the brake and even before the horse came to a complete stop, Kathleen jumped to the ground and circled behind the buggy.

He set the brake and climbed down.

Kathleen paced behind the buggy, muttering to herself in English. "I stood up to Dr. Wilson with all his old-fashioned treatments that weren't evidence-based. I had been right, and the patient lived. I can do this. I can face my family and the community without shame for my disobedience."

He watched her for a moment. "What are you doing?"

"I'm trying to gain my courage. I thought I'd have this whole walk—" she swung one arm back the way she'd come "—to think about what to say to my parents. Planned it all out. And prepared myself if they don't give me a warm welcome."

"I'm sure they'll welc—"

"What will I say to my younger siblings? Are any of them even left at home? The baby that was born the year after I left. Samuel. He'd be thirteen. And Jessica would be only fifteen. They won't even know me. Are Benjamin and Joshua still enjoying *Rumspringa*? Or are they too old? Have they joined church? And Ruby should be considering marriage. I wonder if she's being courted by anyone? And Gloria is certainly married."

She was really worked up. He felt bad that she was so distraught. Dare he try again to console her, to let her know all would be well?

Another buggy came up the lane. Noah motioned for the driver to keep going. He didn't think Kathleen needed someone else to witness her distress.

The young man nodded and kept moving.

Noah nodded back.

"Who was that? Someone I would know? Do you think he recognized me?"

"I think you know him. That was Benjamin Yoder."

Kathleen stopped fidgeting and stared at him. "My brother? Benjamin?"

Her steady blue gaze warmed him. He nodded.

With a wistful expression, Kathleen studied the retreating buggy. "My brother." She sighed. "I wouldn't have recognized him. Do you think he recognized me?"

"I don't think he got a very *gut* loo—"

"Of course he didn't recognize me." Kathleen resumed her pacing. "I've been gone for fourteen years, and he was so young when I left. How could he?"

"Kathleen?"

"How will any of them remember me?"

"Kathleen?"

"I will be as a stranger to them. All of them."

Noah grabbed both of her hands to calm her. "Kathleen, look at me."

Her panicked blue eyes turned to him and slowly focused. "I could diagnose pneumonia. I could set a broken bone. I could take out your appendix. All that, I can do. This I cannot." She meant facing her family.

He squeezed her hands. "Don't be silly."

"I'm not silly." She tried to pull her hands free.

He held fast. He didn't want to let her go. "I didn't say *you* were silly. I said you were *being* silly. You left the community and went against the wishes of the church leaders. You studied for so many years. You have done what no other Amish have dared. Where is that girl? The one who did all those things?"

Her voice came out small. "I think I left her back in the city."

"*Ne.* You didn't. *She* brought you back here." He'd presumed she would be a stout woman who took charge. Not this slip of a thing who appeared scared and unsure of herself. Not this beautiful woman standing before him. "Your parents will be happy to see you."

"How do you know?"

"They've never stopped talking about you."

"You know my parents?"

He gave a nod. "I've spent quite a bit of time with them the past three years. My farm borders theirs. They're proud of all you've accomplished."

"Now I know they've never said that. Pride goes against the church."

"It's the *way* they talk about you."

"So they talk about my being a doctor? Do they think the community will accept me?"

"They don't talk about that."

"You mean my being a doctor?"

He nodded.

"Then how do you know they're proud of my accomplishments, if they don't talk about my being a doctor?"

"Like I said, it's the *way* they talk about you. About their daughter who is in the English world. I can't explain it."

Kathleen pulled free and resumed pacing. "Why did I ever leave? What was I thinking?"

Noah stared at his empty hands, then tucked them into his pockets to keep them from reaching out for her again. "Honestly, I've never been able to figure that out. Did you think the leaders would pat you on the back for your efforts? You know *they* disapprove of your actions? But your *parents* don't."

She stopped and stared at him with wide blue eyes. "I don't know what to do. In a hospital or surgery I do, but not here. Give me a patient, and I'd know what to do."

How could someone be so confident in one area and not in another? "Climb back in the buggy and go see your family. Both you and they have been waiting fourteen years for this. Your reception isn't going to change five minutes from now. Or five hours. Or five days."

"You're right. *Gut* or bad, I must go." She clasped her hands together and bowed her head.

He prayed silently as well. Prayed for a warm welcome. Prayed for Kathleen to be strong. Prayed for Kathleen to become the woman *Gott* meant her to be. Prayed to get to know her better.

After another pickup truck passed, Kathleen marched around the buggy, climbed in and stared straight ahead with her hands folded primly in her lap.

Definitely not how he'd pictured the indomitable Kathleen Yoder. This Kathleen Yoder was never going to make it as a doctor in their Amish district. She would fall back into the traditional Amish role for women or leave the community for *gut* this time. That thought settled uneasily inside him.

Either way, it would be a loss, and he would be disappointed. The community could use her skills and knowledge as a doctor—even if they weren't willing to admit it.

Yet.

No, she wasn't the woman he'd imagined her to be. Hoped her to be.

She was so much better in so many ways.

Chapter Two

❧

Kathleen shifted on the buggy seat as Noah settled next to her. When he flicked the reins and the horse stepped forward, her stomach lurched in tandem with the buggy.

What was wrong with her? She had countered doctors senior to her when a patient was at risk, even grouchy Dr. Wilson. She had taught an undergraduate class. She had stood shoulder to shoulder with other doctors in an operating room.

Or was it this handsome Amish man sitting next to her? Couldn't be. It had to be returning home.

This was her family. Who loved her. And that was the problem. It was one thing to have an arrogant doctor think ill of her, but quite different to have her family view her poorly. That would hurt too much.

Kathleen sat up a little straighter. Regardless of her family's reaction, *Gott* had called her to this path. She had done nothing wrong in His eyes. And wasn't He the one who mattered most?

Noah turned off the road and into her driveway. "Everything will be well. You'll see."

She hoped so. And strangely his words comforted her.

Like the other homes, solar panels sat on the roof.

A tricolor Australian shepherd loped from the barn, barking, announcing their arrival. A dozen or so chickens squawked and scattered.

Noah pulled to a stop and set the brake. When he got out, the dog pranced and leapt around him. "Sit."

The dog raced a few feet away and tore back just as fast.

Making his voice more ominous, he repeated his command. "Sit!" When the dog finally obeyed, it settled at Noah's feet, still wiggling as though it might burst. Noah tousled the shepherd around the neck. "What are you doing here? You should be at home guarding my sheep."

Kathleen stepped down. "This is your dog?"

"*Ja.* She's still young. My other two are supposed to be keeping an eye on her and training her. She does well while I'm on the farm but strays when I'm not there."

She bent toward the dog. "What's her name?"

"Kaleidoscope, on account of her eye."

She looked at the dog's eyes more closely. One brown and the other a patchwork of blues. "Are all your dogs this same breed?"

"I have a black Belgian sheepdog and a black-and-tan Cardigan Welsh corgi."

The Australian shepherd rolled onto her back.

Kathleen obliged by rubbing her tummy. "How old is she?"

"Almost eleven months. She has a lot of growing up to do."

"Noah!" a man called from the barn.

Kathleen froze. Was that her *dat*'s voice? She remained crouched with the dog and stole a glance out of the corner of her eye. The man walking toward them was too young to be her *dat*. Benjamin? He'd grown into a man.

The screen door of the house creaked, and her *mutter* spoke. "Noah, so glad you have come. Who have you brought?"

Air lodged in Kathleen's lungs. She could breathe neither in nor out.

Kaleidoscope flipped from her back to her feet and ran for Benjamin. Fool dog. She was Kathleen's excuse for not looking directly at anyone.

"Someone you're eager to see," Noah said in a light tone. His deep voice brushed over her, calming some of her nerves.

Still looking at the ground, Kathleen saw three pairs of smallish women's shoes come into view. Her *mum* and sisters?

The time had come. Taking a deep breath, Kathleen stood and gazed directly into her *mum*'s face.

Her *mum*'s smile dropped, and her mouth slipped open. "Kathleen? *My* Kathleen?"

Kathleen nodded. *"Ja, Mum."*

Mum cupped her face in both hands. "You're home." Her eyes glistened.

"I'm home." Kathleen's eyes filled with tears as well.

"I cannot believe this." *Mum* pulled her into her arms. "Finally, my child has returned."

After a moment, Ruby's arms wrapped around her and *Mum*.

"Is that my girl?" Her *dat*'s voice came from beside her.

Both women released her, and her *mum* spoke. "Noah has brought our Kathleen home."

Strangely, she liked the sound of that. *Noah* had brought her.

Beside *Dat* stood Benjamin, who had grown into a strapping young man, as well as Joshua and a gangly Samuel.

Dat gave her a pat on the shoulder in greeting. Exuberant for him. "You know Benjamin and Joshua, but you've not met Samuel."

How old were they all now? She counted in her head. Benjamin would be twenty, Joshua eighteen, and Samuel thirteen. She'd missed so much.

Her brothers each gave a nod.

"Pleased to meet you, Samuel."

He gave her another nod.

Mum hooked her arm around Kathleen. "You remember Ruby."

Her twenty-one-year-old sister smiled. "Of course she does. It's Jessica she might have forgotten. She was only one when you left."

Fifteen-year-old Jessica was the spitting image of *Mum*.

Kathleen took one of Jessica's hands and held it in both of hers. "Naturally I remember you. I carried you around wherever I went."

Mum gave half a laugh. "She was quite put out when you left. No one could console her." Her words weren't said as an admonishment but in loving kindness.

Jessica gave Kathleen a quick hug. "Welcome home."

"Supper will be ready in an hour," *Mum* said. "Noah, you'll stay and eat with us."

Not a question but a command.

He chuckled. "I'd love to."

His laugh warmed Kathleen.

Mum shooed the men away. "Get your work finished so you won't keep supper waiting."

The men—including Noah, leading his horse and buggy—tromped off toward the barn.

Noah glanced over his shoulder as he walked away, and a smile jumped to Kathleen's mouth.

Ruby grasped the handle of the suitcase.

Kathleen reached for it. "I can get that."

"Nonsense. You've had a long trip." Ruby struck out across the yard toward the house.

Mum snatched Kathleen's backpack of medical supplies off the bumping suitcase. And when her coat slid to the ground, Jessica retrieved that. With nothing left for Kathleen to carry, she followed in their wake.

She basked in her family's love. All her trials, doubts and time away would be worth the heartache she'd endured to finally be able to help her people.

Jessica and Samuel might be strangers to her, and she to them, but she looked forward to getting to know them.

Standing shoulder to shoulder with her *mutter* and sisters in the kitchen was both familiar and foreign to Kathleen. The other three obviously had their regular tasks and worked in harmony. Kathleen was more of a hindrance than a help until *Mum* sat her at the table to snap the green beans. In time, she would ease back into the flow of the goings-on in and around the house. Hopefully, that wouldn't take too long.

Noah washed up at the outside spigot with the Yoder men. He had always been welcomed at their table. Even more so since losing Rachel three years ago.

He followed the others inside and sat across the table from Kathleen. Though the shortest of the Yoder women,

Kathleen was similar in height to the rest. All between about five-two and five-five. Why had he ever imagined her to be so much taller? And assumed she wouldn't be so pretty?

Seeing Kathleen sitting in the usually empty place always set for her seemed strange. She was finally here to fill the void she'd left. He'd never known this table with her physically here. Her presence had always been felt, even when she wasn't mentioned, by the fact of the vacant chair and unused place setting.

After David said grace, each person filled their plates. Everyone chattered easily except Kathleen. She quietly ate while appearing to enjoy the conversations around her. He tried to listen as she did, a person who had been away for nearly a decade and a half.

Partway through the meal, Samuel asked, "Do we have to call you Doctor now?"

The room became silent. This was what Kathleen had likely feared. Noah wanted to speak up to save Kathleen from having to answer. But why? She was more or less a stranger to him. There was something about her that drew him in. Made him want to protect her.

But her *vater* spoke up. "We'll discuss that another time."

Smoothly avoided, but obviously a tender subject.

Kathleen set her fork down. "I don't mind answering. You are my family. I'm still Kathleen."

Samuel turned back to his plate. One by one, everyone else did the same. Except Kathleen. She looked at each person around the table, then settled her gaze on Noah. He couldn't read her expression, but it flickered between hope and discouragement. He could almost read her thoughts. If her family couldn't accept her being a doctor, how would the rest of the community?

Kathleen averted her gaze first, picking up her fork again and stacking several green beans on it. Nothing but the soft clinking of silverware on plates, swallowing of milk and breathing. The silence in the room resounded as loud as hail pelting the roof.

How much opposition could she take before she gave up? Though not overt opposition, it was opposition nonetheless. How could such a small slip of a woman stand against the whole community? They would wear her down even though what she was offering could help the community greatly. He ached to help her. But what could he say? It wasn't his place. But still he longed to.

After a couple of minutes of the painful silence, and Kathleen shifting in her seat, she spoke up. "How's the garden faring this year?"

Pamela's shoulders relaxed. "It's doing very well. We've planted several new fruit trees since you—in the past few years."

So that was how it was going to be. Would everyone in the community pretend Kathleen had never left? Pretend she hadn't gone to college? Pretend she wasn't a licensed doctor?

He sighed. Too bad Kathleen had caved under the pressure of silence. What would she do if the leadership decided to shun her for her actions? She would give up for sure. But the table conversation relaxed back into typical Amish discussions about farms and gardens, horses and canning, and barn raisings and quilting. She had put order back into the meal.

Later at home, Noah stared into the mirror. He should have shaved off his beard years ago, but since he never planned to marry again, he didn't see the need. The Lord had been niggling him for months to do it, but he'd ignored the prodding.

The image of Kathleen sprang to his mind. She'd mistakenly thought he had a wife.

It was time. He opened the mirror cabinet over the sink and retrieved scissors, a disposable razor and shaving cream. He pinched his two-inch brown chin whiskers between his thumb and index finger and poised the scissors to snip.

Several breaths passed.

Releasing his beard, he lowered the shears. Was he ready to completely let go of Rachel and their child?

Lord, I know I need to let them go. I should be ready, but I'm not. Please heal my heart.

How many times had he asked that of *Gott*? Enough times to fill his barn.

He leaned his hands on the cold porcelain of the sink and stared at his reflection in the mirror. What was wrong with him that he was still hurting after all this time? *Gott* should be all sufficient for him, so why this empty place still inside? He'd given over his anguish and disappointment each day many, many times, yet every morning they were back like old friends to keep him company.

Too bad Kathleen didn't have something in her medicine bag to fix his heart. What ailed him couldn't be remedied by human efforts. Only by *Gott*.

But somehow, Kathleen's return had helped. Strange.

It was time. Raising the shears once again, he snipped one clump of whiskers after another.

After helping to clean up the kitchen, Kathleen sat with her family in the living room for the evening devotional. The hymns rattled around in her brain. She stumbled over the once-familiar words. They would come back to her.

She had missed this time of day to connect with her family. The last fourteen years of evenings had been spent either poring over medical texts, working in a hospital, or sleeping after coming off a double or triple shift. Exhaustion had been her constant companion. The slower pace of life would be a welcome change as well as the routine of a regular schedule, knowing what to expect from one day to the next.

After the Bible reading, discussion and closing prayer, *Dat* said, "Time for bed."

Her younger siblings all stood, as did Kathleen. "Where will I be sleeping?"

Ruby put her arm around Kathleen's shoulder. "Your bed's still in our room."

Mum tucked her sewing into her basket. "Benjamin took your things up earlier."

Kathleen patted her sister's hand. "I'll be up in a few minutes."

Her brothers and sisters tromped up the stairs, and Kathleen sat back down. She wanted to remain standing but didn't want her parents to feel as though she were lording over them.

Dat leaned forward with a warm expression. "We can't tell you how pleased we are to have you back. We prayed for you every day while you were gone."

"I felt them. Knowing you were praying helped me make it through."

Mum leaned forward. "We wanted to write more."

"I know." Kathleen had received letters the first year or so, then came the letter that said it would be the last.

The bishop had requested that they not write her anymore because it would encourage her wayward behavior. Though she hadn't understood the bishop's reasoning, the letter hadn't been a surprise. He would be the toughest of all to convince of the worthiness of her plan.

Dat continued. "We always respected that you needed to make your own decisions."

The point of *Rumspringa*. But she had taken it to an extreme by staying away for fourteen years, just short of half her life, though it felt like more. She wished it hadn't had to be so long, but it had been a necessity to earn her medical degree.

"We appreciate you telling Samuel to call you Kathleen. We must ask you not to refer to yourself as Doctor around the younger ones. They might get the idea we condone your actions and wish it for them as well."

She knew that was a concern and made what she was about to ask all that much harder for them to agree to.

Mum spoke up. "We're proud of you and don't want to tell you what to do. You must make your own choices, but we don't want the others encouraged to do the same. You were always strong-minded and strong in your faith. I always believed that you would return home."

Her *dat* cautioned her further about the church leadership being displeased with her actions. Was Noah disapproving of her actions as well? She hoped not.

She took a deep breath. "I have a request to make." Her parents waited for her to continue, and she did. "I need a place to set up my clinic."

Both her parents leaned back stiffly in their seats.

She hurried on before they could turn her down before hearing her plan. "I want permission to build a small clinic in the side yard. You won't have to do anything. I'll get all the materials and organize the building of it."

After her parents stared at each other for a moment, her *dat* spoke. "What about the church leaders?"

She'd hoped to start building before they realized what she was up to, but she could see that wouldn't be possible. "I'll speak to them after the next community Sunday service. But until then, there wouldn't be anything wrong with putting up a small building on the property. I would like to start staking it out tomorrow."

After a moment of silence, *Dat* said, "I suppose it would be all right to stake it out, but nothing more until you get approval."

He'd said *until* and not *if*. He must believe she would get it. *"Danki."*

"And community church is in three days."

Three days? Kathleen had hoped she was returning with more than a week to polish her planned speech to the leaders. But she supposed that was for the best. No point in putting it off. The sooner she got started the sooner she could start helping people. She went up to bed.

Ruby and Jessica, though in bed, were sitting up, waiting for her. She removed her *kapp* and readied herself for bed.

"Tell us all about living in the English world. What was it like going to university?"

"It was very lonely. People go about doing all manner of things and don't have time for others. They stare at their phones all the time, even when they're talking to you. They bustle around at a frenzied rate. I could hardly catch my breath." *Dat* and *Mum* couldn't have issues with that. Nor the bishop. She had told the truth.

"Every day I wanted to be back here with all of you." She flipped the switch on the wall to turn off the light and climbed into bed.

She smiled to herself. How could something like electric lights and electricity make her feel spoiled? After living in the English world for so long, there were some conveniences she didn't want to give up.

She should thank whoever decided solar panels would be a *gut* thing in her Amish community. So many communities didn't allow electricity in any form. Electricity wouldn't distract people from being close to *Gott* but help their lives be easier so they could focus more on Him.

Her eyes popped open in the dark. Those weren't Amish thoughts. *Watch out, Kathleen, or you'll appear too English.* Then Noah *would* disapprove.

Chapter Three

Kathleen woke at five with the image of Noah Lambright at the forefront of her mind. She had been unable to sleep any longer, her nerves on edge. Because she hadn't been around her people for so long, had she grown slack in using careless words? Would she say something inappropriate for her Amish brethren? Would she say something to Noah—or someone else—beyond repair? There seemed to be so many ways she could slip up. *Lord, guard my lips so I don't say anything that will make another stumble in their faith.*

She climbed out of bed, dressed quietly in a green dress and tiptoed downstairs. In the first-floor bathroom, she wrangled her hair and pinned it to the back of her head then pulled on her white *kapp*. She would ask *Mum* if she was putting her hair up right.

Coffee. She required coffee. She put water and grounds in the machine and turned it on. How she'd come to depend on caffeine. Most days, she literally lived on it. She should wean herself down to one or two cups in the morning. For today, she needed to get started right away to rid herself of the caffeine headache already edging its way in. She thanked the Lord again for electricity.

Her first order of business would be to stake out her clinic in the side yard.

As the coffee maker finished filling, *Dat* entered the kitchen. "I thought I heard someone up. I knew it wasn't your *mum*. She'll be down in a minute."

She held up a cup and the carafe. "Want some?"

"Of course."

Kathleen filled the mug and handed it to him. She filled a second cup and set it on the table for *Mum*. Then poured one for herself and added two teaspoons of sugar. Too hot to drink. She breathed in the aroma and could feel the caffeine taking effect already. Was Noah drinking coffee at this moment as well? She dared a small sip of the hot brew. "*Dat*, do you have stakes and string I could use to plan my clinic?"

"In the barn. I'll put them on the front porch along with a hammer after I finish my before-breakfast chores."

A thrill went through her. He hadn't said *ne*. "*Danki*."

Mum came into the kitchen. "I thought I smelled coffee."

Kathleen pointed to the cup on the table. "That one's cooling for you."

"*Danki*, dear." She brought it to her face and inhaled deeply, much as Kathleen had done. Some family ties stayed with a person regardless of time and distance.

Dat swigged down the rest of his coffee. "I'll go milk. Be back soon." He walked out.

She turned to *Mum*. "How does he do that without scalding himself?"

Mum chuckled. "I think he turned his mouth and

throat to leather so many years ago, he can't feel hot or cold anymore. It's a wonder he can taste anything at all." Her mouth exploded into a smile. "I can't believe you're finally home." With her cup still in hand, she stepped forward and hugged Kathleen.

"I can't believe it either."

Mum released her and wiped her own eyes with her fingertips. "I didn't expect you to be up already. I thought maybe you'd sleep in."

Sleep had eluded her most of the night. It had been a long time since a full eight hours was available for her to sleep. Her body wasn't used to it. It would take time, but she would adjust. "I'm not used to staying in bed for more than three or four hours at a time."

"That's awful. How can you function with so little sleep?"

Kathleen raised her cup aloft. "A lot of caffeine."

"Fresh air and hard work will correct that."

Kathleen nodded. But this work would be easy compared to sixteen-and twenty-four-hour shifts on her feet with only the occasional power nap.

"*Mum*, could you show me how to put my hair up right? I'm afraid I've lost my touch, being away so long." Many days, she'd used a plastic claw clip or had her hair looped through a scrunchie under her *kapp*. Things real Amish women would never do, but she'd usually been too pressed for time. Necessity forced her to find shortcuts. But her hair had always been up and covered. She would not be able to take such measures now.

"Of course. But it'll need to wait until after breakfast."

"I don't want Ruby or Jessica to know."

Mum nodded. "With your *kapp* on, it's fine for now."

"Danki."

After breakfast, *Dat* and the boys left to do their work, and *Mum* sent Ruby and Jessica out to the garden. *Mum* grabbed a chair from the table and guided Kathleen to the bathroom. Kathleen sat, facing the mirror.

Mum removed Kathleen's *kapp* and studied her hair. "You've done pretty well. I'll show you how to make it neater." She pulled the hairpins out. Then, with a spray bottle of water and expert fingers, she twisted the front hair to keep the short hairs under control and wound the rest on the back of Kathleen's head.

Kathleen studied each of *Mum*'s actions so she could get it right on her own tomorrow. Whoever heard of a grown woman needing her *mutter* to put up her hair?

Mum replaced Kathleen's *kapp* and patted her shoulders while gazing at her in the mirror. "There you go."

"Do I look like a proper Amish woman now?" Would Noah approve? Why had she thought of him?

Mum smiled. "Very proper. One more thing—and you're going to like this—buttons!" She pointed to the buttons down the back of her own dress. "A couple of years after you left, they were approved as part of the *Ordnung.*"

Kathleen had noticed them but hesitated to say anything. She feared it was one of those things that wasn't quite approved but people did it anyway and others overlooked the infraction. The numerous pins holding her own dress in place poked her sometimes. The one on her left side at her waist was particularly bothersome this morning. She mustn't have gotten it tucked in just right.

"Only white or black buttons. And they must be plain and five-eighths of an inch—no bigger, no smaller."

A long-overdue change. A few women had even

started using them before Kathleen left. She didn't understand why such a specific size. Would half of an inch or three-quarters of an inch be a sin?

She chided herself. There went those stray *Englisher* thoughts again. The wrong size buttons would be a sin only because as a church member, one promised to abide by the *Ordnung*. To go against that promise would be disobedience. And disobedience was sin. She needed to get her thinking straight if she was ever going to have a chance at convincing the leadership to allow her to practice medicine in their community. And then there was Noah. For some reason, his opinion of her mattered almost as much as her family's. Strange.

Think like the Amish. Think like the Amish.

Kathleen pushed thoughts of their handsome neighbor aside.

Mum grabbed a produce basket from beside the door. "Let's go help Ruby and Jessica."

"I was going to stake out my clinic. *Dat*'s put what I need on the porch."

Mum tilted her head. "Can't that wait? Your sisters will want to spend time with you. Get to know you."

Kathleen wanted to get reacquainted with her sisters as well. How much could she really accomplish before she got approval? Not much. Now she was glad church was only a few days off and headed out to the garden with *Mum*. Young plants rose healthily from the dirt.

Ruby worked the row to one side of Kathleen. "Tell me about going to university."

Again with this question. Hadn't her answer last night been sufficient? Kathleen could feel *Mum*'s gaze on her back. "It was very hard work. I never felt as though I was doing things right." Her parents couldn't have issue with that. The truth, yet not encouraging.

Giggling came from down the row Jessica was in.

"What's so funny?" *Mum* asked.

Jessica shook her head.

Kathleen went on. "The professors had particular ways they wanted assignments completed. Other students didn't like it if you got a higher grade than them. Most everyone didn't think I belonged." Most of the time *she* hadn't felt as though she belonged either. In truth, she *hadn't* belonged. *This* was where she belonged, and yet, she felt out of place here as well.

Jessica giggled again.

Mum straightened. "You can't keep all the fun to yourself."

Jessica bit her lip before she spoke. "She has an accent."

Kathleen straightened now. "In *Deutsch*?" She knew she did in English.

Her youngest sister nodded.

She turned to Ruby and *Mum*. Both nodded. Then *Mum* said, "It doesn't matter."

But it did. It would make her stand out. She didn't need more things to give the church leaders reason to question her Amish integrity. Straightening, she determined to eliminate her accent. She'd thought she could easily slip back into this life without effort. Evidently not. Fourteen years *was* a long time to be absent. What else of her Amish life had been whittled away? Had Noah Lambright noticed her accent? Noticed she wasn't completely Amish anymore? Would everyone? She would work extra hard to make sure she once again looked, sounded and acted Amish. And thought like an Amish.

* * *

At midmorning, Noah rode into the Yoders' yard. He wasn't sure why he'd come. He'd just sort of ended up there.

A woman stood in the side yard pounding a stick into the grass with a hammer.

A smile pulled at his mouth.

Kathleen.

She hadn't been a figment of his imagination. He jumped to the ground and tethered his horse. He stood there and watched her.

After tying a string to the top of the stick, she marched with measured steps.

What was she doing?

She pounded another stick into the ground, tied the string around that one, and strode toward a fourth stick already in the ground. Her enclosure was neither a true square nor a rectangle.

He walked over to her. "What are you doing?"

Looking up, she gifted him with a smile. *"Hallo."* She spread her hands out. "This is my clinic."

"You're building it? Yourself?"

"Ja."

"With those string lines?"

"Ja."

How could he tell her she had no clue what she was doing without hurting her feelings? "And what if you don't get permission from the church leaders?"

"Who says I haven't?"

He folded his arms across his chest. "Have you?"

She hesitated, wiggling her lips back and forth. *"Ne.* But I will. So I want to be prepared."

She had no idea how unprepared she was.

"Have you ever constructed a building before?"

"I went to many barn raisings when I was young. And I earned a medical degree. I don't think putting up a few walls will be that hard. Just nail some boards together. I don't need anything fancy."

Construction was so much harder than she realized. Not so much "hard" as there was a lot more that went into putting up a building than *just nailing some boards together*. He pointed with both index fingers. "Your far *wall* is wider than this one by at least a foot." He indicated the closest string. Probably more, but he was being generous.

She turned and studied the lines. "A foot? That won't really matter once I lay the boards down, will it?"

It would matter. A building needed right angles and straight lines to be sturdy. "You may be able to take out a person's appendix, but you should leave construction to others."

Her blue eyes brightened. "Are you offering to help me?"

"Let's wait and see if you get approval."

"I'll get approved."

He liked her self-assurance. "You're sure?"

She took a deep breath and released it. "One minute, I'm confident they will approve. Or why else would *Gott* have sent me away for so long to become a doctor if not for this?" Her self-assurance held a hint of doubt.

"But?"

Her shoulders drooped slightly. "The next minute, I feel all is hopeless. That I wasted the last fourteen years of my life. Years I could have spent here, with my family."

Her conflict was a valid one. The elders might not

give her approval, then the fourteen years would have been for naught. What would she do then? Leave? That thought rankled him. "If *Gott* did send you away for all that time to become a doctor, then pray for Him to make it happen."

"And if it doesn't? What do I do then?"

"Don't make plans for what may not happen. That invites trouble."

"You're right. I should focus on what I have control of. And that's the building for my clinic."

She had less control over that than she imagined.

"Will you help me get my walls straightened out?"

He wasn't sure there was much point but gladly helped her.

After lunch, Kathleen stood at the table rolling out piecrust, her thoughts on Noah and how he'd helped her stake out her clinic. She sensed he believed it might be a waste of time in the end, but that made his lending a hand all that much more sweet. He'd shaved off his beard and looked even more handsome. And available.

Nonsense. She had to stop thinking that way.

The crunch of buggy wheels alerted her that some- one had entered the yard. "*Mum*, you have company."

Mum peered out the kitchen window. "*Ne*, *you* have company."

"Me?" Who would be visiting her? Noah again? Her heart danced at the thought, but it wasn't likely the visi- tor was him. So who could it be? No one else knew she was back. She covered the partially rolled crust with a damp towel, then tucked the other half of the dough under the corner of the cloth as well to keep them from drying out.

She followed *Mum* through the kitchen doorway outside with Ruby and Jessica tagging along. Her breath caught at the sight of her older sister, Gloria, pulling to a stop.

Mum approached the side where a smiling girl, about ten, sat with a one-year-old on her lap. The baby stretched out his arms, and *Mum* scooped him up. Between the girl and Gloria sat a boy of about four. The girl scooted out and helped the boy down.

Gloria sprang from the buggy and wrapped Kathleen in her arms. "You're home. At long last, you're home." She pulled back to look at her. "You've grown up. I still pictured you as the girl who left. But you've come back a woman." She hugged Kathleen again. "How are you?"

Her older sister was a welcome sight. Even though her family hadn't been allowed to write to her, they all seemed happy to have her home. Kathleen smiled. "I'm *gut*. And you?"

"Wonderful." Gloria turned to her children and pointed to the baby. "This is Luke. He's one. Mark is four. Andrew's with his *vater*. He's six." She paused at the girl. "My oldest is ten. I named her after our sister... Nancy."

Kathleen stared at the girl who looked a lot like their sister. Nancy would have been twenty-six, but she'd had an allergic reaction to a bee sting when she was eight. By the time *Dat* had raced into town at ten miles an hour, she'd succumbed to anaphylactic shock.

That was the day Kathleen became determined to be a doctor. Nancy had died needlessly because there was no medical care close at hand.

Kathleen turned to little Nancy. "You look so much like her. I'm pleased to meet you."

The girl stared up at Kathleen. "*Danki. Mutter* and *Grossmutter* say that too."

Mum waved her hand at Nancy and Mark. "There are cookies in the kitchen."

The pair ran into the house with Ruby and Jessica following.

Kathleen turned to Gloria. "Is your Nancy allergic?"

Gloria hooked her arm through Kathleen's. "Fortunately, she's never been stung, but Andrew and Mark have. I've feared for her. But now that you're back, I won't worry so much."

Her sister and the children stayed for a few hours, then left midafternoon to get home in time to prepare supper. She would see them all in two days for the whole community church services.

After Gloria left, *Mum* brushed her hands down her apron and sighed. "Time to get started on our supper."

Kathleen stood from where she'd been sitting on the porch, sewing buttons onto the men's shirts for her *mum*. "What can I do to help?"

"You stay put," *Mum* said. "We have it all in hand." The three went inside, leaving her alone.

She eased back into the rocking chair. She wasn't needed. She'd been gone too long. She didn't fit into the daily routine of the household. Should she go inside and insist on helping? *Ne*. For today, she would enjoy this little bit of solitude. And once she had her clinic up and running, she wouldn't be available as much to help. So it might be best if they didn't get used to her helping in the kitchen.

Movement by the barn caught her attention.

A tricolor Australian shepherd sniffed around an old stump. It wasn't just any dog, but Kaleidoscope. She looked around for Noah but didn't see him. A smidge of disappointment pinched at her. "Kaleidoscope! Here, girl!" The dog charged toward her. "You're supposed to be at home."

The Australian shepherd rolled onto her back, curving head to tail, this way then that. Her tail thumping, kicking up dust.

Kathleen crouched and scratched the dog's belly. She stood and ordered the dog to do the same.

Kaleidoscope flipped to her feet and wagged her tail, causing her whole body to wiggle.

"Come on." Kathleen patted her thigh as she walked around the house to the kitchen door and spoke through the storm door. "Noah Lambright's dog is here again. Do you have a rope so I can walk her back home?"

Mum stood on the other side of the screen. Shaking her head, she reached beside the door and produced a rope. "This is what we usually use to return her. Kaleidoscope, one of these days, we're going to keep you." She opened the storm door and handed Kathleen the rope. "Wait a minute."

Mum disappeared from view, and Kathleen tied the rope around the collar. When *Mum* opened the door, the Aussie raised up on her haunches to receive the tidbit and licked *Mum*'s hand clean.

No wonder the dog kept coming back. She knew where to get treats.

Kathleen started to tell her *mutter* to stop feeding the dog, but a little Amish voice inside her said that was the way they did things here. "I'll be back soon."

Mum called after her. "Invite Noah for supper. With no one to cook for him, I fear he doesn't eat well."

Noah coming for supper? That sent her insides dancing. "He won't be there, hence the reason for his dog being here."

"There's a key under the rock to the left of the back porch. Write a note and leave it on his table."

Enter someone else's home when they weren't there? The English certainly wouldn't do that. She had much to get used to and relearn.

"All right." Kathleen walked up the driveway with Kaleidoscope happily trotting beside her. She'd seen which way Noah'd left the night before and headed that direction. He'd said his farm was next to her parents'. She found herself smiling at the thought of seeing him again. How silly. She wasn't looking for a husband as most single Amish women were. She couldn't afford to. Not if she was going to succeed at becoming a doctor here.

It didn't take long to get there. His house and that of her parents were both on the sides of their respective properties closest to the other. No wonder Kaleidoscope wandered over so easily. She probably thought their property was part of hers as well.

The house was a typical large home ready for a big family, with an even larger barn as well as a *dawdy haus* for his parents. Did he have one or both of them living in the smaller dwelling? Not likely. *Mum* had said he had no one to cook for him, and he hadn't worried about informing anyone last night when he stayed to supper at their house.

She wished her parents had a *dawdy haus*, then she wouldn't have to build a clinic, but then it might be occupied with her *grosseltern*, which would be nice. Both sets of *grosseltern* lived on her parents' older siblings' properties.

A sleek black shepherd and a small corgi trotted up to her and her detainee, all tails swinging at a different tempo. She petted them each in turn.

If Kathleen had any doubts that this was the right place, they were brushed away with the wagging tails. She untied the rope, feeling it safe to free Kaleidoscope to run with her pals, and walked to the barn. "Noah?"

When she got no answer, she crossed the yard to the big house and knocked on the front door. Still no answer, so she headed around to the back and found the key. She turned it over in her hand. It didn't feel right to walk into someone else's home uninvited. She didn't know Noah well enough. This would be an invasion of his privacy. So she replaced the key and sat in a rocking chair on the front porch, hoping he would return soon.

Some time later, she heard her name being called.

"Kathleen?"

"One more minute." She needed just one more minute of sleep before her shift.

"Kathleen?"

That couldn't be a nurse or orderly. They wouldn't call her by her first name. Where was she? She forced her eyes open and focused on the tall, handsome man standing over her. Not medical personnel. Noah! She smiled, then jerked fully awake. "I'm so sorry. I must have dozed off for a minute." She'd learned to sleep anywhere, and her body knew to catch sleep whenever it could.

"Don't worry." He chuckled. "You weren't snoring."

As she pushed to her feet, the rope on her lap slipped to the porch floor. "I didn't sleep much last night." She was used to taking five-and ten-minute naps throughout the day. No more. She would need to teach herself to sleep at night again and stay awake during the day.

He picked up the makeshift leash and offered it to her. "I must say, the last thing I expected to find when I came home was a pretty lady sleeping on my porch."

She took the rope. "You're not going to let me forget this, are you?"

"Probably not."

His smile did funny things to her stomach. And he'd called her pretty. That didn't matter. She had no room in her life for men. One man in particular. She couldn't have a husband and still be a doctor. She'd made that sacrifice years ago. But still, her heart longed.

She held the lead out and teased him back. "Then maybe next time, we'll keep your dog."

"Kaleidoscope?" He shook his head. "I closed her up in the barn. How did she get out? *Danki* for bringing her back. And because you did, I promise not to mention your afternoon nap."

"*Danki.* I'd appreciate that." Then she remembered her reason for staying. "*Mum* has invited you to supper. Shall I tell her you're coming? Or not?"

"I never pass up an invitation from your *mutter.* Let me hook up the trap, and we can head over."

"What time is it?"

"Nearly supper time. I'll be right back." He jogged to the barn.

How long had she slept? Longer than she'd thought, apparently. She hadn't realized the number of things she'd have to get used to again. No chance of slipping back into her Amish life as though she'd never been gone.

Noah returned shortly, leading a horse and the two-wheeled trap he had been driving yesterday. "Kaleido-scope dug her way out. I'll need to figure some other way to contain her. Hopefully, she'll stay put in that stall. I gave her plenty of food and water."

Kathleen climbed into the vehicle. He settled in be-side her, along with the aromas of wood and honey, and put the trap into motion.

"May I ask you a question? Do you hear an accent when I talk?"

He nodded. "It's slight but comes out on certain words. Nothing to worry about."

"But it is. If the church leaders think I've become too English, they might not accept me back."

"How you talk isn't going to get you thrown out or shunned."

"I need them to accept me as the community's doc-tor. I can't have anything they can use against me. I went through a lot of trouble to gain special permission to be able to wear my plain dresses and *kapp* instead of scrubs while working in the hospitals."

"You did?" He sounded surprised.

"Though I haven't joined church, I *am* Amish."

He didn't respond. What did his silence mean? Would everyone meet her declaration of being a doctor for their district and being Amish with silence? She wanted him to approve.

After a moment, he said, "May I ask *you* a question now?"

She smiled.

"Why are you so determined to be a doctor? As you said, you went to a lot of trouble and time away for something that isn't likely to be sanctioned, regardless how you speak."

"I didn't want to leave," she replied. "*Gott* called me to be a doctor. A doctor for our community." She should tell him about Nancy. It would give her practice for speaking to the church leaders.

"My sister was stung by a bee when she was eight. She went into anaphylactic shock. Because medical treatment was too far away, she died before my *dat* could get her to the help she needed. With a simple injection, she would have lived. A simple injection almost anyone could administer."

She hadn't spoken aloud about Nancy in years. Every other time she'd told someone, her eyes flooded with tears and the words lodged in her throat. Not this time. All of her medical training had wrung those emotions out of her. She couldn't help people if she became overwrought.

"I'm sorry about your sister." The sincerity in his tone touched her heart.

"*Danki.* I made a commitment to do all I could to help prevent future senseless deaths."

"I commend you for your determination. So what are you going to do now?"

"I don't know what you mean."

"What's your next step? Other than planning to build a clinic with your own two hands."

"You don't think I can do it?"

"I think your medical degree didn't include a course in construction."

"*Ne*, it didn't. But I think I can manage."

He harrumphed.

"You don't think I'm capable?"

"I think your time would be better spent on other endeavors."

Other endeavors? Like getting married and keeping house and having babies? A longing tugged at her heart. All things she wanted but couldn't have. "I'm going to petition the leadership to give me a trial period. Like they do for testing out the use of new technology in the community. If they can see the benefits for everyone, and people get used to not having to drive all the way into town, then my being the community doctor will be accepted. Then I'll build my clinic that people can come to." She knew in reality that no one would—even if they wanted to—without the leadership's consent. "Until that time, I have my backpack of medical supplies. I'll take it with me wherever I go and help whomever will allow me to."

"Sounds like you have it all figured out."

But she didn't have it all figured out. She still needed to build her clinic. Something she had no clue how to do. Hopefully when she got approval, *Dat* and her brothers would help her. "I've thought about this for over fourteen years. This isn't some fly-by-night thing."

"I can see that."

"I gave up a lot, all those years with our people and more, to learn the skills to help them. I'm going to help our people, whether they like it or not." Then they would see how much they needed her—a doctor in their community—and she would be accepted.

"What about the bishop and church leadership?"

"I'll make them see this is for the *gut* of the community."

"And what if you can't?"

"As you said, don't make plans for what might not happen. I can do this. I know I can. And I'm believing that they are all smart men who will be able to do what is *gut* for everyone." Saying she could convince them and having the actual words that would sway them were two different things. She would go over her arguments for having a clinic and come up with counters for their arguments against. "You probably think all my efforts are going to be wasted, don't you?"

"Let's just say that you have a very steep uphill battle in front of you. And you think more like an *Englisher* than an Amish."

She was afraid of that. And she had an accent to boot. She would talk to *Dat* and *Mum*—when the others weren't around—to straighten out her thinking.

Lord, guide me in what to say and how to get my Amish brothers and sisters to accept me as their doctor. And...let Noah not think poorly of me for my aspirations.

On Saturday, Noah looked up with a start as Bishop Bontrager drove into his yard. He set aside the dog brush and sent Kaleidoscope off, then crossed to the man's buggy as it came to a stop. "I wasn't expecting you."

The bishop didn't get out of his buggy. "I have a favor to ask of you."

"Of course."

"You're close with the Yoders, *ja*?"

"Ja."

"Keep an eye on Kathleen. Let me know if there is anything I need be concerned about."

Spy on Kathleen? "Do you suspect trouble?"

"I don't know. She's been gone a long time. I don't want her stirring things up."

Kind of like Kathleen's plan with being a doctor. Though her intentions weren't to cause trouble but to help. "I'll let you know."

"Danki." Bishop Bontrager drove off.

Noah watched him leave. Should he have told the bishop Kathleen's plans? He didn't feel it was his place at the moment. Kathleen would let the church leaders know her plans soon enough. Tomorrow. For now, he would see how things played out.

The bishop's visit had pulled Kathleen to the forefront of his mind when he'd worked hard to push thoughts of her back. Now with the bishop's request, she would remain front and center. She had to if he was going to keep an eye on her. He liked the idea of keeping an eye on her, but not spying.

Lord, I don't want to spy on her. How can I do as the bishop asks and not feel as though I'm betraying Kathleen or the Yoders?

Chapter Four

The following day, Kathleen climbed out of the buggy last at the Millers' farm. "*Dat*, you'll tell the leaders I wish to speak to them?"

"*Ja*. Don't worry. They'll hear you. But granting you permission will be another issue altogether."

She didn't want to be noticed or singled out. She wanted to blend seamlessly into the throng. But such was not to be the case.

Mum greeted several women who commented on Kathleen's return. Soon a gathering of women crowded around her and her *mutter*. A number of ladies close to Kathleen's age were among the group. She'd gone to school with these girls. Each one had either a small child or two in tow, a baby on their hip or were expecting. Or a combination of the three with older children scattered about. Kathleen wondered what it would be like to be pregnant and have children of her own. But that was not the path the Lord had laid out for her.

Noah popped into her mind, and she sighed. She was a doctor and would be helping each and every one of these women and their children. They all seemed glad to have her back.

Relief swept over Kathleen when people started filing into the house. That was until it was Kathleen's turn to step inside. This was it. She was back.

After a couple of hymns, the bishop stood in front of the community. Bishop Bontrager had been bishop long before Kathleen had left. He was close to the oldest person in their district. "I'm pleased to say that this Sunday is the first class for our young people who want to join church this fall." His voice was still strong. And he still scared her. He was a gruff, strict man. "Those who plan to become church members please stand."

Kathleen stood, pleased she hadn't missed this opportunity. The timing was perfect. The leaders would see she was serious about her faith and returning to the community before she spoke to them of her plans.

Her brother Benjamin stood as well, but not Joshua. He was still young and likely needed another year or two. She was glad Benjamin would be in class with her.

Two others stood as well, a twenty-one-year-old young man and an eighteen-year-old girl and Benjamin, who was twenty. Kathleen, at thirty, felt old. The others were of an average age to join. She tagged along behind everyone following the bishop into the next room. She hadn't wanted to appear pushy, having just returned. She wanted to be respectful of those who had stayed where they belonged.

After eyeing Kathleen for a moment, Bishop Bontrager went over the first three articles of the *Dordrecht Confession of Faith*. These were familiar from her youth. Before long, they rejoined the rest of the congregation.

The church service was so different from the English ones she'd attended while away. At least twice as long, and didn't have the… What was it that was different? Both groups worshipped *Gott*. Both groups sang. Both groups had a message. Maybe the shorter service allowed her to stay focused. And there was an energy among the people. That was it. That's what was different. Which probably had to do with the music. Though the *Englishers* sang hymns, they also sang what they called "praise and worship" songs. Weren't hymns praising and worshipful? They were to Kathleen.

Then there were the instruments. No harmonicas or accordions, and the guitars had been different. They were electric. There was always a keyboard and drums. One church she'd attended had a huge pipe organ. She'd loved to hear it played. She would close her eyes and feel *Gott*'s presence wash over her.

Though she'd enjoyed the diversity in the English churches, she looked forward to the calmer Amish services where she could think and hear *Gott*'s still small voice. The One who had called her away from her people. The One who had sustained her in her studies. The One she couldn't hear now.

She soon learned a bit about Bishop Bontrager's granddaughter who had gone off on *Rumspringa* four years ago and not returned. Kathleen prayed for her.

After service, the bishop excused everyone for their regular cold lunch to be served outside on this sunny day. The bishop called out. "Kathleen Yoder? Please stay behind for a moment."

Her stomach knotted. "Of course." This was it. The church leaders would hear her plead her case.

Dat held back. "Would you like me to stand with you?"

She wanted to say *ja*, but if she was going to stand on

her own as a doctor, she would need to show the leadership she could stand on her own now. "I can do this, *Dat. Danki.*" Besides, she didn't want her *dat* to get in trouble for appearing as though he condoned her actions. It had been enough that he'd asked them to grant her an audience.

The church leaders sat in chairs along the front of the room the service had been held in while she stood, facing them. Most she knew because they were the same ones from before she'd left. Once a church leader, always a church leader. Two were new. One of those quite surprising.

Noah Lambright.

Why hadn't he told her he was part of the church leadership? She had gone on and on about being a doctor and helping their community. And stupidly, she'd believed he was interested. Had he been gathering information for the church leaders to use against her? How naive and foolish of her. Was there any point to even pleading her case? She looked from face to stoic face. Were their minds already made up?

No matter. *Gott* had called her, and she would obey, even if the leadership told her *ne*.

Noah gave her a nod. Was that for encouragement? Or an I-told-you-so gesture?

She took several deep breaths while she waited.

The bishop cleared his throat. "First, I'd like to say on behalf of the whole church leadership, how pleased we are that you've returned where you belong."

She could hear the "but" coming.

"But you have been away a very long time. You have been involved in things you knew went against the *Ord-*

nung and what we believe as a people. We fear you have been corrupted by the *Englishers* and their world."

She wanted to interrupt but knew it would be better to remain silent. Something she'd learned in the English world. To hold her tongue. She would have her chance to speak. She hoped. Or maybe they would simply dismiss her.

Noah leaned forward to look at Bishop Bontrager. "Since she hasn't joined church, she's not under the *Ordnung*."

The bishop inclined his head. "True." He focused his piercing gray gaze on her. "We'll hear you out."

Preacher Hochstetler stood abruptly. "What's the point? Our children get all the schooling they need right here. She willfully went against everything we stand for."

Noah spoke up. "She's technically been on *Rumspringa* all these years."

"But she went to college and got a degree to be a doctor." Preacher Hochstetler again. "She had to know that wouldn't be allowed."

"There is nothing against going to college if you aren't a church member," Deacon Zook said.

"But she expects to be a doctor! Here! That can never be!" Preacher Hochstetler slammed his fist onto his opposite palm.

He really needed to calm down.

Noah sat with his head down, shaking it. Was that directed at her? She hoped it was meant for Preacher Hochstetler.

Bishop Bontrager held a hand up. "Please sit back down."

Preacher Hochstetler's face had turned red. He sat and scowled at her.

The bishop went on. "*Danki.* I said we'd hear her out."

"It's a waste of time," Preacher Hochstetler mumbled.

"No more!" The bishop glared at the man. He took several breaths, then turned back to Kathleen. "You have our attention for fifteen minutes. Then you'll leave, and we'll discuss the matter."

Noah gave her an encouraging nod.

Grateful for the chance, she unfolded the piece of paper with her notes.

"What is the reason the children of the Amish don't go to school past eighth grade? Because the jobs they might get could take them away from the community. But that is not the case for me. I went to university and beyond so that I could return to help our people. I never intended, nor do I now intend, to remain in or return to the English world. Many of our men have been forced to take jobs outside our community to support their families because farmland is becoming more scarce."

She took a deep breath and continued. "I became a doctor to come back and help our community. We go to *English* doctors all the time, take *English* medicine, stay in *English* hospitals. But what if we didn't have to go to them for everything? What if the money we pay them could stay in our community? What if we could be less dependent on them?" After all, wasn't that the basis for a lot of the rules in the *Ordnung*? Not being dependent on the outside world. Being as self-sufficient a society as possible. That was getting harder and harder as men were forced to take jobs outside the community to support their families.

"We keep ourselves separated from the outside world. We don't drive their cars. We don't connect to their utilities. We don't go to their churches. So why the connection to their medical facilities? Because we don't have the education to be our own doctors."

She searched each face for support. "When my sister Nancy was eight, she was stung by a bee. A normal part of being a child. Who here has been stung by a bee?" She paused in hopes that the men would raise their hands.

Only Noah did. But when he realized no one else did, he lowered his. Peer pressure was great in the community. It was one of the ways people were made to conform.

She gave him a tight smile of appreciation. "One percent of children and three percent of adults are allergic to bee stings. My sister was in that one percent. Because treatment was an hour's buggy ride away, she died when a simple injection could have saved her life if gotten to her soon enough. I watched my little sister die. How many others in our community have died needlessly? Women in childbirth? Men with heart attacks? Others with treatable conditions? Don't let pride of adhering to the past allow our people to die when we can prevent it."

Silence hung heavy in the room. Stiflingly so.

She shouldn't have accused them of pride.

The bishop offered a solution. "If you, as an *Englisher*, were to set up a clinic in the midst of our community, our people would be allowed to see you as a doctor."

"An *Englisher*? But I'm Amish."

Bishop Bontrager leaned forward. "Not yet, you're not. You haven't joined church. And when you do— if you do—you will be under the *Ordnung* and must obey the rules, which don't include being a doctor." He folded his arms.

"But I've started the classes. Today. I want to join church. I always planned to join church."

"Then you shouldn't have stayed away so long and done so many things that go against our *Ordnung*."

"So if I join church, I won't be allowed to help our people? I don't understand why not."

Bontrager continued. "If we sanction your behavior, then others will go off and try the same kinds of thing. Then our society will fall apart, and we'll have chaos. *All* our beliefs we've held to for hundreds of years could fall apart if we sanction *your* actions."

"But we all go to *Englisher* doctors. If an *Englisher* doctor converted to Amish, would you let him practice medicine to our people?"

"That would be different."

She could see no difference. "Couldn't you tell our people that I'm allowed to help them, but if anyone else tried to do what I did, they would not be allowed?"

"I'm sorry. That would be like talking out of two sides of the mouth. It would confuse people on right and wrong."

She was sorry too. Maybe they would feel differently if one of their family members or themselves were to need her expertise. She locked gazes with the bishop. "You said you'd discuss this before making a decision."

"That's right. We have all we need from you. *Danki*."

"In your discussion, keep in mind that you've allowed solar panels and buttons. I'm just asking for the same consideration and chance. A trial period to see if this is *gut* for our community." She knew it was *gut* for the community.

"There's no point in discussing this. She can't be allowed to do this." The ill-tempered preacher's face was red again, and he breathed heavily.

Was he having a heart attack? She rushed forward. "Let me check you."

He thrust out his arm. "Don't touch me."

She froze two feet from the glaring man. She couldn't believe he didn't want help. "Take slow, deep breaths." She took the breaths, willing him to breathe and bring down his obviously elevated blood pressure.

Noah waved her off.

She took a few steps backward.

The bishop motioned toward the door.

She glanced at Noah before she turned and left. She'd said all she could think to say. Any more might kill Preacher Hochstetler.

Why couldn't he accept help? He could be having a stroke or heart attack right now. Would he truly rather die than allow her to assess him? So different from the English world.

Noah left quickly at the conclusion of the meeting to find Kathleen.

Everyone was either gathered around the tables set out with food or seated at the other tables, eating.

He couldn't pick Kathleen out of the crowd. She wasn't among them. Had she gone home? Certainly not. That would be too far to walk.

His *vater* strolled up to him. "You look worried, son. Did you have the dream again?"

Noah took a deep breath to focus on his *vater*. He had had the dream. "How could you tell?"

"When you live with someone their whole life, you can tell. Did you catch up to her this time?"

He meant Noah's *mutter*. *"Ne."* It was always the same, following after his *mutter*, trying to catch her to bring her home. Though the setting changed—the barn, town, Sunday service at someone else's farm—the outcome was always the same. His *mutter* turned a corner and Noah hurried after her. But when he went around the building, she was gone. Always gone.

But this time had been different. His *mutter* still disappeared, but an Amish woman stood with her back to him. He didn't know who she was and stared at her back.

In the beginning, he'd had the dream about his *mutter* every night. Over the years, it had tapered off to once or twice a month. And now thrice in as many nights.

"One of these times, maybe you'll catch her. Ask her that question burning in your heart. Unfortunately, you won't get the answer you seek from your dream." His *vater* walked off.

Noah knew that. Because nowhere in his mind did he know why his *mutter* had left. Maybe that was the reason he could never catch up to her. Maybe the dream was telling him that he would never find the answer to his question. His *vater* seemed as anxious for Noah to catch up to her as Noah was himself.

But his *vater* was right. Noah would never know the answer to his question from his dreams. He needed to stop looking back and focus on the future. But what was before him? Everything he'd cared about was in his past. What lay ahead of him except work and loneliness?

Kathleen.

Kathleen?

Noah pushed the remaining thoughts of his *mutter* out of his head and resumed his search for Kathleen. He caught a glimpse of a red dress on the other side of a huge oak tree trunk on the far side of the yard. He approached. "Why aren't you eating?"

She sucked in a breath as she whirled toward him. "I'm sorry for startling you."

"I didn't think anyone knew where I was. How is Preacher Hochstetler?"

She was thinking of others rather than herself. Someone who was against her plan to help. Admirable. "He's calmed down. I think he'll be fine."

"He should have his blood pressure checked. I was afraid he was going to have a heart attack or a stroke."

"You really do have a doctor's heart. You truly want to help people."

"Of course I do." She shook her head. "Why didn't you tell me you're part of the church leadership? I feel so foolish going on and on about my dreams of building a clinic and of being a doctor."

"Don't be." He'd liked hearing about her dreams and plans.

"Was that your task? To find out about me and report back to the others?"

He opened his mouth to say *ne* even though that was exactly what the bishop had asked of him, but his words were cut off by a high-pitched scream.

Kathleen rushed past him and headed toward the gathering of people and the sound of wailing. Noah followed close behind.

She pressed into the crowd. "Let me through. I'm a doctor."

People with surprised expressions shifted aside for her.

Noah peered over Kathleen's shoulder.

Martha Phillips knelt beside her nine-year-old son, Isaac, who had a half-inch-diameter stick protruding from his thigh.

The boy thrashed about. "Get it out! Get it out! It hurts! It hurts so much!" He reached for the stick.

Kathleen dropped to her knees and grasped the boy's wrist. "Don't touch it." She turned to her brother Joshua. "Get my medical pack from the buggy."

Joshua looked to his *vater*, who nodded his consent. The young man ran off.

Still holding the boy's wrist, she commanded, "Hold him still."

Simon Phillips jerked his son free from Kathleen's grasp. "Get away from my son."

"I'm a doctor. I can help him."

"*Ne!* Don't touch him," Simon growled. "He's my son, and I'll say what's to be done for him."

Kathleen stared at the man as she withdrew her hands, then spoke in a soft voice. "But I can help him."

She sounded so hurt.

Simon ignored her.

Martha stared at her husband. "What will we do?"

Kathleen seemed to steel her resolve with a deep breath. "Move him very carefully to your buggy and get him into town as fast as you can."

Noah chuckled to himself. She was going to help no matter what.

Simon focused on his son. "This is going to hurt. Be brave."

The boy nodded, tears wetting most of his face.

Simon gripped the stick.

Noah held his breath to brace against the boy's pain.

Kathleen lunged forward. "*Ne!* Don't pull it out. Leave it in. Let a doctor remove it."

Noah held her back by thrusting his arm in front

of her. "Stay out of this." He couldn't allow her to go against the *vater*'s wishes for his son.

Simon narrowed his eyes at her, then stared at the stick.

Kathleen tilted her head back to look up at Noah. "Do something."

It wasn't for him to interfere, so he prayed instead. "All we can do now is trust *Gott*."

Kathleen unbuttoned her white apron *Mum* had helped her make and held it out to Martha. "When he pulls the stick out, press this on the wound quickly. Firm pressure."

Martha's hand lifted but went back down when her husband shook his head.

"Please let her take this."

Simon shook his head again and yanked the stick out.

Isaac screamed, then fainted. Blood oozed from the tear in the boy's trousers.

Kathleen shook her apron at Martha. "Take it. Please."

This wasn't right. The boy needed help and Kathleen knew what to do.

Martha knew she must obey her husband, so she removed her own black apron, folded it hastily and pressed it to her son's wound.

Kathleen jerked her head back and forth. "We need something to keep the cloth in place."

Noah removed his suspenders and handed them to Martha. "Tie this around his leg and the apron."

Simon accepted the suspenders and did as Noah instructed. As long as it hadn't been Kathleen to offer the item that was needed, it was all right to accept it. How hypocritical.

Noah accompanied Kathleen as she followed the

three men carrying the boy to the Phillipses' buggy, where two other men had hitched up their horse. "Keep pressure on it the whole time. Don't let up."

Martha nodded to Kathleen and climbed into the back of the buggy with her son.

As the buggy pulled away with another one in pursuit, the rest of the people gathered in a huge cluster with bowed heads. Different people called out prayers for Isaac.

Noah prayed silently for the boy and then for Kathleen that she could accept whatever the outcome of today was. That she'd done all she could under the circumstances. He wanted to take her into his arms and let her know everything would be all right. But that would be wholly inappropriate, and he didn't know if everything would be all right. Poor Isaac could die.

And Kathleen's heart would be broken. She would have to live with the knowledge that she could have saved the boy but was refused that opportunity because of pride. He prayed that his people would abandon their pride and allow Kathleen to do what she was trained for.

By late in the afternoon, there was still no word on how Isaac fared. Kathleen helped load her family's dishes into their buggy.

Noah approached her *vater*. "Your buggy's already full. May I take Kathleen in mine?"

Dat stilled his hands from hitching up the horse.

Kathleen willed her *dat* to say *ne*. She didn't want to sit in Noah's buggy. Not after learning of his deception. She shook her head.

Dat said, "You'll take her straight home?"

"*Ja.* We'll travel directly in front of you."

"Very well," *Dat* said.

Noah escorted her to his waiting buggy, keeping one hand on the waist of his suspenderless trousers. Though *Englishers* rarely ever wore them, she'd already gotten used to the Amish men wearing them. So, to see Noah without his looked odd.

She climbed into his open two-wheeled trap without his help. Did he not have a proper enclosed buggy? "I would have preferred to ride with my family."

He settled in beside her and took up the reins. "I could tell."

"Then why force me to ride with you?"

"I need to talk to you."

"Why didn't you tell me? About being part of the leadership?"

He clucked the horse into motion. "I never really thought about it. Everyone knows who the church leaders are, so I don't go around announcing it to everyone I come in contact with. It never crossed my mind you didn't know. But now that I think about it, unless your parents told you, you wouldn't know. And they obviously hadn't told you."

He was right. Her parents could have told her. But that wasn't something people talked about. And she had been back for only a few days. "I suppose it's reasonable that it wouldn't have come up."

"So am I forgiven?" He turned onto the road.

She knew *Englishers* who withheld forgiveness for weeks, months or even years. She didn't want to freely forgive, but harboring animosity wasn't the Amish way. "Forgiven."

"*Danki.* You asked if I had been tasked with garnering information from you."

That had been the worst of finding out his position. "I don't want to know. I feel foolish enough."

"Though the bishop asked me to keep an eye on you, he didn't ask me to find out about you."

"Isn't that the same thing?"

"I don't believe so. Finding out about you would be to gather information and report back to him. Keeping an eye on you was just that. Seeing that your transition home wasn't complicated."

That surprisingly made her feel better.

"It was *Gott* who set me on the road that day you were walking home. I was intrigued when I found out you were Kathleen Yoder. I couldn't imagine any Amish man—let alone a woman—doing what you did."

He seemed impressed. At least she had that.

"Though I wasn't tasked to get information on you, I have been tasked to tell you the outcome of the leadership."

"Don't bother. I can guess what they decided. When one nearly kills one of the members, the answer is a given." She would have to figure out a different way to help her people. One that didn't strictly go against the leadership. A way that people felt they could come to her for help without being disobedient.

"Because you told me of your hopes and dreams of being a doctor to our community and helping people, I was able to convince the others to allow you to set up a clinic through the summer until you join church in the fall."

"Of course—" She jerked toward him. "What? You did?"

He nodded.

She couldn't believe it. They had approved. She would have liked the trial period to be longer, at least a year, but she'd take what she could get. She sighed. A clinic of her own. Then reality set in. "That doesn't give me much time to build my clinic." If she had help, it could be done in no time. However, if she had to do all the work herself, her trial would be over before she was even finished. Therefore, their approval might mean nothing.

"I have a *dawdy haus* sitting empty."

Had she understood his meaning correctly? "You would let me use it?"

"*Ja*. And setting up on the property of a leader will let people know you have permission. They are more likely to come to you."

Kathleen couldn't believe this. She was going to get her clinic after all, and much sooner than she'd anticipated. "Because you're the one who convinced them to give me a chance, did you *have* to offer your *dawdy haus*?"

"The opposite. Because I offered the place, they agreed to the trial. But you are not to treat anyone nor their children without their consent."

She could abide by that. People would soon see the benefits to her helping them. "Why are you doing this for me? You hardly know me."

He was silent for a minute. "Since my wife and daughter died in childbirth, I've often wondered if I'd called for an ambulance sooner when the midwives first suspected there might be a problem, if my family would have lived. If there had been a trained doctor close at hand, would they have lived? If I'd driven her to the hospital as soon as her labor started, would they have lived?"

Kathleen's heart ached. She didn't want to know the cause of death, because then she would know if there might have been a possibility to save them. And if she knew, she would feel obligated to tell him. He didn't need to carry around the kind of heartache and burden she did for her sister. "I'm so, so sorry for your loss. No words ever make the ache go completely away."

"Most people don't understand that. They go on as though nothing happened and that person never lived to begin with. That hurts as much as their absence."

He understood. He truly understood. How many others who had suffered losses needed someone to tell them that they truly understood? Instead of words of platitudes to placate the grieving.

"Life never goes back to normal. You have to discover a new kind of normal. One that never feels quite right without your loved one. A new way of going about living with part of you missing."

"No one else understands that." He turned into her driveway.

Home already? "I think maybe some people do, but we Amish don't talk about it because we either think we're not supposed to, or more often, we don't know how."

"What time shall I come by in the morning to pick you up?"

"Pick me up for what?" Had she agreed to go somewhere with him and forgotten?

"So you can get set up in the *dawdy haus.*"

"I'll walk over. Let me talk to *Dat* and *Mum* about it first."

"I'll tell them so I can let your *vater* know the leadership's decision." He tethered the horse and walked her inside.

All too soon, he left. During the short buggy ride home, she'd gone from not wanting to be near Noah, to not wanting to be parted from him.

It was a *gut* feeling. But was it wise?

Chapter Five

The following morning, Kathleen gathered her medical pack and the basket of baked goods *Mum* was sending to Noah. The man would never go hungry so long as her *mutter* was near. She trekked the half mile next door. An excitement danced through her at the prospect of seeing Noah again so soon. What was she thinking? The excitement must be for setting up her clinic. But no doubt about it, seeing Noah was exciting too.

He'd phoned later last night to let them know that Isaac Phillips's leg was stitched up, and he'd returned home. That had relieved Kathleen's apprehension over the boy's injury and allowed her to sleep. For nearly a full five hours.

Though she didn't see Noah in the yard, Kaleidoscope bounded up, scattering chickens, and flipped to her back, wiggling from side to side. Kathleen scratched the dog's tummy. The other two dogs quickly joined their young pal, so she gave them attention as well. But where was Noah? Disappointment sank inside her that he wasn't there to greet her.

Giving each dog one last pet, Kathleen laughed. "All right. Enough." She stood. "I have work to do."

The dogs scampered off but not far.

She should go to the house to locate Noah first, but eagerness to see her soon-to-be clinic sent her toward the *dawdy haus*. She crossed the yard and onto the porch with her three new friends tagging along, tails wagging. Her clinic would be up and running in no time, and she would soon have patients flooding to see her. As well as having chairs inside, she would line the porch with them so her patients could wait out in the fresh air.

The little sunshine-yellow house had solar panels on the roof. *Gut.* There would be electricity. Maybe she could talk Noah into letting her install a telephone. Then people could call so she could go to them if they couldn't come to her. People shouldn't have to go without medical treatment because they couldn't travel to her. House calls were a thing of the past in the *Englisher* world. But not so for her Amish brethren. She would need to get herself a buggy.

Stepping up to the door, she peered in the window.

Noah's smiling face appeared on the other side of the glass.

With a gasp, she jerked back. That hadn't been expected.

Noah opened the door. "*Guten Morgen.* You're here. Come in."

She stared at him for a moment before stepping inside the typical *dawdy haus*. A love seat sofa and a couple of recliner rocking chairs occupied the living room that was open to the dining area, which was part of the kitchen. She would need to rearrange things to be more suitable for a doctor's office waiting room. But she wanted to keep the homey feel rather than an institutional one. Over all, it would work nicely.

He took her medical pack and set it on the kitchen table. He gazed at the basket. "What's that?"

Kathleen smiled and held out the basket. "My *mum* sent you some food. She seems to think you never eat unless she cooks for you."

He smiled. "I must admit she cooks a whole lot better than I do."

Of course, being on his own, he had to do all his own cooking. He had no one to help him. "How many other rooms are there?"

"A bathroom, pantry and two bedrooms. One is quite small."

"That will be perfect." One could be her examination room and the other her office to keep supplies and records locked up in.

"Let me know what furniture you want moved out as well as what else you might need."

She hadn't thought until now what she might need beyond what was in her medical pack. First, what to use for an examination table. One of the beds would be too low and a table, though high enough, wouldn't be long enough.

He interrupted her planning. "What are you thinking?"

She turned to him. "Trying to decide what to use for an examination table."

"I can build you a long, narrow table. Just give me the dimensions."

How thoughtful of him to ask. "I want it about this high. And this long."

He blinked at her as though waiting for her to say more.

"What?"

"The numbers. I can't build something with only *this high* and *this long* to go by. I need measurements."

"I don't know. How high is this?" She held her hand about hip high.

He unclipped a measuring tape from the waist of his trousers. "How high again?" She held up her hand while he measured.

When he clipped the tape measure back onto the waist of his trousers, she asked, "Aren't you going to write down the numbers?"

"*Ne.* I've got them."

Interesting. It was probably like her remembering medication dosages.

His face suddenly brightened. "Hold on. I have something for you. I'll be right back." He left.

He would build her a table? He was already doing so much. Why hadn't she considered all the equipment and supplies she would need in her doctor's office? The clinics she'd worked in had all the equipment and supplies already. She always pictured her clinic fully stocked but had no idea how it all got there. Most things would need to wait.

Returning, he held a three-foot by one-foot board. "It's not finished. It still needs to be stained and the letters painted."

He flipped the board around. Carved into the oak was *The DR. KATHLEEN Clinic.*

She touched it gingerly. "You carved this for me?"

"*Ja.*"

She gazed at him in appreciation. He must have been a fine husband to his wife. And he'd make another woman a fine husband in the future.

Her parents knew him well and liked him. Her brothers and sisters treated him like a brother, not just a spiritual one but an earthly brother as well.

She needed to stop looking at him with eyes that might want more than friendship. For he could never be anything more than a friend to her. She would never have a husband. The thought saddened her. Moreover, thinking of him with a wife felt as though the stick that had stabbed Isaac in the leg was jammed in her chest.

"When did you do this? The leaders decided only yesterday."

"Last night. With no one else here, I have a lot of spare time. I like to keep busy in the evenings so I don't think about…things I shouldn't."

"Oh, don't ever feel as though it's wrong to remember your wife and child. Even though gone from this world, they're still a part of you."

He shifted from one foot to the other.

She'd made him uncomfortable talking about his lost family.

He tipped the sign back and forth. "Do you like it?"

How touching. "It's beautiful. I can't believe you made this for me."

"People need to know this is an official clinic. And that they can start coming by. What else are you going to need to open your clinic?"

"I could come up with a whole list of things. But I'll have to get by with what I have in my pack for now."

"Make a list of everything you might need, and I'll see what I can gather up."

"You don't have to do that. You've already done so much." His kindness and generosity touched her deeply.

"If your clinic is going to be a success, it needs to

look like a clinic and be able to meet people's needs." He opened a drawer and pulled out a legal pad and pen. He set them on the table and pulled out a chair. "Write down as many things as you can think of, and while we rearrange things, you can add to it."

"You're going to help me move stuff around?"

"I certainly don't expect you to move the furniture by yourself."

"That's so nice of you."

"Well… I… It's my reputation on the line too. If your clinic doesn't do well, it will be a very long time before I would be able to convince the others to consider anything new."

She hadn't thought about what this meant for him by standing up for her. If she failed, would the others shun him? "If this could get you in trouble, maybe I should find somewhere else."

"Nonsense. I've already committed this place. If you back out now, it would be the same as admitting defeat and failing."

"I never meant to put you in jeopardy, only myself."

"You didn't put me in jeopardy. I volunteered."

She stared at him in disbelief.

"If your being a doctor here can prevent a tragedy like Rachel and our baby's or like your sister, then this will all be worth it. You didn't endure the hardship of being away for fourteen years and working your way through medical school to give up now, did you?"

She shook her head.

"You're going to face a lot more opposition than you did yesterday before you're accepted as a doctor here."

More opposition? "But the leadership approved this. Didn't they?"

"*Ja*, but that won't stop some from discouraging others not to come to you or allow you to treat their families."

This wasn't going to be a simple trial period where people would come and test out having a doctor close at hand. She was going to have to endure the ridicule and scathing glares like she did in medical school and her residencies. Her battle was far from over. She'd thought the hardest part was behind her, but maybe it had just begun.

"Now, sit and make your list."

She sat and wrote down *chairs*. Then she looked at the living room to see how many she thought she should add there. Then she pictured the porch lined with chairs. She wouldn't need the porch *lined* with them. Three or four should be sufficient. In truth, for the number of people who would actually come, just the chairs she could fit in the living room would be sufficient. If she was honest with herself, the current furniture in the living room would be sufficient. With seats to spare.

Was there even any point? Why do all the rearranging and setting up of the clinic if no one would come? It could be a lot of work for nothing.

She stared at the mostly blank yellow paper, overwhelmed by the simple task and everything associated with it.

Noah glanced down at the paper. "Chairs. How many?"

She felt like saying zero but didn't want Noah to know how discouraged she was. "These four table chairs should be enough to add to the living room."

"What about the porch? People might like to wait outside when it's nice."

Matching up in their thinking made her heart happy.

"That would be nice. If you have any extra. But if not, that's fine. I'm sure what's in the living room will be sufficient at first."

He nodded. "What else?"

She didn't even want to think of it all. "Well, the only other things, you wouldn't be able to get."

"Like what?"

"Medical supplies."

He pointed to the paper. "Write them all down so we can work on getting them." When she hesitated, he said, "Write down exam table. Then when I have it done, you can check it off. It always feels *gut*, like you've accomplished something, when you can check it off a list."

She wrote down exam table, sheets to cover it with for each new patient, tongue depressors, gauze, file folders for patient records...

With each new item, she thought of two more. The list became easier and easier to build.

Noah took her list. Most items would need to be purchased. He hitched up his larger covered buggy and drove Kathleen into town.

He liked working alongside her. Not only was she intelligent, but she wasn't looking at him as a potential husband. Too many of the young women hoped he would court them. He'd had a few *vaters* approach him and young ladies who weren't as subtle as they might have thought they were being. Even the others in the church leadership had come right out and said he needed to marry again. But unless *Gott* directed him to take another wife or the leadership *ordered* him to, he would remain contentedly single. He'd had enough pain to last him a lifetime.

So working with Kathleen suited him fine. More than suited him. It pleased him.

In town, he parked near the chain drugstore. It was large enough to have most of the nonprescription items they needed: gauze, tape, Band-Aids, over-the-counter medications, tongue depressors and such. She could get small quantities to start out with, then order more online. He didn't know what the procedure was for a doctor to order controlled medications, but Kathleen would know. He helped her out of the buggy.

Then he saw the woman at the end of the block watching him. The woman from his dream. His *mutter*.

She ducked her head and disappeared around the corner.

How many times had he seen her in town and ignored her? Unlike in his dream, he always pretended she wasn't there. Never pursued her in real life. However, this time, he had the impulse to go after her. Keeping his attention on the corner, he spoke to Kathleen. "I have something I need to do. I'll meet you inside." He took off down the street.

From behind him, Kathleen said weakly, "All right."

He hurried to the corner.

Gone.

Just like in his dream. He glanced around but couldn't see her anywhere. Probably for the best. What would he have said if he'd caught up to her? He headed back and entered the drugstore.

Kathleen's arms brimmed with supplies.

He grabbed a cart and met up with her. "Put them in."

She dropped them into the cart. "*Danki*. I can't get very much, so I thought I could carry it all. I'm ready to go pay."

He stared into the cart. One roll of gauze, one of bandage tape, a box of Band-Aids, one bottle of rubbing alcohol, one of hydrogen peroxide, some antibiotic ointment and a bottle of ibuprofen. "You need more than this to run a clinic."

"That's all I can get today."

Meaning that was all she could afford. "I'll buy what you need."

She shook her head. "I couldn't let you do that. I have some supplies in my pack."

Not enough to run a clinic. He could stand here and argue with her, or he could use the time more wisely by filling the cart. He grabbed duplicates of most of the items she already had and several things she didn't.

"What are you doing?" she asked.

"Shopping." He went down another aisle and added several more items.

She stopped in front of the cart and put a hand on it. Her steady blue eyes locked on his. "I know what you're doing. I can't let you buy all this for my clinic. You have already done so much. I will not take advantage of your kindness and generosity."

He had the urge to just stare at her but knew he shouldn't, so he took a slow breath before replying. "You are not taking advantage of me. Think of this as me investing in the future of our district."

"But—"

"You can't actually stop me." He smiled. "Let me do this." It would make up for allowing her to think he was helping her to spare his own reputation. In reality, he *wanted* to help her succeed. Something deep inside him *needed* to help her.

She sputtered several incoherent syllables before

ceasing and drooping her shoulders in defeat. She was more beautiful than ever, standing there all flustered.

He paid for everything, even the items she'd put in first.

Out at his buggy, he glanced around for the woman again. He didn't see her.

He took Kathleen to a couple other stores and a medical supply store so she could establish relationships with them.

On the ride home, Kathleen twisted her hands in her lap. "*Danki* for all the supplies. I feel foolish having to accept so much help. If you need any medical treatment, it'll be on the house. You never have to pay for any visits."

"I'm glad to help." Very glad.

It did his heart *gut* to be doing something for someone else. Not because he had to, like a barn raising or because the bishop asked him to—he was always glad to help—but because he *didn't* have to. This was completely voluntary.

Kathleen deserved someone on her side. And he wanted to be that person.

Chapter Six

Later in the week, Noah entered the *dawdy haus*. Grunting noises came from one of the bedrooms. What was going on? He went to investigate and couldn't have anticipated the scene he would find.

Kathleen stood with the mattress on end, wrestling with it. The mattress swayed this way and that. *"Ne, ne, ne,"* she muttered. "Don't be so difficult."

What took place next happened fast. The mattress seemed to heave itself in an attempt to throw Kathleen to the floor and pin her there.

"Whoa! Oh, *ne!*" One of Kathleen's feet lifted as though to balance herself and the mattress, but her effort failed.

Noah rushed into the room, grabbed the mattress and leaned it back on its end against the bed frame.

Kathleen tottered with the absence of the weight.

Noah gripped her arm to steady her. "Are you all right?"

"Ja." She breathed heavily from her battle. *"Danki.* I thought it was going to trap me."

No wonder. She was so small. The mattress probably weighed more than her. What had she been thinking?

"You should have waited for me."

"I thought I could slide it into the other room."

He realized he still held on to her arm. He should let go but didn't want to.

Her eyes widened. *"Ne!"*

Before he could ask what the problem was now, something soft and large struck from behind, falling against him. The mattress. It pushed him forward, and he in turn pushed Kathleen backward. He threw out his hands to keep from crushing her against the wall, and his palms smacked the solid surface. His face lingered inches from hers.

He didn't move.

She didn't move.

Each stared at the other. Oddly, he didn't feel uncomfortable with the closeness. She didn't seem to either. Her blue eyes studied him.

And he studied her. He should probably move but made no effort to do so. She also made no effort to get out of this awkward, compromising situation.

Then all of a sudden, giggles burst out of her. A sweet tingling sound that warmed him and sent shivers over his skin. Kathleen should laugh often.

He had to laugh too. "What's so funny?"

She pointed behind him. "This mattress seems to have a mind of its own."

"So it does."

"I thought it was just being difficult for me, and had something against me. But it seems you have fared no better with it."

"Ne, I haven't." But he *had* fared very well at being

so near to her. If the mattress were a person, he would need to thank it for creating such a predicament. He really should move now. Standing this close any longer would soon become awkward. He gazed at her like a man who might contemplate marrying again. Which *he* definitely would not. Ever. No matter how many times the church leaders brought up the subject. He wouldn't put himself through that kind of pain again. He knew men who had been widowed two and three times and still married again. He could never do that. Could he?

He pushed against the mattress with his back and removed one hand from the wall. "I'll let you get clear before I attempt to move this thing."

She laughed again. She definitely needed to do that more. She scooted out of the way.

But she seemed like she was reluctant to do so.

He gave the mattress a shove at the same time he spun around to catch it. Gripping the sides, he hoisted it up and carried it into the living room. "Would you get the door?"

Kathleen did. "Where are you taking that to?"

"The big house. I'll store it in one of the rooms there. Unless you want it in the other bedroom in case someone is ill and needs to lie down."

She shook her head. "I doubt a bed would fit. The other room will be my exam room. With the table, supplies and people in there, it will be stuffed. So to the big house it is. I'll go with you and open the front door."

That wasn't necessary. He could easily enough lower the mattress and then pick it up again. However, he wasn't about to turn her down. "Lead the way."

Outside the *dawdy haus*, he hoisted the mattress onto his head and balanced it there. He watched Kathleen stroll across the yard in front of him, all three dogs at her heels. Such a tiny woman. She ascended the porch steps as though she were floating. How did she do that? She opened his front door and moved aside.

"Danki." He shifted the mattress down and entered. He didn't want her to leave and go back to the *dawdy haus* without him. "Would you get the one upstairs?"

"Ja." She slipped in and trotted up to the second floor.

He followed.

"Which room?"

"The last one on the right."

She opened it, then stepped back out of his way.

When he set the mattress against the wall and turned around, his heart sank. She'd left. Probably gone back. But when he went downstairs, he found her waiting by the open front door.

She gazed at him expectantly. "Would you help me with the mattress in the other room?"

He smiled. "Of course. And with the frames. And any other furniture you need removed from the *dawdy haus.*" He'd gladly help her all day if she needed him to.

After a long morning of moving furniture, Kathleen went about scrubbing the house, top to bottom. She needed a fairly sterile environment.

Noah had gone about his farm chores. She missed his presence. He'd been absent for the last hour. A couple of times when she peeked out the window, she saw him on a ladder against his house. She couldn't figure out what he'd been fiddling with. She had to stop looking for him and wondering where he was every minute.

A thump on the outside of the *dawdy haus* startled

her. Then a drill boring into the siding. The sound of electrical tools and appliances still sounded odd. She wasn't sure she liked them. So much noise.

She laughed to herself. Compared to the *Englisher* world, this was silence. Never a moment's peace in the outside world. She'd fondly anticipated returning to the quiet of her community. But she did like electricity. She couldn't have it both ways.

She could understand why some Amish resisted new things and change. Electricity meant more noise and a faster pace of life. She hadn't felt as though she'd gotten to slow down to the previous leisurely pace of life from before she left. She supposed that was gone. Gone forever. How sad. A part of her longed to have the unhurriedness back. But would she be willing to sacrifice electricity to have it? Probably not, now that it was here.

Noah came inside and nodded to her.

She caught herself smiling at him. "What are you doing?"

He gave her half of a smile in return. "You'll see. No peeking." He pointed. "Wait on the porch."

She folded her arms. "Are you kicking me out of my own clinic?"

He folded his arms with a cordless drill in one hand and a screwdriver in the other. "Your clinic, but my *dawdy haus*. Do you want a surprise or not?"

She did. He seemed almost giddy with his secret. "Will it take long?"

"If you keep detaining me? *Ja*."

She huffed a breath and stepped out onto the porch. What could it possibly be?

The dogs lay sprawled in the shade on the porch. Kaleidoscope lifted her head but didn't get up. The other two only rolled their eyes in her direction. All three probably wondered if it would be worth the effort to get up on the off chance she would pet them. Maybe later.

She settled into the rocking chair Noah had brought over from the big house's porch. She could use a break anyway. Leaning her head back, she put the chair into motion and relaxed into it.

"Kathleen?"

She forced her eyes open. Again? She'd fallen asleep again? She needed to stop sitting down on his porches. They lulled her to sleep faster than anything. *"Ja."*

"It's ready."

She stood. "How long was I asleep this time?"

He shrugged. "Twenty minutes maybe. How is it you can fall asleep anywhere?"

She explained the long work hours at the hospital. "I learned to grab sleep when I could. Often several five- and ten-minute naps throughout the day."

He shook his head. "I can't imagine living like that."

"I couldn't either until I was. It's amazing what the human body will adapt to. I'm trying hard to adjust back to normal sleeping habits, but my brain is resistant to accepting that this is the new way of life." She clapped her hands and rubbed them together. "So…what's this surprise?"

He motioned with his hand toward the door. "Come see."

The dogs jumped to their feet and wiggled over, tails wagging.

"You three stay outside." He led Kathleen inside and back to the smaller of the two rooms, the one she'd designated for her office. "Notice anything different?"

She scanned the empty room and spied it immediately

on the floor below the window. "A phone." She turned to him. "You installed a phone." A cordless phone.

"It's just an extension of the one I have in the house and barn, so it's the same number. But no one usually calls me, so you can tell people that during the day, they can reach you here."

"I love it." She stepped forward and started to give him a hug but stopped herself. Not the Amish thing to do. She'd gotten used to people hugging her in the outside world. Even men. Men hugged women and vice versa. It was a way of greeting each other. But not for the Amish. She would need to retrain herself. "*Danki. Danki* very much."

"I figured it would help with you getting patients and communicating with them."

"*Ja*, it will. You have been very thoughtful."

"The other handset is in the kitchen area."

"Two phones. Is that a little extravagant?"

He chuckled. "I have a desk in the house I don't use that I'll bring out, and I can build you a bookshelf along that wall if that'll be helpful."

"Both of those would be wonderful, but I don't want to trouble you."

"It's no trouble."

She knew it was. How could it not be?

"I'll be right back."

"Back? Back from where?"

"The house to retrieve the desk." And with that, he left.

"Should I help?" she called after him.

"*Ne*, I can get it," he called back.

She liked his consideration and helpfulness. Not everyone would be so accepting of her being a doctor.

Most people probably wouldn't until the leaders gave their full approval.

He returned a few minutes later, hefting a smallish desk in front of him by one end.

How was he managing by himself?

He set the desk down and plunked the phone on top of it. "It's starting to look like a real office in here."

It certainly was.

He left the room and returned with a kitchen chair that he set behind the desk. "Try it out."

She sat and ran her hands across the surface. A long, shallow top drawer ran the width. On either side of her chair were two more of medium depth, and the bottom ones on each side were file-folder depth. She could keep all her records in those.

Though the lines were in a simple Amish style, it was a refreshing change from the industrial metal or ornate wood *Englisher* desks. "It's perfect." She would need to get a computer at some point for both record keeping and researching. That is, if the church leaders would approve it. And a copier-printer. Before she bought anything more, she needed to prove her worth as a doctor.

"So it'll work for you?"

"Oh, *ja*. It's beautiful."

A smile pulled at his mouth. *"Danki."*

She tilted her head. Something in his tone made her wonder. "Did you make this?"

"Ja." His smile widened.

He had a nice smile. Engaging. She wanted to study it as she might a virus under a microscope, cataloging every detail, including the causes as well as the effects.

"Would you like to see my workshop in the barn?"

"Ja, I would." She stood and walked to the barn with him.

The dogs got up from where they lay in the grass and trotted along with them.

The scent of cut wood hung strong in the air. And no wonder, the workshop wasn't just *in* the barn, it took up most of the building. Rows of finished straight-back chairs, dining tables, rocking chairs, benches, porch bench swings, headboards and footboards, dressers, and even wooden spoons and toys. If it was made out of wood, Kathleen suspected it could be found in here. She could tell this was where his heart lay. "Why do I smell honey? And…linseed oil?"

"You have a *gut* nose. I don't use chemical-based finishes. I make my own boiled linseed oil as well as a beeswax furniture wax."

The source of him always smelling so *gut* and sweet.

He ran his hand over a piece. "It's not as durable as polyurethane or varnish, but I like to keep the finish more natural. I feel the chemical finishes smother the wood. Wood needs to breathe."

His pieces were beautiful and smelled fresh.

She pointed toward the door. "I thought the surrounding fields were yours."

"They are. I rent them out to one of the Zook families."

"What about your sheep? Isn't that why you have dogs?"

"I have dogs because I like them. They're *gut* company." He dipped his head. "The sheep were my wife's idea. She wanted to spin her own wool. I have no interest in that. The Troyers shear them and pay me a moderate price for the wool. I should just sell the animals to them. But then what excuse could I have for keeping my dogs?"

She laughed. "Because you want to."

"Come over here." He walked to what appeared to be his work area and pointed to a pile of finished boards. "These will be your bookshelves."

She ran her hand over the smooth wood. "Really?"

He nodded. "I'll put them together tomorrow inside."

She looked more closely. Holes were drilled in the ends of the boards and a pile of wooden dowel pins sat nearby.

"I need you to approve your exam table." He motioned toward a piece of furniture, then lifted one half of the surface that seemed to have a hinge in the middle. "This is so you can sit the patient up if you need to, like I've seen in doctors' offices."

Not the flat piece of wood with legs she'd envisioned. "And drawers underneath for storage."

He nodded. "See if it's the height you wanted."

Standing next to it, she ran her hands across the surface. She would need to sew a thin mattress to cushion the surface. But other than that, she couldn't ask for anything nicer. "It's perfect. You didn't have to go to all this trouble."

"I wanted to. It's nice to have someone appreciate my work."

"What do you do with all your pieces?"

"Nothing yet. Now that I have some stock, I'm trying to decide if I want to have a store in town or set up a website."

"You could do both. These will fetch a fine price in the *Englisher* market. You could set your shop up right here on your farm." Then he wouldn't be so far away during the day.

"I've thought of that. It's one of my many business

decisions. Fortunately, I make enough from renting out my fields to be able to take my time."

"Don't forget the sale of your wool."

He smiled again. "That only covers feeding and housing the sheep. I really should just sell them to the Troyers."

"That would leave you more time for the work you love."

His face brightened.

She smiled in return. *Ja*, a closer study of his smile would be interesting. For now, she should get back to work.

Chapter Seven

Two days later, as Kathleen headed out the door to go to her clinic, she wondered if Noah'd had time to install the bookshelves. He did have livestock to tend to and work to do around his place. He couldn't be expected to wait on her. She'd missed seeing him yesterday, having stayed home to help inventory the pantry and cellar.

Jessica trotted up to her but called back to their *mum* in the kitchen. "Can I go with Kathleen and help out at her clinic?"

Mum came toward them at the front door with a basket in her hands. "I don't want you to be in the way. You don't know any medical stuff. What would you do all day?"

"Oh, answer the telephone and check in the patients and anything else she needs me to do." Jessica turned to Kathleen. "Right?"

"Sure." If the phone rang at all, Jessica was welcome to answer it, and if any patients came, she could certainly greet them. The idea of her sister working with her appealed to her. More likely, Jessica would have nothing to do all day, but the company would be nice.

"That's fine then." *Mum* handed Kathleen the basket. "There should be enough in there for three. Invite Noah for supper."

"Three?" Kathleen said.

"You, Noah and now Jessica. Have a *gut* day, you two." She returned to the kitchen.

Jessica slung a cloth bag over her shoulder. Evidently, she had packed herself a few things for a day away.

Once out on the porch, Kathleen turned to her baby sister. Well, she wasn't so young anymore. She would start *Rumspringa* next summer. "I don't want to give you false hope, but I haven't had a single patient, and no one knows to call, so there won't be anything to do all day. You'll likely get very bored. Don't get me wrong, I'd love to have your company. I just don't want to mislead you into thinking this will be some exciting adventure." Though getting to know her sister as nearly a grown-up would be a blessing. She'd missed so much of Jessica's life.

"Oh, don't worry about any of that. If I get bored, I have a book to read in my bag as well as some sewing. I mostly wanted to spend time with you and get to know my big sister. And to get out of a little work around here at home." Jessica gave a winning smile. "I won't be in your way. I promise."

Kathleen looped her arm through Jessica's. "I welcome your company." She was thrilled that they had the same intentions—to get to know each other. Apparently, some of the attachment they'd shared all those years ago still remained.

Arm in arm, they walked up the driveway. Kathleen said, "Do you have your eye on a special young man? One you hope might ask to court you?"

"*Ne.* I'm not interested in boys yet. I have more important things on my mind. Tell me about college. What kinds of things can you study?"

"Why do you want to know about that?" It would be irresponsible to encourage her sister in this.

"I want to go like you did."

How could she dissuade her sister? "Do you think college is all fun?"

Jessica shook her head. "*Ne.* I think, like you, I would not like it."

"Then why would you want to go?"

"I feel *Gott* calling me to go to college, like He did you."

Kathleen couldn't help but feel as though her sister was saying that because that had been Kathleen's excuse as well. Though, *Gott had* called Kathleen. But she'd tried to persuade Him otherwise. "Have you told *Dat* and *Mum* this?"

"*Ne.* They would tell me not to."

"As I must do. I don't think you should consider college for one more minute."

"But you went. Just tell me about it. Then maybe I can tell if I'm truly supposed to go. Some days I think I'm supposed to, and others it scares me."

It *should* scare her.

"I wouldn't be gone nearly as long as you were."

Kathleen supposed she'd have to have this discussion eventually if Jessica was determined. If not today, then tomorrow or next week or next month. "I went with a purpose. You don't go to college just to take whatever classes you want." Well, technically she could. "You have to study in a particular area. What would you study?"

Jessica didn't hesitate. "Business."

"Business? For what?"

"I think it would be *gut* for me to know about how

to run a business. To make the most of all we do here as Amish. *Englishers* love everything Amish. I don't know if I want to run my own business someday or to help other Amish with their businesses. We could do so much more if we knew how to utilize computers and the internet better. Amish once could do quite well separated from the *Englisher* world, but not so much anymore. We grow food to make them dependent on us, but it also makes us dependent on them. Computers are no different."

Her sister sounded a bit like an *Englisher* herself. "How would you even pay for tuition? It's not free."

"The same way you did."

"It's not that easy. I had a nurse who mentored me and helped me out a great deal. She gave me books and found scholarships and so much more. Without her, I couldn't have done it."

"I'll find someone to help me too. If *Gott* wants me to go, then He'll provide the means."

Kathleen had to talk her sister out of this. Her parents would be angry and blame her. Even though she had nothing to do with it.

By the time they'd concluded the short walk to Noah's, she had still been unsuccessful in dissuading Jessica. A part of her was proud of her baby sister.

Suddenly, Kaleidoscope dashed from around the house to greet them.

Inside the *dawdy haus*, Kathleen checked the office. The bookshelf stood against the wall, but it was much bigger than she'd anticipated and made the room smell of fresh wood and honey. But no Noah. Why should he be here? He had better things to do, no doubt. Even so, disappointment settled inside her.

She went to the other bedroom, hoping her exam

table might be there, and couldn't believe her eyes. Her completed table sat against one wall, but it was so different than what she'd seen two days ago. Rather than plain wood, the top surface had burgundy vinyl padding attached with furniture tacks. A small dresser sat on the other side of the room, for supplies, with a rolling wooden stool next to it.

She couldn't believe he'd done all this.

The beeps of telephone buttons being pressed drew Kathleen's attention. She went to her office doorway. What was Jessica up to?

Jessica's voice held a chipper tone. "Hello, Hannah? This is Jessica Yoder."

Kathleen listened to the back-and-forth chatter for a minute, then went back into her office. If this was why Jessica wanted to come—to use the phone freely so their parents wouldn't overhear—Kathleen would need to put a stop to that. She would broach the subject when they stopped for lunch. For now, she'd let her sister enjoy a little freedom.

Kathleen spent the morning organizing her medical supplies and figuring out a filing system. She created forms by hand she would need when charting people's health concerns and made a list of office supplies for preparing and labeling patients' medical records.

A bit before noon, she exited her office and found Jessica sitting on the kitchen table with her legs swinging, still on the phone. The girl must have made twenty calls by now. Hanging up from one and immediately dialing another. Should Kathleen leave this for *Dat* and *Mum* to deal with? *Ne.* Jessica had come with her, and in so doing, she'd allowed her baby sister to overuse the phone. It was her fault.

Jessica said goodbye, took the phone from her ear and turned it off.

"Jessica."

Her sister held up her hand. "Just a sec." She picked up a spiral notebook, jotted something down, set it aside and then hopped down from the table. "Sorry. I meant to get lunch set out, but time got away from me." She lifted the cloth off the top of the basket. "Is Noah joining us?"

Since Kathleen hadn't seen Noah all morning, she guessed not. "I doubt it. I need to talk to you about what you've done with your time all morning."

Jessica's face brightened, and she retrieved the notebook, turning it to face Kathleen. "You have three appointments this afternoon."

Kathleen stared at the lined page. Hannah Zook at one thirty. Martha Beiler at two. And Grace Troyer at two thirty. She looked from the page to Jessica several times. "How...? How did you...?" Finally, she settled on, "How?"

Jessica patted the community phone book lying on the table. "I just kept calling people. Most turned me down politely. A few sputtered and hung up, claiming they had something urgent that needed attending to. We both know, we Amish aren't the urgent type."

"I can't believe you called all those people and scrounged up appointments for me."

"Well, if we're going to have telephones, we might as well put them to *gut* use. There were a lot of people I couldn't get a hold of because they don't have telephones in their homes, only shared ones out at the street."

Kathleen hugged Jessica. *"Danki."* Her clinic was actually getting started. Her dream realized. Finally.

Everything was coming together. "And here I thought… Oh, never mind."

"You thought I was calling my friends."

Kathleen nodded.

Jessica averted her gaze and pulled her mouth sideways. "I confess. I did call a couple of my friends and quickly told them what I was doing and then asked them if anyone in their house needed to see the doctor."

Kathleen smiled. "As far as I'm concerned, talking to your friends needed to be done in order to get around to the question of a doctor visit. You can't jump right in asking if they need an appointment. I overheard your first call where you were doing just that."

Jessica jumped off the table. "Shall we eat?"

"*Ja.* Would you set everything out? I'll go find Noah. After all, *Mum* did pack that lunch for him too."

"All right." Jessica turned to the basket.

Kathleen would check the barn first and then the house. She opened the door to the *dawdy haus* and hurried out before her sister could change her mind. In her haste to close the door, she wasn't paying attention to where she was going and literally ran into the object of her search and tottered off balance.

Noah grabbed her upper arms and kept her upright.

Kathleen gazed into his brown eyes that appeared as startled as she was. Then she noticed his neck flush. Then she remembered the mattress incident two days ago—the last time she'd seen him—and how long he'd stared at her then. Was he also thinking of the incident that had thrown them so close together?

He didn't say anything. Just stared. As she was doing as well.

The door latch clicked behind her, and she sensed it swing open.

Jessica.

Noah jerked his hands away from Kathleen's arms as though she burned him. He straightened and cleared his throat. "Jessica. I didn't know you would be here today."

Jessica spoke. "Here I am. *Gut.* She found you already. I was just setting out lunch. When *Mum* said there would be enough for all three of us, she must have meant for five."

Everyone laughed. Amish women tended to prepare far more food than the number of people could eat. There seemed to be an unspoken motto that no one should go hungry or even think they might go hungry.

Kathleen's three afternoon appointments turned out to be social visits. Ladies she knew from the community who wanted to catch up.

She was disappointed, to be sure. But it was a start.

Two days later, Noah drove to the Yoders' for Sunday singing, Bible study and fellowship. On the Sundays between regular community church services, they always included him, whether at their house or at their son-in-law and daughter's, Titus and Gloria Schrock. Noah was grateful for their generosity and thoughtfulness. He loathed staying home alone when he knew the rest of the community would be getting together in small and large groups to fellowship with each other.

He often rode on horseback to the Yoders', but today, he drove the two-wheeled trap as the day was sunny and he brought a box of food. He was in no way lacking in provisions. He still had jars of food given to him for six months after Rachel died. The older women wanted to make sure he had enough to eat during his grief, and the young women wanted to show off their homemaking abilities to a potential husband.

The inpouring of generosity had been humbling. He still received occasional jars of food, loaves of bread, muffins, pies and cakes. Because he had plenty to eat, he wanted to contribute to the meals. So he'd brought some hard-boiled eggs, biscuits and a stew he'd made out of jars of canned goods. Green beans, corn, potatoes, tomatoes and beef. Not as *gut* as Rachel's or Pamela's, but edible. They obviously did something more than just pour the contents of jars into a pot and heat them.

He settled in the parlor with the Yoder family, which felt like his own. One of the many blessings of being Amish was one never need be alone if one didn't want to be. Simply drive to a neighbor's to visit. Amish always had time. Kathleen smiled at him, and something inside him shifted slightly. He wasn't sure what it was. Probably just indigestion. But he hadn't eaten anything. So he ignored the feeling and pulled his harmonica from his pants pocket.

Kathleen tilted her head. "You play?"

He nodded. "It keeps me from singing. I'm not so *gut*."

"I'm sure you sing as well as any of us."

He didn't. He hurt his own ears when he tried, which he hadn't done in over two decades. His *vater* had given him the harmonica to help him save face. Everyone was required to "make a joyful noise unto the Lord" unless they played one of the three instruments that were allowed. Harmonica, guitar and accordion. Harmonica being the only one to excuse him from using his voice. But even *Gott* had to be relieved when Noah started playing instead of singing.

After the miniservice and meal, they divvied up into their usual teams for softball. David, Benjamin, Joshua, Jessica and ten-year-old Nancy on one team, and Titus, Noah, Samuel, Ruby and six-year-old Andrew on the other. Pamela sat on the sidelines with the two younger children, Mark and Luke, on a quilt. Kathleen didn't have a place in any of the groups, so she sat with her *mutter* and older sister.

Noah crossed to her. "You can be on our team."

"You already have even teams."

"That's all right. There's always room for one more. Besides, Andrew usually tires out and wanders off. He comes back when it's his turn to bat. You'll even up the sides." He held out a worn baseball glove. "I hear you used to be *gut*."

A smile broke across her face. "I don't know about that, though I could hold my own. But I haven't played in years. I probably won't be any *gut* now."

"That's all right."

She took the glove and stood. "What position do you want me at?"

He smiled back at her. "I hear you were a decent pitcher."

She had played on college intramural teams and on the resident doctors' team. No one had expected much from the little Amish girl, but she'd surprised a few people.

She joined the other players. When it was six-year-old Andrew's turn to bat, the boy asked for Noah's help. Noah stood behind him and gripped the bat with him. On the fifth swing, the bat connected with the ball. No one was counting strikes for him.

Noah hoisted Andrew up and ran for first base. "Drop the bat. Drop the bat."

Andrew did, finally, release the bat once the pair stopped at first base. Safe.

That had been very sweet of Noah to help Kathleen's nephew. She couldn't imagine her fellow doctors doing that. They were far too competitive. But for her Amish people, this was about family and building relationships and having a *gut* time.

Kathleen hadn't had this much fun in a long time. With the other medical residents and interns, the pressure not to make even the smallest mistake and to win had been fierce, as though someone's life depended on them winning. It was the reason she'd quit playing with them long ago.

She was glad Noah had talked her into it. He had a *gut* heart and seemed to understand what she needed.

On Monday, Kathleen walked to Noah's alone. Jessica had gone with their *mum* to Gloria's to help her for the morning. The dark clouds overhead threatened rain. As she strolled into the yard, Noah led his horse and larger, covered buggy out of the barn. She crossed to him. "Are you going into town?"

He seemed startled at her presence and hesitant to answer. *"Ja."*

"Could I tag along? I need to get a few office supplies, file folders and such." She smiled brightly in the hopes of coaxing one out of him.

He remained straight-faced. "Sure." He helped her in and drove off down the road.

Silence weighed heavy in the confined space. Something was troubling him today. He seemed to want to be alone.

"Noah, would you pull over?"

He turned his head and focused his gaze on her. "What? Why?"

"I'll walk back. It's not more than a half a mile."

"I thought you wanted to go into town."

"I did. I do. But I can go another day." The office

supplies could wait. It wasn't as though she had a slew of patients to keep track of.

"It could start raining any moment."

"I don't mind the rain."

But he kept driving. "What changed your mind about going into town?"

She hadn't wanted to mention anything, just to allow him to keep his private thoughts to himself. But now she had no choice. "You didn't seem eager for me to come along." That sounded petty. "I don't mean you should be overjoyed with my presence. I just mean that you seem deep in thought and would probably like to be alone, and I've intruded on that."

"*Ne.* I mean *ja.* I do have a lot of thoughts, but you're not intruding. I want you along."

"Are you sure?"

"*Ja.*"

"All right."

He shifted on the seat. "I'm going into town to look for someone."

"Please don't feel as though you have to explain yourself to me or make conversation. I'm content to just be here." *Beside you and enjoying your presence.*

He remained quiet for some time before he spoke again. "My *mutter.*"

"Your *mutter*? What about her?"

"I'm going to look for her."

"She's in town?"

He nodded. "I've seen her."

"This is none of my business and you don't have to tell me anything, but you've *seen* her? You said you were going to *look* for her. Why is she in town and not with your *vater*?"

"She left us when I was a teenager and we lived on

the other side of the county. After my *vater* and I moved into this community, I never expected to see her again. But I've seen her in town many times over the years. I saw her the other time we came into town together. But I don't know where she lives nor have I ever talked to her."

Kathleen didn't know what to say. She had so many questions, but none of this was her business. He could tell her more if he wanted to.

"I don't know why she left us. And I don't know why she's moved to this town. She still dresses Amish."

"I hope you find her. This is a very personal trip for you, so if need be, I can walk back alone, as I said."

"*Ne.* I want you along. I don't know what to say to her. I don't know how to find her. I don't know if I even want to find her."

"I will go with you." She felt honored he would share so much with her. "Tell me what you would like me to do."

"I don't know. I need to find out where she lives."

"If we locate a city phone book, we can see if she's listed. If she has a phone, she should be in there."

"Why would she have a phone?"

Kathleen tipped her head. "Possibly for a similar reason she's living in town?"

Once in town, they used a phone book at a local business and found an address for a woman who could be his *mutter*. When they got there and knocked, his *mutter* wasn't home. Or if she was, she didn't come to the door.

Noah took up the reins. "It's best this way. *Gott*'s will." He drove out of town without remembering that Kathleen had wanted to pick up a few things.

That was fine. This trip had never been about her. She ached for Noah's loss.

Chapter Eight

Noah stood high on a roof gable truss at the barn raising of the bishop's eldest grandson. His *vater* held a board in place while Noah tapped a nail until it held on its own. Then, making sure his elbow was steady, he took a hard swing and sank the rest of the nail in one blow. He'd practiced many hours when he was young to be consistent in his aim. Some of the younger men and boys tried to copy Noah, but none were quite as successful.

Yet all he received from his *vater* was a slight smirk on one side of his mouth and a shake of his head.

Noah pointed with his hammer as he retrieved another nail from the canvas pouch tied around his waist. "Not like when I was a lad."

"You've come a long way, but this isn't a show."

Noah lined up the next nail and got it to hold in place as he did the other one. "I know."

"Do you?"

Why couldn't his *vater* appreciate Noah's work? "It saves time and energy. Why swing the hammer multiple times when you can get the job done with one?"

"You're quite proud of this ability, aren't you?"

"Ja." Why shouldn't he be?

"If you were truly doing it to save time and energy, then it would be something worthy. But you do it to show off. 'Pride goeth before a fall.'"

"I just want you to be…"

"Proud of you?"

Noah bristled. *"Ja."*

His *vater* wasn't nearly as hard on him as he used to be, but his rebuff still stung.

"I'm pleased when you act as a *gut* Amish should. And a *gut* Amish would not be seeking approval from men but from *Gott.* Honor *Gott,* and I'll be pleased enough."

Though it couldn't hurt to get a little approval now and then, his *vater* was right. The only approval that truly mattered was from *Gott.* But still…

He glanced to the yard below to catch a glimpse of Kathleen among the women setting out the noon meal.

As though she knew he was seeking her out, her gaze turned up to the skeleton of the barn, and she smiled at him. It warmed him all over. *She* appreciated his carpentry skills.

Soon, the call sounded for the lunch break.

Noah scrambled down with all the other men on the upper part of the barn.

As he stood in line with his *vater,* waiting to fill a plate with food, he could still feel the tension of his earlier foolishness of wanting his *vater's* approval. The only way to shake it from his thoughts was to broach an equally tense subject. "I saw her in town."

His *vater* stiffened and turned. "Your *mutter*?"

"Ja."

His *vater's* eyes widened. "Are you sure it was her?"

"Ja." He wouldn't complicate things by telling him he'd seen her more than once and over several years.

After a moment, his *vater* spoke softly. "What did you say to her?"

"Nothing. There wasn't time. Besides, I wouldn't know what to say"

"Ask her the question you kept asking me."

"It doesn't matter anymore why she left. She left us, and she's gone. She could have come home if she'd wanted to." But Noah did still want to know the answer.

Had it been something he'd done? Could he have said or done something to make her stay? A mistake he feared repeating.

Was that the real reason he shied away from marrying again? Not so much fear that a wife would leave him by one means or another, but that her leaving would be his fault.

Kathleen hadn't realized how enjoyable a barn raising could be. The smell of the wood mingled with that of the food. The sounds of children playing, people talking and hammers striking nails mingled together in a beautiful symphony. Women bustled around with the food. Children scampered about. Men constructed and climbed on the ever-growing structure.

She'd missed these kinds of community gatherings while away. *Englishers* gathered, of course, but not as a whole community and not to help someone else. Their get-togethers were more self-serving and usually only for enjoyment. A party for this thing or that, or for nothing at all. They never seemed to lack for a reason to throw a party.

After six weeks back, she'd had only ten patient visits. And half of those were her own family. Likely because they took pity on her. Jessica had been mostly unsuccessful at drumming up patients willing to come in. Preacher Hochstetler must be discouraging them. He'd certainly made the evils of higher education clear in his sermon this past Sunday.

Lord, how can I make him see the gut in having a doctor close by? Even a female Amish doctor.

Ne. It wasn't hers to persuade him or anyone else. That was *Gott*'s responsibility. He was the heart changer.

Don't let our community suffer because of stubbornness or pride.

While away on *Rumspringa*, Kathleen had felt out of place in the English world. And when she first returned, she'd felt the same way in her Amish community. But each week, she found herself more and more at home here. She wanted *gut* things for her people, and the clinic *would* be *gut* for them. No question about that.

She stood at the end of the food line, placing a roll on each man's plate.

Noah stopped in front of her. *"Guten Nachmittag."*

"Guten Nachmittag." She placed a roll on his plate. "You men are doing a fine job."

"Danki. Kathleen, this is my *vater*, Abraham."

"Nice to meet you."

Abraham thinned his lips. "So you're the doctor. Have any patients yet?"

She wished her Amish neighbors weren't so slow to accept her. "A few. You should come by."

"Maybe I will. It's on my son's farm, you know."

Well, that was more open than some people. Many either wouldn't acknowledge her as a doctor or just didn't even talk to her because they didn't know what to say.

Oh, they would smile but then hurry away as though she were contagious.

Noah studied his *vater* with an expression of longing as though he wanted something. Something more. But what? She sensed approval?

A high-pitched scream cut through the air. A scream of pain.

Kathleen whirled around. As fast as she was, her sister Gloria was faster. She was in the midst of three of her children—Nancy, Andrew and Mark—faster than a city taxi driver vying for a fare.

Four-year-old Mark waved his pudgy little hand back and forth. Tears stained his round cheeks and continued to flow while he wailed.

Gloria tried to still her son's hand. Though she had hold of his wrist, he still jerked his hand too much to see what was the matter. Gloria turned to her daughter. "What happened?"

By now, the men had gathered as well.

Nancy planted her hands on her slender hips. "Andrew dared him to pick up a bee."

"Andrew!" Gloria scolded her six-year-old son.

"I didn't think he'd do it. He did it wrong. He wouldn't got hurt if he'd cupped his hands around the clover to pick it up. Not put his hands around the bee."

"I don't care. You shouldn't have told him to do it in the first place. You're supposed to be looking out for him. Go sit on the porch until your *vater* decides what your punishment will be."

Andrew shuffled off.

Kathleen took hold of her nephew's hand. "We need to see if there's a stinger."

Gloria helped pry the four-year-old's hand open. The stinger sat in the middle finger of his shaking left hand.

"I can get that out for you." Kathleen carefully scraped her fingernail across Mark's skin. The stinger dislodged, and she flicked it away. "All gone."

Gloria rubbed her son's arm. "There now, you'll be fine."

But Mark didn't look fine and took a gasping breath.

Kathleen too gasped for breath. *Ne.* This wasn't happening. Not again. He wasn't having an allergic reaction. She was imagining it. Her mind playing a trick on her.

Gloria gazed at her with horror in her eyes. "Do something."

Her sister had seen it too. Kathleen jumped to her feet, dashed for her parents' buggy, retrieved her pack of medical supplies and ran back, out of breath. She had an epinephrine injector. She dug in her pack and quickly had the lifesaving medicine in hand. She knelt beside her sister and nephew.

"*Halt!* You can't do that without his *vater*'s permission," a male voice called from the crowd.

Kathleen glanced around.

Preacher Hochstetler.

Kathleen turned back to her sister.

Gloria lifted her chin and looked as though she was about to nod when Titus spoke up.

"What's going on?" He knelt on the other side of his son from Kathleen, next to his wife.

Preacher Hochstetler spoke. "She's trying to give your son something without your permission. She's not allowed to do that."

Kathleen bristled. "It's epinephrine. It will stop the allergic reaction from closing his throat so he can breathe better." She aimed the device for the boy's small leg.

"Don't!" Preacher Hochstetler barked, then spoke to Titus. "Don't let her do it."

Again Titus asked, "What happened?"

Through short breaths, Kathleen said, "Mark's been stung by a bee and is having an allergic reaction. If he doesn't get this medicine immediately, he could die. He's going into anaphylactic shock." Dare she go against Titus and the church leaders? If she did, she wouldn't be allowed to treat another person in their community. She couldn't stand by and watch her nephew die. She would deal with the consequences later.

She leaned forward on her knees.

Preacher Hochstetler held up his hand, and two men grabbed Kathleen's arms and pulled her to her feet.

"Don't believe her. Our children get stung all the time and don't need to be interfered with and poked with who knows what."

Titus's panicked gaze darted between Kathleen, his son, Gloria and the preacher.

Poor Titus. He was getting too much information all at once. And the pressure from Preacher Hochstetler was great. Titus seemed to want to allow Kathleen to treat his son. He also didn't want to go against one of the church leaders. He couldn't seem to get himself to take action.

Kathleen held out the lifesaving instrument to him. "Hold it firmly against his thigh and press the button."

Gloria spoke in a panicky voice. "Please, Titus. He's going to die. Our son is going to *die*."

Titus chewed his lower lip, obviously unsure what to do. So much peer pressure and tradition to overcome.

Noah said, "The leadership approved a trial period

of her being a doctor for the district. You can let her treat him."

Kathleen continued to hold the epinephrine out. "Please take it. You can do it. It's easy. Hold it against his thigh and press the button."

Titus stared hard at the medicine as though he wanted to take it.

Gloria pleaded. "Please, Titus." Tears rolled down her cheeks. "Please."

Nancy snatched the allergy pen from Kathleen, jammed it into her brother's thigh and pressed the button before anyone protested.

Ja! Kathleen released her captive breath. Bless Nancy's heart for taking action. No one would be upset with her because she was a child.

Kathleen prayed that it hadn't been too late and Mark would recover. The men let go of her, and she watched the boy closely from the distance she was allowed to be, close but not touching him.

Though her nephew lay limp in his *mutter's* arms, his breathing came a little easier.

And so did Kathleen's. "You should take him into town to a doctor. Don't let him scratch his hand. And he might have stomach pain and could vomit."

Titus carried his young son to their buggy.

Gloria turned to *Mum.* "Can you…?"

Mum handed baby Luke to Gloria. "Don't worry. We'll look after Nancy and Andrew."

Gloria squeezed her daughter's shoulder and mouthed, *"Danki."* Then she hustled to the buggy.

Kathleen crouched in front of Nancy. "You did the right thing. I'm very proud of you."

Andrew, who had returned from the porch, sobbed softly.

Kathleen hooked her arm around him. "Your brother is going to be all right."

"I never knowed the bee could do that to him. I've been stung before. He's been stung before too."

"When someone is allergic, each time they are stung the reaction can get worse." Kathleen pulled back and held him by his shoulders. "Do you understand that it's not your fault?"

Nodding, he sniffled and dragged his shirtsleeve across his nose.

Everyone drifted off to eat.

Mum put a hand on Kathleen's shoulder. "Are you all right?"

Kathleen nodded. "I'm fine." Of course she was. However, as *Mum* walked away with Andrew and Nancy, promising them each a cookie, Kathleen thought how close her nephew had come to dying. Had relived her own sister dying. Her hands shook, and her breathing became labored again.

Heat flushed through her body, and she ground her teeth together. Preacher Hochstetler nearly cost Mark his life.

Her *mutter* called to her. "Kathleen, are you coming?"

Kathleen forced a cheery tone to her voice. "I'll be there in a minute." She hurried away and around the side of the house opposite where the men were building the barn and the food was set out. This had been too much like what had happened to Nancy eighteen years ago. She needed to be away from people to pull herself together. If anyone saw her hands shaking, they would never trust her to treat them.

She leaned against a large sugar maple tree, bent at the waist and rested her hands on her thighs. *Breathe in and out.* She obeyed her inner doctor voice. *Don't think about what could have happened. In and out. Don't think about what* did *happen all those years ago. Mark will be fine.*

"Kathleen?" Noah said.

She jerked upright with a small squeal. "Oh. I didn't... I wasn't expecting..."

"Are you all right?"

She pinched her bottom lip hard between her teeth and nodded. She *would* be all right if she could just erase the image of Mark struggling for breath.

"Mark was breathing easier by the time we got him to the buggy. I think he'll be fine."

"I saw my sister lying there in Mark's place. I saw her dying all over again." Tears she had been holding at bay cascaded over the lower rims of her eyes. "If my own brother-in-law won't let me treat his family, what hope do I have that anyone else will? None. I may as well quit right now. Why would *Gott* have me go through all that struggling and hardship for nothing? It doesn't make any sense."

"*Gott*'s ways are different than ours. Isaiah fifty-five, -eight and -nine say, 'For my thoughts are not your thoughts, neither are your ways my ways, saith the Lord. For as the heavens are higher than the earth, so are my ways higher than your ways.' Trust *Gott* to know what He's doing."

She thought she'd been doing that, but this made no sense. If she'd gone to all that trouble to go to med school and now wouldn't be allowed to help anyone, what was the use of it all?

* * *

Noah couldn't bear the anguish on Kathleen's face, so he glanced around. What he was about to do went against so many *Ordnung* rules, and he could be shunned. No one was in sight. He stepped forward and wrapped his arms around her. "It's all right." She needed comforting, and he wanted to comfort her.

She leaned into him and sobbed.

After a few minutes, when her crying softened, he pulled back. "You saved Mark's life."

Tears smeared her cheeks. She shook her head. "Nancy saved his life. I was helpless."

"If not for your medicine on hand, he would have died, so you both saved him." He cupped her face and brushed away her tears with his thumbs. Then, before he realized what he was doing, he pressed his lips to hers. He could *really* be shunned for this.

But she didn't resist. Quite the opposite. She kissed him back. *Definitely shunned.*

He pulled away and released her. "I'm sorry."

She didn't say anything, just stared up at him with her piercing blue eyes.

Though he wanted to stay here with her indefinitely, he knew they couldn't. "We should get back to the gathering."

She nodded.

He wanted to kiss her again, but instead, he turned and pushed the kiss out of his mind.

Chapter Nine

On Monday, Kathleen took her parents' buggy into town by herself. A town doctor had seen her nephew, declared him fit to go home the same day and prescribed an allergy pen so they would always have one on hand. And Titus had apologized to her for hesitating.

She pulled up in front of Noah's *mutter*'s house. As she walked up to the gate, the neighbor lady watering her flowers said, "Heddy's not there."

Kathleen turned. "Excuse me?"

"Heddy, the Amish woman who lives there. She's at work. You'll find her at the library."

"*Danki*—I mean, thank you." This was *gut*. She could tell Noah where his *mutter* worked.

However, to make sure, Kathleen drove to the library and spied a woman dressed in Amish garb in a row of shelves, returning books to their places. Must be Heddy Lambright. Kathleen pretended to be interested in titles nearby. So many questions she'd like to ask this woman. Why had she, who still dressed as an Amish, left her family and community? Why didn't she come back? Why didn't she talk to her son?

When Heddy finished and settled herself behind the checkout desk, Kathleen sauntered up. "I would like to apply for a library card, please."

Heddy stared at her a moment, then turned to the computer screen. "I know you don't have the kind of identification we normally request from patrons, like a driver's license or ID card, but do you have something with your address on it with you?"

Kathleen shook her head.

"I can issue you a library card, but what you can check out will be limited to three items. When you can bring in proof of address, we can lift that limitation." She put her hands on the computer keyboard. "Your full name and address."

Kathleen gave her the information.

Noah's *mutter* retrieved a card from a drawer and scanned in its preprinted bar code number. Then she handed it to Kathleen.

"Danki."

She spoke in a kindly tone. "I've been wondering what your name was."

Kathleen did a double take. "Excuse me?"

"I've seen you in town with my son, Noah. Are you his wife?"

This woman had seen her before? *"Ne."*

Heddy stiffened. "I thought you looked different than her. What are you doing with my son? Where's his wife?"

"She passed away."

Noah's *mutter* took a quick breath. "Oh. I'm sorry to hear that. I didn't know. How long ago?"

"Three years."

"You're why he shaved off his beard. I almost didn't recognize him."

He hadn't shaved it for Kathleen. It had been time. He'd said so. "Noah and I are just friends."

"He looks at you as more than a friend."

Did he? That made her smile inside, but she schooled her expression to not reveal her pleasure to the other woman.

Heddy gave a knowing smile. But just what did she know? "I imagine you have a lot of questions for me."

"They aren't mine to ask."

"Do you think my son will come to visit me?"

Kathleen didn't know if she should tell Heddy that Noah *had* tried, but the woman hadn't been home. That too was Noah's to do or not. It might break the woman's heart to know she missed an opportunity to talk with her son. "I can't say. But he does know that you live in town."

"*Ja*, I've seen him see me."

Kathleen ached for this woman. "Have you thought about going and talking to him?"

"I'm shunned for leaving my husband. I have no right to go to him. He's not allowed to talk to me. You could be shunned for interacting with me."

"I'm not a member yet."

"Why not?" Heddy frowned. "I'm sorry. I have no right to ask."

"I'm going through the classes and will become a member in the fall, but I did something unorthodox. I stayed away for fourteen years, attended college and became a doctor. Now I'm trying to get the community to accept me as *their* physician."

Noah's *mutter* chuckled. "That's not going to be easy. The men in leadership are generally rigid in their ways."

"*Ja*, some of them are. But your son is part of the leadership."

"He is?"

"*Ja*, and he's allowed me to set up my clinic in his *dawdy haus*."

"I'm glad to hear my son is open to new ideas. Not everything new or different is bad."

Kathleen liked this woman.

"Would you tell my Noah that I always set a place for him at my table?"

Heddy's way of saying she'd like a visit from her son warmed Kathleen's heart.

"I feel I've already intruded where maybe I shouldn't have."

The woman dipped her head slightly. "I understand."

When Kathleen left, she yearned to stay and talk with Heddy longer. She felt a kindred spirit with this woman who lived in the *Englisher* world but remained Amish and separated from her people and her son as Kathleen had done when she went to med school.

That Wednesday, Noah headed next door while Kathleen was in her new clinic. He had to talk to David. He'd prayed and tried to talk himself out of needing to make this visit, but he saw no way around it.

As he walked on the edge of the blacktop, Kathleen's *vater* slowed his buggy alongside Noah. "Can we give you a lift?" He and Pamela were coming from the direction of town.

"I was on my way over to see you. I have a matter I

wish to speak with you about." Noah stood beside the buggy.

Pamela turned her focus on him. "You'll come for supper. Would you like to talk then?"

"That would be *gut*." Then he could get back before Kathleen noticed his absence. "I'll drive Kathleen over in time to help with supper preparations." He jogged back toward his house, and the buggy continued down the road.

Before Kathleen finished in her clinic, Noah returned and hitched up the trap. He led the horse out of the barn, up to the *dawdy haus* and looped the reins around the porch rail. He walked inside.

Kathleen sat prim and proper on the sofa with her hands folded in her lap.

He raised an eyebrow. "What are you doing?"

"Seeing what it will be like for my patients to sit here and wait. That is if I ever have any more."

"Aren't your sister and Titus having you oversee Mark after his reaction to the bee sting?"

"*Ja*, but fortunately there's not much for me to do. They're going to the allergy specialist to get Mark desensitized to bee venom."

"But they'll likely come to you for other things now that they know you saved their son's life."

She smiled. "*Danki*. I was feeling sorry for myself, and you just cheered me up."

Not his intention, but he had wanted her to feel better. *"Bitte."* And she was quite pretty when she smiled. "I've hitched up the trap."

She stood and crossed the room. "You don't have to take me home. I can walk."

"Your *mutter* invited me to supper."

She tilted her head in a very cute way. "She did? When?"

"They were passing by on the road. I said *hallo* to them. Are you ready?"

She grabbed her pack of medical supplies and preceded him out the door. She locked it with the key he'd given her.

Once in the buggy, Kathleen fidgeted in the seat next to him.

"Is something the matter?" He was already nervous enough without her twitchiness.

She picked at the folds in her apron. "I've done something you might not be pleased with."

He couldn't imagine what that could be. "It's generally best just to say it quickly."

"I went into town the other day."

He frowned. "Have I given you the impression you need my permission to do things or go places?"

"*Ne.* It's what I *did* in town."

"You have me quite curious. The ride to your house isn't long, so if you're going to tell me, you might want to do so soon."

She took a deep breath. "I—I spoke to your *mutter*."

His breath froze in his lungs. He wished they had already arrived. He wished he hadn't pressed her to tell him. He wished he hadn't asked if something was the matter.

"Please say something. Are you angry with me?"

"I don't know."

"Your *mutter* seems very nice and is interested in you and your life."

"She is?"

"*Ja*. She's said she's sorry for the loss of your wife. And…"

"And what?"

"She sets a place for you at her table. She asked me to tell you that."

So his *mutter* welcomed a visit from him. Was he ready to actually talk to her? He didn't know.

"She works at the library. You can find her there if she's not at home."

Did he *want* to find her? A part of him did and another part didn't. Reconciliation warred with punishment. She was the one who had left and stayed away. He turned into the Yoders' driveway.

"Noah?"

He faced Kathleen. "I don't know just how I feel about you speaking to my *mutter*, but I know I'm not angry."

"*Danki.*"

The tight hold he kept on the unknown loosened inside him, freeing him to wonder what talking to his *mutter* would be like. She set a place for him? So why not return?

Once at a stop, Noah parted ways from Kathleen to unhitch his horse and find her *vater*. He needed to put thoughts of his *mutter* aside for now.

David Yoder sat in the cool of the barn, running a file across an ax blade. He looked up and, seeing Noah, stopped. "Is it that time already?" He rubbed his thumb across the blade, then set the ax aside.

"There's still time." Noah had been sure of himself earlier, but now he wasn't so sure.

Kathleen's *vater* gave Noah his full attention. "You wanted to speak to me?"

He couldn't back down now. He had no choice. After what he'd done, this was the only reasonable action. "I would like your permission to court Kathleen."

A wide smile broke across David's face. "You had me scared for a second. I thought you were going to tell me something terrible. Of course you can court her. I already think of you as a son. I'd be proud to have it official."

If David knew what Noah had done, he might not be so eager. But Noah was fixing his transgression. No need to incriminate Kathleen. He was to blame.

When they went inside, David whispered in Pamela's ear before seating himself at the table. Pamela beamed at Noah. David had obviously told her.

After supper, Noah asked Kathleen to go for a walk with him.

"I can't. I have supper dishes to help with."

Pamela waved her hand toward Kathleen. "You go. Jessica and I will clean up the dishes."

"What?" Jessica said. "It's not my turn."

"Hush now," Pamela chided.

Jessica huffed over to the sink.

Kathleen called after her, "I'll do them the next two times it's your turn."

That made Jessica smile.

As Noah walked Kathleen out to the large black walnut tree with the swing hanging from it, she spoke. "Is this about talking to your *mutter*?"

"Ne." He was actually relieved she'd done that. The ice had been broken. "I told you I wasn't angry at you for that. I'll need to decide what to do, though."

She stared at him a moment as though trying to decide what to say, but instead she sat on the swing and remained quiet for another moment. "*Danki* for reminding me that people will likely start seeking me out for their medical needs. But none so far."

He appreciated the change in subject. She was *gut* at relieving tension that way. "It's true. I heard several men at the barn raising talking about Mark and what you did."

"Did they sound like they would allow their wives and children to come to my clinic?"

They hadn't said anything close to that. They just talked about the incident. "I don't think it will be long before your waiting room is full." At least he hoped that was the case. He walked around behind her. "Here, let me push you."

She gripped the ropes, and he pulled the swing back, then pushed her forward. He pushed her higher and higher.

After a bit, she dragged her feet on the ground and brought herself to a stop. "That was fun. I haven't swung since I was a girl. But I do feel guilty about the work I left to *Mum* and my sisters. I should go inside."

Before she could stand, Noah came around in front of her. "Wait. I have something to ask you first."

She tilted her head back to gaze up at him. So pretty in the waning sunlight.

He couldn't put this off any longer. "I already spoke to your *vater*."

She cocked her head to one side. "About what?"

"Courting you. And he gave his permission."

Her sweet expression turned to confusion. "You what? Why would you do that?"

"Don't tell me you didn't expect this?" And he only asked to court her because he'd crossed a line he shouldn't have. Nothing more. If he hadn't kissed her, he wouldn't even be considering this. Would he?

"Why in the world would I expect this? Is it because you're letting me use your *dawdy haus*? You think I owe you or something?"

"*Ne.* This has nothing to do with the *dawdy haus*. It has to do with me kissing you at the barn raising. I had no right to do that. Now I'm trying to make that right."

"By *courting* me? It was just a kiss. It didn't mean anything."

That was the *Englisher* influence in her talking.

"You didn't tell *Dat* we kissed, did you?"

He shook his head. "Of course not. But he was quite pleased for us to court."

With her feet, she pushed the swing back away from him until she stood with the seat at her back. "You had no right to ask him." She untangled herself from the ropes.

"But he already gave his permission. What will I tell him?"

"I don't know. Don't you understand? I can't court you."

"Why not? Is there someone else?" The thought of someone else courting her twisted his insides.

"I can't court anyone because I'm never going to get married."

"Never? Why not? You're still young."

"Because *Gott* called me to be a doctor. If I marry, I won't be able to be a doctor. It's a sacrifice I made a long time ago. Having the medicine to save my nephew is proof to me that *Gott does* want me to be a doctor."

"Kathleen, we kissed. We *really* kissed. I'm just trying to do the right thing by you."

"The *right thing* is to pretend it never happened. I need to go inside now." She scooted past him.

That moment was seared into his brain. He caught her arm. "But I can't pretend I never kissed you."

"You have to."

Now he wanted to be upset with her for talking to his *mutter.* He needed something to pin his anger on. But his *mutter* had nothing to do with this madness.

He let Kathleen slip from his grasp.

Kathleen ran into the house. She fancied Noah. More than she should. She had to keep herself from accepting his offer. Every fiber of her being wanted to say *ja.* But she couldn't court Noah Lambright or anyone else. Courtship led to a marriage proposal. A proposal led to marriage. No Amish man would allow his wife to continue working as a doctor. Noah *had* supported her and seemed like the type of man who would let her still be a doctor. But when children came along, he would insist she quit. She'd gone through too much, been away from her family for too long, to have it all be for naught.

Tears filled her eyes.

As a young girl, she'd dreamed of marrying a *gut* Amish man exactly like Noah and having lots of children. But when Nancy died and Kathleen decided to become a doctor, not having a husband and family was the price for helping her community. Unlike the English women, she couldn't have it all. She'd had to choose. Wife and *mutter*—or doctor.

Kathleen entered the house as her family sat in the living room for the evening devotional. She hurried past them and ran upstairs. In the room she shared with her sisters, she went to the window and peered out.

Noah stared up at the house, his gaze locking on hers. For a long moment, she watched him watching her. Both knew they saw each other, but neither turned away.

Noah lifted a hand in farewell and trudged off to the barn.

"Why, Lord?" she whispered. "Why send a man like Noah Lambright into my life? A man I could fall in love with, if not for the calling You gave me. Why dangle that dream in front of me? Is this a test? A test to see how committed I am to You?"

A soft knock sounded on the door. "Kathleen? It's *Mum.*"

She didn't want to talk to anyone right now. She needed to sort out her thoughts. But it would be rude to turn her *mum* away. "Come in."

The door creaked slightly, then *Mum* spoke. "Are you coming back down?"

Kathleen shook her head. "Not tonight." She needed time alone to figure things out. Time to think.

Mum joined her by the window. "What's wrong? Did you quarrel with Noah?"

"Not exactly."

Through the window, Kathleen saw Noah coming out of the barn, leading his horse and trap. He climbed aboard, and the dream of a different life drove away.

He didn't rush up the driveway as though he were angry. He didn't glance back to see if she was still watching. He left at the normal, leisurely Amish pace.

"What is it, dear?"

Kathleen continued to stare out the window until Noah was out of sight. "Noah asked to court me."

"I know. Your *dat* and I couldn't be happier. He's already like a son to us."

Kathleen faced her *mum*. "I told him *ne*."

Mum's smile slipped away. "What? Why? He's a *gut* man. He'll make you a *gut* husband and *vater* to your children."

Kathleen's vision blurred. "I can't marry him. I can't marry anyone. *Gott* called me to be a doctor." *Gott* had dangled her childhood dream of a husband and family right in front of her. To tempt her? To tease her? Why?

Why couldn't Noah pretend they'd never kissed? Why did he have to be so honorable? Why did he need to do the right thing?

Mum spoke with compassion in her voice. "Why did you come back home then? Why take the classes to join church?"

"*Gott* didn't call me to just be a doctor, but a doctor for our community. I want to join church because I'm Amish." She tapped her fingertips on her chest. "In here. I know I'm not technically Amish until I join church. All through school and my residency, I continued to dress and behave as though I were still part of our community. One of the things that got me through being away was that I would be coming home and becoming a true member of this community. If I don't join church now, I *could* be a doctor for this community. The church leaders said so, but it would break my heart to not be truly Amish."

"You don't care for Noah at all? You can't picture yourself married to him? You don't wish to marry?"

"As a girl I dreamed of marrying someone like Noah. He is a man I think I could fall in love with. But I can't be a doctor if I marry. No husband, not even Noah, would allow his wife to be a doctor. Then what was all my sacrifice for? I might as well have stayed here and been happy instead of out in the world lonely and struggling."

Mum nodded. "Now I begin to understand all you sacrificed." She wrapped her arms around Kathleen. "You gave up one part of the life you wanted for another." She pulled back. "I think he cares a great deal for you."

She wanted to say that he didn't, that he'd asked out of a sense of duty, but then she would need to explain why she thought that way. And she couldn't tell her *mum* that Noah had kissed her. She would then be pressured to marry him. That would make the church leaders happy. Marry Kathleen Yoder off, and then they wouldn't have to hear any more about her being a doctor. Noah was part of the leadership.

A terrible, eerie, spine-chilling thought crawled up her back. Had Noah been tasked with courting her and marrying her to keep her from being trouble in the community? To keep her under control? Under *their* control? To keep her from being a doctor? To make an example out of her to everyone else to prove that going to college would amount to nothing?

She didn't want to think Noah capable of such manipulation. He seemed genuine in his help. If his request to court her was just some ploy, why would he have offered her the use of his *dawdy haus*? A way to control her? He *was* a member of the church leadership, after all.

Kathleen leaned into her *mum*'s embrace. "What am I going to do?"

"Pray. Ask *Gott* for guidance. Follow *Gott* first, then your heart."

The next day, Kathleen arrived at Noah's *dawdy haus*, but he wasn't inside as he usually was. She wasn't sure what to do. She needed to talk to him. She needed to know if there was even any point to having the clinic. Was it all just a farce?

She went to the big house and knocked. No answer. She went to the barn. He wasn't there either. Out of options, she sat in one of the rocking chairs on his porch to wait.

Sometime later, she heard her name being called. She opened her eyes to see Noah looking down at her. "I'm sorry. I didn't mean to fall asleep." This old habit was going to be a stubborn one to break. But if she was going to fall asleep and wake up to someone's face, she liked it being his. She stood.

He scrubbed his hand across his clean-shaven face. "I wasn't sure you'd come after last night."

"I wasn't sure if I would either. But I thought it best if we talked about this rather than letting it fester under the surface. I need to ask you a question, and I need an honest answer no matter what it is."

"I have always been honest with you. I see no reason not to be."

He might when he heard her question.

"Did the church leadership put you up to asking to court me as a means to control me?"

His mouth dropped open. "Whatever would make you think that?"

"Some of the leadership members aren't pleased with my plans to be a doctor in the community. If I married, I wouldn't be able to be a doctor, and their problems are solved. So?"

"*Ne.* They had nothing to do with my asking to court you. I asked because I stepped over the line by kissing you. I never should have done that. It was wrong of me. But know this, I would never ask to court you or anyone else, because the leaders asked me to. And believe me, they have asked."

She was glad to hear that. "I appreciate your honesty."

"The only reason I asked was because I kissed you."

"The *only* reason?" Not because he might like her even just a little bit. Even though both their *mutters* seemed to think he did.

"The only reason. I promise you."

She hesitated a moment before broaching her next topic. "About my clinic being in your *dawdy haus*. Since I turned down your offer of courtship, I assume you'd like me to find someplace else."

He shook his head. "*Ne*. We have done too much work to get it set up here. By the time you found someplace else and moved everything, the summer would be almost over and you'd be out of time to prove to the leaders that you should be allowed to continue as a doctor."

She couldn't figure him out. He was a member of the church leaders, but he seemed to favor her practicing medicine. "Why are you supporting my clinic so much?"

He lowered his head and rubbed the back of his neck before meeting her gaze. "I often wonder if Rachel and our baby could have been saved if there had been someone like you close at hand."

Her heart ached for him. But she dared not ask the cause of death. Would he want to know if a physician could have made a difference? Or was it better not to know? Kathleen had been haunted with the knowledge that her sister *would* have lived had there been a medical facility close. No amount of medical knowledge or medicines would save everyone, but many could be spared.

"I admire your dedication, perseverance and desire

to become a doctor. What you have done is incredible.
I couldn't have done it."

She drank in his praise. Coming from anyone else, it
wouldn't mean as much.

He picked up a box she hadn't noticed from the porch
floor. "I got a few more supplies for the clinic. File folders, pens, a desk lamp, coffee, tea and sugar for the
kitchen."

"Did you buy all that?"

He didn't answer.

"You didn't have to buy supplies for my clinic. You
have already done so much."

"I wanted to."

She felt indebted to him and really felt guilty for turning him down last night. But he'd asked only because
he felt guilty. Guilt was no reason to begin a courtship.
She'd been right to turn him down. "Will we be able to
go on as though nothing has happened between us?"

He straightened. "Nothing *has* happened."

The words *the kiss* bubbled up in her throat, but she
tamped them down.

Chapter Ten

Kathleen stood in the kitchen with *Mum* and Ruby. She and Ruby had been tasked with peeling the potatoes for supper.

Jessica had been sent out to the garden to pick other vegetables they would need. She rushed back inside with her basket full. Tomatoes, peas, carrots, onions, garlic, as well as rhubarb to make a pie. "Kathleen has company, *Mum*." Her face was beaming from ear to ear.

Kathleen couldn't imagine who would be visiting her. Certainly not anyone to cause Jessica to smile so wide. "Who?"

"I don't know. He's talking to *Dat*. But he drove up in a shiny red sports car."

Kathleen widened her eyes. A sports car? Who could it be? The only people she knew who drove cars were *Englishers*, and the only *Englishers* she knew who would drive a sports car were doctors. What doctor would be visiting her?

Mum said, "Are you expecting anyone?"

"*Ne*. Maybe he has the wrong place."

Jessica shook her head. "I heard him mention your name."

Ruby set down the potato she was peeling and dried her hands. "Kathleen has an admirer." She headed for the front room. "I want to see him."

An admirer? Not likely. Kathleen wiped her hands on a towel and followed Ruby. Jessica and *Mum* followed as well. Ruby drew back the curtain, and all four of them peered out the front window.

"Who is it?" Jessica asked.

"Do you know him?" Ruby asked.

Kathleen shifted into a better position to see. The large black walnut tree out front blocked her view of *Dat* and the man, so she moved to the other end of the window and pulled the curtain back there.

Dat and the man strolled toward the house.

When they came into view, the man looked familiar. Then he smiled.

Kathleen sucked in a breath, dropped the curtain and stepped back, all in one motion.

Ruby studied her. "I'd say Kathleen knows him."

"Who is he?" *Mum* asked.

Kathleen swallowed. "Ethan Parker. He was one of the doctors in the hospital I did my residency in."

"He's cute," Jessica said.

"Come away from the window." *Mum* shooed her hands toward them. "You don't want him to catch you all gawking. Back into the kitchen. All of you."

Jessica and Ruby dutifully obeyed.

Mum caught Kathleen's arm and slowed her down. "Who is this Dr. Parker?"

"Just a doctor."

"He's gone out of his way to see you."

"We don't know he came to see me."

Mum planted her hands on her hips and gave her a look.

"All right. He must have come to see me. But I don't know why. I certainly never expected him."

With the sound of footsteps on the porch, *Mum* quickly ushered Kathleen back into the kitchen. Then spoke to all three of them. "Hush now, girls. No talking about this man."

Ruby spoke up. "Then I'll talk about Jonathan. I'm very excited about getting married this fall."

Kathleen had met Jonathan a couple of times this summer but hadn't gotten to really know him. When he visited, he spent all his time with Ruby, gazing at her.

The front door opened and closed. Kathleen went still and quiet, and quit listening to Ruby talk about her almost fiancé. Engagements weren't announced until the official proposal came through the bishop in the fall.

Kathleen couldn't make out what *Dat* and Ethan were saying. She thought to motion for her sisters and *Mum* to be quiet and realized they weren't talking but listening as well.

Then *Dat*'s voice grew closer.

Mum whispered, "Get back to work."

Everyone resumed their tasks.

Kathleen picked up the half-skinned potato and peeler as *Dat* walked into the kitchen. She glanced up and forced a smile.

Dat narrowed his eyes around the room. "You don't fool me. You all have been eavesdropping."

Mum tilted her head up. "Us? We weren't listening. It's hard to hear people who talk in hushed tones."

Dat chuckled and turned to Kathleen. "So you know Dr. Parker is here to see you."

Kathleen set the potato and peeler down. "What does he want?"

Dat shook his head. "I told you. To see you. Now go."

Kathleen resisted the urge to tell her family not to listen, but it would do no *gut*. She walked into the living room.

"Dr. Parker. This is a surprise."

"Doctor? What happened to calling me Ethan?"

Kathleen lowered her voice. "That wouldn't be appropriate."

He matched her lower voice. "Why not?"

"It just wouldn't. You're an *Englisher.*"

"A what?"

"You're not Amish, and you're not a member of my family."

"Ah. You've picked up an accent."

"What? I have?"

"On some of your *Englisher* words."

She cocked her head, not finding his joke funny.

"Your dad invited me to dinner."

Her first impulse was to correct him and say *supper*, but she stopped. It didn't matter what he called the meal. She knew what he was talking about. But why would *Dat* invite him to stay? "What brings you all the way out here?"

"You."

She waited, but when he didn't elaborate, she asked. "Me? Why?"

"I've come to take you back to the city."

"Back to the city? I'm not going back. This is my home."

"I think you'll reconsider when you hear my offer."

"I won't change my mind."

"Can we go outside?" He moved to the door and held it open. "I feel as though we're being listened to. I'm sure we're not, but it would make me feel better anyway."

That was because they were. But no matter what he said to her or what he offered, her family wouldn't judge and would allow her to make her own decision. She went outside anyway. "Nothing you say will change my mind."

He arced one hand through the air and spoke as though he were reading something. "The Dr. Kathleen Yoder Clinic For Underprivileged Children."

Her clinic idea she'd come up with for an assignment? "I don't understand."

"I got Howard to agree to the funding. It'll start out in the hospital. But as it grows, we can move into our own facility."

"We? Our?"

"Yes. You and I. We'll run it together. It's what you always wanted."

It had been an assignment project. But she had believed in it wholeheartedly. Though not for herself. "You misunderstood. What I always wanted was to return home and care for the people in my Amish community."

He shook his head. "How's that working out? Do you have patients crowding your waiting room? Do you even *have* a waiting room?"

"*Ja.* I have a waiting room. And a clinic."

"What about patients? You yourself said it would be hard to get the Amish to trust you as a doctor."

She had patients. Ten of them. So far. Just because

most of them were her family members who lived under *Dat* and *Mum*'s roof didn't matter.

"Do your church leaders respect you as a doctor? Do any of your people respect you as a doctor."

Her family did and Noah did. "It's going to take time. Amish are slow to embrace new ideas. But they will come around."

"Until then, what will you do? Take temperatures and bandage scraped knees? You worked really hard to become a doctor. You didn't go through all that work to diagnose colds and dispense ibuprofen. I know you want to be respected as a doctor. This clinic can give you that."

She did want respect as a doctor. She wanted it very much. And the children's clinic could do so much *gut*.

"How long will it take you here to earn even a little bit of respect from a few of these people?"

Longer than she wanted to wait. Her nephew had almost died due to that lack of respect and trust. And come this fall, the leaders would decide if she could even keep her clinic and practice medicine. How could she prove herself if she wasn't truly given the chance? If they turned her down, what then? Never be a doctor? "I don't know. The clinic sounds wonderful, but what about my community here? They still need me."

"You can't help people who don't want to be helped. Help those who want and need your help."

"Why would you take my clinic idea and make it happen? You were one of my strongest opposition."

He gave a wry laugh. "This is a great opportunity. And we could work side by side."

Ethan was offering her the respect she desired. After her brother-in-law had refused her help and Preacher Hochstetler spoke out against her, no one had come to her clinic. Everyone was afraid. Was her little practice ever going to truly be allowed to help anyone? "I don't know."

He smiled. "But you're at least tempted."

She nodded. Maybe *Gott* hadn't wanted her to be a doctor for her community but for underprivileged children. Shouldn't she help where she was both needed and wanted? Maybe that's what *Gott* had called her to do. She wanted to stay in her community. But maybe *Gott* wanted to send her out into the world.

Then she remembered that Noah was coming to supper tonight. She didn't want Ethan and Noah at the same table. She walked toward his car. "I promise to think about it."

He chuckled. "Are you trying to get rid of me?"

She turned back to him. *Ja*, she was. "I need to help my *mum* and sisters with supper preparations."

"Your dad invited me to stay for dinner, remember?"

Of course he did.

Now what was she going to do? Nothing she could do but help with supper and hope Noah forgot.

Noah had hitched up the trap and was now headed to the Yoders. He hoped to entice Kathleen for a buggy ride to try to convince her once again to allow him to court her. As he turned into the Yoders' yard, he automatically pulled back on the reins.

A little red sports car sat parked in front of the house.

Whose car could that be? Obviously an *Englisher*'s. But who? The feeling of a hot coal in the pit of his stomach burned. Someone Kathleen knew. Someone from the outside world. Someone enticing her to leave.

He stared for a long moment, wanting to turn around

and leave, then finally put the horse back into motion. After parking by the barn, he meticulously unhitched Fred and turned him out into the corral with David Yoder's three horses.

Time to go inside. It would be rude to keep everyone waiting.

As he climbed the steps, the door opened, and Jessica came out with a worried expression. "You have to do something. An *Englisher* doctor showed up and asked Kathleen to go back with him."

Noah's gut wrenched.

Kathleen wouldn't leave, would she? She'd worked so hard to become a doctor for their people. The community needed her, even if they wouldn't admit it yet. He needed her here. The community needed her. Would there be anything he could say to make her stay? "What did Kathleen say? Did she agree to go with him?"

"She promised to think about it. I don't want her to go away again. Because...this time it would be for *gut*."

He didn't want Kathleen to go away either. "I don't know what I could say to make her stay."

"Ask to court her. I'm sure she'd stay then."

He couldn't tell Jessica he'd already done that and Kathleen had refused him. "That wouldn't make her stay if she doesn't want to."

"*Ja*, it would. She likes you. I can tell."

Could have fooled him. He'd asked, and she'd turned him down faster than his racing heart. Maybe if he told her *vater* that he'd kissed Kathleen, her *vater* would pressure her into courting. Could he do that to her? Would he want her if she'd been forced?

But if she left, that would solve the issue of the kiss. Wouldn't it? He didn't like that solution one bit. She needed to stay, for the community. The community needed her and was long overdue for a doctor. She had to stay. Though she'd only been back for two months, he couldn't imagine life without her here. He'd felt a sense of security knowing she—a doctor—was so close at hand. She couldn't go. There was no way around that. There was no other option. He had to think of a way to make her stay.

He focused his attention back on Jessica's worried face. "The decision is hers. She has been through a lot and done a lot of hard work to become a doctor and return to be a doctor here. She wouldn't give all that up." He hoped his argument soothed her, though it did nothing to assuage his own trepidation.

"She was gone a long time and is as much English as she is Amish. What if she realizes she likes their way of life better than ours?"

"She's taking the classes and will join church in another month."

"She could easily quit those or even leave after she joins. Joining church is no guarantee she'll stay."

Jessica was right. But he didn't know what else to do. "Let's just see what happens." He opened the screen door for her.

Jessica huffed. "If she leaves, I'm blaming you." Then she entered.

Noah followed. He stared at the man standing with David in the living room. This was worse than he thought. This wasn't some old, crotchety doctor. He was young. Not much older than Kathleen. And if he had to guess, he'd say he might be handsome. Someone a young woman would find handsome and be attracted to. He knew that most Amish tried to seek a spouse who had a *gut* heart and didn't much consider looks. But the English were different. Was Kathleen too English, as Jessica had said? Would she consider this doctor because he was attractive to her?

David turned in Noah's direction and spoke in English. "Ah, Noah. I'm glad you're here. This is Kathleen's friend, Dr. Ethan Parker."

Dr. Parker held out his hand. "Glad to meet you. Call me Ethan."

Noah did not want to shake this man's hand, the man who wanted to take Kathleen away from him, but he did anyway. "Nice to meet you." This would be strange, having a meal with the Yoders and everyone speaking in English.

Kathleen came in from the kitchen. When her gaze met Noah's, a broad smile broke on her face. Her gaze flickered to Dr. Parker, her smile fell and she looked from one to the other.

She'd seemed happy to see Noah. Now she seemed uncomfortable with him here while Dr. Parker was as well. If there was any way for Noah to get out of this meal, he would. Especially for her sake. He didn't want to make her uncomfortable.

Kathleen stumbled over awkward introductions of Noah and Dr. Parker.

Dr. Parker chuckled. "Your father already introduced us."

Noah nodded. "Not to worry." He hoped she understood his message was for her not to worry about him being here while Dr. Parker was.

Everyone sat at the table. David blessed the food—in English—and everyone dished up.

Jessica spoke in *Deutsch*. "We found a family of squirrels in our walnut tree."

David pinned her with a glare and spoke in *Deutsch* as well. "You know better than that. We have company. Speak in English. And apologize."

Jessica turned to Dr. Parker and spoke in English. "I'm so sorry. That was rude of me. I forgot to speak in English. Please forgive me." She flashed a smile at Dr. Parker, but Noah could tell it wasn't genuine. She'd spoken in *Deutsch* on purpose. Little imp. It was nice to know she was on his side.

Dr. Parker smiled in return. "No problem."

"All I said was that we found a family of squirrels in our walnut tree."

Dr. Parker glanced around the table. "Do you all usually speak German at your table?"

Kathleen spoke up. "*Ja*, but we all know English very well."

"I took a little German in high school," Dr. Parker said. "Let me see if I can remember any of it."

Of course he did. Dr. Parker was perfect. Dr. Parker could do anything. Dr. Parker could do *everything*.

Dr. Parker switched to German. *"Das...sch...eune schmeckt wunderbar."*

Jessica and Samuel snickered.

Maybe not so perfect after all.

Dr. Parker switched back to English. "Did I muck that all up? What did I say?"

Noah had to admit that Dr. Parker was a likable fellow. Hard to dislike.

When no one translated what the man had said, Samuel jumped in with the translation. "This barn tastes wonderful."

Dr. Parker laughed at his own ineptitude. "I barely passed the class."

Very difficult to dislike.

After dessert, Dr. Parker stood. "I hate to eat and run, but I should go. *Danki.*" He turned to Kathleen. "See me out?"

Kathleen glanced at Noah before she faced her *vater*.

Noah willed him to say *ne*.

But he nodded.

Kathleen glanced at Noah again before she left with Dr. Parker.

Noah's gut wrenched this way and that. He assumed supper had tasted *wunderbar* as Dr. Parker had said. All of Pamela's meals were, but tonight's had tasted like chalk and roiled in his stomach. He shouldn't have eaten so much. Shouldn't have eaten at all. Shouldn't have come.

He wanted to leave quickly before Kathleen came back, but that would mean seeing Kathleen and Dr. Parker together outside. There would be no way to get past them without being seen. He was stuck.

But in only a couple of minutes, he heard the sound of an engine starting and tires crunching in the dirt driveway, and then Kathleen returned inside. She gave him a shy smile.

Noah stood. "I need to go as well."

Kathleen almost appeared disappointed. "I'll walk you out." She didn't even bother to gain permission from her *vater* like she had with Dr. Parker. What did that mean? Did she want to tell him she'd accepted Dr. Parker's offer? He didn't want to hear that.

"You don't have to."

"I want to." She hurried to the door.

He held the door and walked with her in silence out to the corral.

"I'm sorry about Dr. Parker being here. I had no idea he would show up."

"You can't control what others do." He understood that better than most he supposed, considering the present situation.

She glanced at the trap. "You drove here?"

He nodded. He understood her confusion. He usually walked or rode bareback.

"Why?"

"Why did I drive instead of walking?"

She nodded.

Because I wanted to take you for a buggy ride. "I just felt like driving. The trap was already hitched." Because he'd hitched it to come see her.

"Now I feel even worse."

"Why?"

"I suspect you planned to ask me for a buggy ride. Have you changed your mind?"

He walked Fred from the corral and hitched him to the trap. "I didn't figure you'd want to, with the doctor having been here. I know he asked you to go back with him."

She jerked around to him. "You do? How?"

"Jessica overheard."

"You aren't going to tell my *dat*, are you?"

"It's not my place. But I can't vouch for your sister."

"I'll talk to her."

"Are you going to go?"

"I told him I'd think about it."

That wrenched his insides. She was actually considering his offer.

She put one hand on the trap. "I know why you wanted to take me on a buggy ride."

"You do?" He wasn't quite sure himself.

"You wanted to talk me into courting. I don't want to hurt you, but as I said before, I don't ever plan to marry. I can't."

It would be difficult to be a wife, *mutter and* doctor. At least in an Amish community. English women did it all the time. Did Kathleen long to be English so she could be all three?

"If I asked you to still go on a buggy ride with me, would you?"

Her sweet smile tugged at her mouth. "Why are you asking me? It's my *dat* you need to get permission from."

That was a *ja*. "I'll be right back." He jogged off toward the house.

Her *vater* readily gave his permission, as Noah knew he would. Kathleen's *vater* would rather have Kathleen courted by an Amish man than risk her leaving home again. For *gut*.

When he came back out, Kathleen sat on the trap seat with the reins in her hands.

"You were that sure he'd say *ja*?"

She answered with a smile. "Are you coming?" She held the reins aloft as though she was about to put the buggy in motion.

He jumped in and sat next to her.

She offered him the reins.

He waved them away. "You drive."

"Me? I haven't driven much in years."

"Then this will be *gut* practice." He leaned back in the seat.

She flicked the reins and giggled as the horse pulled the trap into motion.

"It'll come back to you." It wasn't like driving a car.

And if she ran into any difficulty, he could give her gentle instructions. But he didn't foresee her having any trouble.

His mind circled around to driving a car. Had Dr. Parker ever let her drive his fancy red car? Had he given her lessons? Noah didn't want to think about the man being that close to Kathleen.

"So if you never plan to marry, why are you considering Dr. Parker's proposal? Isn't that kind of giving him false hope?"

She guided Fred onto the country road. "What does marriage have to do with it?"

Now he was confused. "Isn't that what his offer is? A proposal of marriage?"

Kathleen jerked her gaze to his. "Certainly not. Is that what Jessica told you?"

He thought back to his conversation with her sister. *Ne*, she hadn't said anything about marriage. "She said he asked you to come back with him, and you agreed to think about it."

Kathleen shook her head. "I'll have to remember to move farther away from the house when I have private conversations."

There weren't many secrets in an Amish community.

"The reason he wants me to return is to open a clinic for disadvantaged children. It was a project assignment we worked on as residents."

"But I thought you wanted to be a doctor here?"

"*I* do, but that doesn't mean the community will allow me to. What if *Gott* wanted me to become a doctor to help these children and that's why it's so difficult to be accepted here? What if it was just me wanting to come back and not *Gott*'s will at all? Out there, I could be respected as a doctor. If I'm not allowed to use my hard-earned skills, why did I go through all that trouble? I don't know what to do anymore."

Stay, he wanted to scream. "A man like Dr. Parker wants you back for more than working at a clinic for children."

She gave a little laugh. "You mean like marriage? *Ne.* He's always very professional."

"*Ja*, I mean marriage. He could open a clinic with any doctors. But he came out all this way to ask you."

"That's because I was in the group with him."

"He could have written. That would have been more businesslike."

She was quiet.

So he went on. "I saw the way he looked at you. Trying to fit in with your family."

"I hardly think he wants to be Amish. And he didn't *look* at me in any special way. It's the way he always looks at all people."

She couldn't see it. She truly couldn't see it.

"I don't mean to be disagreeable, but he didn't look at anyone else around the table the way he gazed at you."

She pulled the horse over to the side of the road and stopped. She shifted in the seat to face him. "You're serious, aren't you? You think he wants to marry me?"

"*Ja.*"

She turned back forward and stared. "I… I don't know what to say."

Say you won't go.

She faced him again. "You don't think that's why I'm considering his offer, do you? I'm only considering it to be respected as a doctor."

That was *gut* to know. But the marriage aspect might appeal to her and tip her in Dr. Parker's direction. She could have everything with him. He needed to find a way to stop that. "You know how slow to accept change our people are. It will take time, but I believe they'll come to accept you as a doctor. You can pave the way for others who want to do *gut* and help our community in unconventional ways. Don't give up too easily."

After a moment, she nudged the trap back onto the road. "May I change the subject?"

"Sure."

"I don't think you need to feel like we must court because we kissed. No one knows and nothing really happened. I don't see anything wrong in it."

"That's because you lived in the English world so long. They see things differently."

"You really think of this as a big issue?"

"I do. We have *hands-off* courtships here."

"Not everyone chooses that."

He had hoped she wouldn't remember that. "But most do. If anyone found out, we would be frowned upon."

"Well, I'm not going to tell anyone. Are you?"

He might need to. "That wouldn't change what happened."

She pulled into his driveway.

"What are you doing?"

"I'll walk back home."

"*Ne*, you won't." He couldn't allow her to walk home alone at dusk. He held out his hands for the reins. Would she give up the reins? Would she make a fuss about him taking her home?

With a huge sigh, she handed them over.

It was *gut* to know she could be reasonable.

Now, would she be reasonable enough to stay here where she belonged?

Chapter Eleven

❧

The following morning after breakfast, Kathleen followed *Dat* and her brothers out the side kitchen door. "Benjamin?"

The oldest of her brothers stopped and turned. *"Ja."*

Kathleen quickened her steps to meet up with him in the yard. "May I borrow your courting buggy today?"

His courting buggy was the same open-air variety as Noah's two-wheeled trap. "Sure. Are you leaving right away?"

"Soon."

"I'll hitch it up for you before I leave."

"Danki." Kathleen ran back inside.

Jessica stood in her path. "I'm ready to leave whenever you are."

Kathleen hadn't thought about how to keep Jessica from going with her today. She could make the call from her office and leave Jessica at the clinic. "Be ready in five minutes."

"I'm ready now."

Mum laughed. "It looks like Jessica is back to that little girl who couldn't be parted from you."

Kathleen loved her sister and loved that she wanted to be with her, but today, she would have to cope with a few hours of separation. "I love having her with me." She would set Jessica to work at a task in the clinic.

A few minutes later, Benjamin came in. "The buggy is tied out front."

She hadn't wanted anyone to know. Too late. *"Danki."*

"Buggy?" *Mum* said.

"I didn't feel like walking today." Because she was going all the way into town and *that* would be a long walk indeed.

"Didn't you sleep well last night? I thought your sleeping was getting better."

It had been better than when she first arrived. Now she was getting a *gut* six hours in a row. Except last night. What Noah had told her about Ethan had disturbed her, her thoughts galloping through her mind about the disadvantaged children's clinic Ethan had offered her. A chance to be respected as a doctor. "I didn't sleep as well as I have been. I kept waking up. My body is still adjusting to more normal sleep. I will be fine." Once she talked to Ethan and cleared up any misconceptions.

"All right. Have a *gut* day."

Thankful *Mum* had not questioned her further or detained her, she turned to Jessica. "Pack us a lunch and meet me at the buggy."

"All right." Jessica got to work.

Kathleen went to her room and gathered her things, along with Ethan's business card he'd given her last night just before he left. She should get business cards.

A few minutes later, Kathleen and her sister were seated in the buggy and on their way. She pulled into Noah's driveway and up to the clinic. She thrilled at the sight of the sign Noah had made her, as always. She might not have patients yet, but she had a door sign with her name.

Noah. She hoped this was one of the days he was busy elsewhere. She didn't want to face him until after she'd spoken to Ethan. Even then, she might not want to see Noah. It would depend on what happened in town.

She set the brake, wrapped the reins around the handle and climbed out.

Jessica stepped down and grabbed the lunch basket. "Do you want me to unhitch the horse?"

That would be the thing to do if she weren't going into town. "Not just yet."

Kathleen went inside ahead of her baby sister. As she walked through the waiting area toward her office, she said, "Could you give this whole area a thorough cleaning?" Not that she expected any patients. She'd had only one or two patients a week with minor things to treat: sore throat, burn, scrapes and one case taken care of with butterfly adhesive strips. Her most difficult case to date. But she needed to keep her sister busy. She continued on into her office and shut the door. Something she didn't normally do.

She sat behind the desk and stared at the phone. She picked up the handset and stared at the numbers. Then she slipped Ethan's business card out of her side seam dress pocket.

At the soft knock on the door and the turn of the handle, she clumsily and a bit noisily replaced the handset and secreted the business card onto her lap. *"Ja."*

Jessica poked her head around the door. "Do you want me to scrub the kitchen floor or just sweep it?"

Kathleen didn't know and didn't really care. "If it's

fine with only a sweeping, then don't bother to mop. But if it looks like it needs it, then please do."

"All right." She disappeared and shut the door without a sound.

If Kathleen wanted to get her call made uninterrupted, she needed to be quick about it. She picked up the handset again and retrieved the card. She flipped it over to where Ethan had written his cell phone number.

She wished she knew where he was staying so she could call and leave a message at the front desk. Taking a deep breath, she punched in the numbers.

Ring number one.

Her stomach tightened.

Number two.

Her chest tightened.

Three.

Her breathing became shallow. She wanted to hang up, but he would just call the number back from the caller ID. And she certainly didn't want Jessica picking up.

Four?

Where was he? If he'd turned his phone off, it would have gone straight to voice mail.

Then the slight click of the phone being answered with a sleepy "Hello—" Then a clunking and clacking that sounded as though the phone might have been dropped.

"Hello?" she ventured.

More clacking and scratching sounds, then Ethan came back on the line with another sleepy "Hello?"

At least she thought it was him. "Ethan? This is Kathleen Yoder."

He cleared his throat, and his voice seemed to wake up. "Kathleen? I wasn't expecting you to call."

Then why had he given her his phone number? "Did I wake you up?"

"No. Of course not. Okay. Yes, you did. You know how it is with irregular sleeping schedules that are always changing. I slept for a couple of hours, then was up for several, and then I dropped off again around six. But you didn't call to hear about that. Have you decided to accept my offer?"

"I would like to talk to you about that."

"Sure. What do you want to know?"

"Not on the phone. There is a coffee shop on the corner of Chicago Avenue and Lincoln Highway. Can you meet me there at ten?"

"Of course. But I can come pick you up. Then we could meet sooner."

That wouldn't do. "No, ten will be fine. I'll meet you then. Goodbye."

"Kathleen?"

"Ja."

His voice took on a wistful quality. "I'm really glad you called."

Her insides flopped. She didn't know how to respond to that. Fortunately, she didn't have to because he spoke again.

"See you at ten." He hung up, and so did she.

She hoped this was the right course of action. Leaving now would allow her to make the hour and a half drive and arrive before ten. She wanted to be seated and ready. The last one to a meeting was at a disadvantage.

After leaving her office, she found Jessica crouching with the broom in one hand and the dustpan in the other, corralling the dirt from the floor into the dustpan.

Jessica straightened and dumped the dirt into the waste pail. "I don't think the floor needs to be mopped. What do you think?"

Kathleen glanced at the floor. It did look fine. Why shouldn't it? It had been walked on very little since the last time it was mopped. Jessica didn't need to do unnecessary work, but at the same time, she wanted to keep her sister busy. "It looks fine. I'm going into town. I'll be back by lunch."

Jessica quickly tucked the broom back into the utility closet. "Oh *gut*. I'd love to go into town."

Not what Kathleen had planned. "I was going to go alone."

"Oh, please let me go with you. I love going into town. *Mum* thinks I like too much about town and doesn't like me to go."

Mum was probably right. And if *Mum* didn't want Jessica going all the time, it was best if Kathleen didn't take her. "How do you think *Mum* will react when she learns I took you into town without her permission?"

"I won't tell her." Then her face brightened. "*That's* the reason you drove the buggy."

Her little sister was perceptive. "I don't—"

The front door opened, and Kathleen whirled around.

Noah entered. "Would you like me to unhitch your horse?"

"*Ne. Danki.* I'm heading into town."

"I can go with you."

Not Noah too. Was that hope she heard in his voice? Jessica latched onto Kathleen's arm. "Sorry. I'm going with her. Benjamin's buggy doesn't seat more than two."

Given the choice between the two, Jessica would be the better one for the errand Kathleen needed to make.

Noah nodded. "Then I'll see you later." The hope gone from his voice.

Kathleen wanted it back. "We should be back for lunch. If you're around, you can join us. We have plenty of food."

His face brightened. "I'll see you then."

All three walked out, and Noah held on to the harness while Kathleen and Jessica climbed aboard.

"Can I drive?" Jessica reached for the reins.

Kathleen laughed. "I'll drive. I need the practice."

Noah waved as Kathleen drove off. She nodded in reply.

Jessica waved to Noah, then situated herself forward. "He likes you, you know?"

"Who?" Her sister couldn't mean Ethan. How would she know? Did she suspect Kathleen was going to meet him? How would she excuse herself from Jessica?

Jessica guffawed. "Noah, silly."

"Noah?"

How could Jessica know that? Had she seen Noah kiss her? This could not be *gut*.

"He hangs around the clinic. He looks at you a lot. And he acts happier now that you're home."

Noah certainly didn't care for her in that way. But the thought made her giddy inside anyway. *Ne.* She needed to stop that. She could never marry, and that was that. She would have to put Noah Lambright right out of her mind.

She had assumed that Noah had asked to court her

only because he'd kissed her as he said. And he'd only kissed her because she'd been so upset. But had that all been an excuse? Hadn't he said that he never planned to marry?

At the edge of town, Kathleen knew she needed to part from her sister. "Can I drop you at the library?"

"So you can meet Dr. Parker?"

"What? How did you know about that?"

"I heard you on the phone."

"It's nothing. I'm just meeting him for coffee. I'll let you off at the library."

"*Gut.* I want to check out some books on business."

When Kathleen pulled to a stop in front of the library, she put her hand on her baby sister's arm. "Please reconsider going to college. What do you want to study business for?"

"So I can learn to run a successful business."

But would the lure of the outside world be too much for Jessica to resist? Would Kathleen's disobedience cause her sister to stumble and leave their community? She wouldn't be able to forgive herself for that.

Jessica flashed a smile, like she did when she was a baby. "Don't worry about me." She climbed down.

"I'll be back by ten thirty." Her conversation with Ethan shouldn't take long.

Jessica nodded and waved, then disappeared through the library doors.

Kathleen clucked the horse into motion. She would need to hurry if she was going to arrive before Ethan.

She pulled up to the coffee shop ten minutes early. She went inside to find Ethan already seated at a table in the far corner.

He waved her over.

He was early?

She hadn't anticipated that. So much for getting herself a cup of coffee.

With his charming smile, he stood as she approached the table and held a chair out for her.

She sat across from him.

He waved to the barista before seating himself again. "Your coffee will be here in a minute."

"My coffee? But I haven't ordered anything."

"I ordered it ahead of time."

"*Danki*—I mean thank you. You didn't have to do that."

"I know how much we doctors live on coffee. Some days I wish I could have a caffeine IV drip. Say fifty milligrams an hour."

Kathleen didn't have the heart to tell him that she'd cut way back on her consumption. But with her lack of sleep last night, she could use it.

The coffees arrived. Two extra larges.

She inhaled the aroma. Strong, dark and loaded with sugar. "You had them add sugar."

"Three heaping teaspoons. I know you like yours sweet."

He remembered? This wasn't *gut*. He was too cheerful and happy to see her. Trying too hard. "You didn't have to wait for me to get your coffee."

He dipped his head, then looked up sideways, sheepishly. "This is my third."

"How long have you been here?"

"Since five after nine. I wanted to make sure I didn't miss you."

Well, he'd made sure of that. So, no matter how early

she'd intended to arrive, he still would have been here before her. She sat awkwardly for a minute.

He cleared his throat. "Please tell me you're going to accept my offer and work with me at the clinic."

"I haven't decided." The idea appealed to her. A lot. She would have no trouble getting patients or being respected. But she would have to leave her people for *gut*. And leave Noah. Her breath caught.

"Then why did you want to talk to me?"

She might as well dive right in. "Someone said that your offer was for more than just working at the clinic."

He shifted in his chair and studied his coffee. "Like what?"

She felt foolish saying it but couldn't back out now. "Like your offer might include more than working at the clinic."

"More?" He took a long sip of his coffee as though he were hiding behind it.

If she decided to accept his offer, she needed to know exactly where she stood. "Me."

He set his cup down and took several deep breaths, gazing at her.

Ne. Noah had been right.

Ethan stretched out his hand and rested it on hers. "You had to know I care about you. I pushed for the clinic for you."

This was what she'd been afraid of. She slipped her hand from his. "You know I'm never going to get married. I can't be a doctor and a wife. It can't be done."

"Not with the Amish. But out here—" he spread his hands wide "—it's done all the time."

That was true. Could she actually have a career as a doctor as well as being a wife and *mutter*?

He reached across the table and recaptured her hand in both of his. "I care a lot for you. I might even go so far as to say that I love you."

"Don't say that." She knew she didn't love him. But she loved what he was offering her. Something no Amish man could. Or would. Besides, *Englishers* threw around the word *love* like it was nothing more than a chocolate candy to be savored for the moment then on to the next thing they loved. It wasn't something lasting.

"If you accept the position at the clinic, I won't pressure you. We can date like everyone else, and you can let your feelings for me grow."

He assumed they would. Would they? In Amish marriages, there wasn't always love when a couple married. But it always grew after marriage. Didn't it?

"I don't know. I'll think about it. About all of it." She stood, pulling her hand free again.

He stood as well. "Don't go. I feel as though I just messed everything up between us."

"You have given me a lot to consider. I need time."

"How much time? I just want to know when I should stop hoping."

"Next month I must make the decision to join church or not. I'll let you know by then."

"Just so you know, if you accept the clinic position, I won't assume I'm part of that. I'll give you all the time you need."

She appreciated that, nodded and left without so much as one sip of her coffee.

It was only ten o'clock. Too early to pick up Jessica.

So she stopped by a big box store to pick up supplies for her clinic. She had to have something to prove she went into town with a purpose other than to see Ethan.

After that, she headed to the library, parked and went inside. Heddy wasn't sitting behind the desk. Nor did she see the woman as Kathleen searched for her sister.

Jessica checked out an armload of books, several on business and two on getting a GED. Should Kathleen tell her parents? Or let this play out and see where it led? Maybe her sister would grow tired of the idea. After helping with the plethora, Kathleen drove back to her clinic.

"How did your meeting go with Dr. Parker?" Jessica asked.

How did it go? "All right, I guess."

"What did he want?"

What should she tell her sister? Until she made a decision, it was best not to tell her anything. "Nothing really."

Jessica's voice took on a concerned quality. "Are you going leave again? For *gut*?"

"Ne." The word shot out of Kathleen's mouth before she knew it. Was that how she truly felt? Or just a practiced response due to years of conditioning? "I don't know. I always dreamed of coming back and helping our community."

"But no one is making that easy for you."

"Ne, they're not." Except Noah. "Don't say anything to anyone. All right?" Especially Noah.

"All right. But I'm going to be praying for you to stay. Forever."

Chapter Twelve

Noah sat at his *vater*'s kitchen table, cradling a cup of coffee in his hands. He couldn't shake the feeling of needing to talk to his *mutter*. The only person who really knew about her was his *vater*. Which had propelled him here. But he didn't know how to bring up the subject. His *vater* only ever talked about Noah's *mutter* in general terms, but mostly avoided the subject.

His *vater* cradled his own cup. "I can't remember the last time you sat at my table."

"It's been a while." Though they saw each other every other week at church service and sometimes in between, they didn't see each other on a regular basis.

Staring into his coffee, his *vater* spoke. "When a man gets on in years, he thinks back over his life and can see his mistakes clearly. One of my biggest regrets is pushing you away."

"You never pushed me away."

"I did by being harsh with you. I promised myself that if I ever had the blessing of having you at my table again, I'd let you know I was sorry. Sorry for a lot of things."

His *vater* had always seemed strong and self-assured.

But the man before Noah looked humbled. Maybe his *vater* was ready to talk about Noah's *mutter*. "Why did *Mutter* leave?"

He stared into his coffee. "Another regret. I did and said things when I was younger that were unkind and unfair. I couldn't see what I had. Only what I *didn't* have."

"I remember you and *Mutter* fighting, but I never saw you hit her or anything. Nothing that would give her reason to leave."

His *vater* took a deep breath before speaking again. "The wounds I inflicted and the scars I created were on the inside. On her heart."

Noah waited for his *vater* to go on.

"I know you want me to tell you the rest, but it's your *mutter*'s story to tell, not mine. If she's in town, you should go talk to her."

"I don't know what to say to her after all these years."

"Ask her to explain, and then just listen."

"So you're not going to tell me anything."

"After you speak to her, if you still have questions, I'll see what I can answer. But you need to talk with her first."

This had not been very helpful. Noah stood, went out to the corral and retrieved his horse.

As he swung up onto his horse, his *vater* came to his side. "Two things, Noah. No matter what your *mutter* tells you, I do love you, son."

"I've never doubted your love." But his *vater* feared he might. "And the second thing?"

"I've never stopped loving her either."

He still loved *Mutter*?

"Would you welcome her back after all these years?"

"I might."

That was unexpected. But it shouldn't be. The Amish forgave no matter the transgression if the guilty party confessed and asked for forgiveness. Would his *mutter* be willing?

Noah worked in his barn on a filing cabinet for Kathleen. He had sanded the wood smooth. When she had more patient records, she would need a place to store them. He had to believe she would have more patients. She had to. If not, she might be tempted by Dr. Parker's offer to leave.

When he heard barking, Noah peeked out of the barn. All three dogs ran out to greet the incoming buggy. His heart relaxed at the sight of Kathleen.

He went back inside and threw a canvas tarp over the filing cabinet. He wanted it to be a surprise.

Then he strolled over to the *dawdy haus* to unhitch her horse. He took hold of the harness. "I'll take care of her and then be in for lunch. If the offer still stands."

Kathleen gifted him with a genuine smile. Not the forced one she'd had before she left. "Of course. We'll get everything set out." She grabbed several plastic bags by the handles.

Jessica hoisted a tall stack of what appeared to be library books. "Don't be long."

He didn't intend to. "Can I get those for you? Either of you?"

"We have them," Jessica said. *"Danki."*

She seemed eager.

He wondered why, though it really didn't matter. Jessica wasn't the only one who wanted him to hurry. He longed to sit in Kathleen's company.

Once the horse was settled in the corral, he went

inside. The table had been set with a white tablecloth, plates and flatware. A little fancy for a picnic-style lunch.

Jessica grinned. "Have a seat. I'll tell Kathleen everything is ready." She sauntered to her sister's office, looking back over her shoulder. She motioned for him to sit.

He did and stared at the table.

Jessica had made a mistake. There were only two plates set out.

Maybe he wasn't welcome at lunch after all. He would just get another plate. But he was too late.

Jessica returned with Kathleen.

He stood anyway.

Pulling out a chair, Jessica spoke to her sister. "Have a seat."

Kathleen sat. "Certainly we don't need plates. And there's one short."

"I'll get it," Noah said.

Jessica waved him away. "Don't bother. I have to go back home. I remembered something *Mum* needed help with this afternoon. Bye." She scooped up her books and darted out the door.

Kathleen jerked her head back. "What was that all about?" Though her expression told him she knew.

Noah chuckled and sat back down. "Not very subtle."

"*Ne*, she's not. I'm sorry about her."

"Don't be."

"We can pretend this is just an ordinary lunch like we've shared many times, can't we?"

Ordinary? There was nothing ordinary about Kathleen. "Sure." He said a blessing over the meal, and they ate in companionable silence.

When Kathleen served him a piece of peach cobbler, he said, "Can I ask you a question?"

She smiled. "Of course."

He wanted to get lost in her smile but turned his thoughts back to his question. "Earlier, when you left for town, you seemed uneasy around me. Did I do something? Or was it because of last night?"

"*Ne—ja—ne—*"

What had made her so flustered? "I don't mean to upset you."

"You haven't. You haven't done anything. And *ja*, it does have to do with last night." She was silent for a few moments.

"You don't have to tell me if you don't want to."

"*Ne.* You deserve to know. I didn't sleep well thinking about what you said."

He wanted to ask which thing that he said had disturbed her so much but decided to wait for her to tell him on her own.

"I just couldn't see what you saw where Eth—Dr. Parker was concerned."

He didn't want to think or talk about Dr. Parker.

"It made no sense that he had anything more in mind than a position at the new clinic."

But he had.

"I went into town to talk to him. He admitted he… has feelings for me."

She seemed sort of upset, but not fully. Did this revelation change her mind? "So have you reconsidered thinking over his offer?"

"I'm still considering it."

Ne!

"I would have real patients that would *want* me to treat them. I'd be respected as a doctor."

And she would have Dr. Parker. Noah wished he'd never told her that the *Englisher* doctor had more in mind than just a clinic. He'd thought it would turn her off the idea. But it hadn't. He pushed back from the table and to his feet. "I have work to do."

Kathleen stood as well. "What about your cobbler?"

"I'm full. *Danki* for the food." He strode out, off the porch and into the barn.

He'd been a fool to think the Amish way of life could compete with everything Dr. Parker could offer Kathleen. She'd been young when she left and had been gone so long that it was natural for her to think more like an *Englisher* than an Amish. *Ja*, after all that time, she could never truly think like an Amish again.

He pulled the tarp back from the file cabinet. Should he bother to even finish it? She wasn't likely to stay. He kicked it with his boot and dented the wood on the bottom.

"Noah?"

At the sound of Kathleen's voice, he jerked the tarp back into place and spun around. *"Ja."* He walked toward the entrance where she stood.

"I feel as though I should apologize for upsetting you."

"You have nothing to apologize for."

"But you seem upset that I went to see Ethan."

Why did she have to use his first name? It was too familiar. Dr. Parker was an outsider. "You are free to see whomever you like. I'm upset that you're considering his offer. What happened to helping our community? What about everything you went through? What about your sister Nancy? Was all that just an excuse? Was I wrong to stand up for you to the other church leaders?" Had he been wrong to allow his feelings to grow for her?

"They don't want me as a doctor here."

"So you are just going to give up after three months? You knew it was going to be hard. You knew it would take time and convincing. You said you would have to convince our community. Where did all your aspirations go? This community needs you, whether they want to admit it or not. What about your nephew? Without you, he would have suffered the same fate as your sister."

Her eyes filled with tears.

He hadn't meant to hurt her. He'd just wanted her to come to her senses. "I'm sorry. I shouldn't have said all those things."

She shook her head. "Don't be sorry. Everything you said is true. I'll hitch up my horse and leave."

He stepped toward her. "Don't go, Kathleen. Please."

"I have a lot to think about."

"You can't do that at home with your *mutter* and sisters around. You know Jessica will pester you as to why you are home already. Stay at the *dawdy haus* for the afternoon. I promise not to bother you."

After a moment, she nodded and walked away.

A part of him went with her. And he realized, a part of him would always go with her.

Kathleen went back to the *dawdy haus*. She had much to consider and think over. Everything Noah had said was true.

Where had all of her hopes and dreams gone? Where *had* her aspirations gone? Where had her convictions gone?

Lord, what should I do?

She spent the afternoon flip-flopping between trying to figure out what to do and worrying that Noah would come and try to sway her to stay. Then there was always the disappointment when he hadn't come. He'd been true to his word. And the solitude of the house did offer her a quiet place and the time to think.

But now that it was time to go home, she hoped Noah didn't try to talk her into anything or ask her if she'd made a decision. Because she hadn't. She was no closer to knowing what she was going to do than four hours ago.

Maybe she could slip out and walk home without him noticing. But what about the horse and Benjamin's buggy? *Ne*, she couldn't leave them here. That would be irresponsible. If Noah was anywhere around when she hitched up the horse and buggy, she prayed he wouldn't pressure her.

She collected her backpack of traveling medical supplies and the picnic basket. Lunch had been a disaster. She opened the door, stepped out onto the porch and stopped.

Tied to the porch railing stood her horse hitched to her brother's buggy.

She looked around.

Noah was nowhere to be seen.

He'd been true to his word and thoughtful to boot.

She locked the clinic and stowed her things in the buggy before climbing aboard. As she drove out of his driveway and turned onto the road, she glanced back but still didn't see Noah.

She arrived home way too quickly for her liking.

When had buggy travel seemed so fast? She could use more time to herself.

Neither *Dat* nor her brothers were in the barn, so she unhitched the horse and turned him out into the corral, then she wheeled the buggy into its place in the barn.

When Kathleen entered the house through the kitchen door, *Mum* glanced up from cutting biscuit dough and did a double take. "Gracious, Kathleen. You look peaked. Are you feeling all right?"

"*Ja.* I'm fine." Though she did feel absolutely drained, between little sleep and the upheaval of her emotions. "I'll put my things away and come back down to help."

"You lay down and rest. We have supper well in hand."

Kathleen climbed the stairs.

In her wake came Jessica. "Did you have a fight with Noah?"

Kathleen wouldn't call it a fight, exactly. She shook her head. "Don't think we both don't know what you were up to by setting the table like that and leaving so conspicuously."

Her baby sister grinned. "Did it work?"

Kathleen offered a withering look. "What do you think?" She didn't need her sister playing matchmaker.

Jessica straightened. "I think I need to try harder."

"Don't bother. I don't plan to ever marry. I gave up that option when I decided to become a doctor."

Jessica's expression changed to concern. "Why?"

"No Amish man is going to want their wife busy being a doctor."

"No *Amish* man? Is that why you met with Dr. Parker? Are you going to marry him?"

"I haven't made any decisions yet."

"So you're considering marrying him?"

"Ne." At least Kathleen didn't think so.

"Noah would let you be a doctor. I know he would."

Would he? Even if he would, he deserved better than a wife who would be busy with patients all day and might be gone at all hours. "He doesn't wish to marry again. So your little matchmaking schemes won't work."

"But—"

"Please let me rest."

Jessica huffed as she left the room.

Kathleen flopped back onto her bed. Life had been so much easier as an Amish before she left. Now it seemed as though every time she turned around, her life was getting more and more complicated.

Noah had kissed her and wanted to court because of it. If she said *ja*, he would eventually offer her marriage. If she married him, what would become of all her medical training?

And Ethan wanted her to go back to the English world with him. And marry him? Out there she could be a doctor *and* a wife. But did she want that? Did she want to marry Ethan?

But what about Noah? He'd stood up for her and helped her get her clinic going. If she left, she would disappoint him.

She had a lot to think about.

Chapter Thirteen

Two days later, Noah jumped down from his covered buggy in the Yoders' yard. He had made a decision. He was going to see his *mutter*. And he wanted Kathleen to come along. Not because he needed her there when he spoke to his *mutter* for the first time in over a decade and a half. Not because she'd talked to his *mutter* already. And not because he need a mediator.

He wanted her along simply because he enjoyed her company. But if he was being honest with himself, her support would encourage him. And with her beside him, he wouldn't be able to change his mind.

As he climbed the porch steps, Jessica came out the door. "Noah. We weren't expecting you. Kathleen and I were just about to head over to the clinic."

"I have a favor to ask you. Don't head over until the afternoon. I'm taking Kathleen into town."

Jessica wiggled her eyebrows, leaned close and lowered her voice. "Does she know that?"

He chuckled. "Not yet."

She put one hand on her hip. "How do you feel about Ada Mae Hershberger being a *mutter* of five and running her Plain & Simple shop of Amish novelties?" Her voice took on a wistful quality, and she no longer looked at him. "And Sarah Kuhns runs a fruit stand with her children. And Hannah Lapp does custom quilting, and she has children. You don't have anything against a wife and *mutter* helping contribute to the family, do you?"

"Ne." He wasn't sure what Jessica was going on about, but felt as though he was answering more than her straightforward question. "Is Kathleen here?"

"I'll go get her."

"Danki."

Jessica dashed inside and spoke in a singsong voice. "Kathleen, there's a dashing man waiting for you on the porch."

That girl needed to learn to be a little more subtle.

When Kathleen came out, she wore a concerned expression that quickly brightened. "Oh. It's you."

"Who were you expecting?"

"No one. I mean I wasn't expecting anyone first thing in the morning. Jessica and I are just on our way to the clinic."

From inside the house, Jessica called, "I'm going to head over after lunch. So you two go on without me."

Kathleen opened her mouth to reply, but Noah spoke first. "I asked her to come over later."

"Oh. I can come over later as well if there's a problem."

"No problem. I just wanted you to go into town with me."

She narrowed her eyes and stepped back. "Why?"

He had two reasons and neither were the one he would give her. "I'm going to visit my *mutter*. I'd like to have you along."

She straightened. "Oh. I'd be happy to. But you don't need me to go with you. She was very nice."

Noah thought back and remembered his *mutter* being a kind and caring woman. "I'd like you there."

"Then I'd be happy to go. Let me get my things."

He'd had the dream again, but when he rounded the corner, his *mutter was* there… With Kathleen at her side.

In no time, Kathleen sat at *his* side as he drove into town. So the first reason for inviting her was accomplished. Now for the second. "Have you made a decision about Dr. Parker's offer?"

Kathleen remained silent for a minute. "I don't want to talk about his offer or him. But *ne*, I haven't decided."

Well, at least she hadn't chosen to leave. "All right, but I'd like to say one thing, then I'll drop it."

"What's that?"

"You left and went to college with a clear purpose, to return and help our people. I don't believe that has changed. If our people didn't need a doctor so badly, you never would have left. But they did then and still do now."

"They need a doctor who can help them. I'm not so sure I'm that doctor. If no one will come to me, then I'm useless here, and it would be better that there were no doctor than an ineffective one. It would be better for an *Englisher* doctor to be brought in than to have me standing in the way of help for this community."

He noticed she didn't say *my* or *our* community. Was she detaching herself? "I believe you are meant to be *our* doctor."

"But how many people have to die before the leaders come around? I don't want to be responsible for people dying because I'm an impediment for another doctor coming in to practice. Can we please drop this now?"

He didn't want to because he hadn't convinced her to stay yet, but he would, because she asked. If he pushed any further, she might jump out and walk back.

The silence that hung in the air became strained. He wanted to ease the unspoken tension. "You asked me if I was angry with you for talking to my *mutter* without asking me."

"I should have asked you first."

"*Ne*. It's not mine to say who you can speak to." He'd taken his *mutter* not being home last time as a sign from *Gott* that he didn't need to reconcile with her. She'd made her choice and it was up to her to take the first step. But after Kathleen had visited her, he'd had this odd feeling. It took him a few days to figure out what it was. *She'd* talked his *mutter*, and now he wanted to. "I'm a bit envious that you have gotten to speak to her and I haven't."

"And you're changing that today."

He still didn't know what to say to her. Should he just blurt out, *Why did you leave us? Why did you leave* me? That was the crux of it. He'd felt abandoned. And why the thought of Kathleen considering leaving felt like she was abandoning him too, even though he knew he had no history or real connection with her.

When they pulled into town, Noah's insides felt all twisted up. "You said she works at the library?"

"It won't be open yet. You'll have better luck if you go to her house."

He pulled up in front of the little cottage about the size of the *dawdy haus*. He didn't get out.

But Kathleen did. "Are you coming?"

"I don't know." He wanted to say just the right thing to his *mutter*.

"No hurry." She leaned against the side of the buggy and waited.

After a few minutes, the front door opened, and an Amish woman stepped out onto the small porch but no farther. His *mutter*.

Pushing away from the rig, Kathleen glanced between *mutter* and son. "She'll speak to you. I know she will."

"But will I be able to speak to her?"

"She's your *mutter*. The words will come."

Would they? "You go. I'll be along in a minute."

She nodded and headed up the walk to the porch. They spoke, but he couldn't tell what they said.

His *mutter* gave him a nod and disappeared inside with Kathleen.

He wanted to say mean things to her. Accuse her of her misdeeds. Hurl pent-up questions and frustrations at her. Make her feel the pain he felt the first time she left. And the second. And the third and final time. The anger and hurt he'd tamped down over the years rose and burned. He wanted her to know how much she'd hurt him. But at the same time, he didn't want to push her away again.

Lord, take away this burning inside me and give me the right words to say.

He felt no different, but something inside him propelled him out of the buggy and up the walk. He stopped just outside the threshold.

His *mutter* and Kathleen sat in the small sitting room. His *mutter* stood from an overstuffed rocker.

When the first word crossed his lips—*"Mutter"*—
the bitterness washed away and love consumed him.

"My son. I've been praying for this moment every
day." Her eyes glistened with tears.

Eyes that mirrored his. He'd forgotten he got most of
his looks from her.

Staring at her, he realized he'd been wrong to stay
away. Wrong to hold this bitterness in his heart. Wrong
not to forgive her. She had suffered as much as he had.
But he still wanted some answers and hoped she would
tell him more than his *vater* had.

She motioned to the love seat Kathleen sat on. "Please
have a seat. I've made tea." She picked up a cup and
handed it to him.

He took it and sat next to Kathleen, as it was the only
available seat in the sitting room.

His *mutter* returned to her chair. "You must have a
lot of questions for me."

"Too many. I scarcely know where to begin."

Kathleen inched forward and set her cup on the coffee table. "I'll leave the two of you to talk privately."

"Don't go." He had the urge to take her hand but
didn't. She was supposed to be here.

"But I thought you two would like to speak freely."

Though his *mutter* looked as though she would like
to be alone, she gave a nod. "You may stay."

He handed Kathleen her tea.

She took it and settled back in the seat.

His *mutter* spoke. "I can't tell you how happy I am
that you've come."

"I should have come sooner."

"Ne. All in *Gott*'s timing. You probably want to know
why I left. What has your *vater* told you?"

"He said he'd scarred your heart. That no matter what you told me that he loved me. And that…he still loves you."

"He does?"

"That's what he said. Why didn't you come back?" He glanced around the room. If he didn't know better, he would think he was in a *dawdy haus*. "You seem to live and dress as an Amish. Why live apart?"

"Your *vater* and I hurled bitter words at each other. I didn't come back because I didn't think your *vater* wanted me back."

"Why would you think that?"

"The last time I left, I told him if he wanted me back, he would have to come to me this time. He never came."

"I don't think he knows you're in town."

"He knows. Just as you knew."

His *vater* had seen her? Why hadn't he said anything?

"I was both hurt and proud of you for staying with him."

"How so?"

"Hurt, obviously, because you—my son—didn't choose to leave with me."

"I thought if *Vater* and I were both in one place, you'd come back to us. Why proud?"

"You chose the Amish way of life."

The English world held no appeal to him. "I know you and *Vater* fought, but was it so bad that you had to leave? I never saw him hit you or anything."

"It was his words that wounded. He blamed me that we couldn't have any more children."

"But you had me. You should have been able to have more."

"It's not that simple. But, I suppose, you deserve to

know. Though your *vater* is your *vater* in every way that matters…he's not your biological *vater*."

Noah tried to make sense of her words. "I don't understand."

"When I went on *Rumspringa*, I was a foolish girl. In our community, everyone looked out for each other. And I never imagined someone hurting another. I believed what anyone told me. There was this English boy who was quite cute, and I liked it when he paid attention to me. He kept trying to get me to drink alcohol. I didn't like the taste and wouldn't. He gave me a cola instead. I started feeling dizzy. I don't remember much after that. Two months later, I realized I was pregnant. Your *vater* and I were already planning to marry. I told him about you. He said it didn't matter, that he would love you as his own as he would love all the children that came after you. He wanted a big family."

"But no more children came."

She shook her head. "He became more and more agitated about it. He said it was my sinful, wicked ways that denied him his own children. He said he'd been wrong to marry me. I'd hoped he didn't mean it, that it was his own pain talking. All I know about your biological *vater* is that his first name was Justin."

No matter what your mutter tells you, know that I love you, son. This news didn't surprise him as much as he thought it should. He always knew he didn't resemble his *vater* and looked only partially like his *mutter.* "My *vater*'s name is Abraham. As you said, he is a *vater* in every way that matters." So his *vater* had been afraid of losing Noah and was hard on him to make sure his English blood didn't take him away. There was nothing to worry about. In no way did Noah feel English.

His *mutter* held her cup in her lap. "He must be very proud of you."

Noah thought back to the barn raising. His *vater* always wanted him to behave Amish so Noah wouldn't be tempted by the outside world. *Behave as an Amish should, and I'll be pleased enough.* "I think that maybe he is. Will you come back now?"

"If he wants me back. But I doubt he does."

"I'll talk to him."

After another hour and a half, Noah rose to leave. Kathleen stood up after him. He'd forgotten she was even there. Noah stepped forward and hugged his *mutter*. "Forgive me for staying away."

"Of course."

Too many years had been lost. "If *Vater* won't welcome you back, come live with me."

"In your *dawdy haus*?"

"Kathleen has her medical clinic in there, but my house has plenty of room for you."

"What about a wife and children?"

That pained him, thinking about what he'd lost and would never have. But his mind turned immediately to Kathleen at his side. "I don't have a wife or children. Not anymore."

His *mutter* patted his hand. "You will again one day."

Three months ago, he would have told her with certainly that he would never marry again. But now, he didn't know. He didn't plan to marry, but he wasn't as much opposed to it as he once was. "You are still welcome in my home." He stumbled over his next words but managed to get his sentence out fairly smoothly. "I have room." He'd almost said *we* have room. He and Kathleen weren't a *we*. Why would he think of them as such?

"I'll think about it. I don't want to foist myself upon your *vater* and make him uncomfortable."

"You wouldn't be. I'll come visit you again." Noah needed to convince one of his parents to make the first move.

Noah waited until Sunday to approach his *vater*. He helped him unhitch his buggy. "She told me that another man is my biological *vater*."

His *vater* paused in unhooking the shaft from the harness. "I've always loved you as my own. I was hard on you because I wanted you to be a *gut* Amish and not go into the English world."

"I know you do. I think of no one else as my *vater* but you. You raised me, and you *are* my *vater*. And I *am* Amish." It surprised Noah how much he felt both of those things.

His *vater*'s eyes watered, and he gripped Noah's shoulders. "You have always made me…proud."

"If you go to her and ask her to come home, she will."

He released Noah. "She doesn't want me anymore. I've caused too much pain."

"*Ja*, she does. She's been waiting for you to ask her. When she left she told you—"

"That if I wanted her back, I would need to go to her."

"She said you have seen her in town. Why didn't you ever tell me?"

"At first, I was still angry with her. Then in time, I was too ashamed of my actions. I didn't want you to think poorly of me."

If his *vater* didn't make an effort, Noah feared he would think poorly of him.

"I always pictured myself having a big family. Lots of children. When we didn't, I blamed your *mutter*."

"It wasn't her fault or yours. *Gott* determines the number of children families have."

"But it *is* my fault. I'm the reason we couldn't have more children. I've come to realize that the Lord blessed me with you because I couldn't have any others." His *vater* took a deep breath. "If I could do it all over, I'd treat her better."

"You can. You always encouraged me to be a *gut* Amish man. What would a *gut* Amish man do in this situation?" Though they both knew the answer, he spoke it aloud anyway. "Reconcile."

His *vater* didn't look convinced.

He could bring his parents' separation up to the other leaders and have Bishop Bontrager talk to him. If his *vater* refused to reconcile with his *mutter*, his *vater* would eventually be shunned. Noah couldn't do that to him. For now, he would let his parents find their own way back to each other.

Chapter Fourteen

Decision Sunday had arrived, and Kathleen still didn't know what she was going to do. Her family congratulated her and Benjamin on finishing the classes to join church. She sat in church feeling like a hypocrite.

Again she pleaded, *Lord, what would You have me do?*

Stay or go? Both options seemed right in their own way. To stay would allow her to help her people as she'd always wanted to do, if they would allow her. If she left, she would have plenty of patients and respect as a doctor. If she stayed, she would be close to Noah. That thought made her smile. If she left, she could have everything—a respected medical practice, a husband and children. Ethan would expect her to marry him. Could she be happy with him?

Standing up front, the bishop gave his oration about the importance of church membership and called those forward who wished to complete the process to become church members.

Noah stared hard at her as though willing her to stand.

Noah's *mutter*, Heddy Lambright, sat with her husband. She seemed to have come back. Hopefully for *gut*.

All Kathleen had wanted was to be a respected doctor in her community. There was nothing wrong in that. Then a realization struck her as hard as if someone had slapped her.

Gott had not called her to be *respected*. Just a doctor for her people, in whatever form that took. For all those years away in school and hospitals, if she saved just one life—which she'd done—then that was how it was to be. Was everything she'd worked for just to have the medicine on hand to save her nephew's life?

She glanced around the room. These were her people, and she would serve them in whatever manner *Gott* saw fit. She was a doctor. A very *gut* doctor. But that wasn't what defined her. She was Amish. That too didn't define her. Being a child of *Gott*, *that* was what defined her. She would obey His calling on her life.

As she stood, Noah released his breath. This would make him happy, which pleased her.

Ethan would need to be told of her final decision. He wouldn't be pleased, but she had to follow her heart. And her heart belonged to *Gott*. *Gott* wanted her here in her community.

When the membership ceremony was completed, Kathleen felt a stifling weight lift from her. She hadn't realized that the burden of not being a member of church had weighed so heavily on her. She was finally fully Amish. Now maybe the church leaders would see that she was serious about her commitment and start accepting her as their resident doctor.

Kathleen walked out of the Zooks' home into the warm fall day. She had definitely made the right decision. *Gott*'s peace had enveloped her. The sun seemed brighter and the sky clearer. Though she'd committed herself to this community for the rest of her life, bound by the rules of the *Ordnung*, she felt somehow freer.

Noah strolled up next to her. Along with him came his familiar scent of wood and honey. "The leadership is pleased you decided to join."

"I'm pleased as well."

"You seem happier than you did before the service."

She smiled. "I am."

"Had something been concerning you?"

She didn't know if she should tell him. But she took a deep breath and spoke. "When I arrived this morning, I hadn't decided if I was going to stay and join or not."

He pulled his head back as though surprised. "Really? You don't regret your decision, do you?"

"*Ne*, of course not."

"What helped make up your mind? Because there are still certain members of the leadership who haven't changed their opinions about your being a doctor."

"I thought I wanted respect as a doctor from our people. If I couldn't get it from them, then I thought maybe I was supposed to seek it elsewhere."

"And now?"

"I was looking in the wrong places. I realized I needed to be seeking approval from *Gott* and only *Gott*."

"And are you?"

"*Ja.*"

"Even if you aren't granted continuing permission to be a doctor here?"

"*Ja.* But will you promise me something?"

"If I can."

"If you think I'm seeking approval from anyone but

Gott, would you tell me? I don't want to become misguided again." That was a lot to ask of someone who wasn't a family member. But she sensed she could trust him to be honest with her. And she wanted to confide in him. She felt as close to him as her family. And he lived nearby. And she would see him often with her clinic on his property.

"I'm honored you would ask such a thing of me. I'll do my best."

"Danki."

"I suppose we should see if there is any food left."

With a chuckle, she headed toward the tables. "Amish women *always* prepare more food than what could ever be eaten."

He chuckled too. "Then let's get food before all the *gut* stuff is gone."

She turned a withering look on him. "*Gut* stuff? What here will not be *gut*?"

He heaved a deep breath. "Let me say it this way. Will you join me for lunch?"

Oh. She should say *ne*. If she agreed, he might take it as permission to court her. Courting, marriage, family were still sadly not an option. She shouldn't encourage him, but she said, *"Ja."*

As she reached the buffet line, she noticed Preacher Hochstetler.

Though he stood in line, his eyes were closed, his face red and his breathing strained and fast.

Kathleen left Noah and maneuvered around several people. "Preacher Hochstetler, are you feeling all right?"

His eyes opened, and he scowled at her. "I'm fine. Leave me alone." Sweat beaded on his upper lip. Even on this warm fall day, he shouldn't be sweating with zero exertion.

She took his arm. "Come sit down."

He pulled free. "Don't touch me. I don't need your meddling ways."

Noah had caught up to her. "Paul, you don't look well."

His wife, Elizabeth, spoke up. "That's what I've been telling him all morning, but he won't listen to me."

Just then, he set his plate on the edge of the buffet table and rubbed his left arm. "I'm fine, I tell all of you."

He was *not* fine. If he wasn't already having a heart attack, he soon would.

Kathleen turned to Noah. "Call 911."

"What? Why?"

Staring at him, she willed him to understand.

He mouthed, "Heart attack?"

She nodded.

He turned to someone else and whispered in his ear. That person ran off.

Kathleen glanced around and saw her youngest brother close by, probably back for seconds. "Get my medical pack out of the buggy."

Samuel nodded and walked off.

"Run!"

He leapt into a run.

Kathleen focused her attention back on Preacher Hochstetler.

He wadded up his hand and pressed it to his chest. "Don't touch me," he ground out between clenched teeth.

Kathleen stepped toward him. "You're likely having a heart attack. Let me help."

He shook his head.

Just as she was about to grip his arm, Noah grasped hers and held her back.

She jerked her head around. "What are you doing?"

"The leadership was clear that you weren't allowed to give medical treatment to anyone who didn't want it or to their family members."

She shifted her gaze from Noah to the ailing preacher and back. "He's going to die. Shun me if you want."

Thankfully, he released her.

By now, those closest to them had backed away, and those who had been seated, eating or milling around had closed in to form a dense, wide circle.

As Kathleen took hold of the preacher's arm, he dropped to his knees. She went down with him.

He grasped her arm and opened his mouth, but no words came out. He stared hard at her with glassy eyes.

"Don't worry. You're going to be all right." Even if he didn't make it, that statement was true, because he would be in heaven with the Lord. She glanced around the crowd. Where was Samuel with her medical kit? "Did someone call for an ambulance?"

Noah answered. "I sent Jacob."

Samuel called from the back of the crowd. "I can't get through!"

"Let him through!" Kathleen yelled.

The crowd shuffled enough to let her brother pass. He dropped the bag next to her.

"Help me lay him on his back."

Noah did.

"Roll up his sleeve as far as you can get it."

Noah complied.

Kathleen wrenched the zipper on the pack open and yanked supplies out and dropped them in the grass. She pulled out a pair of latex-free surgical gloves and put them on. She set her stethoscope in her lap. Seizing her blood pressure cuff, she jerked that free. She wrapped it around Preacher Hochstetler's arm and pumped it up. She jammed the earpieces of her stethoscope into place and put the round end in the inside crook of his arm. She slowly released the air pressure.

Two-ten over one-oh-five.

Panic rose in her. The preacher would die for sure.

His face was red. His eyes were closed. No detectable rise or fall of his chest.

She reached for the preacher's shirt buttons.

Noah gripped her hands. "What are you doing?"

"Trying to save his life."

"But you can't undo his shirt."

"I'm a doctor." True, it was very inappropriate for an Amish woman to half undress an Amish man, but this was an emergency. "*You* unbutton his shirt while I get the AED."

He released her hand and went to work on the shirt. "What's an AED?"

"A portable defibrillator. I can restart his heart with it."

He nodded as he finished unbuttoning the shirt. "Everyone turn around. And pray."

The crowd shifted as one until all backs faced the inside of the circle.

How had she ever become a doctor when she'd come from such a reserved upbringing? She'd been forced to get over her discomfort fast.

She pulled out the red-and-yellow AED case, then opened the lid and removed the package with the defibrillator pads.

The AED spoke, "Begin by removing all clothing from the patient's chest. Tear open package and remove pads."

She did so and untangled the attached cords.

"Peel one pad from plastic liner. Place one pad on bare upper chest," the mechanical machine's voice instructed.

She peeled the pad and reached to stick it to the preacher's chest.

Noah stopped her. "It would be better if I do it. Tell me what to do." He took the pad.

"Place one pad on bare upper chest," the machine repeated.

She pointed. "Put it there and press it down firmly."

He followed her instructions.

"Remove second pad and place second pad on bare lower chest," the machine instructed.

Kathleen pointed again. "Press it down firmly. It needs to have *gut* adhesion."

He did so.

"Now take your hands away so the machine can read his signs." Kathleen held her hands up.

"Do not touch patient," the machine said.

Noah pulled his hands back.

Kathleen spoke to the crowd. "Stand clear everyone. Don't touch him." That was a foolish thing to say. Everyone was several feet away. And all but the leaders had their backs turned.

The machine spoke again. "Analyzing rhythm. Do not touch the patient. Analyzing rhythm. Shock advised. Charging. Stand clear. Press flashing button to deliver shock."

"Clear! Don't touch him!" Kathleen pressed the flashing red heart-shaped button. She prayed this worked.

The preacher's body jerked.

"Shock delivered," the machine announced. "It is now safe to touch the patient. Give thirty compressions then two breaths."

Kathleen clasped one hand over the other and pressed on the preacher's chest.

Noah held out his hands. "Let me do that. It's not right for you to be touching him in that manner."

She gave him a withering glance and continued.

He'd done his due diligence in asking.

Kathleen inclined her head toward the AED. "There's a mouth barrier mask in the kit. Take it out and extend it."

He did.

"When I tell you to, place it over his mouth and nose and give him two breaths. Now." She pulled her hands away.

After two minutes of this back-and-forth between compressions and breaths, the machine spoke. "Do not touch patient. Reanalyzing."

Kathleen took her hands away.

"Shock advised."

"Clear!" *Please, Lord, make this work.* She pressed the button, and the preacher's body jerked again. She resumed the chest compressions.

After another two minutes, the AED did not advise another shock, and Preacher Hochstetler blinked his eyes.

He was alive.

She drew in a relieved breath and patted his shoulder. "Lie still. An ambulance is on its way." She monitored his vitals and wrote down his blood pressure every few minutes on the palm of her rubber glove.

This was why she had become a doctor. This was why she wanted to stay in her community to be a doctor. This was why she'd made the right decision to stay.

Soon sirens wailed in the distance.

"Everyone move back so the paramedics can get to him," Kathleen said.

Noah stood and made sure the people cleared a path.

When the paramedics rushed over, Kathleen gave them Preacher Hochstetler's pertinent information and all that had been done to help him.

One of the paramedics stared at her. "Even though you look like one, you don't talk or act like any Amish I've ever met."

She would likely always be part English in her Amish body, clothes and world. But that was finally all right with her. "I'm a doctor."

Soon the preacher was secured on a gurney and put into the back of the ambulance. Elizabeth Hochstetler climbed in as well.

Kathleen stared at her hands. They shook from the aftereffects of the adrenaline rush. She hoped no one noticed, or they wouldn't trust her.

Noah stood next to Kathleen as several people congratulated her. He couldn't believe what she had done. "You saved his life."

"I need to go to the hospital."

He nodded. "I'll take you."

She knelt down and crammed her supplies back into her medical kit.

"You could have easily obeyed the leadership's decision and done nothing. Then your main opposition would no longer be a problem, and you would not be blamed."

"I couldn't do that."

"I know. That's why I released you. Let's go." Noah drove his larger, covered buggy. He was glad he'd opted for this vehicle instead of the smaller open one. With the cooler fall evenings, he hadn't wanted Kathleen to get cold if she agreed to a buggy ride later. But this wasn't exactly what he'd had in mind.

"Could you drive faster?"

"The *Ordnung* is specific about the speed at which we are permitted to drive."

"We can have solar panels for electricity and telephones, but in an emergency, we can travel no faster than a fast trot."

"If this truly were an emergency, it would be permissible to run the horse. But it's not."

"Not an emergency? Preacher Hochstetler went into cardiac arrest. If that's not an emergency, then what is?"

"He was taken by ambulance and is receiving medical treatment. He's getting the best care he can. Whether the horse runs, trots, or walks, there is nothing more *you* can do at the moment."

She let out a quick breath. "I know. You're right. I just want to be there in case they have any questions, and so I can know what's going on."

"Ah. So that's it. You don't like not knowing something."

She huffed out a single laugh. "I guess not. *Danki* for driving me."

"Of course."

Once at the hospital, Kathleen dismissed him. "You

don't have to stay. I'll get in touch with my parents to get a ride home."

"I'm staying. I might not have to, but I am."

Tears filled her eyes. "*Danki.* I can't tell you how much your being here means to me."

He'd hoped she would appreciate his presence. He didn't want to be anywhere else except at her side. He'd seen her hands shaking. "I'm happy to stay. Just let me know what you need. I'll help in whatever way I can." He parked the buggy in the designated buggy parking area.

Kathleen rushed to Elizabeth Hochstetler's side. "Have you heard any news?"

Elizabeth gripped her hand. "They say he's stable. They said he is only alive because you used that machine on him. *Danki* for saving his life."

"*Ne*, I'm just a person. It was *Gott*. Without Him, nothing I did would have been enough."

The woman hugged Kathleen. "*Danki* for listening to *Gott* rather than man. Your obedience has given me back my husband."

Kathleen opened her mouth again, most likely to protest who should get the credit.

But Noah touched her arm to stop her. "Let's sit."

Soon the waiting room filled with their Amish brothers and sisters. People huddled in the center of the room, round after round of people, praying. This was the heart of the Amish. Coming together to help others in need. Noah was proud to be Amish and among such faithful people.

And to be here for Kathleen.

Chapter Fifteen

The next morning, Kathleen sat at her desk in her clinic and called the hospital to check on Preacher Hochstetler.

"I'm sorry. I can't give you any information on him. HIPAA, you know."

Ja, Kathleen knew. She was just hoping the nurse would give her a little information because she'd been the first attending physician. She didn't want to get the nurse in trouble by pressing the matter. "Thanks anyway."

She pressed the end button and stared at the phone. She had another call to make. Though it had to be done, she didn't relish it. Putting it off wouldn't make it any easier. Maybe she could simply "forget" and never make the call.

That wouldn't work. Besides being rude and breaking a promise, Ethan would likely show up here at some point soon and ask for her decision. She'd told him she would be making it around this time.

She removed his business card from her top desk drawer. She flipped it over to stare at the handwritten cell number on the back. Maybe she could call his office and leave a message. *Ne*. That would be rude as well.

If she could defy her Amish leaders by going to college, medical school, becoming a doctor and returning to be a doctor for them when they didn't want her to be, she could make a simple phone call.

She took a deep breath and punched in the number.

It rang several times with no answer.

Maybe he was in surgery.

That would be perfect. She could leave a message on his personal phone and not have to talk to him.

"This better be important." His gruff voice sounded tired.

No hello or pleasantries.

"Ethan? Is that you?"

"Who—Kathleen?"

"Ja."

His voice brightened. "Kathleen. I'm so glad you called."

"Ne, you're not. I woke you up again, didn't I?"

"I just got off a double. I might not have been glad to be woken up, but I *am* glad you called."

He wouldn't be when she told him.

"I'm sorry for waking you. You should turn your phone off when you're sleeping."

"I do, but I have it programmed to let two numbers through. The hospital and your clinic. I didn't look at the caller ID. Thought it was my office."

Ugh. This wasn't going to be *gut*. He was going to be disappointed. She wanted to ask him how the children's clinic was progressing, but small talk would not be fitting. "You told me to let you know when I came to a decision."

"Stop right there. I can hear the hesitancy in your voice. You're not going to tell me good news, are you?"

"I'm sorry."

"Don't say that. You should see the kids. They need you so much. I met this little boy Nicky last week. He has a cleft palate. We could help him."

"You'll have to help him on your own. I'm needed here."

"You're needed *here* too. The *clinic* needs you. The *children* need you." His voice dropped. "*I* need you."

He was once again offering her everything. But instead of being tempted as she had been before, it made her feel sad. Sad for him. "I'm where I'm supposed to be. I saved a man's life yesterday." She left out *Gott*'s part in all of it because Ethan wouldn't understand. And maybe that was it. Ethan didn't need *Gott*. He was an excellent doctor and believed he'd become one all on his own with no help from anyone, let alone an invisible *Gott* he didn't believe in. She felt sad for him in a different, deeper way. She would pray more fervently for him.

"You could save lives here too."

"That would be true anywhere I went. You're meant to do great things as a doctor. I'm meant to be here. Just being a doctor for my community is a big thing. I wish you all the best."

"Don't say that. It sounds so final."

"This is final, Ethan. I've made my decision."

He hung up without another word or argument.

She had done the right thing. Ethan had a different path. One that didn't include her. Her path was here. And she had no regrets about that.

With no appointments scheduled and nothing to keep her at the clinic, she headed back home to help her *mut-*

ter and sisters harvest the garden and start some canning.

Later in the morning, Kathleen opened the front door of her parents' home for Bishop Bontrager. *"Hallo."* She ushered him into the living room where *Mum* and *Dat* were. "Have you heard any word on Preacher Hochstetler?"

Nodding, the bishop sat. "He is doing well because of you."

She corrected him. "Because of *Gott*. My efforts would go only as far as *Gott* would allow them to."

"Kathleen," *Dat* admonished.

"It's all right." The bishop's smile widened. *"Gott's* part is a given. But don't minimize what you did. No one else had the training, knowledge and equipment."

This bishop was so different from the hard man he'd been when she'd left.

"I want to visit him at the hospital."

"I think it's best to wait until he comes home."

She didn't want to wait. She was his doctor. *Ne.* She wasn't. And never would be. He likely wouldn't let her anywhere near him or permit her to help him or anyone else in the community.

"Now—" the bishop inclined his head "—if you'll allow me to speak with your parents."

"Of course. I'll get some refreshments." Kathleen left for the kitchen. She quickly filled a plate with old-time cinnamon jumbo cookies and poured three cups of coffee.

When she returned to the living room, both her parents were beaming.

Kathleen set the tray on the coffee table, handed a cup to each of them and offered cookies all around.

Dat caught her gaze. "Would you find Ruby and tell her to come in here?"

A visit from Bishop Bontrager in the fall, asking to speak to the parents of a young woman who had a serious beau could mean only one thing. A proposal! "I'll get her." Kathleen hurried outside to where she'd last seen Ruby in the garden. The English thought the Amish way of delivering a proposal offer through the bishop was a bit odd, but it had its own sense that one couldn't fully appreciate when one wasn't raised Amish.

She found she was a little jealous of Ruby. She would marry, be a wife and *mutter*. Things Kathleen would never do or be. She steeled herself to be who *Gott* had called her to be. A doctor. *Gott* had already demonstrated that this was what He wanted for her life. And she was grateful to be back with her Amish people and determined to be content with that.

She got to the garden and called, "Ruby?"

"At the end by the pumpkins," came her sister's voice from beyond the green leaves, vegetation and foliage.

Kathleen hurried along and jumped over a row of carrots.

Ruby held her apron up filled with red ripe tomatoes and pea pods. "What's got you in a rush?"

"You have to come to the house."

"Let me finish picking tomatoes from this plant."

In both of her hands, Kathleen took her sister's free hand, the one that wasn't holding up her apron. "You have to come right away. No time to dally."

Ruby straightened. "You asked me to tell you when you were acting too English. Now is one of those times. There is nothing to rush so much about."

"There is today. Bishop Bontrager is at the house. He's waiting for you. You know what that means."

Ruby's eyes widened, and she bit her bottom lip. "I knew Jonathan was anxious for us to marry, but I never expected him to ask for me the very first day he could."

Kathleen hugged her sister. "I'm so happy for you."

"You'll deliver all my babies, won't you?"

"Of course. I'd be honored." A feeling of loss flowed through Kathleen. Loss for things she would never have. She thought of Noah.

"Your turn will be next. I just know it."

Kathleen knew differently. Yesterday had been confirmation from *Gott* that she was right—or rather *Gott* was right—about where she was supposed to be. Here in the Amish world, being a doctor for her people. Most of them might not understand her decision to remain single and be a doctor rather than marry and have children. Might not understand her call from *Gott*. But she did, and that was what mattered.

But she wouldn't ruin her sister's day with her gloomy thoughts for herself. She'd made her choice all those years ago, and was honored to have been given such a calling by *Gott*. His ways were higher than her ways, His thoughts higher than hers. How could helping to save a life compare to selfishly wanting a husband— Noah—and children?

Later that same afternoon, Kathleen opened the door once again for Bishop Bontrager. "You're back. What a nice surprise. Come in."

The bishop had a strange expression. "Are your parents here?"

"*Ja.* Is something wrong? Preacher Hochstetler didn't

take a turn for the worse, did he?" She knew she should have gone to the hospital.

"Relax. Paul is fine. This is a completely different matter."

She was glad to know the preacher was fine. "I'll go find them." She went to the kitchen and retrieved a cup of coffee and another plate of cookies, and brought them back to the bishop. "For you, while you wait."

She went out to the garden, where her *mum* and sisters picked vegetables to can. *"Mum?"*

Her *mutter*'s head popped up from behind a row of climbing pea vines. "What is it?"

Kathleen picked her way over, making sure not to step on any plants or vegetables. "Bishop Bontrager is back. He wants to talk to you and *Dat*."

Mum furrowed her eyebrows. "He is? We weren't expecting him again."

Ruby hurried over. "It's not Jonathan, do you think? He didn't change his mind, did he? I hope nothing happened to him."

Mum turned to Ruby. "You better come with me." *Mum* turned back to Kathleen. "Can you find your *dat*?"

Kathleen nodded. She'd planned to and took off toward the barn as *Mum* and Ruby headed for the house. She found *Dat*, and they headed to the house as well. As they entered through the kitchen, Ruby sauntered from the living room with a smile. "Told you so." She continued out to the garden.

Kathleen turned to *Dat*. "What was that about?"

"I'll go find out," *Dat* headed into the living room.

"I'll bring you and *Mum* coffee."

She prepared cups of coffee and carried them into the living room. The trio abruptly stopped talking. Obviously, the topic wasn't for her. She handed *Dat* and *Mum* their cups. "Is there anything else I can get?"

Mum shook her head.

Dat motioned to the open spot on the couch next to *Mum*. "Have a seat, Kathleen."

She gave him a quizzical look. This couldn't be *gut*. If the bishop was here for her, she was likely to be shunned for her actions yesterday when Preacher Hochstetler went into cardiac arrest. She was not sorry for allowing *Gott* to use her to save his life. She straightened. She would take whatever punishment the leaders saw fit.

Bishop Bontrager cleared his throat. "Had I known about this earlier, I would have conducted this business then. Now you all will just think I came for more of these cookies." He chuckled.

Why was he making light of the situation? This was obviously a serious matter for him to return so soon and not put it off for another day. "Am I to be shunned?"

The bishop's eyes widened. "Is that what you think? The leaders haven't met on the events that transpired yesterday. *Ne*, I'm here on another matter. There has been an offer of marriage for you."

"What?" Kathleen stared. Who would want to marry her?

The bishop chuckled again. "Apparently you weren't expecting an offer. Interesting."

"Who would offer for me? I've gone against so many points of the *Ordnung*, no man would want a wife like me. And most know that I never plan to marry. I wouldn't make any man a *gut* wife."

"Well, obviously Noah Lambright thinks you would."

Her heart leapt for joy, and then was dashed into pieces. "Noah?" This couldn't be right. Noah also never planned to marry. Losing his wife had been too painful.

"*Ja*. Noah. What shall I tell him?"

Why would Noah offer for her? Part of her wanted to say *ja*. If she were ever to marry, Noah would be whom she would choose. But she couldn't marry. Hadn't *Gott* made that clear? She was to be a doctor. Not a wife and *mutter*. That made her heart ache. She wanted to be all three. "Tell him I'm very honored by his offer, but I can't marry him."

Mum gasped. "Kathleen. Why would you turn him down? He's a *gut* man and will make you a wonderful husband."

She knew that, and he already fit so well into their family. "*Gott* called me to be a doctor. Not a wife." Tears pricked her eyes. "I need to obey Him."

The bishop studied her a moment before he spoke. "I think you should reconsider. I'll give you time to think about your decision."

"I don't need time. I've made my decision. I can't marry Noah." The words choked out. "Tell him my answer is *ne*." A chasm of pain opened up inside her, and she shot to her feet and ran upstairs.

She stood by the window. How could he have offered for her when he knew she would say *ne*? She recalled his warm lips on hers. All those years ago, when she'd decided to become a doctor, had she known it would be Noah she couldn't marry, she might not have had the strength of will to become a doctor.

Then a terrible thought occurred to her. What if the bishop and other leaders had successfully pressured Noah into this? He'd said he wouldn't court anyone if they asked, but maybe he hadn't had a choice. If she had a husband, she would have to obey him. And if he said she couldn't be a doctor, she would be honor bound to obey. But she'd already committed to *Gott* to be a doctor. She couldn't go against Him. *Ne.* Sadly, she couldn't marry Noah.

Noah stood in his yard when Bishop Bontrager's buggy pulled up. This was it. The bishop would have an answer from Kathleen. He'd wanted to talk to her directly and was going to after the service yesterday, but then Paul Hochstetler'd had a heart attack and nothing else mattered. He wanted to talk to her directly so he could tell her so much more than what she'd hear from the bishop. But this way was probably better, because she would know he was serious. That his offer was genuine.

Bishop Bontrager pulled his buggy to a stop and got out. "*Hallo*, Noah."

Why did the bishop seem reserved? And why wasn't he smiling? "Has something happened in the community?" Maybe he hadn't had a chance to talk to Kathleen and her parents yet.

The bishop shook his head. "It's Kathleen Yoder."

His gut wrenched. "Is she all right?"

"*Ja.* But I'm sorry to say that she turned down your offer of marriage."

His heart dropped to his shoes. "Turned me down?"

"I'm afraid so. Said she can't be both a doctor and a wife. She said she will never marry. I'm so sorry."

What was he going to do now? "*Danki*, Bishop." Should he try to persuade her? Should he move to the far side of the community so he would only have to see her every other Sunday? The one consolation was that he wouldn't have to see her married to another man.

Unless…she fell in love and changed her mind.

He'd never considered that she would turn him down. In his mind, he'd pictured her delighted. She would have thrown her arms around him in a fit of overwhelming joy, then have to control herself. Then one day, he could tell their children how English their *mutter* was. She obviously didn't care as much for him as he'd thought and hoped.

He had never planned to marry again after Rachel died. After about six months, people started encouraging him to marry again. It hadn't seemed right so soon. Then he just wasn't interested. Then he felt *Gott* calling him to remain single, which suited him fine. He had been enjoying his single life with only a small niggling every once in a while that he should contribute to the continuation of the Amish people and their Amish way of life. But those moments were brief and passed quickly. And they came more and more seldom. *Gott* had called him to a different life than his Amish brothers and sisters. Being alone had become a comfortable habit. He had been content. And happy.

Until…

Until Kathleen returned and turned his contentment into longing and his happiness into dissatisfaction. He wanted more. It had been as though he'd been waiting for more than contentment. Though he hadn't known he'd been waiting, he realized he had.

When Kathleen showed up, walking along the roadside, his heart came back to life. As though he'd been waiting for *her*. Everything he'd done for the past three years was in preparation for her. He could see that now.

So if he'd been preparing for her return, why didn't she feel the same way about him? It made no sense. Why would *Gott* do that to him? Why get Noah's hopes up just to dash them? Too many questions and no answers.

Well, one answer.

Ne.

Chapter Sixteen

On Friday, Preacher Hochstetler was released from the hospital.

Bishop Bontrager sent word that Kathleen's presence was required at the preacher's home. *Dat* insisted on driving her even though she told him she would be fine going by herself.

"If my daughter is going to be summoned by the bishop after…after all that has happened—and I'm including the time you were away—then I'm going to be there."

"Me too." *Mum* put on her coat.

Kathleen didn't need a babysitter, let alone two. Now that the preacher was home, the bishop and Preacher Hochstetler probably wanted to chastise her for going against the preacher's wishes. Helping him when she was told in no uncertain terms not to touch him. They would likely shun her for her disobedience now that she was a member. But she didn't mind. Elizabeth Hochstetler had her husband and her children still had their *vater*. She would never be sorry for that. This visit would give her a chance to check on him.

Even if Preacher Hochstetler would never welcome her medical expertise, others in the community had to see how vital her presence as a doctor was. Whether approved or not, others would seek her out. Even if they didn't, they would feel more reassured having her near, knowing she would be there if needed. They had seen it with Isaac being stabbed with that stick in his thigh. Though she hadn't been allowed to physically tend to the boy, he was doing well and his wound had healed. He still had a slight limp but was running around again.

Then, she hadn't been allowed to aid her nephew Mark. But because she was there with her medical supplies, he had been treated and was alive today. Bless little Nancy for stepping in where the adults were stymied by rules and tradition. What a blessing that Nancy didn't have to watch her younger sibling die as Kathleen and Gloria had so many years ago.

And then there was the preacher. She had been able to be the one to administer medical treatment to him.

But she hadn't done any of those things to get her community to accept her as a doctor. She had done them because she wanted to help her people. So she would hold her head high regardless of what Preacher Hochstetler, the bishop or any of the leaders had to say.

Deacon Zook came out of the house when *Dat* pulled to a stop.

What was he doing here? She saw several buggies. Were all the church leaders here? If so, this meeting was definitely to shun her. She'd hoped to check on how Preacher Hochstetler was doing. But that wouldn't be likely now.

She took a deep breath and got out of the buggy.

Deacon Zook smiled.

Why? Was he trying to confuse her? Trying to lower her defenses?

She squared her shoulders and smiled back. *"Guten Morgen."*

"Guten Morgen. Please come inside. Everyone is waiting for you."

Everyone. That wasn't daunting.

Preacher Hochstetler's oldest son, Eli, walked the horse and buggy away.

Dat flanked Kathleen on one side and *Mum* on the other. Kathleen was grateful for their support and glad they had insisted on coming.

Mum leaned closer and whispered. "We are very proud of you."

Dat nodded. "Very proud."

Her parents were proud of her, even after disobeying the leaders and being away so long? That meant more to her than any number of patients. Their pleasure in her was magnified by the pleasure she sensed from *Gott.* Like a confirmation. *Well done, my gut and faithful servant. Gott*'s words from the book of Matthew ministered to her like a salve on a burn, cooling and comforting.

Inside, Preacher Hochstetler sat in the living room with all the other leaders, including Noah, as Kathleen had suspected. Noah didn't look directly at her. Not after her turning down his offer of marriage. So now she would have at least two church leadership members openly against her. Noah's opposition hurt worse.

She would be respectful but would refuse to stop practicing medicine. If she had to spend the rest of her life in the community as a shunned member, she would. And she would help any of them every chance she got.

The preacher's wife crossed to Kathleen. "I just want to say—"

Preacher Hochstetler spoke abruptly. "Sit down, woman, and let us conduct our business first."

Elizabeth Hochstetler squeezed Kathleen's hand and mouthed with a smile, *"Danki."*

Kathleen gave her a nod, then turned to Preacher Hochstetler. "You shouldn't excite yourself. You need rest so your heart can heal."

He waved his hand back and forth in front of him. *"Ja, ja.* The doctors at the hospital told me all that. We have important matters to take care of."

"But you will do as they advised?"

"Ja. Now have a seat."

All the leaders were standing except Preacher Hochstetler.

She didn't want to be the only other one in the room sitting. "I'll stand, *danki.*"

He narrowed his eyes at her. "You are a stubborn one."

Rather than taking his comment as an insult, she would look at it as a compliment. *"Danki."*

He widened his eyes at that and raised one eyebrow. "About the matter of you running a medical clinic and helping people—who, by the way, expressly told you not to."

"I regret nothing I've done." She wouldn't add that without her, he wouldn't be here to criticize her actions.

"I'm sure you don't. The bishop has allowed me to be the one to tell you the outcome of our vote on these matters."

She braced herself, and her anger rose even before he started speaking.

"First the matter of your clinic. You have permission to run your clinic for the *gut* of the community."

"But… What?"

He chuckled. Preacher Hochstetler actually chuckled. Had she ever seen him do that?

"The vote was unanimous. We believe your clinic will help the community tremendously."

Unanimous? She looked around the room at each member of the leadership. Each returned her gaze with a nod. She let her gaze linger on Noah. He too gave her a nod, then averted his gaze. She couldn't believe they all voted for her to continue her clinic. "How long of a trial period am I allowed?"

"No more trial period. The clinic is in the best interest of everyone. There are other communities who bring in an *Englisher* doctor. We have no need for that. As to your disobedience in going to college and becoming a doctor, we decided since you hadn't joined church, you weren't breaking any rules. But don't let that become common knowledge to others. We still disapprove of higher education because it takes our young people out of the community for so long, and we will discourage anyone who tries to do as you did. But what's done is done."

This was what she wanted from the start. To be accepted in her community as a doctor. And now that the church leaders had declared her clinic admissible, her fellow Amish brothers and sisters wouldn't hesitate to come and allow her to treat them.

"On the matter of helping someone, or their family, who have expressly told you not to, you *must* refrain. If someone, or their family member, dies because they refuse your medical treatment, then their blood is *not* on your hands."

This, she might not be able to abide by. If she saw a life-threatening situation, how could she not step in? She would have to pray about that one and see how the Lord directed her.

"As for me and my family, you have my permission to treat us as you see fit. And I won't intervene in your assistance with any community member." He held out his hand to her.

She stepped forward and took it. She wasn't sure why he was offering his hand nor why she took it.

He squeezed her hand. "*Danki* for being stubborn and saving my life."

Kathleen stared. She never expected gratitude. "*Bitte.* But it was *Gott* who actually saved your life. I did what I could and the rest was up to Him."

"*Danki* for allowing Him to use you."

"*Bitte.*"

She couldn't believe this turn of events. She looked to Noah, who stared at the ground. Had he given up his chance to marry her by voting in favor of her clinic?

As soon as the business at hand was completed at Preacher Hochstetler's, Noah backed out of the room and stepped into the kitchen. He'd positioned himself to be able to escape without notice. The oldest Hochstetler daughter, a willowy twelve-year-old, blinked at him as he passed through the room. He gave her a smile and a nod before exiting.

He hurried to the corral where he'd left his coat hanging over the railing. He swung it on.

From behind him came Kathleen's voice. "*Danki.*"

He turned but didn't meet her gaze. Why had she broken his heart? "For what?"

"For voting in favor of my clinic."

"We need a doctor. It was the right thing to do." He hurried into the corral and walked out his horse.

"I didn't expect you to vote in my favor."

He swung up onto his horse's bare back. "The clinic is right for the community."

Though true, he'd also wanted to give Kathleen what she wanted. Even if that didn't include him.

Why couldn't Kathleen accept his offer of marriage? Hadn't he always supported her efforts? Why couldn't she see she could be both a doctor *and* a wife? Maybe she just didn't care for him enough. Maybe she didn't care for him as much as he did her.

He would need to pray to figure out what the Lord wanted of him. He'd thought he knew, hence the reason for offering for Kathleen. Now he didn't know what his next steps were.

Kathleen stared up at Noah on his horse. She hadn't been to the clinic at all this past week after refusing his offer of marriage. And he, in turn, hadn't been to a single meal at their home. He had been avoiding her. Well, hadn't she been avoiding him first by not going to the clinic all week? She didn't know what to say. Anything she could think of would likely make matters worse. But she didn't want him to leave like this.

If they were going to be neighbors and in the same community for the rest of their lives, they were going to need to find a way to coexist.

The cold fall air seeped through her clothes and bit her skin. She didn't care.

She wrapped her arms around herself. "Noah? I need to know something."

He didn't dismount. "What?"

"Why did you offer for me?"

His voice came out flat. "The same reason any man offers for a woman. Because he wants to marry her."

She rubbed her hands vigorously on her upper arms. "Was your offer a ploy to keep me from being a doctor?"

He stared hard down at her. "Is that really what you thought?"

She had hurt and insulted him. "I didn't want to."

"But you did."

"You said you'd never marry again."

"Sometimes things change."

"I want to hear from you that you weren't trying to manipulate me. That the other leaders didn't pressure you into it."

"You think someone put me up to offering for you?"

She continued to rub her arms. "You made it very clear when we first met that you weren't looking for another wife, ever, and wouldn't marry again. You were going to remain single."

He climbed down. "That was how I felt when we first met. Most of the eligible Amish women knew that about me, though some chose to ignore it. You being new—or at least not knowing—I didn't want you to get any ideas." He took off his coat and wrapped it around her.

His warmth enveloped her.

He continued. "Little did I know that you had the same outlook. You didn't want to get married either. It made you easy to talk to and be around, without feeling like there had to be something more. But then things changed. I guess I misjudged what we had. My mistake."

"What we had? I thought it was friendship. Wasn't it?"

"It started out that way, but it changed along the way.

I saw life differently. I saw *my* life differently. Instead of a solitary life, I saw you in it with me."

She'd had no idea. She'd had to keep reining in her own heart because she knew he wouldn't marry and she couldn't. Maybe that was why she was so adamant about not marrying because she knew there was no chance that he would offer for her. "So you truly do care for me?"

"Care? What I feel is so much more than care. I love you. That's why I offered for you."

"Oh, Noah. I love you too."

"Could have fooled me. You said *ne*. You thought I was coerced by the other leaders. You thought I'd stoop that low." His expression changed from hurt to expectation. "Now that you know I wasn't compelled by anyone or anything but my heart, will you reconsider my offer?"

"What about my being a doctor? I can't exactly marry and do that too."

He took both of her hands in his. "Your drive and determination are only two of the reasons I fell in love with you. We'll work out the doctor thing. If you marry me, you'll be a lot closer to your clinic. Jessica reminded me that several married women—women with children—run fruit and vegetable stands and make quilts and more."

"You would let me continue to be a doctor?"

"Provided the leaders are agreeable. If they aren't, we might be shunned."

We? He would stand with her? "You would risk shunning for me?"

"For you. For us. For the *gut* of our community."

He was offering her everything, just as Ethan had done. But this was so much different, because she loved Noah. "But we haven't even been courting."

He smiled. "Not in the conventional way."

She thought about him letting her use his *dawdy haus*, him taking out all the furniture she couldn't use, the desk he'd brought out for her, the exam table and bookshelf he'd built her—built *for* her—the filing cabinet he'd also built *for* her to put her records in—not that she had many yet—and putting in a telephone line, and standing up for her to even be able to start the clinic. And mostly preventing her from administering medical help in the beginning to show she could follow the leaders' instructions. "Sneaky. *Ja*, I'll marry you."

He took her in his arms and kissed her.

He pulled back. "I shouldn't have done that. We aren't married yet."

Kathleen shook her head. "I see nothing wrong in an engaged couple holding hands or sharing an occasional hug or kiss." She guessed that was her English side coming out.

"Your English side?"

"Do you mind?"

"Not in the least."

He glanced around and, after making sure they were alone, kissed her again. "We better go tell your parents. And the bishop."

Enveloped in his scent of wood and honey, Kathleen closed her eyes. "Once more."

She rose up on her tiptoes and kissed him again.

* * * * *

WE HOPE YOU
ENJOYED THIS

LOVE
INSPIRED®
BOOK.

If you were **inspired** by this

uplifting, **heartwarming** romance,

be sure to look for all six Love

Inspired® books every month.

Love Inspired®

www.LoveInspired.com

Love Inspired®

Save $1.00

on the purchase of ANY
Love Inspired® book.

Available wherever books are sold,
including most bookstores, supermarkets,
drugstores and discount stores.

Save $1.00

on the purchase of ANY Love Inspired® book.

Coupon valid until May 31, 2019.
Redeemable at participating retail outlets in the U.S. and Canada only.
Limit one coupon per customer.

52616365

5 65373 00076 2   (8100)0 12420

*With a new job at Big Heart Ranch, pregnant single
mom Hannah Vincent's ready for a fresh start.
But as she and her boss, horse trainer Tripp Walker,
grow closer, Hannah can't help but wonder if she's
prepared for a new love.*

Read on for a sneak preview of
Her Last Chance Cowboy *by Tina Radcliffe,
available March 2019 from Love Inspired!*

Hannah exhaled. "My point is that you should consider doing the
100-Day Mustang Challenge."

Tripp looked her up and down. The woman was a sassy thing
for a stranger who'd only arrived a few days ago.

"You don't even know if you'll be here in one hundred days,"
he returned.

Though her eyes said she was dumbstruck by his bold
statement, her mouth kept moving. "You don't believe I'm related
to the Maxwells, do you?"

Tripp raised both hands. "I don't know what to believe."
Though he tried not to judge, there was a part of him that had
already stamped the woman's card and dismissed her.

"I am, and I'm willing to stick around to find out if it will help
Clementine."

"Help Clementine?"

Hannah offered a shrug "We could use a little nest egg to start
over."

"The prize money?"

"Sure. Why not? If I make it possible for you to train, maybe
it would be worth some of the purse." The flush of her cheeks told
him that her words were all bravado.

"What makes you think I'm going to win?" Tripp asked.

"I've seen you with the horses." She paused. "I know a winner when I see one."

He nearly laughed aloud. "So what kind of split are we talking about here?" he asked.

"Fifty-fifty."

Tripp released a scoffing sound. "In your dreams, lady. I'm the trainer and I'm paying for fees and feed and everything else out of my pocket."

"Sixty-forty?"

"More like seventy-thirty, and you have a deal." The words slipped from his mouth before he could take them back. What was he thinking, making a pact with a pregnant single mother who might very well prove to be a seasoned con artist? His mouth hadn't run off on him in years. Yet here he was, with his good sense galloping away.

"I, um…"

Despite his misstep, Hannah seemed reluctant to commit, and that stuck in his craw. Was she having second thoughts about his ability to win the challenge?

"What's the problem?" he asked. "Your bravado seems to be fading the closer it gets to the chute."

"Seventy-thirty?" She shook her head in disagreement.

"Are you telling me that you couldn't start over with fifteen thousand dollars? If you can't, then you're doing it all wrong, my friend."

"We aren't friends," Hannah said. Then she stood and walked over to his desk. She offered him her hand, and he stared at it for a moment before accepting the handshake.

"Deal," she said.

Tripp stared at her small hand in his.

The day had started off like any other. In a heartbeat, everything was sideways.

Looking for inspiration in tales
of hope, faith and heartfelt romance?

Check out **Love Inspired**® and
Love Inspired® **Suspense** books!

New books available every month!

CONNECT WITH US AT:

Facebook.com/groups/HarlequinConnection

Facebook.com/HarlequinBooks

Twitter.com/HarlequinBooks

Instagram.com/HarlequinBooks

Pinterest.com/HarlequinBooks

ReaderService.com